T0398021

Praise for
IN THE COMPANY OF KILLERS

"**Wild and unpredictable**, Elora Cook's *In the Company of Killers* is a fast-paced, addictive debut that draws you into a perilous world dripping with glamour and opulence. I was so gripped by the story that I didn't want it to end—**this book is wickedly fun!**"
—**JUNE HUR**, *New York Times* bestselling author of *A Crane Among Wolves*

"In this dazzling YA debut, Elora Cook invites readers into the glamorous lives of two teenage Mafia heirs who run Manhattan's elite social circles. **Sizzling romance and pulse-pounding twists will have readers devouring this book from start to finish!**"
—**KATIE ZHAO**, author of *How We Fall Apart* and *Zodiac Rising*

"An **epic modern-day *Romeo and Juliet*** story between rival Mafia families that will leave you on the edge of your seat. *In the Company of Killers* had me kicking my feet and flipping the pages as fast as I could to see what would happen next. **Fans of *Gossip Girl* will be thrilled by this edgier version of New York high society.**"
—**LISELLE SAMBURY**, author of *Blood Like Magic* and *Delicious Monsters*

"Elora Cook's page-turning debut is a thrilling ride from beginning to end. With two morally gray protagonists you can't help but root for, an immersive crime world where everyone's a suspect, and a romance that leaves you breathless and craving more, *In the Company of Killers* is a standout read you won't want to miss."
—**MACKENZIE REED**, author of *The Wilde Trials* and *The Rosewood Hunt*

IN THE COMPANY OF

Killers

IN THE COMPANY OF

Killers

ELORA COOK

LITTLE, BROWN AND COMPANY
New York Boston

Copyright © 2025 by Elora Cook

Chandelier art © berez_ka/Shutterstock.com
Lion art © sewonboy/Shutterstock.com
Calla lily art © Plawarn/Shutterstock.com
Feather art © Roman Malyshev/Shutterstock.com

Cover art copyright © 2025 by Elena Masci. Cover design by Karina Granda and Jenny Kimura. Cover copyright © 2025 by Hachette Book Group, Inc. Interior design by Michelle Gengaro-Kokmen.

Little, Brown and Company
Hachette Book Group
1290 Avenue of the Americas, New York, NY 10104
Visit us at LBYR.com

First Edition: March 2025

Little, Brown and Company is a division of Hachette Book Group, Inc. The Little, Brown name and logo are registered trademarks of Hachette Book Group, Inc.

The publisher is not responsible for websites (or their content) that are not owned by the publisher.

Little, Brown and Company books may be purchased in bulk for business, educational, or promotional use. For information, please contact your local bookseller or the Hachette Book Group Special Markets Department at special.markets@hbgusa.com.

Library of Congress Cataloging-in-Publication Data
Names: Cook, Elora, author.
Title: In the company of killers / Elora Cook.
Description: First edition. | New York : Little, Brown and Company, 2025. | Summary: "After her family is brutally murdered, a teenage Mafia princess must team up with the heir to her family's rival Mafia to catch the killer." —Provided by publisher.
Identifiers: LCCN 2024009530 | ISBN 9780316574150 (trade paperback) | ISBN 9780316574167 (ebook)
Subjects: CYAC: Mafia—Fiction. | Murder—Fiction. | New York (N.Y.)—Fiction. | Romance stories. | Mystery and detective stories. | LCGFT: Romance fiction. | Detective and mystery fiction. | Novels.
Classification: LCC PZ7.1.C64738 In 2025 | DDC [Fic]—dc23
LC record available at https://lccn.loc.gov/2024009530

ISBNs: 978-0-316-57415-0 (trade paperback), 978-0-316-57416-7 (ebook)

Printed in Indiana, USA

LSC-C, 04/25

Printing 2, 2025

To my parents, for giving me a name and a voice
that helped me soar

CHAPTER ONE

Tasha

THE LIGHTS FROM THE CHANDELIERS GLIMMERED ABOVE MY party guests, illuminating every whispered secret and haute couture gown. Plopping one more caviar-spread cracker into my mouth, I turned to survey the glamor. Every student at Scarsdale Country Day milled around my home. Elaborate satin and chiffon dresses in intoxicating colors grazed the polished floors while their tux counterparts were smoothed to perfection.

I'd made it clear in the invites that anyone dressed less than perfect wouldn't be allowed in. From all the beauty surrounding me, it was clear my influence hadn't faltered over the summer. Thank God for that. It was always a hassle to remind my peers who was in charge around here when their minds were so mutable, ready to change their opinions and support with the shift of the tide. But with everyone already following my lead, tonight's fourth and final Return to Scarsdale Soirée was destined to go well.

It *had* to. Or else.

The serpent-green satin of my custom Vivienne Westwood gown moved with the shape of my legs as I headed into the thick of the party, the crowd parting to let me through. Anyone worthy enough to get an invite to a Nicastro event knew better than to stand in our way.

"Look at them, lapping it all up," I said, sliding next to my older sister, Amelia. She stood alone by the grand piano, as the pianist played *Primavera* by Ludovico Einaudi. "And you said the extra food stations and aerial performers would be too much."

As per tradition, the first half of the party was when everyone floated around the room indulging in the caviar or oyster stations and taking pictures by the custom floral installations. The second half was when the DJ arrived and phones were locked away so the next round of fun could begin.

Amelia sipped her champagne, each bubble like a perfect diamond to enjoy. Her warm caramel-brown curls fell down her shoulders, accentuating the lavender purple in her Chloé dress and soft beige skin. We both inherited most of our looks from our father, but only I got his midnight-black hair and "excitable temperament" as our mother used to put it before she packed only a carry-on to Milan and never returned.

Please. I wore my bitch badge with pride. There was nothing excitable about it.

"I never doubted you'd make this a showstopper of a party," Amelia replied. "I'm only surprised Dad let you blow the budget more than last year."

I shrugged, grabbing a glass of the Dom Perignon being passed around.

"He knows how necessary my soirée is for the school year."

My sister delicately laughed. "Please, Tasha. It's because he'd do anything for you."

I smiled in return and found my gaze wandering out of our oversize living room to the closed office door down the hall. Our father wasn't in his personal office right now—he made a point of going down to our Upper East Side penthouse tonight—but his presence still hovered throughout the wings of our home and really, anywhere else he went. We might rule over this town and all of Westchester as a family, but it was my father who wore the crown. The adoration and respect I got from my Scarsdale Country Day classmates was child's play compared to the level he received from every person he met.

I nudged her in the side. "You make it sound like I'm the only one."

Amelia sighed, then opened her mouth again to say something else when the doorbell chimed through the rooms. Her attention caught on the sound immediately, because only one person in our circle rang the bell.

"What's Julian doing here?" I couldn't help but scrunch my face up.

Amelia turned to me, her hazel eyes apologetic. She grabbed my hand, giving it a squeeze, and I relished in the softness of it...save for the hard, ugly band nestled on her ring finger. "He's taking me to Midtown for dinner."

"But what about my soirée?" I asked, gesturing around. "You never miss it."

"I'm sorry, Tasha." My sister let go of my hand. "You always make sure I have a good time, but I'm twenty-three and engaged now. This isn't a party I can enjoy anymore."

I followed Amelia to the front doors, a knife twisting deeper in my stomach when her face beamed bright as she revealed her fiancé. It was bad enough Julian stole our father's attention every time he could. He had to rip Amelia away, too.

Julian's sharp cheekbones and flimsy arms pulled Amelia in for a kiss. "There you are, my darling," he said. He presented a small box in a mint-green tint with the name of a French patisserie embossed on it. "I brought you an opera cake. But only the one—wouldn't want that beautiful dress to tighten."

Amelia smirked as she took the gift while it took all *my* willpower not to shove him and his Armani suit back down the stairs he'd walked up.

How she found him charming I would never know. The Henderson family owned a global hotel chain, but all the top positions to run a major enterprise like that were taken by his siblings when it became clear Julian would rather trash their Presidential Suites and get caught in one scandalous situation after another than take their family empire seriously. So his little head decided the next best plan was to get cozy with my sister and kiss my father's ass to try to take over our empire. The worst part was our father adored him for it.

I glanced at the box and then to him. He didn't deserve the suit. He didn't deserve a lot of things in this house. "If you're so concerned about her dress, why don't you do us all a favor and stuff the cake into that wide, gaping mouth of yours instead?"

My sister threw me a glare and I inwardly rolled my eyes. She hated when I dug a wedge between my future brother-in-law and me. But I didn't care what he thought of me. The chance that I would ever like him was as possible as drinking beer out of a dirty funnel.

As in, never happening.

"We'll be going now," Amelia said pointedly, grabbing Julian's hand and stepping out into the cooling night air.

As usual, our house manager, Charles, appeared like a puff of smoke, holding Amelia's favorite light jacket out to her.

"If it gets cold, Miss Nicastro," he said.

Amelia took her coat, smiling at Charles, before bringing her attention back to me. "Be good. And don't embarrass the poor freshmen too much this year."

Right. With my sister making an abrupt exit, I'd gotten off track.

"Won't make any promises," I replied, but Amelia had already turned away.

"Tasha!"

From the crowd, my life preserver emerged in Dior and Versace. I exchanged grins with Val, success already glinting in her eyes. If I could rely on anyone to keep me focused, it was my best friend.

"I've picked our contestants out." Val frowned. "What happened to Amelia?"

I waved her question off, moving back to the thick of the party. "Julian happened."

Val flicked her cat-lined eyes over to the dance floor, each movement she made showing new shades in her ombre gown. We'd gone to the same private schools since kindergarten, growing closer with each grade we graduated to. It was easy to stay close when her father, Richard Costa, worked as the chief legal officer of Nicastro Developments.

"Her loss." She handed me a small stack of flash cards and a microphone. "Now it's showtime. Remember, I expect only the best performance from you."

I chuckled, pulling a few of my short locks behind my ear and shaking my bangs from my eyes. Maybe it was excitement—and nerves—making me laugh. I *was* about to put myself on display to the hundreds of students in attendance for the final time.

I winked at her. "Enjoy the show."

With a flick of my wrist, I silenced the pianist and moved toward the dance floor, ready to take this song to its crescendo.

"It's that time, everyone!" I exclaimed, thrusting my hand in the air as I strutted onto the black-and-gold dance floor. A grin spread wide across my face when the crowd cheered and whooped. "I'm happy to see so many of you are as excited as I am. As you should all know, and if you *don't*, you'll soon find out, each year during my Return to Scarsdale Soirée, a cluster of freshmen are plucked from the crowd and called upon to answer some crucial questions before they can be properly welcomed into our school. And if they don't answer correctly?" I cocked a brow, a thrill running through my veins when the crowd shouted out the answer. "Exactly. One item off. Without further ado, these are the freshmen I want on the dance floor with me."

I listed off the names of thirteen students Val had randomly chosen and caught sight of them immediately from the way their shoulders went as rigid as an overstuffed sales rack.

"Hurry, hurry," I cooed into the microphone. Finally, the thirteen of them made their way toward me. "The questions are easy, I promise."

Not, but they'd figure that out soon enough.

"Now," I continued, "any question you answer correctly means all of you are in the clear. Any wrong answers mean you discard something you're wearing into this basket over here. Are we clear?" When the crowd cheered in response, I exclaimed, "Then let's get started!"

I strutted around the room, letting everyone get a good look at the work I'd put into my legs over the summer, and grinned wickedly at the first three questions on the card. There was no way these freshmen would have a clue what the answers were.

"Our first question of the night"—I spun around to face the chosen freshmen like a lioness spotting her next meal—"has to do with my older sister, Amelia. In her junior year at Scarsdale Country Day, what designer did she wear to homecom—"

Boom. Boom. Boom.

I paused as every head in the room turned toward the front doors. Anyone who was fashionably late already arrived over an hour ago. So who the hell was banging on my door?

Charles materialized right away and opened the door to inspect the guest. Before he could greet them, the person shoved the door fully open and stormed in.

Oh, for the love of—

"What are you doing here?" I demanded, curling my lip up.

Scarlett Green flipped her blond blowout over her tanned shoulder and sneered at me as her friends pushed in after her. "To enjoy the party, obviously. And look, we're just in time for your little Scarsdale hazing ceremony to make you feel relevant. Perfect."

Flames licked at the insides of my chest, ready to unleash all over her baby face. Everyone from Scarsdale Country Day was invited to my soirée, *except* for Scarlett and her group of cancerous cells she called friends. That tradition started after they torched the kitchen trying to make flaming cocktails during my first party. Scarlett spent the rest of freshman year trying to humiliate me for kicking her out.

"Oooh, so mean. How will I ever survive such a burn," I replied. "Does it hurt your feelings that you weren't invited again?"

At one time, we had actually been friends. But the memories felt like a fabrication, something I'd dreamt up that my mind tricked me into thinking were real.

Scarlett let out a sharp laugh. "Not at all. I would never be caught dead at this party and your pathetic attempt to be liked. But a certain *someone* came home from boarding school for his senior year, and I thought, *What a perfect opportunity for a reunion with everyone already here.*"

My stomach dropped as I lowered the microphone. I didn't ask who she was referring to, because there was only one person she could bring here that would rattle me.

I was desperate to be wrong.

But then he stepped through the door.

"How's everyone doing tonight?" He hollered, throwing his arms high and wide and showing off the large bottle of champagne he held at the neck. "The one and only Leonardo Danesi is *back*, baby!"

Leo's cocky grin spread wide when the room roared with excitement.

Even after four years away, he could still get everyone who knew him to think he was some god descended from the heavens.

"Get out." Venom laced itself in every word. When he didn't notice—or listen to—me, I screamed, *"Get out of my house!"*

Leo's honey-brown eyes cut to me. The intensity in them could make another girl weak in the knees, but I stood my ground.

I hadn't seen him since I was thirteen years old. Since that day we stood in my old riding stable and he tore my heart in two.

Almost every piece of his boyish self then was peeled away and the body of a near man had been stitched over him. His dark roots were now sun-kissed from his time in California, swept back in the messy style of a guy who barely put in any effort, yet somehow looked good anyway. The first three buttons on his black dress shirt were undone, showing off bits of his smooth skin while he stretched his neck. The only thing I still recognized was the faint dimple on his chin. Everything else about him was different. New.

And I still hated every bit of it.

"Hello to you, too, Nicastro," he said.

"I know you heard what I said." I stayed locked in place, shoulders rigid and ready to fight. "Get out of my house and out of Scarsdale before I have security throw you out. And it won't be pretty." Tilting my head to the side, I purred, "Though it would be fun to see."

Leo barely hesitated before he moved closer. Enough to smell his rich, peppery cologne as he stared down at me. He held the champagne out. "But I brought you a special gift. Scarlett told me how much you like to drink now."

I glared at Scarlett. "Did she?"

A glint danced in his horrible eyes. "I'd hate to start off senior year in the great Natasha Nicastro's bad books."

Others might have believed his act of sincerity. Maybe I would've, too, if it weren't for the smirk stretched wide across his face.

This champagne wasn't an olive branch. It was a test to see how easily I could fall for his lies.

If I gave in now, I'd be throwing a grenade at my carefully formed reputation. All anyone would see at school and beyond was a Nicastro bending at the first pretty word out of a Danesi's mouth despite the hatred our families had shot at one another since his father's death.

No. I wouldn't accept Leo's fake peace offering.

But I could twist it in my favor.

I clicked my heels along the dance floor, leaving no distance between us. It was the only sound now that the party had gone silent. "May I?"

Leo studied me. After a few tense seconds, he complied and handed the champagne over.

The bottle was dense, weighed down by the amber liquid encased in thick glass with a gold seal wrapped around the neck. The size of it could easily fill half the empty glasses in this room. "It's lovely. How much?"

Leo flexed his arms as he propped them behind his head. "Just shy of six grand."

I nodded.

Then hurled it to the floor.

Champagne and glass splattered across the black-and-gold tiles and onto my shoes. A rupture of gasps rippled through the crowd, but I kept my composure and gaze leveled on Leo.

"Oops."

Leo stayed completely still. No heat in his face, no spluttering or angry words thrown at me. I wanted him to lash out. To make a scene. That was easier to navigate than a masked face whose moves I couldn't predict. If this was the way he'd always react when I tried to put him in his place, I had no idea what to expect for the rest of the school year.

"That's what I get for coming all this way?" he finally replied. "And here I thought we might finally get along again."

I picked up the top of the broken bottle, wanting nothing more than to plunge it into his chest. How *dare* he say that after what he said to me, what he did. "You and I both know that'll never happen, Danesi."

Saying his family's name coated my tongue with a vile taste, but the gaze of hundreds of eyes rippled like electricity down my skin. I had them all. Now they waited for the final act.

Grabbing Leo's hand, I slapped the bottle neck into his open palm. "Now for the last time, take your discount friends and get out of here."

Leo stared me down for a long, breathless moment. I hadn't held his attention like this for years. I put up a fortress of steel walls after our last encounter, promising to keep him out for good. But the longer he looked at me now, the harder those walls shook, wanting to bring me right back to that naïve thirteen-year-old girl I used to be.

Finally, he closed his fingers around the glass, his gaze never leaving mine. "Fine, Nicastro. You win."

I smiled, pride draping over me like a warm mink coat. Of course I won. It was what I did best.

Turning away, Leo gestured for his friends to follow him back to the foyer. Scarlett's scowl sent an adrenaline rush through me that was sweeter than any gold-coated treat. If she hated this, it could only have gone perfectly.

The household staff stepped in armed with mops and brooms to quickly clean up the mess. I moved out of the way and onto dry ground, catching Val's approving eye.

"You really do shine when all eyes are on you," she said. "Especially when you're humiliating Leo."

I fluffed my dress. "It's a natural instinct."

Scarlett and the others hurried out, but Leo paused at the doors and glanced back at me. Our eyes locked through the crowd and held on to each other.

"Miss?" A server appeared, offering a fresh glass of bubbling champagne.

I accepted and raised it to Leo. A smile played on my lips as he scowled, but it vanished once he slipped out into the night.

Four years away. Four years of silence. Of hatred. And he waltzes back in here, into my life, as if nothing happened.

I wanted to be disgusted by it, but really, I was at the edge of a skyscraper, wondering if I was one push away from ruin.

CHAPTER TWO

Tasha

My bones still hummed with the success of my party two days later. I'd put on a fantastic soirée, positioning myself as Scarsdale Country Day's queen for the last, and most important, year of my high school life. All while stomping a much-desired foot into Leo's cocky scheme. Nothing was coming between me and my power over this school.

I packed up my things when the last bell rang and texted Val, telling her to meet me in the Donor Lounge.

Students quickly moved out of the way like weeds bowing to the wind as I walked by with my chin held high. No one had the nerve to look me in the eye—just the way I liked it. All day, I'd heard whispers of gossip about what happened at my soirée. Thankfully, the conversations were in my favor. Leo Danesi thought he could humiliate me in front of our whole school, and I'd gladly served him up a large platter of it instead.

The freshly buffed DONOR LOUNGE sign came into view a few minutes later. It was reserved for students with families who supported the school aside from tuition fees, the Donor Students as we were called. The room was designed so we had a view of the courtyard and weren't too far from any of our classrooms. We had our own bathrooms, constant refreshments, plush couches...

And the best part of it? The mark of exclusivity.

Although everyone paid hefty fees to get into the school, Scarsdale Country Day needed far more money to keep it well maintained. The main building was built like a miniature castle nearly a century ago with three expansive levels and sprawling east and west wings. Every floor and room had been renovated to fit modern needs with only the best materials and staff to keep it running. Students had access to every type of sport imaginable, and they were all available on the school's property. With tennis, lacrosse, and polo being our specialties.

At the farthest edge of campus was the Scarsdale Polo Club—one of the nicest in New York—and definitely the nicest for a private school. The twenty-stall stable sat like an elegant swan watching over the field where the team practiced and held games. It was one of the most difficult clubs in school to join.

Obviously, that was the one I was part of.

I scanned my key card against the Donor Lounge's door and opened it when the light turned green.

Five students relaxed on the dark emerald couches. Three girls, two guys. One of them sat with his back to me while two of the girls stretched their exposed legs across his lap. Non-donor students weren't allowed in the lounge. But naturally the lure to bring some in anyway and piss off the other Donor Students was too strong of an urge for some.

I crossed my arms. "Danesi."

Resting his toned arm on the back of the couch, Leo craned his neck around. His hooded eyes did a bored sweep of me. "Yes?"

I cocked a brow at the girls lounging with him. One of them, of course, was Scarlett. When the feud between my family and Leo's started, the

Greens quickly became the Danesis' lapdogs, desperate to raise Evergreen Pharmaceutical's stock price by establishing stores in all the real estate the Danesis owned when my father refused to partner with them.

The second guy among their group was a donor, Jonathan Bakker, but the two extra girls were not. "I see you're already back to breaking the rules," I said to Leo.

"I have no idea what you're talking about." A grin stretched across Leo's lips as he turned to his friends. I could've slapped it off his face.

"This is our space, too." Scarlett leaned against the couch, rubbing her smooth leg against Leo's thighs. "We can do anything—and invite anyone—we want. You don't have any power in here."

My mouth itched to snap a few choice names I had for both of them, but I thought of what my father had engrained in me. A Nicastro didn't show all their cards, even if those cards held enough power to throw someone to their knees.

Leo looked back at me again. "If you're done now, we'd like to get back to relaxing in peace and not listening to your dull bitching."

My brows shot up my forehead. Oh, that was *it*. I'd remember my father's words starting tomorrow.

"Look, you little shit," I hissed, stepping closer.

I was ready to tear his throat out and eat it raw when the door clicked open and a familiar voice spoke.

"What's going on?"

I turned, my breath hitching, as I looked up at a boy with gel-smoothed hair, silky olive skin, and full lips on a face I knew far too well. It was a face I'd kissed and dumped not two weeks ago on the final day of his family's trip to St. Barts.

Ravi Ferreira. My ex-boyfriend.

He swept one look over the scene, his quiet, dominating energy expanding through the room, before he looked down at me. "Are they bothering you, Tasha?"

"Who the fuck cares if we are?" Jonathan replied like a fool.

Nerves rattled in my windpipe. I couldn't keep my gaze on Ravi's and instead stared at a photograph hanging on the wall. I'd broken his heart, yet here he was protecting me like nothing had changed between us. And here *I* was getting the same fluttering anxiety in my chest when he was around, quelling the fire roaring inside.

"It's not anything you need to worry about."

"Yeah, listen to her, Ferreira," Jonathan said. "She's not your bitch to take care of anymore."

The girls gasped on my behalf. That comment was welcoming a world of pain from my fist, but I stayed quiet with Ravi here. In the three years we dated, he was the one who jumped to my defense before I could say anything. It was an easy habit to fall into—apparently even after we broke up.

Ravi stalked over to Jonathan; his glare strong enough to melt skin. "Speak to her like that again, Bakker," he growled, "and this will be your last day at this school."

Jonathan had the decency to show a hint of concern. As he should. The Ferreiras weren't just another wealthy family. They were tech billionaires who held more power in the influential people they knew than they did in cash. No one was immune from their wrath, especially not a loudmouth like Jonathan.

"Whoa, man, no need to get so harsh," Jonathan replied, raising his hands in front of him. "It was a stupid joke. No one here thinks it's true."

We all knew he was full of it, but Ravi let him get away with his insult. This time.

He pulled back, cutting his dark gaze to the last person I wanted him to notice.

"You look familiar," Ravi said to Leo. "Have we met before?"

Leo rubbed his chin, keeping his expression wiped free of emotion. "Nah, man. Can't say I've ever seen your face."

"Come on, Leo, you've heard of Ravi Ferreira," Scarlett replied, swatting him playfully on the arm. "His family owns Aurora Technology."

He held his focus on Ravi, still with that blank look on his face. "Oh yeah. I think I've heard of you."

"What an honor," Ravi replied dryly. He moved back to stand beside me, and his hand brushed briefly against mine. I knew it was deliberate. Apparently, so did Leo. His gaze caught the movement and went down to our hands before he looked back up, staring straight at me.

I went warm all over against my will. I didn't need to explain anything to him. He shoved his way out of my life long ago.

"It's best if you and your friends find another area to occupy," Ravi continued.

Leo didn't look away from me. "Does he always speak for you, Nicastro?"

Of course not, caught on the edge of my lips and hovered there— taunting me. I glared at him, willing myself to answer.

"Only when she needs me to," Ravi replied.

A ghost of a look passed over Leo's face. Quick enough that I could've missed it. I wished I had. The last thing I needed was for *him* to show an ounce of judgment.

I crossed my arms, digging my nails into my palms to distract from the anger coursing through my bloodstream.

"So?" Ravi asked. "Are you going to make this more difficult for yourself or not?"

Silence passed. The stereo played. The mini fridge hummed. Muffled chatter swelled from other students in the hall. I held my breath through it all. I never would've expected Leo Danesi to have a power standoff with my ex-boyfriend. Guess God could have a bad sense of humor, too.

Finally though, Leo slowly rose from the couch, prompting his friends to follow suit.

"Fine, Ferreira," he said. "You win. Enjoy your alone time with Nicastro."

I held myself together, raising my chin at him instead. "Welcome back, Danesi."

The hairs on the back of my neck stood up as he brushed past me before he disappeared out into the hall.

Once they were all gone, I cleared my throat and faced Ravi. "Thanks for your help, but I could've handled it myself."

"You know I can't stand by when you need protecting." His eyes, the color of summer's green grass, softened. "No matter where we stand."

My jaw clenched. "When did you get back from Brasília?"

"Late last night," he replied. "My mother wanted me to stay home a few nights longer after what ... happened in St. Barts."

I nodded, not quite meeting his eye. Three years ago, Ravi had only ever visited New York as a tourist. Now he lived nearby in Bedford Corners. The Ferreiras bought an estate there so his oldest sister could work for a distinguished New York law firm known for their pro bono work for vulnerable women and children. Ravi followed her to go to private school in the States, fatefully making us meet on the first day of freshman year.

He'd set his sights on me immediately, and I'd gladly accepted his pursuit. Throughout our relationship, I'd stayed wrapped in his arms. Until things ... shifted.

I started feeling fidgety when we were together, a sensation I couldn't push away. It didn't help that my father, drinking up our relationship like it were his own, started musing over me *marrying* Ravi. Like it was an inevitability, a choice already made for me. On the Ferreiras' recent family trip, Mrs. Ferreira started showing me photos of engagement rings. That was it. I broke things off, needing to think, to *breathe*, and it was the only way I would get it. Even if it meant hurting Ravi in the process.

I had no interest in making small talk with him, but he made no move to leave, and from the look on his face, he had a reason to stay. I glanced at the closed door, willing my best friend to materialize. What was taking Val so damn long?

"Can we talk?" Ravi asked.

And there it was.

I stepped back from him, shaking my head weakly. "Ravi, I still need more time."

"Ignore what our families think," he replied, closing the distance between us and grasping my hands before I had a chance to hide them. "We don't need to take the next step in our relationship right away. All I want to do is make you happy, and it's killing me that you think being apart is the way you can get that."

"It's *not* the only way I can be happy," I said. "But it's what I need right now as I figure things out."

Ravi pressed his lips into a thin line, looking ready to continue this argument, but I was saved when the lounge door opened with a flourish and Val finally strutted into the room.

She halted when she saw us. Her long highlighted brown hair hung over her shoulders and a soft blush accentuated her high cheekbones, complimenting the natural tan she got from summering in Santorini. "Hello?"

"Val!" I exclaimed, pulling my hands free of Ravi's. "There you are." I hurried over and linked arms with her before turning to Ravi. "We need to get going. But I'll see you later, okay?"

Ravi rubbed his mouth, giving a solemn nod. "I'll be here when you're ready to talk."

My ears immediately burned, but I forced a smile to keep him happy and guided the two of us down the hall—fast.

"What the hell did I walk in on?" Val said when we were far from the lounge. "Are you two getting back together? Knew it."

"Nothing happened, and no, we're not. Where were you?"

"I was handling some last-minute stuff for my trip to Scottsdale with Mom," she replied as we made our way to the donors' parking lot where her silver Mercedes waited for us. "She wants to leave Friday morning now."

I groaned. "I really wish you weren't. Who's going to be my buffer on Saturday?"

My father was throwing one last hurrah to celebrate Amelia and Julian's engagement before the wedding next month. Everyone connected to our family was invited to see his enthusiasm for the nuptials. Julian's family wasn't coming until the big day, but one Henderson was plenty to deal with. I thought I would have Val to keep me from making a scene and embarrassing Amelia, but then she had to go and accept a girls' weekend to Arizona with her mother instead.

Usually, I loved parties, but this one was going to test that.

"You'll be fine," Val replied as she unlocked her car. "Latte before I drop you home?"

I shook my head and climbed in the passenger seat. "Can't. I've got a date with the shooting range."

The blast vibrated through my arms, rattling every nerve inside me. I didn't waste any time hanging on my perfect shot when the next target swept by faster, pulling the trigger and firing the bullet right into the bullseye again.

Bang, bang, bitch.

The target machine groaned before coming to a halt. Victor pulled his hand away from the switch, lips puckered and nodding.

He was my trainer, but also my father's best friend and right hand in the family business. Knowing him all my life, Victor fit into the uncle role with ease since my actual extended family couldn't be bothered. Or had died in Uncle Luca's case.

"Nice work. I knew that extra practice would pay off."

I grinned and pulled my earmuffs off. "I aim to please."

Victor gave me a rough pat on the back, revealing the fresh river of bruises running along his left bicep and down to his knuckles. Unease went through me as I glanced at them again. He wore bruises and scars like his tattoos, new ones popping up every week and overlapping with the ones still fading. I wasn't allowed to ask where he got them, and he never explained.

"Then you can go bench-press for me, too."

The grin fell from my face. I shouldn't have said anything. I could do the other weights, but the bench press was the worst. Victor turned into a sadist when I used it, not letting me stop until I leaked sweat like a fountain.

Our personal gym held regular equipment, but our father insisted years ago that Amelia and I train with Victor in combat fighting and learn how to shoot. He always promised us we were safe with our security dutifully around, but he wanted the extra peace of mind in knowing his daughters could take care of themselves, if necessary. According to him, operating in the one percent meant we had to stay constantly vigilant.

I dragged myself into the weights room and straddled the bench. "Forty pounds. No more."

Victor scratched the gray stubble on his chin, cutting me a look that said otherwise. "Sure." He added the weights and stepped behind my head to spot me, his T-shirt barely containing the years of muscle he'd built to make up for his lack of height.

When I heaved the cold metal rod off its stand though, I swore. Should've known. "I said *forty*. Not *fifty-five*."

Victor arched a brow. "Are you admitting you can't handle the pressure?"

I suppressed the urge to roll my eyes.

I jerked my chin at the two-and-a-half-pound weights nearby. "Add another five."

Victor smirked as I set the bar down and lifted myself to a sitting position. While he secured the extra two and a half pounds to each side of my bar, I fidgeted with my gloves, ignoring the dull ache in my muscles from weight lifting over the weekend, too.

"I've always been impressed by how often you push past your comfort level," a steady voice said.

I spooked, whipping around to look at my father.

He stood by the open doorway in an impeccable suit, one hand resting easy in his jacket pocket. When people saw my father, they hurried to say hello, charming their way into his good graces. It was an easy thing to want when he was a man who could make nearly any wish come true. We'd held influence in New York for decades, ever since we brought the family business, Nicastro Developments, to the States three generations ago.

All I cared about though was the sly smile playing on his weathered, handsome face. A smile as rare as a black pearl and one that he only let his daughters see.

"Dad!" I slid off the bench press and stood. My first instinct was to rush over and give him a hug, but the large sweat patch on my tank top from my earlier cardio stopped me. "How long have you been standing there?"

"Long enough to see you're getting much better at your marksmanship. Though there is one habit you still haven't broken."

I stayed quiet as he headed over to the shooting range and picked up one of the handguns with ease. After flicking the machine back on, he raised the weapon and sent four bullets flying to the same target before it had moved into center frame.

"You're still twisting your wrist too much to the right when you fire." He faced me, demonstrating what he was referring to. "You need to tighten it to keep your aim true. Understand?"

I nodded, hoping he didn't notice the flush in my skin. He was one of the best shooters I knew. The easiest way to make him proud was to get just as good as him.

"Trying to show me up, Gabriel?" Victor asked.

"I'd never dream of it," he replied, strolling over and slapping his friend playfully on the back. "Except for every time I do."

Their grins would look feral to an outsider, but to me they were endearing.

"Are you here to watch the rest of my training?" I asked, already knowing the answer was no. He hadn't done anything spontaneous in years, putting everything in his life into a schedule. Including family time with Amelia and me.

My father tipped his chin to me. "I wanted to talk to you. It's about Saturday's party."

I cut my attention to Victor when he grunted softly. Whatever this was, he already knew about it.

"I'll go grab us some fresh water," Victor said, already en route to the exit.

I frowned as he closed the door behind him and turned back to my father. "I'm getting the feeling I should be concerned."

He chuckled, placing a gentle hand on my shoulder. "I've updated the guest list. I'm telling you this so you won't be thrown off when they arrive on Saturday."

My heart quickened like my body already knew what name he would say before my mind could catch up. "Who?"

His gaze was unwavering. "The Danesis."

"*What?*" I ripped away from his touch. He hated when someone raised their voice, but it was impossible in a moment like this. "Why would you *ever* do that? Sloane Danesi tried to ruin your name!"

The Danesis used to be our closest family friends. My father and Angelo Danesi were always full of roaring laughter and flowing wine whenever we got together. But after Angelo died in a head-on collision, everything changed.

My father wouldn't let us see them. With the things Leo said to me before he stormed out of my life...I understood why. The Danesis were looking for someone to throw their anger at, to drag down with them, so they chose us. I'd never seen my father so stressed trying to weather that storm and come out the other side with our reputation still intact. Thankfully, we'd made it through, but not without first losing my mother to Milan and then later Uncle Luca to a boating accident.

All that pain and loss was too much for a thirteen-year-old to experience, and yet, somehow, I made it through alive.

"Because I've invited many powerful families to celebrate my first daughter's upcoming wedding," he replied. "Families that are friends and those who are in debt to me from the times I've saved them from their own greed and stupidity. Just because we've had our share of issues with the Danesis doesn't mean they should sit out from such a joy-filled celebration. Sloane has known Amelia since she was a toddler."

I stared blankly at him. There had to be more to it. I could hear the instinct whispering in my ear, nudging me to probe his explanation further. "Dad, it sounds like you're using Amelia as a pawn in some game. Don't you care how she'll feel about this?"

He scoffed, folding his hands tight enough to make the knuckles go white. "She's far from a pawn. Amelia has plenty on her mind right now that I doubt she'll notice their presence. There will be a lot more security on the night, too."

My eyes widened. "Is something going on?"

"For now, let's be on a need-to-know basis." He took a few steps back and shot me a discerning look. "And remember our rules about the Danesis. My invite does not mean you're welcome to drop your guard around them. Specifically when it comes to Leo. I know you two were close, but we still need them at arm's length. Can you promise me that?"

"That's an easy promise to make," I replied.

My father nodded, rolling his shoulders back. "Good to hear."

"What if I were your extra eyes for the night?" I asked. "Everyone will be so focused on you and Amelia, no one will notice me. I can watch the Danesis...or anyone else."

But really, I meant *only* the Danesis. If Leo was stepping into my house a second time in a week, I needed to make sure he didn't touch anything other than what the caterers brought in. I didn't trust that family not to use this party as an opportunity to humiliate us in some way.

My father's dark eyes searched my face, his a fortress I couldn't decipher. "Are you sure you want to do that?"

I crossed my arms. "Do you think I'm not capable?"

"The opposite." He came closer to me, cupping my cheek in his warm hand. "I've known how capable you are for a long time."

My brows pulled close while I leaned into his touch. "Why do I feel like there's more to this?"

He chuckled and let his hand fall back to his side. "What do you think about the family business?"

"It's given us the life we have, so I'd say I'm a fan." My eyes tightened. "Why?"

He paused for a moment before finally replying, "Because I'd like to bring you in. There'd be some...cultural hiccups that'd take some time to get used to, but I think you can handle it."

Shock rushed through my body and stole my voice for a few seconds. He'd never hinted at wanting me involved before.

Nicastro Developments acquired and developed real estate across the East Coast. No one could go with a better developer than ours. At one point my family owned nearly all of Lower Manhattan as we created the city's current real estate. The business had steadily grown since my father took over.

"Have you asked Amelia to work for you, too?"

Although I doubted she'd say yes. My sister loved her job as a curator at the Met.

"No, I don't think that would be a good idea," he replied, the fortress reappearing on his face. "But do you like the sounds of it for yourself?"

I mused over my answer. Until now, I'd been so focused on maintaining power in Scarsdale Country Day, I hadn't considered what I would want afterward. With such a clear invitation from my father though, I had the chance to soar higher than I'd ever imagined. Maybe even shove Julian out of the top spot if I felt like it. I would never know if I didn't dip my toes in.

I nodded, a grin spreading across my face. "I don't see why not. As long as you promise I won't be doing data entry until my fingers bleed. If I had to sit at a laptop all day, I think I'd combust."

My father replicated my grin, grabbing my shoulder and giving it a loving squeeze. "That's my girl. And of course I wouldn't. You're too much like me; I can never sit still for long either."

"What's got you two grinning widely?"

I turned as Amelia walked into the gym with a white Met tote slung over her shoulder and a lush bouquet cradled in her arms like a newborn baby.

"I've let Tasha know Ravi accepted his invitation to the party," our father answered before I could. "We may be back in the Ferreiras good graces before the end of the week. Isn't that wonderful?"

I wasn't sure why he was lying to Amelia about our conversation, but I wasn't going to be foolish enough to contradict him.

"Yes," my sister replied, glancing my way. "Assuming you want to get back together with him, Tasha?"

I stiffly nodded. "I'm thinking about it."

It wasn't a total lie.

"I have to go. I have a meeting with some suppliers in ten minutes." Our father leaned over and kissed my cheek before moving toward the doorway. "I'll see you two at dinnertime."

He stopped when he reached Amelia, kissing her cheek as well. When he pulled away and slipped back down the hall, my sister turned to me.

"Now that he's gone," she came closer, her eyes brightening, "tell me what you two *really* talked about. A boy has never made you grin that widely. Not even Ravi."

I pressed a hand to my mouth to try and hide my smile, but it was pointless. My sister knew me too well.

So I spilled everything to her.

CHAPTER THREE

I should've jumped in the damn ocean rather than come to this place.

The clock on the wall clicked to two thirty in the afternoon, marking two hours since I'd fallen for Mom's strings-attached gift and ended up at Greenwich Country Club for this meeting. She'd offered Dad's black Ferrari in exchange for coming with her instead of going to school. *Just once*, she promised. I regretted that choice the second my sorry ass sat in this chair. I wanted nothing to do with the business Mom and her associates discussed, but I was locked in until she set me free.

Before Dad's death, I used to enjoy coming to the club for rounds of golf or causing trouble with friends. But ever since Mom took over the family business, all visits were hijacked to this private room where a group of wolves dressed like sheep sat around figuring out how to make our empire richer—by whatever means necessary. She didn't want to hold *these* types of meetings at the office near our house in Greenwich, Connecticut. One of our long-standing hangouts had to be seized instead.

I turned to my older brother seated beside me. Carter leaned against his cushioned leather chair, one loafered foot crossed over the other, and held a pen in his hand like a Marlboro. When he noticed my gaze, his ocean-gray eyes jumped to me, and he smirked.

Carter was just as much at fault for this. He'd worked for Mom and the rest of Danesi Properties since he graduated high school two years ago and could've made an excuse to get me out of this.

I'd been home for less than a week and already I was being hauled into the world I ran from. I'd avoided—and tried to forget—a lot of things while I was in California, but Mom made it clear the second I returned, those years were over. All because I got expelled from the Thacher School for drunkenly brawling with another student on the anniversary of Dad's death.

"I've tried convincing the owners of the land we need in Worcester to sell to us, but they aren't budging," one of the associates said, continuing the conversation they'd had for the past hour over some new casino Mom wanted to build in Massachusetts. "If we can't get them to sell for our expansion, we'll need to rethink this entire location. The city's already made it clear they'll be down our throats if we try to build on our current acreage."

"I'm getting tired of your indifferent attitude, Samson. We have *many* forms of persuasion in our arsenal and yet, all you want to do is roll over and play dead?" Mom stabbed her laptop's keyboard with her red-coated nails. "We're getting that property and that's final. Or do I need to find myself a more competent group?"

Her associates shook their heads aggressively, satisfying Mom—for now. I pissed her off for being a son she couldn't control easily. Dealing with that was brutal enough; I couldn't imagine what it was like to sit at this table staring down her wrath without the protection of familial blood.

My family owned a long list of casinos and racetracks across New

England and a handful in the Midwest with the first opening in the sixties. At one point, Danesi Properties was seen as a true rival of Vegas casinos. But that power and reputation sunk as quickly as our cash flow when Dad died. Mom took over not long after that, trying to claw her way back up to our old status ever since.

"We'll make it happen, Sloane," another one of the associates said. "I've heard the husband's an addict. We could plant some shit on them. Go big enough that the property's seized. I have an in with the Worcester force that could get it in our hands easy."

Carter scoffed. "Did you start your job yesterday? Might as well wait 'til they drop dead at that point, and we *don't* involve any law enforcement. Let's torch the place so they're forced to sell when they realize insurance will take forever. We could be breaking ground before the first snowfall—if they make it out alive."

I rubbed a hand across my forehead, mumbling, "Jesus, Carter." Unfortunately for me, my brother heard. So did Mom.

He elbowed my side. "Look at that, the second Danesi son *can* speak."

"Do you have a suggestion you'd like to share, Leo?" Mom asked coolly.

I shifted in my chair. "I'll pass."

Mom could drag me to these meetings, make me transport briefcases full of unmarked cash, or whatever else she demanded of me, but she was never going to convince me to be an actual member of our twisted empire. Let alone inherit her position one day and risk dealing with a mess of dead bodies.

"It is a foolish idea though, burning their house down." She narrowed her eyes at Carter, disdain deepening in the lines around her mouth. "We do things *discreetly*. Not light up our intentions for all to see. Either give me smart ideas or none at all. Or do you need to be demoted a second time?"

My brother cleared his throat, shifting in his seat. "My apologies, boss."

The room stretched with silence while Mom went back to her laptop, not noticing—or caring—about the discomfort that formed with it.

I flicked my attention back to Carter who had pulled out his phone. A year later, and Mom still hadn't forgiven him for his screw up. I hadn't asked for the details. All I knew was Carter went behind her back and agreed to an under-the-table scheme with a union leader for a hospitality group. He didn't like how slow she was to give him responsibility and power within the business.

His grand plan to prove her wrong blew up in his face when that union head ended up working for the FBI and nearly got our entire organization shut down. Whatever ideas she had to groom him for her position erupted that day. Now here I was, the pound of flesh Mom thought she could mold into her perfect heir instead. *Thanks*, Carter.

"I'm getting a call from our supplier for the Boston racetrack," Carter said, pushing to his feet abruptly. "Permission to leave?"

Mom waved a hand at him, already moving on to another topic related to the Worcester casino. I zoned out for too long, not noticing Mom was trying to get my attention until she slapped the table. I jolted back to the room with everyone staring hard at me—most of all my mother.

"Sorry, what?"

Mom gave me a tight smile. "Go check on your brother. Make sure he realizes I expect him back at this meeting and not at the bar."

I nodded, rising from my chair. All *I* wanted to do was hang at the bar, but I kept that comment to myself.

Slipping out into the hall, I moved across the polished hardwood and past the floor-to-ceiling windows that gave an unobstructed view of the club's lush golf course. My brother wasn't right outside the doors, so I kept walking through the seating area and one of the dining rooms. When I was near the entrance, I caught sight of him standing outside talking to someone.

The stranger was a foot taller than Carter with a willowy figure underneath his unassuming collared shirt and navy dress pants. I couldn't make out much other than the profile of his face, but I could see Carter's. The look he gave the man put me on high alert.

Every line on his face was severe as he listened to the stranger speak. About what, I couldn't say. Whatever it was had my brother's full attention—and fury. He glanced around, then yelled something at the man before storming back to the main doors.

I stepped away from the windows right before Carter came back inside. He spooked when he saw me, but quickly recovered, melting back into his usual self.

"What are you doing out here?" he asked.

"Mom sent me to look for you."

Carter cocked a brow, stopping to fix his mousy-brown hair in a mirror. "Look at you following orders. And here I thought you'd put up a bigger fight before getting sucked into the family business."

I kept pace with him while walking back to the meeting. My brother swaggered through the club, grinning at a group of pretty girls heading out to the patio like nothing was amiss. Like the guy I saw out front was a mirage.

"Who was that you were talking to?" I asked. "Looked heated."

My brother glanced absently behind us and shrugged. "A guy named Ivan. He's some local antique dealer who's been harassing me for weeks trying to sell rare art to us. I've told him we're not interested, but he's persistent. As you saw."

I tilted my head, studying him closely. "And that's all he's selling? Rare art?"

In my family's world, you could never be sure.

Carter laughed, patting me lightly on the back as we reached the closed doors to the meeting space. "What happened to not caring about the business? Don't worry about it, Leo. That guy won't bother us again."

Not waiting for me to respond, he knocked lightly and opened the door, pulling us right back into the belly of the beast.

The front door closed behind me, echoing throughout the cold interior of home. It was muffled by the scuff of my shoes as I headed upstairs before Mom and Carter arrived, too. The second the meeting was over, I'd sped out of the club, wanting distance between that slog of an afternoon and getting ready for a fun night out with my friends.

I moved through a stark, quiet house. No staff mopping the floors, no sounds of our chef moving around the kitchen. I nearly shouted hello to make sure they all hadn't collectively quit when I stiffened.

One of our guards lay face down at the base of the stairs.

A cold sweat broke out over my skin. The guy wasn't moving and when I trailed my eyes up the rest of the stairs, I caught sight of three more toppled to the ground.

Oh, shit.

I nearly turned and bolted in the other direction if it weren't for one sound that broke through the sharp silence. A choked sob. And from the last person I wanted to hear it from.

With nausea thumping against the base of my throat, I stalked up the stairs, careful not to make any noise or trip over the bodies. I wanted to be wrong, but as I crept down the hall, a new smell hit my senses.

The staff kept the entire house scrubbed with a delicate lavender and jasmine scent Mom was strict about using. But this wasn't floral. It was metallic mixed with a subtle decaying musk.

And it was coming from my little sister's bedroom.

The door was slightly ajar as I approached, and rustling noises of multiple feet came from within. I hovered with my heart in my throat. Whoever was in there was good enough to break in and take down all our security, and here I was without even a switchblade. What the hell did I do now?

"Okay, I'm done. Let's take the girl and get out of here."

I saw red.

Chucking logic off a cliff, I hurled through the door—and froze.

Blood.

Smeared across her duvet and pillowcases, her bookshelves and wallpaper. All from the broken bodies of a dozen white doves thrown across the room.

But all that gore was irrelevant compared to the horror in front of me.

Two masked men stood in the bedroom with one holding a gun to my sister's head.

Tears streamed down Sophia's round cheeks, the nozzle of the gun digging through her golden-brown hair. Her body trembled violently underneath her junior high uniform, and the items in her bag were scattered on the floor.

"If you want her to live, you'll back the hell off," the one holding a gun to her head growled.

A storm lashed in my chest. In the moment my little sister needed me the most, I was useless to her.

"Let her go," I croaked, hating myself for how weak I sounded.

The two men laughed, flashing their yellowed teeth at me through the holes in their masks.

"Yeah, fucking right," the second one said. "Do you hear this Danesi kid? He's lucky we don't mow him down, too."

"Why don't you give him a little taste though? Nothing that'll maim him for life."

The second man grinned and pointed his gun at me. "I like the way you think."

I nearly lunged for their guns, ready to push through their bullets to save my sister, when two gunshots fired behind me.

The masked men collapsed instantly. Sophia shrieked and fell to her knees, curling into herself. A shock of panic went through me thinking she was hurt until I realized she wasn't bleeding.

I looked behind me, clocking Mom lowering her handgun with Carter hovering beside her.

Relief cleared my vision, and I took in the two bodies. Their blood leaked out onto the hardwood below, eyes wide and mouths drooped open like they were in awe.

Bile burned in my stomach.

It wasn't my first time seeing freshly dead men, but it hadn't gotten easier. I hoped it never did.

I rushed over to Sophia, holding tight to her as she cried into my arms. This was the first time she had witnessed a murder. And it was one more way our world stripped away someone's innocence without any warning.

"Secure the room," Mom ordered Carter.

He didn't spring into action at first. Instead, Carter stared down at us, his face sheet white, before he snapped out of it and swept through the space, throwing open the ensuite bathroom door.

"Well, here's all the staff." Carter grimaced at the strained whimpers. "Everyone looks to be alive."

Mom stepped into the room and crouched in front of me and Sophia. "Are you hurt, honey?"

When she pulled her face away from me to shake her head, Mom straightened and went over to the bodies, jerking back their masks to look at their faces. I didn't recognize either man.

I faced my sister. "What happened?"

Sophia's entire upper body shook underneath my grip. She wouldn't look at me as she replied, "I got home early and th-they must've been waiting for me. I screamed and the guards c-came running, but…"

A heavy weight settled onto my chest, pressing and pressing and pressing. If Mom and Carter hadn't shown up, if we were one minute too late…Sophia could have been taken from us. Just like the day I watched Dad die. When tires screeched, bullets punctured metal, and my hands covered both eyes while I wondered if I'd ever open them again.

It was the reason I spiraled so much that I needed to redo freshman year.

But I wasn't that fourteen-year-old kid anymore. Right now, I had to be strong. For Sophia and for myself. "Did they say what they wanted with you?"

A fresh set of tears formed in Sophia's eyes. She wiped at them, but it did nothing to stop the steady flow. "All they said was something about 'the boss' wanting me to be brought in alive."

Blood pulsed behind my eyes and roared in my ears. I glanced up at Mom and met her murderous gaze. Usually I had to hold myself back from cowering underneath it, but I was grateful for it now.

She jerked her chin to one of the bodies. "Look at this."

I gently let go of Sophia and moved over to Mom, my skin breaking out in a cold sweat the closer I got to the bodies.

I swore under my breath.

She'd pulled back the sleeves of the dead men. And there, on both of their left forearms, was the tattoo of a lion.

The Nicastros' symbol.

"They've cut through it though," she said, pointing to a long knife-point scar running diagonally through the tattoos. "It's fresh, too."

"Doesn't matter," I replied. They could slash through their tattoos a hundred times and it still wouldn't change the fact that they worked for

Gabriel Nicastro. The man I pictured burning in hell each time I said a prayer at church.

I reached down and grabbed one of the guns laying a few feet away and took out the bullets to verify my suspicions.

Seeing them again didn't make it any easier.

Etched into the side of the bullets was the lion. The one I knew far too well.

All at once, I was fourteen again. Cracking open the back seat door, crawling on the asphalt thinking more gunshots would fire if I rose. Looking ahead so I wouldn't see the bodies lying on the road around me. My bare knees had pressed into one of the bullets. The pain had been so fierce that at first, I'd thought it punctured my skin.

When I'd seen the outline of the lion, I wanted to believe it was another family. That it was a terrible misunderstanding. But it wasn't. It was deliberate. A message. Like this was.

"Take your sister out of here while Carter and I deal with everything," Mom ordered. "Carter, get a team over here *immediately*. Leo, are you listening to me?"

I snapped out of the nightmare and looked over at her. "What?"

Mom snapped her fingers toward Sophia. "Take your sister and leave. *Now.*"

Pocketing the bullet, I moved on instinct, helping Sophia to her feet and gently guiding her out of the room. When we eventually made it down to the kitchen, I helped her sit on one of the barstools at the large island. The tea towels still hung out of place; dirty cutlery still sat beside the sink. Nothing was out of the ordinary down here despite how much had changed one floor above us.

"Sophia," I said softly, taking the seat beside her. When she stared off, fading into a husk of herself right in front of my eyes, I grabbed her clenched hands. "Hey, look at me."

She did, her breaths ragged and her face puffy. I pulled her wavy locks behind her ear, brushing my fingertips over her hot cheek. "I swear on my life that I'm going to get to the bottom of this so it won't happen again."

She shook her head. "Never swear anything on your life, Leo. Please."

I nodded, brushing a fresh set of tears off her face.

"What's going to happen next?" Sophia asked, her voice hoarse and wobbly.

I clutched her hands tighter in mine. The image of the gun pressed against her head was seared in my mind. Right beside the image of Dad dead at the wheel. "I don't know."

But I did know. Turning my head, I looked across the island to an invite we'd received this morning. The thick paper and gold lettering were too beautiful to be connected to such a nasty family. And yet, now it was the key I needed to protect my sister.

I might reject every attempt Mom made to join her world, but when it came to Sophia, I'd put on the suit and do whatever vile, horrific thing needed to keep her safe. Even if that meant going into the lions' den and confronting the one person I was supposed to stay far away from.

The girl I once knew better than myself.

Tasha.

CHAPTER FOUR

Lambos to Rolls-Royces lined the long circular driveway like jewels dotting a crown. Right in the center was the Nicastros' sprawling white mansion, chandeliers in the windows bouncing light throughout the home and lavish gardens that could rival Buckingham Palace surrounding the property. I'd forgotten how much larger the Nicastro house was to ours. More room for dark secrets behind the luxury.

Our driver pushed the Cadillac SUV closer to the front. I glanced behind us to make sure Carter was still behind me and Mom. Arriving anywhere in two cars was always Mom's policy. She hated the idea of relying on one car to get away in even when all she was doing was something as simple as shopping at a boutique store in a random little town. With us waltzing into enemy territory, I was surprised there weren't five vehicles following behind.

After Sophia's bedroom was cleaned up and Mom wrote out checks with eye-watering amounts for each of the staff members to stay quiet, she declared she was marching straight into the Nicastros' party. She wanted to know what game Gabriel Nicastro was playing by sending the invite—and such a blatant threat—to our home.

My mother, Sloane Danesi, was entering the Nicastro household again for the first time in four years.

My brother was already handing his car keys to the attendant as I got out of the SUV. He had chosen a crisp dove-gray Tom Ford suit while I'd chosen a raven-black Dolce & Gabbana tux. The Nicastros were the type of people who would kick guests out if they didn't show up dripping in wealth.

Carter slid up beside me. "Crazy to be back here, isn't it?"

I grunted a response while I looked up at the mansion. He and Mom didn't need to know I'd already been back a week ago.

Mom walked up to us in her five-inch heels. She had on a rose-gold dress with frilly ends that fluttered every time she moved and a collection of Danesi security guards trailing behind her.

"Now, I better hear the correct answer out of you two. What are we *not* going to do tonight?"

"Make a scene," Carter and I said in unison. What I wanted to point out was how *much* of a scene she would make trying to walk inside with a bunch of angry men pumped full of steroids and who knows what else, but I kept my mouth shut.

"Good," she replied, her pearl earrings swaying when she nodded. "Let's go."

We walked up to the front doors, where the Nicastros' long-time house manager Charles was waiting for us. A smooth female singer's voice drifted into the large foyer along with the laughter and chatter of over a hundred voices.

He eyed us without a smile as he took our invitation. When I used to come over to hang with Tasha, his smile used to lift every wrinkled corner of his face. Now, not so much. "No weapons are permitted inside."

Mom raised her chin. "Then it's a good thing we don't have any on us."

Her answer wasn't enough though. Charles jerked his head, and one of the Nicastro security guards stepped forward with a metal detector wand. After painstakingly hovering it over every one of Mom's guards and us, they let us through.

Sweat immediately formed on my palms as my legs drew me closer and closer in. The walls were lined with more Nicastro security guards than art. Their stares flicked around the rooms we passed through, looking for someone to breathe the wrong way.

Privately interrogating Tasha would be more difficult than I thought.

Down one of the hallways, we reached a ballroom where the main event was happening. Most of the guests mingled in here. I didn't know many, but anyone could see the power draped over them like a second skin. This was the real elite. The people who held the keys to society's control board, the ones who could make any problem go away with one call and used blackmail—and more—as currency.

Every head turned sharply toward us, and hurried whispers erupted across the room the moment we stepped inside.

"This is going to be a long night," I mumbled to myself.

Unfortunately for me, Carter heard. "Aw, don't be close-minded, little brother. We're here to have *fun*." He stopped a passing server and grabbed flutes of champagne. When Mom declined, he handed one to me.

If I didn't know his bullshit meter so well, I might have believed him. I had a plan of action in my head, but I had no clue what Mom was thinking. And from the rigid stances and furrowed brows on the other guests' faces, they were thinking the same.

What I needed to do was get away from my family. That was the only way I had a marginal chance of speaking to Tasha alone.

But when a glint caught in Carter's eye, I knew that meant one thing: trouble.

I followed his gaze to another doorway. Amelia Nicastro entered the party with her fiancé at her side. She wore a sapphire-blue dress with long flowing sleeves that fell around her like she was a cloud floating through air. She was a beautiful bride-to-be, but my attention snapped to the person following behind her.

Tasha strutted into view; smoky eyes studying the crowd. Her short hair was curled at the ends and a long gold necklace dangled over the exposed front of her gown. I couldn't help it, my eyes trailed down the red fabric clinging to her in new ways each time she moved. I inhaled sharply.

No one told me in Sunday school that the devil could appear as a girl dressed in a killer gown.

"Damn, that's hot," Carter said.

The chill of my drink pressed deep into my palm. "What's wrong with you? They're Nicastros."

"Yeah, but I'm not dead either."

Tasha laughed at something her sister said and leaned close to whisper in her ear. But when she pulled away, her dark brown eyes cut across the room—catching me staring.

My breath hitched at the way she looked at me, despite it being laced with venom. I faced my brother and chugged back the rest of my champagne, trying to wash away the dryness in my mouth. The girl I once knew had morphed into a lioness, ready and eager to tear me apart.

"There he is."

I startled at Mom's voice, completely forgetting for a moment why we were here. Her gaze seared a line through the room to the man who caused us a world of pain. Gabriel Nicastro had arrived, his face clean-shaven to show off his hard jaw and his black-as-tar hair pulled back in a typical tough-guy style. A colorful handkerchief was placed in his suit's breast pocket and gold rings adorned his fingers. He swept one look over the room before he noticed Mom.

Then it was game over.

Sweat broke out along my brow. This was a bad idea. A very, very bad idea. One look alone between my mom and Gabriel was enough to release a shockwave. All the months of attacks thrown at each other with the torturous pauses in between tore back into my mind. I couldn't go through that again.

"Sloane," he said when he was within earshot.

Our security stiffened, some reaching for guns that weren't there, while others glared at him with open rage.

Mom held perfectly still. But I could see her lip curling upward before she spoke.

"Gabriel."

Hovering behind him was a shorter man with muscles barely restrained by his suit and a buzz cut that showed off every scar dotting his skin. I recognized him instantly. Victor Callan.

Gabriel pointed to me and Carter. "I see you and your sons have made it to my eldest's celebration. It's good of you to come. You remember Amelia, correct?"

"Naturally." Mom brushed a strand of hair away from her face... with her middle finger. "Memory loss isn't a consequence of having my life ruined by you, though there are many days I wish it was."

Gabriel's expression stayed fixed in place. "And yet from my knowledge, Danesi Properties has risen in value exponentially since I allegedly ruined your life. Or was all the excessive spending you've been throwing in peoples' faces for show?"

A flush appeared in Mom's cheeks as every line on her face deepened with her fury. Gabriel's eyes simply narrowed in response. Baiting her to make a scene.

Damn, we weren't starting off small. I glanced at my brother to gauge his reaction, but he was just as engrossed in Mom's first semi-peaceful interaction with Gabriel as the rest of the room.

Wait a minute. . . .

I looked around at the other guests. If they weren't directly watching this conversation go down, they were pretending not to be. No one was looking at me. Which meant no one was looking at—

I trailed my eyes over every guest until I landed on the one in the red dress weaving away from the party.

Where are you going?

Slowly placing my empty flute glass on a nearby surface, I carefully inched away. As long as no one asked me to jump into this chess game, I could slip farther and farther into the depths of this party until . . .

Boom. I was gone.

With a solid twenty people between me and my family, I finally picked up the pace to reach Tasha.

She moved like she was on a mission. I was almost within reach of her when I heard Gabriel's voice sound through the room.

"Excuse me, Sloane. I need to speak privately with Amelia. We'll continue this conversation later."

Shit, I was about to run out of time. And worse, within the few seconds I had turned to look back at Mom, Tasha had left the room all together.

I had to make a choice.

So I followed after her.

I hid behind a corner when Tasha placed a hand on a wall light, glanced around her, then twisted it. The wall groaned as it shifted sideways, letting her disappear inside.

A hidden passage.

Right. I'd completely forgotten that the Nicastros had a secret way to travel through their house without being seen. As kids, we'd run through the maze lurking behind the walls of the house to eavesdrop on anyone we could.

Should I go after her? It was one thing to confront her in the open halls of the mansion. It was a whole other to confront her while hidden somewhere no one on my side could find me.

But it was also the perfect place to talk. There'd be no witnesses.

I stepped out from around the corner and hurried over to the wall light.

Twisting the light, I exhaled when the secret door reopened, blood pounding in my ears. There was no going back now.

"Ready or not, Nicastro," I mumbled, pulling the wall shut and letting the darkness close around me.

CHAPTER FIVE

Tasha

LIGHTS FLICKERED TO LIFE AS I WALKED THROUGH THE PAS-
sage, each of the ignitions jumpstarting a new wave of nerves through
me. Anybody important wouldn't notice I was missing at first. It gave
me enough time to do a proper sweep through the house and make sure
no one was skulking in a place they shouldn't.

I still couldn't believe my father invited that family. Allowing them
to strut into our home with all those uglies patrolling behind. What
kind of message was that sending? I hated this for Amelia, but my
father had his reasons and my job tonight was to be his secret pair of
eyes like I'd offered.

Ten steps in though, a movement caught my eye. I straightened,
flicking my gaze backward to the darkness creeping at the edge of the
light. The hairs on my neck stood on end. Obviously, there was nothing
there. There was no way I could've missed someone following me.

But then a shoe scuffed against the ground.

I whirled, all the nerves in my body suddenly on high alert. In the
dim lighting a figure moved in the shadows.

Holy shit. I grabbed for my handgun—strapped and hidden at my left thigh where the slit of my dress ended—and held it where the figure darted. My father added it to my outfit before the party began, stating it was an extra safety measure since I knew how to use one responsibly. Clearly, that was the right move.

Heart in my throat, I called out, "Come out before I shoot."

In slow, careful steps, the figure emerged, their face bathed in the light. A growl escaped my lips.

"What the *fuck*?"

I kept my gun aimed on Leo. He held completely still, hands slightly raised, with a brow arched. "Is this how you usually greet people?"

"Only the ones who sneak into places no one—especially *you*—is supposed to know about," I snapped.

Leo cocked a brow at me. "You should bring up that complaint with seven-year-old Tasha. Seeing as she was the one who introduced me to it."

My chest rose and fell. This could not possibly be real. Yet every time I blinked, his smooth hair and sharp tux were still there. Dammit.

"What do you want?"

"To talk."

He moved closer, keeping his eyes leveled on me. I rolled my shoulders, willing the goose bumps caked on my skin to settle.

"Problem is, I don't react well to an ambush." I cocked my head to the side. "Or to demands."

He shook his head. "No demands."

"Then?"

He let out a frustrated sigh. "Why are you sneaking around inside your home like a ghost?"

"*That* is none of your business," I replied. "It's one thing for you and your awful family to take my father's bait and show up here and a whole other to stalk me into a place that warrants shooting you. Or did that viper mother of yours not warn you to play nice tonight?"

Every muscle in his face hardened, becoming more brutal from the harshly cast shadows. "And what trap is your dad trying to lay?"

I swallowed, wishing I could take that flippant comment back. I had no idea why my father invited them.

"He's not laying any traps," I replied. "That skill is all your mother's. Seeing as she tried to get my dad thrown in prison countless times on baseless accusations."

Leo let out a harsh. "Don't play the innocent act, Nicastro. We all know by now what kind of man your father is. Prison would be a gift for everything he's done."

I tensed, fighting all the rage inside me not to lash out completely. "Don't you *dare* tell any lies about my father. He's a good man. Now you have five seconds to explain why you followed me."

A curious look danced through Leo's eyes, barely masked by the blend of light and shadow. I wanted to rip that curiosity off his face. Because whatever Leo was thinking put an infuriating glint in his eye and a heavy lump of dread in my core.

"Do you still not know?"

I clenched my jaw. Did I not know *what*? There was no way I'd ever ask that question out loud though, so I repeated, "Tell me right now why you're here before I decide what to shoot first."

At first, Leo went tight-lipped. I willed him to speak, since I wasn't sure I wanted to shoot any part of him, but then something shifted in his face. A taut rope seemed to unravel within Leo, and his eyes went near black as he released more fury than I'd ever known him to be capable of.

"Yeah, I'll tell you," he snapped, and slipped a hand into his pocket. "Yesterday I came home to find blood strewn around Sophia's room like some fucked-up real-life horror show with two freaks about to *kidnap* her."

I inhaled sharply. Whatever resentment and anger I felt toward the Danesis didn't include Sophia. She was barely nine when the feud between our families broke out. This revelation I could be horrified by. "Why are you coming to *me* about this instead of the police?"

Leo's nostrils flared. "Because I know your father had something to do with it."

The rage and confusion pressing against my insides poured out, making my hand fly to his neck and press the gun to his stomach. "*How dare you* accuse my father of trying to kidnap a thirteen-year-old."

Leo didn't flinch despite the restraint of my hand, the muscles in his neck and face instead throbbing harder under the weight of his own fury. "I *can* and I *will* when those two kidnappers had *lions* tattooed to their forearms, and *these*"—he pulled a small object from his pocket, shoving it in my face—"were used to shoot our security."

I glanced down to the object held between his two fingers. It was a bullet with a tracing of a lion etched into the side. I smacked it out of his hand, its small metallic body letting out a clatter when it hit the ground. "What the hell are you spewing? I've never seen that and men having lions tattooed on them has *nothing* to do with my dad."

Though the moment I spoke, Victor's lion tattoo flashed through my mind. It wasn't the same, was it? It couldn't be.

He curled his lip up at me. "Liar."

"Call me a liar again, Danesi." I shoved the gun deeper into his gut, my fingers deeper into his neck. It was what I should've done the day he accused me of being a killer. Saying I was disgusting and weak and a person he never wanted to be around ever again while I stood there, taking it without any defenses.

A silence passed between us, ripe with the pressure of an incoming tsunami.

Leo leaned closer despite the gun, making my knuckles press against his abs.

"At least I pay attention to what goes on in my family. You're too busy running through the walls of your house like some rat to notice what kind of home you actually live in."

A slow, taunting smile curved onto my face. Oh, so he wanted to play this game? I could do that—with pleasure.

"A rat, huh?" I pressed myself up against his torso, not missing the heavy thump of his heart or the way his chest held still for a second too long. "If I'm a rat then you're a roach crawling after me. And do you know, Danesi, what rats are willing to eat?"

A muscle in his jaw ticked.

I lifted my hand up to his chin, moving his face left and right, my thumb flicking over his smooth bottom lip.

"You've taken some big risks tonight. We're hidden in the walls of my home, and I bet you didn't tell anyone you followed me. This little rat could do whatever she wanted to you."

Eyes locked on mine, his breath spread over my skin, luring me in. "I'd like to see you try."

I pressed my nail into the softness of his cheek, ready to draw blood, when—

A sound like an exploding balloon shook my eardrums.

I jerked away from Leo, the air squeezing out of my lungs. "Did you hear that?"

Another muffled pop.

Leo's eyes bulged. He opened his mouth, but no words came out.

Oh my God.

I didn't think and immediately sprinted down the tunnel. Security checked people for weapons at the door; how did one get in? The sound seemed to come from the dining room, so I raced toward it.

Chest heaving, I stumbled to a stop in front of the one-way mirror my father had installed long ago. It let me see that the secret door into the passages was wide open while the regular doors into the room were shut tight. I was about to sprint for it when I noticed three people inside.

And one of them was masked and armed.

My body went numb as the gunman aimed at someone. But not just anyone.

My father.

He clutched his right arm as blood soaked his sleeve, lunging for the gunman.

My lips parted, chest clenching at the sight. I had to—

Bang.

Icy horror spilled over me as my father cried out and fell to his knees, clutching his stomach. "N—"

A large hand slapped against my mouth and another wrapped around my chest, stopping me from crying out or running into the room.

I struggled anyway, kicking and screaming into the hand. *My father.* This was a nightmare. Not reality. It couldn't possibly be real.

"Don't let the hitman hear you," Leo urged in my ear. Panic braided itself through his voice. He paused, sucking in air through his teeth. "We have to get out of here. *Now.*"

But I didn't hear Leo. I was suddenly all too aware of who the third person was. She was the most important person in that room, staring down at my father as the gunman turned their attention toward her.

I thrust Leo away, screaming at my sister to run.

The gunman flinched at the sound of my voice. If I could distract them long enough, I could get in there and stop this. I *had* to. I—

Whirling around, they aimed their gun at the mirror.

Leo grabbed me, pulling us to the ground as a bullet fired through the air and shattered the glass. The sharp pieces dropped on top of us in a piercing cacophony of sound as suddenly more gunshots fired in rapid succession and screams erupted. I could've sworn I heard my sister shout my name.

I tried to reorient myself, only to press my right knee into a jagged piece of glass as I tried to find my dropped gun. Before I knew what was happening, Leo had pulled the fragment out and got me to my feet, the rest of the glass crunching beneath our shoes as he dragged me away from the gaping mouth of where the one-way mirror used to be.

We raced deeper into the tunnel system, farther away from the bullets firing and the force of many footsteps echoing through the air. My mind was spinning in a frantic loop, losing connection to the rest of me. It was the reason I let Leo pull me along without a fight.

It didn't matter how much I tried to shake myself awake though. There was no waking from this nightmare. My world, my identity, my life.

My family.

My family.

Laying in a pool of their own blood.

CHAPTER SIX

Tasha

Shouts from someplace farther away chased after us, shaking me out of my daze. I could still hear the gunshots ringing in my ears, the image of the bullets firing into my father.

Leo jerked backward at my sudden stop. "What are you doing?"

I broke free of him. The shooter was still here. I didn't care if it was reckless; they were *in my home*.

"*Not* running away!" I shouted, swearing when I realized he had dragged me far from the dining room.

Leo yelled after me as I bolted back down the passage.

They could be *dead*. The thought taunted me.

Down a corridor.

Dead.

Past the shattered mirror.

Dead.

I turned a corner when a gun blasted through the passage and a bullet flew inches past my face. I quickly ducked back, gulping down air while a wave of dizziness swam through me. Maybe running into danger was a terrible idea, but I was committed now.

"Don't run *straight* toward them, Nicastro!" Leo yelled.

Leo's voice was a muffled annoyance in my ears as I charged forward looking for any signs of the attacker.

Another gunshot exploded, and someone cried out down the left fork in a passage. I skidded to a halt and went down it, watching large shadows move around with my heart in my throat. But when I reached the spot, shock cracked like a whip through me.

My father had dragged himself into the passages, one hand clenched against his torso with the other one raising a Glock. My eyes followed the aim of his weapon and caught sight of the gunman darting around a corner with a gash in their upper left arm where the bullet had grazed them.

"Dad!" I screamed, rushing over when he collapsed to the ground, his face laced with pain.

I fell to my knees beside him, barely noticing the shock of pain from my cut knee. His face was too pale, and sweat poured from his forehead. A trail of smeared blood showed his path from the dining room where he'd tried to pursue the shooter.

My vision blurred in and out with tears. All I could see was my father's white dress shirt drenched in red, his hand doing nothing to stop the bleeding. "I need to call Dr. Morris!"

I was about to leap to my feet, but his hand grasped my wrist, stopping me.

"*No*, Tasha," he gasped, each word a strangled sound. "He won't get here in time."

As my father spoke, his skin drained of color and his dark eyes turned glassy. A blade of fear went through my chest. *No, no, no.* I had to keep him awake, keep him looking at me.

I pressed my hands over his. "Stay with me, Dad."

His eyes went wide, jumping around the tunnel like he was

searching for someone. He turned back to me, a heavy wheeze coming from his throat. "Where is she? Amelia?"

Dread kicked me in the gut. *My sister.* I'd been so wrapped up in our father, I'd forgotten about her. "I . . ."

"Tasha." With a shaky hand, he pulled something from his jacket pocket and pressed it into my palm. The item was small and wet with blood, but all I could focus on was his voice threaded with fear, the beads of sweat coating his skin. "Find her."

A rage of coughs burst from him, and blood spilled from his lips. I screamed.

I tried to keep him settled, calling out for others to help me, hating with a passion that these passages were too thick to be heard. Finally, my father stopped breathing.

But this time, he didn't move.

A sob broke from me. I grabbed his face, willing him to take a breath, blink, do *anything.* His blood soaked into my red gown, smeared across my arms and fingers.

But it didn't matter. He was gone.

"*Daddy,*" I cried,

My grief was a noose around my throat, ready to choke me, when a hand grabbed my arm, pulling me back.

I screamed, only to realize it was Leo again.

"What the fuck, Danesi!" I wobbled to my feet, shoving the small item my father had given me down the front of my dress for safe-keeping, before flinging off my heels to help my shaking legs—or use as a weapon. "Don't *touch* me!"

His face was ghostly white and shellshocked. But that didn't stop me from wanting to hurl all my grief and rage directly at him.

"You need to get out of here," he said. "In case that hitman comes back with more reinforcements to finish you off, too. They almost always take out the whole family."

Hitman? The person who shot my father was a *hitman*?

I pointed my father's Glock at him, but I couldn't keep the tremor out of my hand. "And why should I listen to *you*?"

He leveled his gaze with me, the intensity in them too much for me to bear. "Because we have no idea what kind of danger you're in. A bullet could strike you at any moment."

Chest heaving, I stopped fighting him and took in what he was saying just as a woman's screams erupted.

I snapped my attention to where it came from—the dining room.

I gasped. *Amelia.*

Bolting away from him, I raced toward my sister's voice—

And slammed immediately into a muscular wall.

Large, gruff hands grabbed my shoulders. I tried to wrench myself away until a familiar voice shouted at me to calm down.

"What's happened?" Victor demanded. "You're covered in blood. Are you hurt?"

I stopped moving, my whirling thoughts and rattled body quieting long enough for me to take in Victor and our guests staring at me with wide eyes. The room was now filled with security. Some stood at the door stopping the guests from coming inside while others hovered around a body on the floor lying beside the long twenty-person table.

A body.

Oh God, *a body.*

"Amelia!" I screeched.

She was curled up in a fetal position with her back to me, her poofy blue dress sprawled out around her like a jellyfish. She looked like she had fallen asleep underneath the dining table, an old habit we had as kids during dinner parties before our parents noticed we were ready for bed.

But now. *Now.*

There was blood soaked into the carpet. So much blood.

I tried to lunge forward, but Victor pulled me back and into his arms, forcing me to keep my face pressed against his chest.

"Don't look, Tasha," he said, his voice softer than I'd ever heard before.

That was when I knew.

I sobbed into his chest, repeating *they're gone, they're gone*, until Victor pulled back to look at me.

"Where's your father?"

My lips trembled, but I somehow managed to reply. "He's in the passages. This is his blood."

Victor's throat bobbed, but otherwise he didn't give his emotions away. He barked at some of the security to go retrieve my father's body, before guiding me out of the dining room.

Victor roared at everyone to get back and many did, gasping and shrieking when they saw me covered in crimson. He pushed through all of them though, taking me into the library. When we were out of the chaos, I realized Leo had disappeared on me and my anger returned.

"Where were you?" I shouted. "You were supposed to be at my dad's side the *entire* night! Why weren't you in the dining room when the shooter came in?"

Victor shook his head, every wrinkle on his forehead deepening right to his skull. "He wanted to be alone with Amelia, so I went looking for *you*. No one realized what had happened until one of Amelia's friends from work tried to find her. She walked in on her already..." He put a bloodied palm up to his forehead. "It was too late. We were too late."

His words were a knife plunging through my chest. I stumbled back a few steps, gasping for air. I stood helplessly while my eyes burned from the tears pouring down my cheeks.

Sirens wailed in the distance.

"Someone called the cops!" I heard a person shout.

Through the library's doorway, I could see guests shoving at one another to flee the party, their faces strained with fear. What did they have to be scared of? My father and sister were *killed*, the police needed to be here.

"Victor!" Richard Costa exclaimed, storming into the room with a group of security guards. "What do you want us to do?"

Instantly, Victor started throwing orders around like an anchored ship among a thrashing storm. "Tell all the Nicastro soldiers to get out of here through the western edge of the property and meet at your house. And call Matteo to tell him what's happened and to get the fuck back from Miami *now*."

I whipped my head between the men. What did Val's father and my cousin Matteo have to do with any of this?

I wanted to ask a million and one questions, but once Victor's orders were given, Richard and the rest of them hurried off, shouting for security to follow suit.

"Victor. *Victor!*" I grabbed his forearm when he was about to rush off, too. "What's going on? *Please.*"

He took my hands in his, the strength and warmth in them helping to keep me upright. "I'm sorry, Tasha. I'll explain everything to you soon. But right now, I need to make one thing very clear to you. Okay?"

I nodded through my hot tears.

"Don't say *anything* to the cops, you understand? They are not your friends tonight. And frankly, they never have been."

Without giving me a chance to respond, he dropped my hands, rushing out of the library to yell orders at more security guards hovering nearby.

I lowered myself onto a nearby seat and shoved my hand down the front of my dress to grab the small item my father had given me. It was also bathed in his blood, but when I wiped some of it away, the image was clearly visible.

A dove pin.

"Tasha! Thank goodness you're alive."

I closed my hand and looked up as Ravi's beautiful, devastated face rushed in. He fell to his knees in front of me and clasped my hands in his. "You're covered in blood."

My vision blurred, a sob breaking through me. "It's not mine."

Without thinking, I threw my arms around him. His presence was aloe on a burn, soothing the searing pain engulfing my body and trying to consume me. I breathed in his familiar scent between gasps of air.

"I want to get you medical attention to be on the safe side," he said into my hair. "I know Gabriel would want me taking care of you right now. Boyfriend or not."

I pulled back, rapidly blinking the remaining tears away, as his words caused a question to form in my mind.

"Where's Julian?"

Ravi frowned. "I haven't seen him."

I didn't have a chance to think anymore about Julian when the police burst into the party, yelling for everyone to stay where they were while they locked down the house.

The chaos grew. We were rounded up, yellow tape draping around each doorway. Ravi and I were escorted outside to an ambulance by two officers.

"Sit here," one paramedic said, throwing a blanket over me while Ravi sat by my side. "We'll check your vitals first."

I did as I was told, too exhausted and numb to fight anymore. My mind was both sharp and in a fog, grasping certain details while losing sight of others.

It wasn't right. I should be inside, whispering jokes to my sister. I should be planting kisses on our father's cheek. I should have protected them. I should have saved them.

None of this was ever supposed to happen.

At some point, the police shouted orders for people to move out of the way. I turned my attention to the front doors and my heart immediately dropped to my stomach.

A body bag was brought out on a stretcher.

The police carefully carried the stretcher down the front steps, giving me enough time to see the shape of my father underneath.

My eyes stayed fixed on his body, a new rush of painful tears aching to burst from me, until he was taken out of sight.

Then the second stretcher came outside. In those seconds, I forgot how to breathe.

Gone. They were both gone.

My father.

My sister.

I looked around the front yard of my home. At all the flushed skin and shaking limbs now accompanying the layers of couture clothes and bejeweled accessories. I spotted Sloane and Carter Danesi speaking quickly to each other as they watched the stretchers go by. I wanted to claw out the glint in their eyes, the whisper of a smile on their lips. But I forced myself to look away.

And that's when I noticed him.

Leo stood by himself, watching me. He held my gaze, his brows knitted together as the police and ambulance lights swept over his face. The lights flashed over mine for a moment, too, making me squeeze my eyes shut from the brightness.

For one second in the darkness, I could forget.

But when I opened them again, the police were still there, the party guests were still crowded in supervised groups, my family was still dead.

And the life I knew would never be the same.

CHAPTER
SEVEN

Two FBI agents showed up the next day. Noon sharp.

Mom brought the two agents to the sitting room reserved for visitors who weren't staying long.

Inside, her team of lawyers waited patiently.

I leaned against one of the walls. The agents asked for the entire family to be present. Even Sophia. So far, the law-abiding heads in the room hadn't objected. It was surprising, since I was sure they'd put as many walls up in our favor as possible. Back when Dad was freshly dead and Mom was in full attack mode, we had cops and feds knocking on our door at least twice a week trying to get a crumb of evidence to prove we were more than a regular grieving family. Mom's lawyers basically lived with us for months because of it. Another reason why I wanted to get as far away from my family as possible.

"Kids, these are agents Philip Marquez and Liam Stein. Your answers are to be truthful, understand?"

That was Mom's way of telling us to lie. She'd established that coded sentence into our lives years ago, so we never said something she deemed a threat to our way of life. Whether it was toward others in our world or, in this case, the law.

"Mrs. Danesi," Agent Stein, the younger of the two, said. "We've heard you and the Nicastros didn't get along. Is that true?"

A loaded question. The agents knew how much bad blood was between our families. The real question layered underneath his pleasant tone was simple. Was Mom behind the deaths of Gabriel and Amelia Nicastro?

I could be truthful if the agents ever outright asked me. Because the answer would be simple. I didn't know. She was the obvious conclusion after what happened to Luca Nicastro. Tasha's uncle was the reason this conversation was happening even though they could never pin his death on Mom.

"You don't need to answer that," one of the lawyers said.

I glanced at my brother, turning away when he caught my eye. Mom kept her attention on the two agents, an artificial look of remorse painted on her face.

"I'll reply," she said, turning back to the agent. "It is. More squabbles over status, really. Things our society cares about."

"Oh?" Agent Marquez asked. Despite his beard, I could still see a muscle flex in his jaw. "And what kind of 'society' are you a part of?"

Mom gave him one of her signature foxglove smiles. Of beauty and allure, ready to poison with the slightest taste.

"A society that has no idea what polyester feels like."

Any other day, I would've laughed at their pinched noses and confused side-eyes. But it was impossible with the image of Tasha covered in her dad's blood—completely helpless and frantic—lodged in my mind.

I shouldn't care at all.

I flicked my gaze to my little sister sitting on one of the couches with her hands clasped in her lap. The same nightmare Tasha was living almost took place again in our home.

Agent Stein pursed his lips and glanced down at his notepad. "Did you notice anything suspicious before the shooting last night? We heard from other witnesses at the party that it was unusual to see your family there."

"Our clients will *not* be responding to that last statement," one of our lawyers replied.

The agents ignored them and glanced at us. I swallowed a lump in my throat. No one stood out to me before the hitman arrived, but that was because I was too preoccupied with talking to Tasha about Sophia's near kidnapping.

"Not at all," Carter replied. "Mom and I were busy chatting with some guests after Gabriel left the ballroom. I hadn't had a chance to touch the caviar tower before someone started screaming."

Agent Stein turned to me. "And where were you when the shooting started?"

"Um..." I glanced at my family then back to him. Shit, I was about to lie to a federal agent. Hadn't done that in a hot minute. "I was by the buffet. I didn't really know anyone there and decided to take advantage of the good food."

The agents narrowed their eyes at me, but otherwise didn't look like they smelled my bullshit. There was no way I was saying out loud that I was in the Nicastros' tunnel system alone with Tasha. It wouldn't matter what my intentions were, Mom would rake me over hot coals immediately.

"We're very distraught from this." Mom clasped her hands together, the knuckles turning white. "I keep thinking what might've happened if the shooter decided to go after more targets."

Now *that* was usually cause for my bullshit alarm to go off. But it didn't. And all because of the deep lines around her eyes and the dark circles hidden underneath her makeup. Maybe Mom was thinking of the violence that had traveled through our home. The possibility it could happen again.

"I can understand that this was a traumatic event for the three of you to witness," Agent Marquez replied.

"Have you found the shooter yet?" she asked.

Agent Marquez kept his face neutral. "I can't give out that kind of classified information during an ongoing investigation."

"That is a good place to end this interview," one of the lawyers said. He rose to his feet, prompting the others to follow suit. "Agent Marquez and Stein, if you have any further questions for our clients, you'll contact our firm first."

"All right," Agent Stein replied. "Thank you for your time."

My shoulders relaxed the minute the agents were escorted out of the room. That was one thing I couldn't shake, the tension that built up inside me whenever the law was around. Side effects of being raised in the Danesi household.

"What *really* happened last night?" I asked.

Mom's dark eyes pierced into me. "I don't know, Leo. I already said that. Or were you not listening a minute ago?"

I glanced at Carter who seemed almost amused by this and then back to her. "I was. But this is us, Mom."

We didn't get a reply at first. Instead, she turned to my sister, tapping her on the nose. "Sophia, honey, can you please go into the kitchen and boil the kettle for tea? I think we should all have some."

My sister frowned but knew better than to object.

Mom turned back to me once she was out of earshot. "I'm a perfectionist, Leo. That's why there are names that will never be associated with this family. So let me make one thing absolutely clear to you." She leaned forward, resting her arm on her crossed leg. "Yes, I've tried to have Gabriel killed in the past, but none of them were in such a flashy, public way. I don't believe in having multiple witnesses. Let alone over a hundred. I didn't order this hit, but I have a feeling I know who did."

I couldn't detect any lies in her answer, but I didn't fully believe her either.

"Who do you think is behind it?" I asked.

Before she could give me an answer, Mom's lawyers appeared in the doorway. "Mrs. Danesi, we need to spend some time strategizing how to handle this situation right away."

Mom nodded. She rose to her feet, but before she slipped out, she turned once more to us. "Until I find out what's going on, I want nothing interesting happening in this household, understood? You're to be the most boring people around."

"Darn," Carter replied. "And here I was planning on robbing a bank and hijacking a couple of transport trucks this week."

She cut him a look, then the same one to me. "*Nothing*, are we clear?"

"Christ's sake," Carter said after she was gone. "She knows how much work I have to do—all piled on by her. I *wish* I could have a boring day."

I almost held my tongue—any work he was doing wasn't the kind of work I wanted to be associated with—but my curiosity got the better of me. "What kind of work?"

"There's a group of small-time criminals in Hartford who think they're big scary boys loansharking and extorting small businesses under our protection. I've been given the lovely task of reining them in."

Carter smirked, waiting for a reaction, but I kept my face as impassive as possible. I didn't need to ask. I could already hear the crack of bone and the wails of grown men.

He headed for the doorway, but just when I thought he'd leave without saying goodbye, he turned to me. "By the way, I'm leaving early tomorrow morning for a work trip to Aspen. There's a big opportunity to get us established there and I'm not passing it up. I'll be gone for about a week."

"How could you pass up a chance to scam a horde of rich people out of their money?" I replied dryly, making him laugh. "See you later then, Carter."

When he was gone, I went over Mom's words again. She swore she wasn't involved. Did I believe her? I wanted to. Despite how much it might turn my stomach, it was true she kept the violence she inflicted discreet and indirect.

Who did she think orchestrated it, then? And if they had also ordered Sophia's kidnapping, what were they planning next?

"Hey! Where did Mom and Carter go?" Sophia asked, carrying a tray of empty mugs and a teapot back in. She sat the tray on an ottoman.

"Forget them," I said, sitting down. "What tea did you bring?"

"Chamomile," she replied, pouring the steaming water into a mug. "It was the first one I found, and I couldn't be bothered to look for anything else."

I forced a smile. Chamomile tasted like a wet rag, but I didn't object.

Sophia finished pouring my tea, smiling as she moved on to her own cup. I tried to stay cheerful for her, but my thoughts forced me back to last night. Hearing Tasha's screams, seeing the anguish etched into her skin as the life in Gabriel's eyes flickered out. The images morphed into my memory of Sophia, of a gun pressed to her temple, and how so many horrible, horrible things could have gone wrong that day.

"The people who killed the Nicastros..." Sophia suddenly said. "Do you think they'll kill us? Or do you think they'll go after Tasha next?"

My stomach dropped as she calmly looked at me. I hated how she asked such horrendous questions like it was an acceptable part of her life.

I placed my mug back on the tray and kneeled in front of my sister, taking her hands in mine. "I never want you to ask me that question again. Okay? Nothing will ever happen to you while I'm around."

A deep line appeared between her brows. All at once, she looked too grown up for a girl still harboring her childhood softness. "You won't be able to protect me forever, Leo. If the Nicastros aren't safe, neither are we."

"I don't agree," I replied, squeezing her hands. "And I'll spend my whole life proving that to you."

She gave a tiny smile, but it felt like it was only to appease me. It was the truth though. I would spend the rest of my godforsaken life protecting her, so at least one of us in this fucked-up family had a chance to come out unscathed.

But she was right about Tasha. What if she was meant to die in that dining room, too? A dozen questions bloomed where her dad and sister had fallen. A dozen more were bound to pop up.

And after the conversation I'd had with her, I was willing to bet that Tasha didn't know just how much of a hell she had fallen into.

Because hiding underneath all the glamor, the wealth, and the power my family had was a gruesome truth. We weren't only known for owning and operating Danesi Properties. We were the Danesi Family. Known for controlling one of the most powerful Mafias along our side of the East Coast. All thanks to Dad's family who dragged us into the underworld decades before any of us were born, building our family name, our wealth, our power, and the number of watch lists we lived on.

But we weren't number one. That title was left for the one family that outranked us. A family who had influence over enough people, ruled over enough areas, that they could follow their own set of rules. A family that shot lions into the hearts of men.

And one girl was about to inherit it all.

Tasha

A SIMPLE DOVE PIN. IT DIDN'T MAKE SENSE.

I turned the small item from left to right, looking for a sign. It had to be important enough for my father to hand it to me before he died. But so far nothing clicked.

I shoved it back into my black Chanel purse and pulled out my phone. The time read 1:20 PM. Val got back from her trip with her mom late last night and was in AP English like it was any other Monday, yet here I was across from Howard Waldmann, my father's personal lawyer.

With a father and sister who were still dead.

Rows of book spines lined the built-in shelves in the library, moving in a tidal wave of colors from stark blacks to delicate pastels. Elaborate Portuguese-inspired wallpaper covered every inch of the room with peacocks resting on branches and flowers in full bloom. Every room of the Costas' house was styled with a similar artfully classic look that was a balm of comfort in the devastating chaos.

Richard and Isabel Costa swept me into their protective arms the moment I was released from police custody. I had to stay with them while my home was part of the investigation and the swarm of news vans circled every inch of the property. Even the police who questioned me acted like amateur journalists, pressing me for the strangest details and growing frustrated when all I could say was *I don't know*. But if I did know the answers to their bizarre questions, I wouldn't say. Not when Victor warned me not to trust them.

Howard made a point to write one endless email while we waited for the reading of the will. I didn't blame him. It was better than a staring contest or painful small talk when I was already two breaths away from screaming until my lungs ached. I'd done a lot of that in the forty-odd hours since I'd lost the two pieces of my world I cherished the most.

The large chestnut doors clicked open, and Richard and Victor stepped inside.

I flew to my feet, running over and throwing my arms around Victor. I hadn't seen him since that night, when he promised to tell me everything after the suffocating dust had settled. I had no idea where he went after leaving me in the library. Richard wouldn't tell me despite being in constant communication with him. All I could assume was Victor had to immediately go into crisis mode, keeping the roof of my family's empire from caving in.

I pressed into his shoulder and breathed in his scent of mint after-shave. It was insignificant to me before, but his scent now reminded me of my father. Of home.

"Thank God you're here," I said. "I wasn't sure you'd come."

Victor gave me another squeeze and pulled away. "Of course I'd be here. I'm sorry for going silent, but I had a lot to deal with before I could come up for air again."

I tried to nod, to stay strong, but a sheen coated my eyes. "I don't know if I can do this alone."

He cupped my cheek. "You won't."

I bit my lip as his hands fell back to his sides. All my life, Victor had never shown physical affection toward me, but every drop of it now stirred a desperate need for more. To know that there were still people who cared about me and would hold my hand through this darkness, while I pretended not to need it.

"Someone important flew in today, too," Victor said, turning to the door.

I didn't have a chance to ask him who he was referring to when a young man wearing a familiar pair of bright red glasses walked through the door.

"Tasha, darling." Matteo glided over and wrapped his arms around me, his neatly trimmed beard tickling my skin. "I'm so sorry I couldn't get here sooner. I tried to leave right away, but a storm in Miami kept me grounded until now. I'm devastated by what's happened to Uncle Gabriel and Amelia."

"It's okay," I replied. "You're here now."

Matteo worked for the college and university side of Nicastro Developments. My father gave him the job of convincing schools to award us their contracts for new campus developments or the remodeling of existing buildings. It sent him all across the country and away from us all the time, but it was better than nothing, given that Matteo was the only extended family I ever spoke to and had regular Sunday dinners with.

"I need to warn you though," Matteo said, a shadow crossing over his face. "I'm not the only family who arrived."

"Who?"

My mind went through all the possible people who would show up. Aunt Giana and Uncle Edward, my father's sister and her husband, lived in a suburb outside Chicago with Matteo's three sisters close by. I had no clue how they were doing since they refused to speak to us and their son. I doubted it was Nonna Donatella. She never left her beach house in Long Island these days because of her poor health. Then there was Aunt Céline, my mother's younger sister, and her husband, my uncle

Wade, but I hadn't spoken to them or my cousins since the day my mother abandoned us.

Matteo scrunched his face up like it was painful to say the name. I glanced at Victor and Richard, thinking they would answer my question for me.

But then I heard it—stiletto heels. The click of them echoed into the room just before they reached the doorway.

"Natasha! Oh, thank goodness."

I balked as a woman dripping in gold jewelry and bright, outlandish clothes entered the library. Her hair had fresh highlights and her skin was practically glowing, looking more like a person who stepped out of a day spa and not off a nine-hour flight.

"Mom?"

My mother dropped her purse on the floor, her full lashes blinking away tears, before she hurried over to wrap her arms around me. "I'm so relieved you're okay. Look how much you've grown, my darling."

She had barely touched me before I was shoving out of her embrace.

"Who called you?" I spat.

She flinched, flicking her eyes over to Victor. "He did."

"I tried to tell her not to come," he replied gruffly.

I glared at him. "What makes you think she deserves to know they died? She could've found out from the news like the rest of the strangers out there."

My sister's voice spoke in my mind, telling me I was being too harsh. But frankly, the words didn't come out harsh enough. My *real* family was dead. My mother made that clear when she abandoned us. Subtlety wasn't a high priority right now.

Victor sighed. "I had to tell her. To keep the situation—and story—contained."

"I did not fly over here for you to *contain* me, Victor," my mother snapped. "I came here to be with my youngest child. Nothing else. Even when she looks at me like I'm the devil because of all the lies my ex-husband fed her." She turned to me, sighing deeply. "There are many things your father kept a secret from you that are going to come out today. Things that will be devastating to hear. I couldn't let you go through it alone."

"I'm not alone," I replied, voice clipped. "I have people who *actually* care about me to lean on. Not someone who hasn't contacted me since I was thirteen."

Just because my father and sister were dead didn't mean she could waltz in here acting supportive not forty-eight hours later. I wasn't a discarded phone. I was her daughter, and I had enough heartache to deal with. I didn't need my mother ripping open an old wound with a pearl-white smile on her face.

"Let's reapproach this subject in due time," Matteo said, deliberately stepping between us. His smile was far too genuine. But that was Matteo for you. Always on good terms with everyone. "Good to see you again, Aunt Adriana. You're looking sun-kissed and half your age."

She tapped his shoulder affectionally. "Still such a gentleman. Gabriel didn't deserve you."

I met Victor's gaze, mouthing a *what the hell* to him. This day had gone from a sinkhole of misery to an earthquake of fresh pain within thirty seconds.

Of all the people. *Of all the people* and he let her get on a plane and strut back into my life like nothing had changed. I could've strangled him.

"It's one thirty now. We don't want to get behind schedule." My mother moved over to Howard, extending her hand to him. "Adriana Lemieux. Natasha's mother."

I didn't immediately follow her when she took a seat on the couch. I was still busy glaring at Victor. All he could give me was a gesture to sit as well. So I took the loveseat across from Howard, *not* the couch where my mother was sitting. Victor pulled up a chair while Matteo and Richard stood.

Howard put his glasses on, opened a sealed envelope, and let out a heavy sigh.

"What's wrong?" Victor asked.

"Gabriel's will is fairly straightforward," Howard replied. "It explains which properties in the States he wants to give the girls and how they're to share the villa in the South of France and the penthouse in Tokyo. The majority of the money is split nearly the same for them with a percentage going to you, Victor, some to his sister, Giana, and to funding his mother's expenses and live-in caretaker until she passes. The money was to go into separate trusts until the girls turned twenty-one." He cleared his throat, looking around at all of us. "Under the tragic circumstances, we are all aware Amelia isn't here to receive her share."

A shock of tears welled up behind my eyes.

It wasn't right. Why would someone kill Amelia? In an awful way, there was some logic to why my father was targeted. He was a powerful man in New York making choices some people didn't like. Maybe even hated him for. But it didn't make sense why my sister was killed, too.

I should've protected her better. And now my beautiful, patient, loving sister was dead. A future she could've had ripped away forever.

I wasn't worthy of inheriting anything from the Nicastro empire. Not when I failed her so greatly.

"I've yet to understand what the problem is," my mother replied. "Shouldn't Natasha receive Amelia's portion of the will?"

Howard cleared his throat as he took off his glasses. "In theory, yes. But it appears Amelia married her fiancé, Julian Henderson, in a private court ceremony on September first. As the widower, Mr. Henderson is entitled to Amelia's portion of the Nicastro estate since there was no prenup. My firm uncovered this information a few hours ago."

A silence fell. I stared at him, not quite knowing—or letting—myself process what he said. All that planning, all those dress fittings, and Amelia was already married to that prick for nearly *two weeks?*

"Are you fucking kidding me?"

My mother gasped. "Natasha! *Language*."

Ignoring her, I pushed to my feet, making sure Howard saw the wrath billowing off me. "You're going to sit here and tell me the guy who has conveniently gone missing since my sister was shot will inherit multimillions? This is a textbook definition of foul play!"

"I realize how suspicious this is, which is why the firm hasn't released her share of the money yet. Hopefully Julian is found soon, and the authorities can give us answers." Howard cleared his throat. "But as it stands, he is legally allowed to inherit Amelia's portion if he's deemed not criminally responsible for her death."

I paced back and forth. If I didn't, either my knees would give out or I'd start shattering every breakable thing in sight. It wasn't about the money. Clearly, I would receive a ton of it. What I cared about was the fact that this contagious rash of a man had weaseled his way into our lives and was now too spineless to look me in the eye as he stole money from our estate.

"But why would she secretly marry Julian?" I ran a hand through my hair. "Did he convince her to? Two weeks later my sister dies. He could easily have wanted her dead to get it."

"We shouldn't jump to conclusions," my mother replied. "There are many people who could be behind your father and Amelia's deaths."

I ignored her comment and focused on the one man my father trusted completely. "You really haven't found anything about where he is, Victor?"

Victor shook his head. "He's gone off the grid, but we have a team looking for him. They have ways of finding people the cops can't access."

"What about Nicastro Developments, then?" I asked, whirling between Howard and Victor. "Dad told me he wanted to bring me in. What does the will say about it?"

Instead of a response, every single person in the room stiffened.

Matteo and Richard exchanged a look I couldn't read and even my mother and Victor held each other's gazes for far too long. Howard rubbed his forehead and focused on the will.

"Um, what's happening?" I asked. "Why do you all look so weird right now?"

Victor winced. *Winced.* I had never seen the man wince. "Tasha…"

"Your father lied to you about the true nature of the family business," my mother interrupted. There was a hard set to her mouth with fine lines eroding through her Botox. "Nicastro Developments isn't *just* about building new real estate, Natasha. It never has been."

My heart picked up speed, climbing further up my throat with each breath. "What are you talking about?"

She rose from the couch, slowly moving toward me. "Gabriel Nicastro, the father you loved so much, ran the most powerful criminal organization in New York and along most of the East Coast. The Nicastro Mafia."

The floor opened wide, waiting for me to stumble and fall into its eternal hell.

"You're lying."

I whipped my attention to Victor. To Matteo. To Richard. One of them *had* to confirm my mother was a vicious, crazy woman trying to drive the knife deeper into my exposed wounds.

"*Tell me* she's lying," I said, jabbing my finger in her direction.

"I can't," Victor replied.

I let out a harsh, maybe hysterical, laugh. "Now you're lying, too. Is this some kind of weird grief prank you're all playing on me? I get it. Ha ha. We can all stop now."

Pain laced Victor's face. "I've lied most of my life, Tasha. This isn't one of those times."

My hand dropped to my side and with it any remaining hope that I'd wake from this new reality.

"*What?*" I shouted, my voice cracking.

My mother pushed a lock of hair behind her ear. "This is one of the main reasons I came right away. I figured Gabriel never told you girls the truth. He thought keeping you in the dark of his nefarious life would ensure your safety—and stop you from despising him. He never prepared you for this reality. That man always thought he was invincible.

"I need you to know that I never wanted to leave you and Amelia behind," she continued, grasping my hands in hers. "I wanted to leave your father and take you two with me; I couldn't handle the world I'd married into anymore. But he forced my hand. He threatened your Aunt Céline if I tried to take you two with me or if I attempted to contact you. I had an hour to throw a bag together and flee. I went to the first place I could think of—Milan."

I swallowed, willing myself to continue fanning the flames of hatred I felt for her and to not believe a word she said. It was easier to sit in my anger toward my mother than admit that maybe I didn't know the whole story. That maybe my father played a massive part in ruining my life long before he died.

My mother let out a dry laugh. "I still can't believe I went to the place where we had our honeymoon. I don't know what I was thinking. Once I got there though, I couldn't leave, because I knew he'd tell you where I went. And if there was ever a chance..." She cleared her throat and stepped away from me to pick up my purse. "Anyway. This is the timeline we're living in, and next steps need to be taken."

Before I could stop her, she grabbed my phone and ripped out the SIM card, putting both items into her own purse.

"What are you doing?"

"I'm taking the first step in protecting you," she replied, pulling out a new phone and handing it to me. "Your phone is likely compromised now. This one is from France with a French VPN. It'll make you difficult to trace. I assume you haven't forgotten the language."

"Who would try to trace me?"

"Law enforcement," Richard replied. "Other mobs. You're a prime target right now for different reasons. We'll need to have a security detail escort you everywhere you go from now on until we resolve who issued and made the hit on Gabriel and Amelia."

A hit? Security detail? Other mobs?

I ran a hand over my chest, trying to calm the storm raging inside.

"Tasha, listen."

Victor approached me. I used to see a man who had a heart of gold despite a few rough edges, but that was a lie. Those edges were a darkness that stemmed from a place where horror stories were born.

He stopped when I put my hands up, shaking his head. "Your father had planned to reveal the truth to you. He had high hopes that you'd work well within the organization as his close aide. Obviously now... none of those plans are going to happen. But we still need to know if you want to be part of it."

"Absolutely *not*!" my mother exclaimed, baring her teeth at him. "I've already lost my first daughter to that horrific world you live in. I will not let you drag my second baby into it!"

"You gave up your rights to your daughters, Adriana. So you have no say in what Tasha decides to do."

"And I wonder who forced me to do that!"

The storm inside me expanded, pooling in my stomach, choking any air I could breathe. I couldn't contain it anymore. Not unless I wanted it to crack me in two.

"Stop it!"

When I accepted my father's offer, I had pictured myself sitting in his office in Midtown, listening and learning from him as he told a room full of employees what big plans he had.

That was what I had agreed to. There was never supposed to be any Mafias or hitmen or dead family involved. And now Victor was asking me if I still *wanted* it? I wasn't sure I could *comprehend* it.

Heat flooded my face. Tears swarmed my vision. My world had already shattered in my hand and they had the audacity to argue with each other?

I fled from the room, shoving a chair over on my way out. I didn't know where I was going or what my next decisions were. All I could think about was screaming at the top of my lungs until my throat cracked and bled.

"Tasha!" Victor called. "Tasha, wait!"

I whirled around. He and Matteo had followed me out into the hall, both in a defensive stance as if I might lunge forward at any second.

"You lied to me!" I screamed. "All my life you made me believe I was from this powerful, virtuous family, when really it was bullshit. Even the respect I thought people had for us was based on fear, wasn't it?"

Matteo stepped forward, pained creased in his face. "Not everyone who associated with Uncle Gabriel knew. The Danesis tried to expose us after Angelo's death, but we put an end to that when we threatened to expose their Mafia as well. He kept it separate from Nicastro Developments employees and from many he was friendly with."

The Danesis were criminals, too. I couldn't feel the shock of that news when so much of it already raged inside me.

"And now he's *dead* because of it." I snapped out each word like bullets, aiming to pierce through their composure. "He and Amelia were murdered in cold blood because my father decided getting rich and powerful the legal way was taking too long."

Matteo pressed his lips into a thin line. "This didn't start with him. At the beginning of the twentieth century other development firms tried to crush us by stealing projects and blocking property sales. Our family changed tactics to survive and has been wrapped up in the underground world ever since."

I crossed my arms. "And how exactly are we wrapped up in it?"

Matteo exchanged a look with Victor before replying, "Well, let's see ... There's the smuggling through our unfinished projects. Then the money laundering. Those two have kept this company afloat and running smoothly for decades. Sometimes when we're very motivated to purchase a property and negotiations aren't going well, we have to sweeten the deal." My cousin winced. "Though it's not always 'sweet' to the other party."

"That's enough, Matteo. Tasha doesn't need to know the whole grim breakdown right now," Victor said. He turned to me. "We don't know who's behind their deaths. Or if it's related to the family business. All we know is that the hitman knew about your home's tunnel system and how to navigate them. That's it."

My thoughts jumped to one face and name. Leo. He'd known about the secret passages since we were kids and had followed me that night demanding answers to questions he expected me to understand. Mafia-related questions. We all knew how much Sloane Danesi hated every inch of my father, and now I knew they had a Mafia of their own.

"Was it the Danesis?" I asked, spotting my mother and Richard stepping out into the hall. "They were the only people at the party who actively hate us and don't try to hide it."

"It's possible. The Danesi Mafia has been around long enough to gain a significant amount of power," my mother replied. "They always had a chip on their shoulder over being considered new money. Maybe all that resentment finally got to Sloane."

Richard shook his head. "They haven't declared it theirs. We'll continue to investigate to see if that's true ... but as it stands, I can't see Sloane Danesi refusing to take credit. This kind of hit sends a monumental message through the entire underground world. Other Mafias, gangs, and cartels would take notice of and respect her power more than ever. So it's likely not her."

"*Respect?*" I hissed. "Respected for killing my *father* and *sister*?"

Richard sighed deeply. "Yes."

I ran my fingers through my hair. My family had a Mafia. One powerful enough that someone gunning them down was seen as some grand accomplishment instead of what it was—heinous murder.

"And Dad didn't talk to them?" I asked, looking straight at Victor. "Other than at the party? He hadn't reached out beforehand to talk or... intimidate them?"

Victor's brows pulled close. "Not at all. What would make you ask that?"

I shook my head, thinking of the bullet Leo showed me, his accusation that the two men trying to kidnap Sophia were linked to my father. "I don't know."

"We can investigate who's behind their deaths later, but right now, we have a crucial meeting we need to get to," Victor said. His harsh eyes were on me, but a fragment of softness reflected in them. "You are a Nicastro, Tasha. Whatever your mother says doesn't change that. You need to finally meet the people who run the foundation of your life. From there, we can talk about what comes next."

I glanced at my mother who shook her head, mouthing a silent plea for me not to go.

Shock still rang in my ears and muddled my thoughts, but I was clear about one thing: I needed to see it for myself to believe it. All the monstrous details that had been hidden away from me for the last seventeen years. The grisly details that had been layered within the beauty. I wanted to know what my father saw when he looked at me. What he thought I could handle.

Turning to Victor, I replied, "Let's go."

CHAPTER NINE

Tasha

HORNS BLARED AND THE THICK SMELL OF DIESEL ENVEL-oped me the moment I stepped out of the car in Hudson Yards. Victor had taken the four of us down in one of our black SUVs, leaving my mother back at the Costas. While he wanted to keep her close, he warned that everyone who worked for my family saw her as nothing but a traitor. Seeing her was bound to rile them up, so it was better for everyone if she stayed behind. I didn't object.

"Ready?" Matteo asked, resting his hand on my back.

I pulled my gaze away from the Hudson River and to the building we'd parked in front of. NICASTRO DEVELOPMENTS signs and DO NOT ENTER warnings decorated the tall fence surrounding the property. No passersby could see into the construction zone. Not unless they craned their necks way back to look up at the towering high-rise taking over another piece of the Manhattan skyline.

"The meeting is happening in *here*?" I gawked as Victor unlocked the fence's door, dust and garbage flying into the air when it swung open.

"It wouldn't be the first time," Victor replied. "Now hurry up. Before we get an audience."

He fixed his jacket and I caught sight of a handgun attached to his belt. My heart did a double thump. Until now, I'd never seen Victor wear a weapon outside the shooting range. And here he was, carrying one like how I carried a handbag.

Why did I never question my father's insistence that I learn how to shoot? His late night meetings? The multiple cell phones he used? The strange people he let into our home? It had been right in front of me since the beginning, but there had been the reality I was allowed to live in and the one shielded from me. And now they'd collided, and I had to readjust fast.

I did as I was told and carefully stepped into the construction zone. Silent cranes loomed above us while tarps covering materials flapped in a passing wind. The high-rise had all its windows installed—thank God—but not much else.

"The main elevators were put in," Victor said, guiding us into the lobby. "I called in a small group of our soldiers and associates to attend this meeting. They're waiting for us on the fifteenth floor."

Every muscle in me wanted to freeze up and stop any attempt to go further into this new reality. But I'd come this far and I couldn't back out now. Even if no one warned me I'd be walking around a construction site in white tennis shoes.

The four of us crammed into one of the elevators. Blood pumped in my eardrums as Richard pressed the number fifteen button and the ground slid away from us.

"What are they expecting?" I asked to anyone who would answer. "Definitely not me."

Victor clasped my shoulder. "They're expecting a plan."

"Do we have one?"

"Not one they're going to like," Matteo replied.

The elevator whooshed open, revealing barren subfloors and exposed lights spanning through an open concept office. The view of the river and New Jersey was blocked by *hundreds* of men. They varied from Wall Street–ready to grimy creeps you crossed the street to get away from. The contrast was stark, but one detail was the same. A detail that made a knot in my stomach.

They were all mobsters. Dangerous, merciless mobsters.

And they all went dead quiet when we walked in.

"Gentlemen," Richard boomed, his voice bouncing off the unfinished walls. "Thank you for gathering here on short notice. We're all aware of the terrible circumstances we now have to face. We're here to assure you we'll not be wavered for long. Our esteemed underboss, Victor Callan, is here to provide you with more details."

It was Victor they were all supposed to be looking at, but they stared directly at me. I kept my shoulders pulled back and my chin lifted despite my shirt clinging to me from sweat. I was meant to be here, so I needed to act like it.

"You're takin' over, Victor?" someone yelled from the back.

"Is it true the Great Lion was gunned down by Danesi scum?" another asked.

Matteo leaned in close. "He means your father."

"Right," I whispered as if that was a normal piece of information.

I'd never heard someone call my father the Great Lion. Not in passing or when I eavesdropped. I used to think I was good at sneaking around, quietly listening in on my father's private conversations. The more I learned though, the more I realized how good he was at making me *think* I was outmaneuvering him. He probably knew every time I listened in. It would make sense why I never learned anything of true value.

"Of course it was those fuckers," one of the men spat. "They took Luca and brutalized the shit out of his body before tossin' him back to us. Those animals are capable of anything."

The room shouted their agreement and muted my gasp. They were talking about Uncle Luca. He died in a *boating* accident, not—

I flicked my gaze to my cousin who looked back grimly. God. Another truth wrapped in a sea of messy lies. My poor uncle. Did he know about this world? And that it would end him before his thirty-second birthday?

Victor stepped onto a glass staircase leading to the next floor, staying calm as the crowd rippled with heated tension. "Everything you've heard is bullshit. What I'm *not* gonna allow is anyone goin' rogue to get retribution. I don't want none of you fuckers sparking war with the Danesis just 'cause you're pissed off." When the room remained silent, a murderous anger flooded Victor's face. "We clear?"

I tried to keep my face neutral. I'd *never* heard Victor speak in such an obnoxious way. But he knew these men better than me, so I wasn't going to question his way of communicating with them.

The majority of the men grumbled in agreement, satisfying Victor enough to relax again.

"I called you here, in honor of the Great Lion, to tell you what his plans were." A jolt went head to toe through my body when Victor turned his attention to me. He reached out his hand, coaxing me to stand on the staircase with him. "You all know who the Great Lion's daughters are. His first daughter, Amelia, was caught in the shooting, too. God rest her soul. But today I've brought his second daughter, Natasha, with me."

Rubbing my sweaty palm against my jeans, I stepped onto the first level of the stairs. Victor placed both hands on my shoulders and faced me to the crowd.

"The Great Lion knew she could be a strong member of our organization. I've watched her grow, making choices that prove she's her father's daughter. We've been training since she was young, and I know she could put most of you in a chokehold before you knew what was happening."

Despite my still fresh shock over everything, I smiled. I'd never known my father felt that way, but then, he never revealed he was running a *Mafia* underneath Nicastro Developments. Victor's form of compliments usually looked like a tip of the head. A grunt of approval if I was lucky. So this was more than I could ever hope for from him, too.

"Which is why we plan to induct her into the Nicastro Mafia as the organization's next boss," Victor suddenly declared.

The room went feral. Every man began hurling insults at Victor and me, each one crueler than the last. I could barely breathe as their faces turned monstrous. Their hands swiping through the air like razors trying to rip at skin. I could barely breathe through it.

The Nicastro Mafia's *boss*? Was Victor out of his mind?

The blast of a gunshot shocked my system. I nearly stumbled forward and off the stairs before Matteo jumped forward to catch me.

"*Enough!*" Victor roared, his handgun raised toward the ceiling. He bared his teeth as the room silenced. "All of you deserve a death sentence for disrespecting the Great Lion and his daughter."

"You can't kill us all," a man near the front of the crowd with a wicked scar across his face shouted. "I respected the Great Lion more than any man, but we ain't following someone so young and weak and... *female*."

I couldn't say whether it was his words or his tone. Each was humiliating, sending a wave of heat through me and lighting fire to my senses. It didn't matter what I wanted, all I knew was I immediately hated him.

"Fuck you," I spat. "I'm nowhere near weak. You'd be lucky to have me as your boss."

The man smirked. "It's cute when you cuss."

The fire inside me roared louder when the room chuckled and sneered at me.

"Thank you, Tasha," Victor said. "You've made your point."

"How can we believe this was the Great Lion's idea when we never heard it from him?" someone shouted.

The scarred man raised his chin, his upper lip twisting. "Yeah. Last we heard that Henderson kid was all set for the role."

Richard let out a laugh. "That idiot was never gonna be boss. The Great Lion used him and his family for their money and connections. All he's proven to be good at now is playing hide-and-seek."

"Exactly," Victor replied. "Gabriel always had plans for Natasha to take over one day."

My brows rose up my forehead and could've jumped off my face entirely. My father *hadn't* wanted Julian to take over our empire one day? That role was meant for *me*? Julian's position seemed set in stone no matter what Amelia or I thought. My father made it clear he thought I was capable of working for our empire, wanting me to dip my toes into its not-so-crystal-clear depths before I knew the truth, but he never revealed he wanted me to sit on the throne, ruling it all. What did that say about me if he thought I was a worthy successor to his *Mafia*?

"We've already decided I'll be acting boss," Victor added. "You disrespect the Great Lion's judgment *and* mine by assuming I want to put Natasha in the role right away. Especially when your sorry asses could never handle it."

A rumbling went through them as most turned to feel out their peers and see if someone would be bold enough to disagree.

Unfortunately for me, they weren't done using their peanut-sized brains.

"That's not good enough," one hollered from the back. "I'll desert before I ever let a fucking little girl be in charge of me!"

Victor snapped threatening orders for everyone to calm down, but this time his authority wasn't good enough. A blade of fear plunged through my stomach when they turned their growing anger onto me, some with fists at their sides or fingers toying with the guns strapped to their waists.

These were malicious men, nurtured in an environment that strengthened their dark instincts. If they decided I was a threat, there was no way Victor could stop them from eliminating me.

"What if Tasha were to marry?" Matteo said, his usual soft voice thundering through the room. "Her boyfriend is Ravi Ferreira, son of the Ferreiras who own Aurora Technology. He'd do anything for her. We'd *all* be stronger with them connected to us."

My eyes widened at my cousin, but he refused to glance my way. He couldn't be serious. For one, Ravi was *not* my boyfriend, and I wasn't going to *marry him* to gain favor with my father's Mafia.

Matteo rested his hands on his hips, staring out at the crowd as— to my horror—an immediate rumble of satisfaction traveled through them. *What?* These men knew nothing about Ravi's family and yet they would jump right into that arrangement?

"He'd take over then?" the man with the scar asked. "Or would we still have to put up with her hysteria?"

"Oh, don't worry," I snapped. "I would only subject *you* to it."

Victor put his hand on my shoulder, a silent warning to keep my thoughts to myself.

"Richard and I will talk," he replied. "As I've said, I'll be acting boss. So you better follow whatever orders are given. We clear?" When the room hesitated, Victor gritted his teeth and roared again, "I said, *are we fucking clear?*"

Every man balled their left hand into a fist, raising it above their head, shouting, "*Yes, sir,*" in unison. I spotted a tattoo on all their left forearms. A lion. Like the one Leo described on those two kidnappers.

He knew they were connected to my father. What else in this secret world did Leo already know about?

Victor gave a curt nod. "Good. Richard or I will deal out new information when we're ready. Until then, it's business as usual. Don't forget."

Wrapping his arm protectively around me, Victor led me off the stairs and back toward the elevators with Matteo and Richard in tow. We didn't speak until we were down in the lobby when I spun around to face the three men.

"What the hell, Matteo?" I exclaimed. "You're trying to sell me off like cattle?"

Matteo winced, raising his hands protectively. "Of course not, Tasha. I'm just trying to help your case. As you noticed, our organization doesn't take kindly to a woman in power."

"No shit." I turned away from them, putting my palms up to my face and letting out a frustrated scream.

Victor pulled my hands down, forcing me to hold his gaze. "When I brought you here, I didn't expect them to welcome you with open arms. That response was exactly what I anticipated."

"You let me be humiliated," I replied. "For a role I haven't said I *want* or *knew* about until today."

"I brought you here," Victor continued, "to show you what you're up against and to explain the severity of the situation. This isn't a normal inheritance, Tasha. You don't get to pick and choose what parts of your family's empire to keep and what to throw away. That small group represents the thousands we have working for us in New York and beyond. While it may be difficult to wrap your head around it now, we need you to fight for the Mafia to accept you as their new boss."

"And why's that?" I replied. "What's stopping me from throwing up two middle fingers at those pricks upstairs and walking away from it all?"

Matteo cleared his throat, shifting from his left to right foot. "You'd have to leave New York, possibly the US, and move somewhere under a different name to protect yourself. There'd be no coming back for your own safety. Whoever is behind Uncle Gabriel's and Amelia's deaths did something no one has ever been able to do to our family. And we don't know if they're also after you."

"Nicastro Developments would also crumble without the Mafia. It's too wrapped up in it now to detach. You'd lose a hefty chunk of your family's estate and likely get the feds pounding on your door," Victor said. "Matteo is failing to mention the other, uglier, issue though. If you don't stay and fight for the role of boss, you'll be creating a death sentence for the rest of your remaining family. While you'll get away safely, anyone related to you will be tracked down and killed by others to eliminate any chance of the Nicastro Mafia retaining their power."

My heart dropped into my stomach. "*No*, you're lying to me. Right, Matteo? Tell me he is." I turned to my cousin, desperate for reassurance that this was a sick joke Victor was telling, but all I got from him were downcast eyes.

"I would never lie about something like this, Tasha," Victor replied instead. "When I mean everyone, I mean everyone. Matteo will be targeted, your aunts and uncles, all your other cousins. Even your grandmother, Donatella, will be eliminated. The level of power your empire has means more groups wanting to destroy it for good. But if you stay, fight for your legacy and win it, they'll have no choice but to back off."

I ran my fingers through my hair, tugging at the roots until it pinched. And here I thought the nightmare I was already living couldn't get any *worse*.

"Why does this have to be me?" I demanded, whipping my attention between Matteo, Victor, and Richard. "You three were already running things with my dad. Why can't one of *you* take over?"

Richard shook his head, gesturing between himself and Victor. "We can't take the role because we're not Nicastros. The title can only go to someone within the family."

I huffed, forced to accept that answer, and shifted to Matteo. I stepped closer to him until he finally raised his head and looked at me again.

"Matteo...," I started. "Can't you be the one?"

My cousin searched my face through his red glasses. "I'm not the right choice. We've been down this road already.... They see me as too soft and they're right. I can't make the kind of difficult decisions the role demands."

My mouth went dry. "And I can?"

Matteo was quiet for a moment, the bob of his Adam's apple the one sign that he was hesitant about his answer.

"You're a fighter, Tasha," he finally said. "That's why I know you can do this."

I pulled back, a tremble starting in my hands. I didn't know what to say anymore. There were two options I could choose from—destroy my family's lives or destroy my own.

"I meant every word I said up there," Victor said. "You have what it takes to run the Nicastro empire. It might not feel like it now, but it's true. If you stay, I'll push hard for you as your father planned to do. Not by getting you to marry Ravi, but by showing every single one of them that *you* are enough. That you are as strong as your father. If not more so."

My skin warmed with the genuineness, but it didn't stop my throat from tightening. The world my father had lived in was filled with violence. It was immoral. Illegal. It was a thousand other things I wasn't part of. But whether I liked it or not, it had always been there pumping life into me. Now I had to ask myself if I was willing to let it take every part of my existence. All because of some mystery person I couldn't even scream at.

"What if I found the person responsible for Dad's and Amelia's deaths?" I asked as an idea sprang into my thoughts. "Would that be enough for the other Mafias to back off so I wouldn't need to take over?"

Victor quickly shook his head. "Absolutely *not*. Whoever is behind this hit is too dangerous for you to be looking for them."

"Leave the investigative work to us, Tasha," Matteo added. "The cops will be useless, but we have ways of finding answers."

"None of this is making me feel better," I said. "You're telling me there isn't another option? Something that doesn't involve running a Mafia or going into hiding?"

Victor walked to the entrance, the evening light catching on the side of his buzzed hair and highlighting three scars above his ear. "That's the question Nicastros have had to ask themselves for generations."

And I already knew the choice each of them made.

Tasha

WHAT A NIGHTMARE.

I leaned down and rubbed again at the dark stain clearly visible on the side of my riding boot. With my level of patience recently, I was ready to chuck them into the nearest trash bin rather than walk around less than perfect, but I couldn't turn around now. Not when this was my first time out of the house in days.

"We've arrived, miss," my head of security said.

I looked out the car window as we pulled up to my school's stable and the polo field situated in front of it. Victor insisted I stay locked inside the Costas' home while he and Richard worked on finding Julian, those behind the hit on my family, and getting me a security detail.

The only thing they'd accomplished in those three days was hiring five high-level bodyguards to follow me around indefinitely. I couldn't go anywhere outside the house without them. They were always around, whether directly in my line of sight or slinking around corners, waiting for someone to do the worst.

"Miss, please." Eric reached out a hand from the passenger seat, stopping me from opening my door. "Don't get out of the vehicle until we've done a sweep of the grounds to determine it's safe."

I rolled my eyes and unlocked the door. "No one knows I'm showing up to practice, Eric. We're fine."

He threw out another protest, but I barely heard him as I got out of the car and speed-walked over to the stable, the first flush of morning sweeping over me. Victor and my mother insisted I stay home from school until next week, but there was no damn way I was missing the Scarsdale Polo Club's first practice of the season. I had ten minutes to get my white Arabian mare ready to go. Every season we were assigned one horse to ride, and I made sure since my first season in the club that Dahlia was mine.

My security team hovered around me while I got the mare ready for practice and continued to hover when I walked her down to the field. Already my teammates were in their saddles, either standing around chatting or giving their horse a warm-up ride as they waited for Coach Samaras to start.

I was the beacon of everyone's attention long before I made it to the field. Everyone came to a halt so they could gawk, but I kept my focus on the task at hand. Normalcy. Victor said the version I was used to would never exist again, but I was *not* about to roll over and accept it. My father and sister were dead. My whole life had been a lie. I had to decide if I wanted to lead a notorious Mafia or run and leave bullseyes on my remaining family's backs. And yet I wouldn't let any of that stand in the way of my polo practice.

Ravi handed his horse's reins over to a sophomore member and jogged over to me. He had on a crisp white polo shirt tucked into a pair of slim polo jeans with a large 2 resting over his heart. My shirt had 1 stitched in a bold black font. We'd been co-captains of our team since last season—the dream duo—with unbridled confidence raining off all of us that our team would be unstoppable come competition time.

That energy had dried up after I dumped Ravi. Now it was probably a withering husk, gasping for air while it crumbled into obscurity. But I wouldn't contribute to that failing confidence by abandoning my team.

His dark brows furrowed as he approached me, wrinkling his otherwise smooth olive skin. "Tasha? What are you doing here?"

I walked Dahlia onto the field, my fingers pressed deep into my helmet as I stopped to put it on. "Arriving for practice. Did you think I would miss the first one of the season?"

"I—" Ravi slid his gaze over to our coach and back to me. "We all thought you'd need more time to grieve. It hasn't been a week."

"Thank you for the lovely reminder, Ravi," I snapped. My chest ached to cave in on itself under his scrutinizing gaze, but I hid it by pressing my lips firmly together. "I can't stay isolated. Or sit in the pain. Can you please just...give me one thing that feels normal?"

His rigid shoulders softened. "Okay. But please find a way to rein in the anger. The Tasha I know isn't like this."

I swallowed the shame that crept up my throat as Ravi turned his back and approached our coach. They exchanged a quick conversation, Coach Samaras looking over at me briefly, and broke away soon after.

"Coach is fine with you joining us," Ravi said, coming back over with a mallet for me in hand. "Let's get started."

I moved through the motions of practice, perfectly following Coach Samaras's instructions as we cantered around the field, swinging our mallets at the ball. I savored the sensation of the sweat forming underneath my helmet and the ache of my muscles as minute after minute passed.

He blew the whistle when the sun had crested fully into the sky. "Okay, team, take five! We'll divide into two groups for a match next!"

I slowed Dahlia to a walk. Scarsdale Country Day's grand building stretched out in front of me, sitting on the most elevated piece of campus so no matter where someone was, it was the focal point.

"Hey." Ravi rode his Thoroughbred up beside me, giving a sad smile. "Are you sure you're okay? I've tried calling and texting you with no answer, so I came over to Valentina's house to see you, but Mrs. Costa said you weren't taking visitors."

I cringed at the disappointment in his gaze. "I'm sorry. I have a new phone and number, and everyone is being extra protective of me lately." I nodded to my security detail spread out around the outskirts of the field. "As you've already seen."

Which was all true, but when Ravi came over, I'd asked Isabel Costa not to let him inside. I wasn't ready to put on a good face for him and hide the true depths of my pain. How ugly it could be. He wasn't there when Angelo Danesi died and my mother left, so he didn't know that side of me, and I didn't want to see how he would react to it now.

"I can imagine." Ravi frowned, looking down at his reins. "Saturday was a nightmare. I've had trouble sleeping ever since. Amelia was amazing; she always made me feel like a part of the family. And your father was a great man. He never said it with words, but I'm sure I was in his good books."

I focused on my breathing when a snake of pain slid through my chest. Ravi's words were loaded in ways he didn't seem to realize. I couldn't fault him for still living in my former reality.

"I've laid awake most nights wondering how any of this is real. Even my mom is back. Can you believe it?"

We simultaneously turned our horses toward the center of the field. No matter what, there was no way I could tell him the biggest truth: My father had been the boss of New York's most powerful Mafia.

Ravi pursed his lips. "That *is* cause for questioning reality."

I couldn't help but smile. "She's already driving me crazy with all her worries about my safety and how to navigate being the sole heir of Nicastro Developments at my age."

When he didn't say anything, I glanced over to see him pensively staring forward.

"What is it?"

Ravi shook his head, a dark cloud settling over him. "I hadn't thought about that. Your mom has every right to be freaked out."

I frowned. "You don't think I can handle my family's empire?"

Ravi didn't say anything for a long minute before he shook his head. "You know I'm your biggest supporter. But this is huge, Tasha. There will be a lot of vultures circling who want to steal as much as possible from you. It happened when my avô was retiring, and Mom's siblings fought over who was taking over as CEO. The reason he gave the role to her was because she was the one not trying to backstab everyone else." He sighed. "People's ugly sides come out when heaps of power are on the table."

I sat with his response. Over by the refreshment table, our teammates chugged water and wiped towels across the back of their necks. Some of them laughed as they returned to their horses standing patiently with the club's student assistants. All their lives were beautifully simple. Not long ago, I thought I was one of them. But I'd never been like them. And it took a double homicide to find that out.

"You have no idea how right you are," I mumbled.

Suddenly, Ravi's hand wrapped around mine, his horse pressed far too close to Dahlia. But I didn't pull away and instead let him look at me with wide open eyes.

"I can protect you from it," he said. "We can go back to how things used to be and then whatever support you need from my family is yours."

I savored the feel of Ravi's hand. When we were together, he always knew how to comfort me when I needed it most. If I was ready to break something, I would go to him or call right away. I hated to disappoint him with my bad mood, especially when he was gentle and loving toward me, so it always worked. Despite us breaking up, I wanted to see him smiling even if that meant only showing him the side of me he loved.

But I didn't have the energy to be that girl right now.

I delicately lifted his hand from mine and put some distance between our horses. "I know, but I need to figure this out on my own. At least for now. Are you okay with that?"

He let out a long sigh before nodding. "Fine. What are you going to do then?"

That was the biggest question of all. What *was* I going to do? I was supposed to decide what future I would shackle myself to. That was enough stress to make anyone an insomniac, but more than anything, I lay awake at night thinking about who was behind the deaths of my father and sister. If I wanted to sleep well again, I needed to find them and have my heel pressed into their face while they begged me not to destroy their life the way they had mine.

And yet no one was okay with me looking for answers. They wanted me to sit on my hands and wait for them to figure everything out while I stayed out of the way, proving the Nicastro Mafia's point that I wasn't worthy of leading them.

But then, where did I go from here? I couldn't do this alone with my limited knowledge of the criminal world. I needed someone who already understood it. Who had something to lose from these mystery murderers, too.

I groaned quietly, hating how quickly the most aggravating, the most *repulsive*, face out there popped into my mind.

"I don't like that look," Ravi said.

I clenched the reins a little tighter, hiding it with a teasing pout. "And why's that?"

"It always means trouble," he replied. "And you've had enough of it to last you a lifetime."

I laughed his observation off and silently breathed a sigh of relief when Coach Samaras called us back over to continue practice. It was better if Ravi stayed in the dark about my plans. I already knew he'd try to stop me, and while he'd do it with my safety in mind, I couldn't let that happen.

"You don't have to worry about me," I said, taking my phone out of my side pouch. "I need to text Victor and tell him I'm still alive. He's demanding I let him know every half hour."

"I'm glad you have him to keep an eye on you." Ravi pushed his horse forward and called over his shoulder. "Don't take too long."

When his back was turned, I quickly opened my phone and went to my contacts list.

I scrolled down to a name I hadn't looked at, much less texted or called, in four years. Despite all the horrible things he said to me then, I didn't have it in me to delete his contact details. The last part that connected me to him.

Before I could psych myself out, my fingers flew over the screen, writing out a direct, simple message.

We need to meet—T.

When the text sent, I immediately shuddered at my own assumption. Why did I ever think he would respond? He probably had my old number blocked. Once he saw this one, he'd probably block it, too.

My embarrassment boiled over. This was a terrible idea. Probably my worst. I nearly chucked my phone across the field when it buzzed in my palm.

I stared down at a new message. From him.

Where?

For one long minute, all I could do was stare dumbfounded at the screen. He responded. I didn't know what to make of it and I had no interest in starting now, so I pushed away all my thoughts and sent off a reply.

> The school's stables. 7:50 AM. Come around the back and don't be late.

Tasha

I clipped Dahlia to the leads in the middle of the stable's long hall, breathing in the scent of hay and horsehair. The rest of the Polo Club was still down at the field, finishing their last round of practice for the day. I'd asked to leave a few minutes early and blamed it on a headache. Coach Samaras was more than happy to let me go. Being in the presence of grief really brought out the cooperation in people.

On the way back, I convinced Eric to stay behind to talk security details with Coach Samaras. The rest of my guards were a bit trickier, but after they did a sweep of the stables to make sure it was secure, I got all of them scrambling to fulfill my demand for an arbitrary list of items I wanted for a "headache." It would give me a few minutes at least.

I checked my watch. 7:48 AM. He better show up on time.

Dahlia flicked her ears toward a noise. I steeled myself and turned as the back doors pulled wide open.

The morning light washed over Leo as he stood in the entranceway with a baseball cap on. His backpack hung loosely from one shoulder, and he had his hands in his pockets.

"You came."

"Looks like it."

I placed my hand on Dahlia's warm, soft neck, letting her steady me. It didn't get past me that the last time we were in a stable together was the day Leo broke our friendship—and my heart—for good.

"We only have a few minutes," I said. "So I won't waste time. I know about the secret my father kept from me."

Leo lowered his head, taking a deep breath. "It's tough news to learn."

A dry laugh escaped me. "That's putting it lightly." I paused. "Did you always know about your family?"

"Not always." He paused, searching my face. I wondered briefly if he was thinking about the last time we stood in a stable, too. "But I found out when my dad died. After that, I wanted to get out of here."

I tried to keep my sharp inhale subtle, but Leo's gaze flicked down to my open mouth and back up.

That was why he left for boarding school. I never did find out, seeing as he left for California without ever saying goodbye.

It was a few days after Angelo Danesi's fateful car ride. Another car ran a red light and smashed into the driver's side where Angelo sat while fourteen-year-old Leo was in the passenger seat. Angelo died on impact, and Leo was rushed to the hospital with minor injuries. That was what my father told me. I believed him because he never gave me a reason to think otherwise.

When Leo asked to meet me at the riding stable, I thought I would be comforting my closest friend in the height of his grief. Instead, he was a storm of rage and devastation, ready to uproot everything we once were to each other.

Shaking the memory away, I quickly asked, "Why don't you have any security then? You're the second son of a boss. Shouldn't you have a swarm of guards keeping you from getting shot like me?"

Leo shrugged. "I can take care of myself."

I frowned, irritation stirring in my stomach. So *he* could handle watching his own back, but *I* had to have someone breathing down my neck every time I decided to leave the house?

"Why did you ask me to come here, Nicastro?"

My boot heels sounded along the cement as I moved closer. "I don't trust you, Danesi, let's make that clear."

"You don't, huh?" he replied dryly. "How shocking."

I pressed my lips into a thin line. "But I've been thinking about what happened and what you told me about Sophia. My father wasn't behind it. Just like I have a hunch your mother isn't behind the hit."

He stayed quiet for a moment, giving nothing away. "She said it wasn't her call. That another mob is behind it."

"Exactly," I said quietly, more to myself than him. "I need to find those responsible for the hit and I want you to help me do it."

Leo's brows rose. "And why's that?"

"Because you know more about the world of the Mafia than I do. You know it's another Mafia who's behind the hit, *not* a lone wolf. And you have your own reasons to find these people, because I have a feeling they're also the ones behind what happened to Sophia. Something I'm sure you've considered already." I paused, steeling myself to show my hand. "That's why I asked you to meet me here. We have a common enemy. And I think we should be the ones to find out who that is."

Leo's gaze locked with mine, his black pupils consuming the honey-brown in his eyes. "That's a tall ask, Nicastro. Last time we were alone together, you were waving a gun in my face."

"True." A smirk played on my lips, but it faded as quickly as it appeared. That night would be a black line in my life. "And the time before that, you called me a killer and accused me of ruining your life."

I nestled in the satisfaction of Leo flinching. He deserved it and a lot more. All I'd wanted was to be there for him, a shoulder to cry on and a person to hold. Instead, he accused me of helping orchestrate the "attack" against his father because I'd convinced him to change his plans last minute.

You were the one who gave me the tickets to see the Yankees with my dad, Leo had roared. *All I'd wanted to do was go sailing with him, but* you *were the one who changed my mind. His body is filled with bullets because of* you. *You're a fucking killer, Tasha. Like the rest of your fucked-up family. I bet you wanted me dead in that car, too.*

I'd been devastated and confused by his accusations that I'd let instinct take over, speaking declarations I could never take back.

Go to hell, Leo, I'd screamed. *Since that's the only way you'll reunite with your dad.*

It was the last time I ever saw or spoke to him until he crashed my soirée.

"My security will be back any second," I said. "So tell me now. Are you in?"

A long silence drew out between us as he searched my face. For what, I wasn't sure. The more I remembered that awful day, the more Leo's accusation muddled over my father's reassurances. I always assumed Leo had been fed some vile lies by his mother to blame us for his father's death. But with everything I'd learned, a gnawing uncertainty clouded the confidence I used to have over what happened that day.

"Yeah," he eventually said. "I'm in."

I turned and walked back to my horse, holding my stance. No matter what short-term alliance we might have, I would never let him see how much being around him rattled me.

"You're one of the most powerful girls in New York now. Do you know that?" Leo added. "If you don't, you're about to find out."

I stayed quiet when I looked back at him.

"But you're also the most vulnerable." Leo pulled out a pair of sunglasses from his back pocket. "Be careful out there, Nicastro."

I crossed my arms and dug my fingernails into my forearms, hating the way my chest clenched. It shouldn't be so easy for him to get under my skin, even when he was telling the truth.

"Don't make me regret this, Danesi."

He stared at me for a moment before putting his sunglasses on and disappearing back outside.

"What was Leo Danesi doing here?" Ravi asked, appearing beside me.

I held completely still. Not trusting myself to look anywhere but forward. It was the only way I could keep myself steady against a guy like Leo who already knew how to knock me off my axis.

"Offering his condolences," I replied quietly.

CHAPTER
TWELVE

Tasha

THE CLICK OF MY HEELS BOUNCED OFF THE EMPTY HALLS, causing a grumbling hum through the building as lights flicked on above me and pipes hissed awake for the day. Students and teachers wouldn't start trickling in for another hour, giving me plenty of time to do the one thing I thought I would never do.

Join forces with Leo Danesi.

I stepped into the Donor Lounge. It came to life at my presence, which meant my new ally wasn't here yet. What did I expect.

We'd made plans right after our agreement in the stables to meet here early the next morning. I still wasn't supposed to be back at school, but I was willing to take the chance. Especially when I successfully snuck out of the Costas' house and away from my oblivious security team. I should have a few hours of them assuming they were guarding a depressed girl who refused to get out of bed. Plenty of time to brainstorm with Leo and get back to the house undetected.

I laid out my notebook and laptop on the four-chair table, tapping my foot and staring at the doorway. The muted walls brightened from the fresh light streaming in through the courtyard-facing window. There wasn't much in terms of décor in the lounge. Not when a view of lush trees and gardens of vibrant flowers took up a quarter of the room and shifted with the seasons.

I checked my phone, but there were no new texts from Leo. Somehow in the span of twenty-four hours, I was a person who regularly texted a Danesi again. My father would be raging with disappointment. Amelia would either be appalled or find it amusing. I'd never know which theory was true.

Finally, he appeared in a whirlwind of ruffled clothes and hair. He pulled off his uniform's jacket and laid it on one of the ivy-green couches, pushing up his white shirt sleeves.

I glared at him. "You're late."

"By, like, three minutes. There was traffic." Leo grabbed one of the many bottles of water in the fridge and took a long swig, swiping his knuckles over his full lips afterward.

"Boo-hoo," I replied, looking down at my laptop and opening it. "We have a lot to go over before I need to get out of here."

"You mean when your security team realizes their client is willingly dodging their protection when she has a target on her back?"

I shot my attention back up to him, flashing my teeth. "If I didn't, we'd get nowhere with this plan."

"Oh, I know," he replied, holding up his hands. "Doesn't change how risky it is. Your father had dozens of security guards at your sister's party and well..."

My chest deflated with the weight of his words. "I get it. It still wasn't enough." A stretch of silence built between us before I lowered my head and closed my eyes. "Did you ever suspect? About your family's...secret?"

"You mean their Mafia?" He took another swig of water and let out a heavy sigh. "I guess I always had a hunch that Dad was doing something shady when he started asking us to lie to the cops about seeing the cargo boxes that'd come through our house. And when we had to pretend like we'd never heard of certain people when they'd visit him all the time. One time when I was six or something, I woke up in the middle of the night and heard a guy's muffled screams." He shrugged. "I fell back asleep and let myself believe I was still dreaming."

I searched for similar memories I'd glazed over or rewritten but came up empty. "I don't remember anything like that. My father would invite people over sometimes that were questionable, but I thought it was all part of the real estate development industry. Maybe mob-adjacent at worst."

"Then he hid it well from you," Leo replied. "Lucky."

I shook my head. "More like unlucky. I was so, so naïve."

"You weren't naïve." Leo locked his eyes on mine his routine smugness replaced with a sincerity I couldn't look directly at. "You trusted your dad. There's nothing to be ashamed of for that."

My throat tightened, making it difficult to swallow. I needed to change the subject right away, but Leo beat me to it when the bit of sincerity he showed dissolved in a blink.

"You called me here. What big, scary mobster shit do you want me to explain to you to help get this crusade off the ground?"

I was about to snap a few choice words at him when he grabbed a yellow-packaged breakfast bar from the snack tray and ripped it open.

"Don't eat that!" I exclaimed, flying over to him and swatting the bar from his hands.

Leo stepped back, his eyes going wide. "What the hell, Nicastro?"

I huffed, a flush rising up my neck and heating my cheeks. Guess some things stuck with you. Like knowing what food could kill a former close friend. I crossed my arms, replying, "Those bars have banana in them."

Leo's exasperation shifted into amused surprise as he glanced at the dropped bar and back to me. "Look at you going soft. You could've had one less Danesi to deal with if you let me take a bite out of that."

I shrugged, turning back to my laptop. "You're more useful to me alive." I tapped my freshly done nails on my laptop where I'd already pulled up one of Amelia's credit card accounts. "I've been tracking my sister's statement for the black card she and Julian shared. See if he slips up and uses it."

"He's your prime suspect right now?" Leo asked, trying to get a look at my computer screen.

I shot a brow up and turned the screen away from his view. "Yes. He conveniently went missing right after my father and sister were shot. He's hiding out somewhere, avoiding the police and my father's men, and I want to know why."

"Makes sense you want to find him. I'd have suggested him, too. It generally doesn't go well when outsiders try to marry into our world," he replied.

"How would you know that?" I asked warily.

Leo shrugged. "I heard the son of a family in Chicago tried to elope with a girl. His family smuggled loads of illegal shit across the Canadian border. It turned out the girl he was trying to marry was the daughter of a pastor who ran the largest church in the area. It got messy fast when it went public, and his family suddenly had a spotlight on their shipments and what exactly their business was. But anyway, we should also look at your sister. Did she have enemies? Or get involved in something she shouldn't have?"

All my muscles tensed at his accusations. "Of course not! She works at the Met and has big dreams of traveling to every country's major museums. The only terrible choice she's made is marrying Julian."

My tongue went numb as I realized I spoke about her in the present tense. But Leo gave me the kindness of not correcting me.

"We can't disregard anything at this point, whether you like it or not. What involvement did Julian have with your mob? Does he know it exists? Carter dated a girl not long ago that turned out to be secretly working for the FBI. She was trying to use my brother to get concrete evidence against my family. You never know what agenda outsiders have."

I mentally laid out all the information I currently knew about Julian. If I wanted this partnership to work, I had to tell Leo some details, but I wasn't about to show all my cards to him just yet either.

"I don't think he knew, but he probably does now. My father never planned on giving Julian the role of boss if that's what you're asking." I eyed him carefully, weighing if it was a risk or not to tell him the next truth. "Amelia and him secretly got married two weeks before the hit."

I wasn't about to tell him the last key detail. That I had to decide if I wanted to take over a Mafia that didn't want me.

Leo let out a low whistle. "Damn. So you have a brother-in-law now."

I ground my teeth together. "Yes."

"We really need to find this guy," Leo went on. "But it's clear he didn't work alone. Like I said before, this wasn't a lone-wolf hit. Julian might be the one who made the call, but if he's not going to come out of hiding to answer our questions directly, we need to find his supporters who will lead us to him."

He went over to one of the couches and flopped himself down on it. "If the guys behind my sister's attack are related, we know at least two of the supporters are Nicastro soldiers who deserted. The deliberate cut across their lion tattoo symbolized that. There could be more."

If not now, then soon, I thought, but kept it to myself. The men in that Hudson Yards tower already made it clear that I had to give them a good reason to follow me if I decided to take over or they'd desert, too.

"They threw dead doves around Sophia's bedroom, too. An intentional message," Leo continued. "My guess is this other Mafia uses it as their symbol the way my family uses white lilies and yours uses lions.

It's a common way for organizations to differentiate themselves. I've never heard of or seen a mob using doves before. Not here or Chicago or Miami or any other major city they tend to operate in. If my guess is correct, they're new and keeping their presence minimal for now."

I stared at him blankly for the briefest moment before I realized what I was doing and quickly looked away. But I wasn't fast enough.

Leo sat up straighter. "You didn't know about that either? Wow, you really were in the dark. Your house has two lion statues placed out front at the gates. And your dad had that lion painting hanging over top of the fireplace in your front living room."

"Gee, thanks for pointing out the obvious," I snapped while my cheeks burned. All my life I had assumed my father simply loved the animal and what it represented. But after seeing the identical tattoos on his soldiers, I'd never believe that again. "You're really an expert for someone who tried to stay away from his family for years."

Leo rested his hands behind his head, the cut of his jaw hardening as he stared at the wall. "Unfortunately."

His mind was clearly elsewhere, so I sat at the table, opening a new Search tab. My thoughts went to the dove pin my father gave me right before he passed. The one that was currently in a drawer in my room at the Costas' house. There had to be a connection between it and the dead doves Leo talked about. I needed to figure out what that was.

"What are you looking up?" Leo asked a minute later.

I squinted at my web results after typing in "Mafias associated with doves"—nothing, like Leo said—then moved to a different angle.

"What doves symbolize," I replied, scrolling through the web results. "It might lead us to a detail you missed."

A ton of random websites popped up relating to doves in a religious context or how someone could interpret them in dreams. Nothing substantial. When I clicked on the second page of results though, the first link made me pause.

"Hey, it's Jesus."

I spooked at Leo's sudden appearance pressed close to me. Instinctively, my hand flew to his throat. He held completely still as my acrylic nails dug into his tender skin, staring at me with heavy-lidded eyes while my chest rose and fell.

Our gazes seared into each other. His hot, mint-touched breaths mixed with mine and tickled my chin, my lips, my cheek. Black pooled wide and large over Leo's irises. I watched it up close, mesmerized, until he spoke.

"Not good with surprises, are you?" Leo asked, his voice low and thick.

I flicked the briefest look down to his slightly parted lips and back up.

"Not when they come from you," I replied.

Letting my hand fall to my side, I shook off the lingering adrenaline rattling my nerves and turned back to the laptop. Usually, I wasn't easily spooked, but it was impossible not to be now. "What did you say? Before I went for your throat?"

"I was noticing that picture of Jesus." Leo pointed to the top web result with a drop-down image of a painting.

"That's not just *a* painting," I replied, clicking on the link. It brought me to an article from a top news site talking about the origins of the painting. "That's the famous painting da Vinci did of Jesus Christ. It's called *Salvator Mundi.*"

"Okay, art snob. Sorry for not knowing about one painting out of millions."

"And here I thought you'd be all over Leonardo's work since you two share a name."

Leo took the empty chair across from me, resting his right leg over his left. "Doesn't seem necessary when I'm the more interesting one."

I didn't try to hide the annoyance on my face.

"I wonder why this article came up about the painting," I mused.

Starting a new web search, I typed in the name *Salvator Mundi* and got a slew of results for the painting but nothing else. I narrowed it down to the word *Salvator* and propped my elbow up on the table as a new list of results appeared.

"Still reading about that painting?" Leo asked.

"Not exactly," I replied. The results included links to a slew of different websites from academic articles to hotels using the name, but tucked between all of that was one company that stood out to me. "But there is a company calling itself Salvator that looks interesting."

Leo leaned forward, gesturing for me to shift my laptop enough for him to get a better look. I did and clicked onto the website. The page automatically changed from their French to English version, revealing that Salvator was an art dealer out of Nantes, France, who sold rare and exclusive art to people who wanted to own museum-worthy pieces. Their website was bland and two-dimensional, begging to be taken out of the soft-launch look it had.

"Doesn't look like much," Leo said. "Reminds me of a discount version of Sotheby's or Christie's."

I clicked around on the website for a little bit longer and nearly exited the page when Leo's hand was suddenly on top of mine, stopping me.

"Wait," he said, pointing to a list of countries and states Salvator had partnerships in. "New York."

At first, my mind was too busy focusing on his hand to listen, until finally, I remembered myself and swatted it away. "And what about it? This isn't exactly a unique place to conduct business."

"Because I remembered something from the other day." Leo reached past me, forcing me to smell his freshly showered, citrusy scent, while he typed in three keywords. *Ivan, art dealer, New York.*

"I was at a meeting my mom forced me to go to with Carter," he continued. "There was nothing special about it, but during the meeting, he left to take a call. I followed and spotted him talking to a man I'd never seen before. I tried to eavesdrop and didn't get much out of it, but Carter told me his name was Ivan and that he was a local art dealer. There could be a connection."

That got my attention. "What was your brother doing talking to him?"

Leo shrugged. "That's all he told me. Apparently, Ivan's been pestering my brother to buy stuff from his collection for weeks."

"Pestering him to buy *art*?" I replied, raising a brow.

"That's what I was thinking," he replied. "But it could be a coincidence. We shouldn't get too excited until we find some more information on this guy."

I couldn't argue with that and kept quiet while Leo tried searching for more details on this mystery Ivan.

Working with a first name proved as difficult as I expected. A list of different Ivans in New York and in the surrounding states came up, taking us to dead end after dead end each time. It was only when Leo narrowed his search from New York to Westchester that he finally found him.

"That's him," Leo said, swiveling my laptop to show me a website's "About" page where a picture of an unremarkable man stood smiling at the camera. "Ivan Romano, owner of Golden Age Antiques and Collectibles in Rye, New York."

"Are you sure?"

He nodded. "I saw enough of his face. It's him."

"Well done, Danesi." I looked up, letting a smirk dance across my lips. "We got our first lead without killing each other."

All the satisfaction I felt at this win paused when my ears heard the sound of shoes clicking on the school's polished floors. It could have been anyone walking the halls early...if a familiar voice didn't grow closer to the door.

"Yeah, I see a light on. I'll check if it's her and call you back."

I shot to my feet, jabbing a finger at the bathroom door. "That's Val! Get in there *now*!"

The corners of Leo's eyes pinched like he wasn't sure he believed what I was saying. I didn't have time for this. Our agreement was not going up in flames on day one because my best friend found us out. Victor would put a stop to this before I had a chance to state my plea, and I was sure Sloane Danesi would do the same with Leo.

Grabbing his forearm, I dragged his ass toward the lounge's private bathroom. I'd barely shoved him in and closed the door when Val reached the doorway.

"Tasha! There you are, thank God," she exclaimed, rushing over to me. Her hair hung in a relaxed blowout with the latest pearled headband from Chanel pulling it away from her face.

"My dad and Victor and all your security are looking for you. What were you thinking sneaking off by yourself? It's way too dangerous for you to do that."

I stepped away from her and over to my stuff, making a deliberate point to close my laptop before she looked. "I needed some space. How mad is Victor right now?"

Val crossed her arms, narrowing her lined eyes at me. "Victor's royally pissed off. He said you *better* be kidnapped. I'm supposed to bring you back to my house before class starts."

Ugh, how did I go from having a couple hours to none at all? I checked my phone for the time and instead got an onslaught of notifications for missed calls and texts from everyone that knew I wasn't supposed to sneak out. Lovely.

"Let's get going then," I replied, packing up my few things. I didn't want her to ask any more questions while we were here or decide she needed to use the bathroom before we left.

Val tilted her head as she analyzed me. "Why did you come all the way here?"

"I wanted to work on an AP History essay in peace," I replied, ushering her out the door. "No offense, Val, but your house has a lot of distractions or someone breathing down my neck every damn minute."

She rolled her eyes at me. "Most of those are from *your* people."

I sighed dramatically. "Fair."

Val was nearly out of the lounge when she stopped, her pointed chin nodding to the couches. "Is that yours?"

My barely relaxed shoulders stiffened again as I turned to see what she was referring to. There, dangling off one of the couches, was Leo's uniform jacket.

Good one, Danesi, I thought, adding a few choice swear words while I was at it.

With my best acting skills on display, I played it off with an indifferent shrug and shake of the head. "Someone must've left it overnight."

I prayed she would accept my lie without a second thought, but Val was too quick for her own good. She stared at the jacket with a blank expression. I knew her better than most. That look was her way of trying to stop any thoughts from creeping onto her face. The type of thoughts that almost always led to interrogations and secrets spilled.

"Val?" I asked, gently touching her arm while my body screamed with stress. "Are you coming?"

She finally turned to me and smiled, flipping her long, highlighted hair over one shoulder. "Of course."

I returned her smile, looping my left arm around hers as she started rambling about the couture pop-up shop she wanted to go to in SoHo this weekend. I focused on her excitement. As long as I did, I wouldn't have to think about the moment her attention had snapped to the bathroom door. How she held her gaze on it for a second too long.

"Hey," Val said, bumping her elbow in my ribs after she was done telling me all about the audacious style this particular designer was known for. "You really shouldn't go off on your own right now. You never know what freaks might take advantage of that."

I nodded. "I know."

"No secrets, okay?"

I hadn't told Val the truth of how my family built their wealth and power. The title her father *actually* possessed working under mine. I didn't know if she suspected anything, but today was not going to be the day we talked about it. Or anything related to what I was doing.

I wove a blank expression onto my face, hoping my best friend didn't see her own technique reflected back at her. "None at all."

CHAPTER
THIRTEEN

I HELD COMPLETELY STILL FOR AN UNEASY THREE MINUTES. Not trusting myself to screw this whole thing up by scuffing my shoe or my phone clattering out of my pocket.

There was no way I could let my family or any of my friends know about the agreement I'd made with Tasha. I was still processing my decision. Already, I had deliberately gotten out of bed *way* before my usual alarm to meet her here. Who the hell was I? Anybody who knew me might think I'd snapped completely. It was better for everyone if I kept this under wraps for now. Maybe forever.

My phone buzzed and I groaned when I saw the name on the caller ID. Mom.

"What?" I answered.

"Cut the disrespect," she snapped. "You answer with a *hello* or a *good morning, Mom.* Though I should be hearing you say it to my face as I drink my espresso. Where are you?"

I closed my eyes. By the tone of her voice, my first mistake was answering this call. "I went to a café on the Ave, and now I'm at school."

"In what world do you go to school early?"

"Appreciate the belief in my academic career," I replied, though she was right. Typically, I was in class thirty seconds after the bell. I should have anticipated Mom would question my sudden punctual attitude. "Jonathan has an early lacrosse practice that I told him I'd watch."

The lie went down smoother than Dad's forty-year-old whiskey I'd drained after his death. Burned less, too.

"Hm." She let silence stretch between us for a long minute, but I didn't care. The fact that Mom wasn't badgering me with questions or accusations meant she believed me. "Since you decided to charge out of here so early, I'll have to tell you over the phone."

I gripped my phone harder, my brain going into overdrive at what she would say. "What's going on? Is Sophia okay?"

Mom scoffed. "Honey, she's fine. I want you to come with me after school to our racetrack in Saratoga Springs so you can be part of meeting a new client. He's interested in getting to know the next heir of Danesi Properties."

And there it was. The reason I regretted picking up the phone. Mom was relentless. It was the reason she thought she could get anything she wanted even if it took years.

"I don't kn—"

"Leo." Her voice was washed of any niceties, leaving the cold, unforgiving one she saved for people who defied her. "This is nonnegotiable."

I leaned against the sink, tilting my head back to stare at the ceiling. "Can't this wait until Carter comes back from Aspen?"

Mom took her time replying. Long enough that I nearly wondered if she'd already hung up. "Your brother isn't needed for this meeting. *You* are the one the client wants to meet. The driver and I will be at the front entrance promptly when your last class ends. Someone is already on their way to stand by your car all day to make sure you don't get any ideas, too. Have a good day, Leo."

Then she hung up.

I rubbed my forehead and put my phone away. It wasn't nine in the morning and already this day was gearing up to be brutal.

Unlatching the bathroom door, I stepped into an empty lounge. If I hung around here until class started, nothing was off the table for what I might end up doing. Not when I had the types of violent memories waiting for a quiet moment like this to torture me all over again.

I grabbed my jacket, wincing that I let it lay blatantly out in the open, and shoved my arms in. If I moved fast enough, I could get to the Ferrari before Mom's goons showed up and grab something to eat nearby.

Striding into the hall, I twirled the car keys around my finger, already salivating at the thought of getting caffeine in me.

All those thoughts abruptly ended though when I rounded a corner and nearly collided with the last face I wanted to see.

"Oof, sorry, man," I said, jumping back. "Didn't see you."

Ravi Ferreira slid around me, his tall and lanky body standing nearly as high as mine. He already irritated me. I may have only seen him around school a few times, but I'd already endured countless conversations where his family name came up ever since Mom decided to make me the Danesi heir. She even suggested I befriend him when I moved home. Yeah, right.

Girls and guys in all grades did a double take when they saw him. His shock of dark hair neatly trimmed on all sides. The unique curves to his face. Those bright green eyes. Yet he acted oblivious to all of it. Like Tasha's attention was all that mattered. Anyone could see it in the way he looked at her so longingly. Pathetically.

I continued forward without much thought but froze when he spoke.

"What are you doing here early?"

I turned around, giving him a once over. "What does it matter to you?"

He shrugged, resting his hands in the pockets of his school dress pants. "Not much."

"Okay..." Whatever this was, I didn't have time for it. I'd nearly spun back around when Ravi spoke again.

"I thought it was odd that you showed up to the stables yesterday," he said. "We may not know each other, but I've heard stories about you—and I'm sure you've heard them about me—and none of them make you sound like the horse-loving type."

I stared at him. If I'd learned anything from Mom, it was to never let my face give anything away. Whether I pulled it off or not was another story.

"Stories can leave out a lot of details."

"True, but I have a feeling my instinct on this one is right." Ravi took a few steps forward. Close enough that I could stab my car keys into him if I wanted to. "Whatever plans you have need to stay yours. Tasha's dealing with enough emotional baggage and turmoil. She doesn't need anyone to add to it."

A hard pit formed in my gut. It took everything in me to keep my cool. To not throw at him that Tasha had asked *me* for help and not him. Instead, I replied, "That's a lot of big talk coming from a guy who's now the ex-boyfriend."

He smiled, but there was nothing pleasant about it. "I can still love her. And I know her well enough that I see she's trying desperately to keep it together. She needs support from all sides. Even when she isn't aware of it."

"How nice of you to offer yourself like a dog," I replied.

Ravi wasn't fazed by my taunt. Instead, he stepped closer without breaking his gaze. "What she doesn't need is a hurricane to come through—indifferent to the destruction it causes."

My nostrils flared, every knuckle on my hands itching to throw a good punch to his judgmental face. But I forced myself not to and moved away from him. No good would come out of brawling with this prick.

"Fuck you, Ferreira."

I whirled on my heel and headed for the foyer, crushing the car keys tight enough in my fist I wouldn't be surprised if they cracked in half.

"Stay away from her, Leo," Ravi called behind me. "You won't like what happens if you don't."

I ignored him and kept walking while a rope of anger coiled inside me. He didn't have any right to be so protective of her. Not anymore. I was around long before he ever came on the scene anyway. I'd watched Tasha grow from a soft-spoken kid to a girl with fire in her eyes. What happened between our families, what I said to her four years ago, didn't change any of our history. And there was no damn way I was letting some jealous ex of hers stop us from going after our shared enemy.

Other early-bird students trickled in, some giving me double takes like they also couldn't believe who they were seeing. Maybe I underestimated how large the spotlight on me was.

Just before I reached the front entrance, my phone buzzed again. I grabbed it, reading a new message from Tasha.

I can't sit in this house for the rest of the day, her text read. Come with me to spy on I.R. after school?

My answer was the fastest text I'd ever sent.

Hell yeah.

CHAPTER
FOURTEEN

Tasha

"THERE IT IS."

The charming storefronts in Rye lined the sides of the narrow roads with young trees bowing against the blustering winds. Beautifully dressed moms hurried from store to store with their beautifully dressed children to purchase more beautiful things for their beautiful, perfect lives.

While I was planted in a car with the last person I ever thought I'd be with.

Leo pulled into an empty spot next to the curb and put the gray Bentley in park. We'd still get onlookers ogling the vehicle, but at least it was better than that beast of a Ferrari roaring in.

Across the street was a store that had the words GOLDEN AGE ANTIQUES AND COLLECTIBLES in large serifed lettering. It was 3:40, and the shop was open until six. It gave us plenty of time to see this Ivan Romano man in action.

Well, long enough before someone called my brainiac classmate Margaret and realized I was *not* having a study session at her house.

After a tense conversation with Victor and my mother, where I swore I would *never* think about sneaking out again, security dropped me off at Margaret's. Obviously, I immediately hopped the backyard fence and hurried to where Leo waited.

"Let's go in," I said.

Leo threw out a hand, his fingers brushing my arm. "Hold up! You can't barge in there looking for answers. If he is involved, we need to tread carefully."

I shifted away. "What do *you* want to do then?"

"Get a feel for him and his business from here," he replied. "See who goes in and out. We could sneak around back, too, if it feels right. See what kind of deliveries he might get."

I couldn't stop myself from rolling my eyes. "Are you serious? This is not what I meant when I asked you to come spy on Ivan Romano with me. What kind of information are we going to get from *staring* at the store like a couple of pigeons?"

Leo leaned his head back against the headrest, wiggling his damn butt around on the leather seats. "No idea. That's the point. We're *spying.*"

After an excruciating seven minutes of nothingness, where I was painfully aware of every movement from Leo, I couldn't hold still anymore. I had to do *something* other than sit here staring at a quiet shop with him breathing loudly beside me. Without giving him any warning, I threw open the passenger door and jumped out.

"Hey! Nicastro!" Leo exclaimed, "You can't jus—"

I slammed the door behind me, cutting off whatever nagging lecture he was about to give.

My heartbeat picked up as I moved closer to the store's front door. I didn't know what to expect, but I'd brace for all of it if it brought me one step closer to finding answers.

Behind me, Leo's footsteps slapped against the cobblestones as he jogged to catch up. "Are you *trying* to get us thrown in a trunk at gunpoint?"

"If it'll help, yes, " I replied.

My hand wrapped around the door handle, but before I could turn it, Leo's hand was over mine, his chest pressing into my back, stopping me.

Electricity zinged through me as I leaped back and away from him. I whipped around, flashing him my clenched teeth.

"*Don't* touch me."

"Then *don't* be reckless," he snapped. "I didn't agree to this just for you to get us killed. I know how these groups work. You need to scope out your situation before you go storming in all hotheaded. People in our world are always looking for a fight. We won't get answers if we give them one."

I glared at him. *Now* he decided he'd be the reasonable one? I wanted to argue, but after casting a glance into the store, I realized there was no point.

Crossing my arms, I replied, "Well, it's your lucky day, Danesi. Because the place is closed."

Leo's eyes widened. He squinted to look and pulled back when he realized it was pitch-black inside. "So much for our plan."

"You think I'm wasting an afternoon of being away from my security team?" I replied, stepping off the sidewalk. "Hurry up before someone recognizes us."

He followed, unlocking the car as we approached. "Then what do you want to do?"

I threw myself back on the passenger seat, letting out a heavy sigh. My mind was blank at first, until I remembered something Leo mentioned earlier.

"You said your mom thinks she knows who's behind the hit," I said.

Leo eyed me warily, turning the ignition on. "She does."

"Then it's settled." I shook my bangs free from my eyes and slipped my Prada sunglasses on. "We're going to your house to search through her stuff."

"Don't screw with me, Nicastro. That's a *terrible* idea. We're not supposed to go anywhere near each other's homes now. Territory rules are a thing."

"And yet, that didn't stop *you* from crashing my soirée," I replied, shifting my body to face him. "Is anyone home?"

Leo frowned. "No. Mom's at one of our company properties and Sophia's at her riding lesson until five thirty. Carter's in Aspen."

"Then put this car in drive and let's get going."

He looked ready to argue with me some more but must've thought better of it and started driving.

We drove in silence for the first few minutes of the short trek. The lack of sound closed in around me, forcing in memories of the many times I used to take this route to go see Leo. I had no business going down memory lane, so I blurted out the first thing to get my mind away from it.

"Why did you go to California?"

It was a genuine question. I only learned he transferred to the Thacher School through word of mouth.

Leo massaged his lips together, clearly deciding if it was worth a response. "I couldn't stand being around the fighting. Between our families, but mostly in my own head."

"What do you mean?"

He rubbed the back of his neck. "I watched my dad get gunned down. It screwed me up badly enough I had to drop out of our school freshman year. Staying at home wasn't any better though, and I insisted on transferring there."

I let out a long, shaky breath. I'd expected a dozen other answers, but that wasn't the reason for the uneasiness building in me.

My father told me Angelo Danesi was in a car crash with Leo. There was never any mention of being *gunned down*.

But Leo had screamed accusations at me about his father's death when we were younger. I hadn't believed him, trusting my father's version of events instead.

"You don't know how my dad died, do you?"

I spooked, glancing at Leo. He kept his eyes on the road, but his fingers gripped the steering wheel too tightly.

I could tell myself he was lying. That this was the continued Danesi ploy to tear my family's reputation apart. But my father hid so much from me. It was naïve to pretend like the story I was told about Angelo Danesi's death was immune to those secrets.

We fell back into silence. I thought this time it'd stick, but then Leo went and threw a bomb between us.

"I talked to Ravi at school."

My eyes bulged. "*What?* When?"

"This morning after you left," he replied. "We bumped into each other. He's observant. Already suspects something's going on with us."

My heart did a double thump. "What makes you think that?"

He took his focus off the road to look at me. "Because he told me to stay away from you."

I was lost for words. Of all people, Ravi had already noticed I was up to something. In a way, I shouldn't be surprised. We'd dated for three years. It gave us lots of time to pick up on the slightest shift in each other.

Leo turned back to the road. "You've got one protective ex-boyfriend."

I cleared my throat and looked down at my hands. I'd die happy if I never had to hear him talk about my ex again.

"Why'd you break up with him?"

Guess I was destined to be miserable.

"Seriously?"

Leo shrugged. "It's something to fill the quiet."

"I'd listen to silence for hours before ever talking to *you* about my ex," I replied. A wicked smile curled my lips as I thought of a question to fire back at him. "Have *you* figured out what you want out of Scarlett yet? Or are you going to date and dump her every time you come home?"

"Um." A rosy hue flushed over Leo's cheeks as he ran a hand through his hair. Good. I wanted him to get a taste of his own medicine. "Scarlett is...great. And always there. I don't know. It's easy to fall into old habits with her."

Scarlett wasn't my friend anymore, but I got the urge to throttle him anyway for that answer.

"Why would you keep going back to someone who's a habit? Wouldn't you want to be with someone you love?" I genuinely wanted to know. It wasn't a concept I'd ever explored before. If I was going to date someone, it had to be real. I wasn't going to waste my time on half-hearted romance.

He cut a look to me, the edges of his warm eyes crinkling. "It's easier than loving someone I could lose."

We held each other's gazes for too long. My chest ached, and I turned away first.

Thankfully, we reached Leo's street a couple minutes later, giving us the excuse to focus on the task at hand.

"Hide until we're in the garage," Leo instructed as he pulled onto his driveway. "There shouldn't be any guards hanging around the house, but there might be some walking the grounds."

I snuck a quick look at the front of the Danesis' massive home. I hadn't been here since the feud started and yet nothing had changed except for the new manicured cypress trees out front. It still jutted up into the sky with its pointed roof, arched in different heights to make it look like a golden crown. The long driveway circled to the home's front staircase, beckoning everyone to glide into the labyrinth of luxury inside.

The Danesis' house sat on more land than mine, and Sloane had wasted none of it. Gardens bloomed in between pathways, and the edge of the resort-style pool area and tennis courts peeked into view. I could still taste the saltwater droplets that used to hit my tongue every time I swam in it. No thanks to Leo splashing me.

When Leo turned toward the garage, I ducked and stayed that way until the garage door had closed with my nails pressed deep into my palm.

This was *actually* happening. I was inside the Danesi house after all this time. When I'd told Leo to take us here, I hadn't fully processed what I was saying, but it was too late to back out now.

"Her office is still on the first floor," Leo said as we got out of the Bentley. "Follow me and stay quiet."

We slipped into the house, treading on light footsteps in case someone was home. Though I was following Leo, I didn't need his guidance to tell me where to go. I remembered the exact layout of this place.

Sloane's office appeared. Leo hovered at the door long enough to make my temple throb with irritation.

"Will you open it already?" I hissed.

He locked eyes with me. "I've never snooped through her stuff."

"Oh, for the love of—" I rolled my eyes and shoved him out of the way, turning the handle with no issue. "Don't be such a baby."

"A *baby?*" Leo replied as he skulked into the room after me.

I whirled around, placing my hand on my hip. "Do you want to search for what your mom might know, or should we wait until she and Sophia come home and make this a big party?"

Leo clamped his mouth shut. I took the opportunity to riffle through the drawers of the large designer desk. Sloane had bookshelves lining every wall save for a few spots for paintings and windows bringing in natural light.

"She'd ring my neck if she knew you were going through her stuff."

"I don't care about your family business," I replied. "Not unless it relates to my family's murders. Now are you going to help me look or am I on my own here?"

He grumbled something under his breath and started on the binders lining the shelves. We searched for a solid amount of time, but none of our efforts produced results. I shoved the last drawer closed, giving a loud huff.

"There's nothing here." I twisted my lips, considering our next move. "What about Carter? He's the one who talked to this Ivan guy. We could look through his things and see if there's anything he's got."

Leo opened his mouth. Maybe to agree or maybe to object. I would never know, because one heartbeat later, I caught movement out in the hall.

There was no time to escape or warn Leo. I fell to my knees, pressing up against the desk and praying the unannounced guest didn't notice me hiding.

"Carter!" Leo exclaimed, shoving the binder he was holding back in its spot and hurrying to the open doorway. "You're back. I thought you were in Aspen until tomorrow."

"Change of plans," he replied. There was a pause, forcing me to listen to the blood pounding in my head. "You look like someone caught red-handed. What're you doing in there?"

"I—"

I clenched my teeth together. Come on, Leo, make up *some* good excuse.

"I'm looking for some document Mom wanted for the Saratoga Springs property. She's up there now meeting with a new client."

My chest deflated—slightly. It was a decent enough excuse, but until Carter moved away from the door, I wasn't in the clear.

"Did you find it?"

"Ah, yeah," Leo replied. "I sent her a picture just now. All good."

There was another pause. I pictured Carter's ocean-gray eyes peering closely at Leo's face, searching for cracks in his story. As kids, he was always the most suspicious. Not trusting if he got his fair share of dessert or if Leo and I were about to play a prank on him. But this wasn't some trivial issue. Carter was a mobster now. If he found me, there was no saying what he might do.

"Then I guess there's no other reason you need to be in here."

It was Leo's turn to take a beat. I held my breath as long as possible while neither of them spoke.

"You don't need to tell me twice," Leo finally said. "You have any plans?"

Carter's reply was too muffled for me to hear as Leo pulled the door shut behind him, trapping me in this godforsaken place.

I waited a few more minutes before shakily getting to my feet. My options were to creep out the office's door and pray no one but Leo spotted me or kick at the sealed windows and hope I didn't slice a tendon while crawling out. How *perfect*.

The door shoved open a second later, making me jump out of my skin and bang my knee hard against the desk. I stiffened, ready for a fight, only to see Leo staring at me.

"Carter's not coming back until tomorrow, huh?"

Leo glanced out at the hall before stepping farther into Sloane's office. "Shut *up*, Nicastro. He's upstairs for now, but he could come down any moment. I can drive you back to Scarsdale. You need to hide out in the car for a bit before I can leave. I can't make my brother any more suspicious than he already is."

I ground my teeth together. I hated this, but I didn't have much of a choice since it was my idea to come here.

"Fine," I whispered.

Moving gingerly, I made my way to the garage with Leo, the ends of my hair sticking to my neck.

"Okay, wait here," Leo said once I was hiding in the Bentley.

I did. For five minutes. Ten. All the way up to twenty. My bladder throbbed with an urgency that grew while Leo showed no sign of returning.

"Screw this," I hissed, throwing open the passenger door. What was I doing putting this much trust in *Leo*? I had no idea what was going on in the house and I wasn't waiting around to find out.

I went to the garage's side door and snuck through it, pausing long enough to check my surroundings before hurrying to the street. I kept to the edges of the property, shrouded by the bushes and trees, then hopped the closed gate when I reached it.

I was in the clear—for now.

Once I was at the corner of Leo's street, I pulled out my phone and dialed the number of the person who would ask the fewest questions.

My cousin picked up immediately.

"Matteo, I need a favor," I said, skipping past the greeting. "But you can't get mad or tell anyone. Especially Victor."

He sighed, and I heard the distinct cough of another man in the background. A slice of guilt went through me for likely interrupting one of Matteo's dates, but it was too late to change course now. "I feel like I might regret making this promise to you, but okay. You have my word."

"Great," I replied. "I need you to pick me up right now. I'm a tad stranded."

"And where are you?"

I pursed my lips. "Greenwich."

Matteo swore. I could picture him pushing up his glasses to rub at the bridge of his nose, only because I'd put him in plenty of stressful situations to warrant it. But wasn't this what responsible older cousins were for? "One of these days, I'm not going to bail you out of your bad ideas."

I grinned. "And thankfully, today is not that day."

CHAPTER FIFTEEN

I GROANED, PUSHING AWAY FROM MY DESK, LETTING MY GUR-gling stomach take me downstairs. After I found the Bentley empty yesterday and saw a text from Tasha telling me she found her own way home, I'd locked myself in my room searching for information on Ivan Romano.

My legs ached from the position I'd sat in for the past ... three hours. Ruining my eyesight was a waste. Nothing interesting or new lived on the internet about this guy other than an old Getty image of him at some grand opening for an art gallery in Rhode Island.

Early afternoon light flooded onto the recently mopped floors as I crept across them and over to the kitchen. Saturdays were a wild card day when it came to Mom. While Carter was God knows where and Sophia had hurried off to hang with friends, Mom could be ruining someone's life, getting a facial, or reading a magazine in the sunroom. This was her day to spin the wheel. And I had to hope it landed on something that kept her too busy to yell at me.

I reached an empty kitchen, breathing a sigh of relief, and immediately went to the fridge to see what leftover lunch platter our new chef put together.

"So. My little mouse finally got the confidence to scurry down here for a meal."

I jerked upright and nearly banged my head against a shelf, coming face-to-face with Mom. She wiped her dirt-caked shoes on a mat and carried her bouquet of freshly cut purple roses to the sink, laying them and a pair of shears on the counter.

"I—"

"Save it," she snapped. "You crossed me with your little disappearing stunt yesterday and now you have the nerve to fix yourself a plate of food? The food paid for by the work you stick your nose up at?"

I closed the fridge and set the platter on the kitchen island, my gut tangling into a weighted heap inside me. Guess I wasn't getting off easy today. "You can say whatever you like, Mom, but it's not going to change my opinion. I've already told you I don't want anything to do with the family business."

Waves of guilt flowed through me from time to time. Making me stop and wonder how I could wear the clothes and drive the cars paid for by the world my family built. But it surrounded me in every way. I'd have to completely sever my life from them, leaving everything—leaving Sophia and Carter—behind for good. And I couldn't do that. Not to my sister. My brother. Or myself.

"And I've already told you this isn't up for negotiation," she replied, grabbing a vase and putting the roses in without a care for the thorns. "You embarrassed me with our new client. I had to show up to the racetrack empty-handed and explain why my son, the one I *confidently* told him was eager to take over one day, somehow couldn't make it."

Mom's voice rose another octave throughout her speech until each word thrashed out of her. It didn't matter what I said. She was convinced my life plan was the one she laid out for me; my only purpose to be a puppet for her grand ambitions.

"Where were you?" she asked when I stayed silent.

The image of Tasha sitting beside me, her raven-black hair tucked behind one ear while her blouse crept open just enough, vaulted into my thoughts. Then they shifted, reminding me of the smell of her sweet floral perfume as she snuck through the house with me.

Mom had no clue where I'd snuck off to or why. I'd damn well make sure that didn't change, but I couldn't stop my heart from racing as she stared me down. Like if I wasn't careful, she might see a crack in my armor and pry me open, revealing just how far I was willing to go to betray her.

"I was with Scarlett," I said. It wasn't a total lie. After Tasha left, I'd called her over. I'd needed the distraction to stop my thoughts from creeping to places they shouldn't. We'd both gotten some fun and sore lips out of it. A win-win. "She gave me a better offer than you."

Red as bright as her lipstick flooded Mom's face. She stalked closer to me with enough ferocity that I instinctively stepped back and bumped into one of the barstools. "Your father lived and died for this family as did your grandfather and his father before him. Everything has been for your benefit, so you can flourish more than them. What choices go through your mind for you to blatantly disrespect their memory by denying your responsibilities?"

My insides twisted into knots thinking of Dad's hand on my shoulder or his fleeting smiles filled with approval. Getting a drop of his affection was enough to keep my roots watered for months. But I was no longer the kid willing to do anything, to ignore anything, to maintain his love. Mom wanted me to sacrifice myself to the beast that controlled our lives and never ask what I would lose in the process.

I put a good amount of space between us. "Are you serious, Mom? I'm disrespecting them because I don't want to maintain this cruel world the Danesis brought us into?"

"The entire world is cruel, Leo," she replied. "They saw a way to leverage it like my family did. We wouldn't have maintained our position if it weren't for our Sullivan relatives sending extra muscle and weapons right away after your father died. Because they understand that cruelty well. Do you truly think you'd magically avoid the rest of the world's cruelties by working anywhere else? I didn't raise you to be naïve."

"I'm not naïve," I shouted, an intense throb forming in my head. "I don't know why you won't give Carter the role when you're set on keeping this family business alive. He's the firstborn and wants it. Who cares if he screwed up one time?" I grabbed my phone from my back pocket, my vision blurring as I scrolled to my brother's name.

"What're you doing?"

I showed the screen to her while it rang. Carter picked up immediately.

"Hey, Carter, you want to take over the family business, right?"

A stretch of time passed before he answered. "I'm game."

"Then I bequeath it to you," I replied, bowing like a fool. "Your screwup has been pardoned."

Carter chuckled. "Are you drunk, little brother?"

I never replied. Mom snatched the phone from my hand and ended the call. If I thought she was enraged before, I'd turned that dial to one hundred.

"This isn't a joke, Leo. This is your future legacy. The *family's* future legacy."

A dry laugh escaped me. "But it is a joke, Mom. I'm not the guy to take over. You should give that kind of power to Carter. He's your son, too, and he wants the job."

My muscles braced for another round of her anger. For her to start hurling insults—or maybe plates—at me. What I didn't expect was for a hush to fall over her, the entire force that made up my mom going very, very still.

Then she turned back to the roses like nothing had happened. "I won't risk putting it in the hands of Carter after what he did. You're the one I trust with this responsibility. And one day you'll understand why I needed to push you so hard."

I hated that she refused to accept my choices. How nothing I did swayed her. I could murder someone and she'd nod with satisfaction, telling me I was strengthening my reputation within our world. What kind of mom was like that? Our lives were destroyed when the Nicastros murdered Dad. Then Mom decided to throw herself into the flames of our Mafia, getting so engulfed by it that she became agitated and obsessive over fixing what should've stayed broken. Every day she kept this lifestyle alive was a reminder she was willing to risk our lives imploding again. Now she wanted to pass that torch over to me.

I picked up my phone and opened the chat I had with my Scarsdale group. I sent them a quick message telling everyone we were starting the fun early tonight. Thankfully, I got immediate thumbs ups and gleeful yeses. The fuel I needed to get the hell out of here until tomorrow morning.

"Where do you think you're going?" Mom asked when I grabbed a cold sandwich from the leftovers platter and headed for the garage.

"Out," I replied, biting into my sandwich. Pastrami on rye. Not my first choice, but it'd have to do. "Or are you going to ground me for the rest of the week?"

Yeah, I was taunting her. Others my age might balk at it, knowing if they did that to their parents, they'd end up royally screwed for weeks on end. Mom was all talk with her threats though, never using an iron fist on me so I'd discover what an actual consequence felt like. She was too busy using all her energy to convince me to sign my life away instead.

I could feel badly, but it was much easier to take advantage of it when all I wanted was to get away from everything.

Which was why I wasn't prepared for a human blockade to stop me from leaving the kitchen.

I stumbled back from the archway, nearly dropping my sandwich in the process. Three bulked-up, oversized men stood between me and the garage, materializing from who knows where. I spotted a white lily tattoo on one of the guy's necks when he arched it to the side, a bemused expression on his face as he watched me fumble to keep my lunch in my hand.

Danesi soldiers.

"No, Leo, I won't be grounding you," Mom replied. "But you won't be leaving this house yet. I've got a project I'd like for you to work on to make up for your deliberate absence yesterday."

I turned back to her wearily, already feeling a pit of dread forming in my gut. She finished her bouquet and slid it into the center of the kitchen island.

"And what's that?"

Flicking her wrist, Mom headed for one of the closed doors off the kitchen, revealing a darkened staircase when she opened it. It led down to a small set of cellars separate from our basement. I never went down there other than to steal a bottle or two from the wine cellar. But I had a strong feeling this *project* had nothing to do with food or booze.

"Come with me," was all she said.

I followed her down into the cellar, her three mobsters never far behind. The lights lining the stone hallway bathed her in gold, but the deceiving warmth couldn't stop the chill in the air from raising goose bumps across my arms.

When Mom reached the wine cellar door, she stopped and unlocked it, beckoning me inside. The dread inside my stomach intensified as I stepped into the room and saw just what this "project" was.

A man huddled in one of the corners of the cellar, tucked between two shelves of wine. I didn't know who he was, but from the sharp cut of fearful understanding that appeared across his face, he knew exactly who we were.

"What the hell is this?" I hissed.

"A chance for retribution," she replied, circling around the wooden island at the center of the cellar. "And for you to practice your leadership skills."

I glanced at the doorway as two of the soldiers clicked it shut while the third one waited outside.

"I don't want whatever 'leadership' lesson you have for me," I replied.

Mom trailed her fingertips over the smooth counter, her sharp gaze unwavering on the prisoner. "Maybe you'd think differently if you knew who he was." She walked over to me. "This man is an employee of our Saratoga Springs racetrack. We discovered he's been skimming off our profits for months."

"Please, ma'am." The employee clasped his hands in a prayer as he looked up at her. "I only did it to pay for my past due medical bills. I would never dream of taking from you if I wasn't desperate."

My throat thickened, but Mom's face remained stony. She gently squeezed my forearm the way she used to when I was a kid.

"I want you to show him that no one takes from us. It'll send a proper message that we don't let anyone get away with it unscathed. Do you understand?"

The heat in my blood cooled. "You want me to fight this guy?"

"It won't be," she replied calmly. "Because he won't fight back."

I'd never witnessed someone get punished by our Mafia. And yet here I was, getting thrown straight into the deep end, expected to kick and punch like I was no different than them. But despite the Danesi name flowing through me, I wouldn't let myself get swallowed by the darkness my family thrived in.

"I can't do that." My voice was strained, each word coated in bile and a struggle to say.

Mom's hand on me tightened. "You think a thief deserves to get away with stealing from us, Leo?"

I clenched my jaw, glancing at the man again. His skin shone with sweat, his hands trembling. I doubted this guy had ever been involved in a fight. It didn't matter what his reasons were for stealing from us, hurting him would make us worse.

I shook my head, lighting a spark in Mom's eyes, until I spoke. "He doesn't deserve to be punished like this."

"What he deserves is a crowbar to the knees, but I'm keeping things civil today." Her nostrils flared, and she cut a look to her soldiers watching us closely. "You *will* follow through with this order. I won't let you refuse this."

"Punish me then," I replied. "Because I am."

She stared me down. I almost thought she would relent when she snapped her fingers and said, "Restrain my son."

Before I could react, one of her men sprang on me and clasped my hands behind me.

"What're you doing?"

Mom turned her back on me. "Blocking any heroic impulses you might have."

Her second mobster stepped toward the cowering man. I tried to break free, but it was useless. Just like the protest I made right before his foot smashed into the man's ribs.

The man cried out, but that didn't stop Mom's soldier from sending another one to his stomach.

He kicked a few more times, stomping once on the man's exposed hand, before hauling the employee to his feet and letting his fist take over. Each punch the soldier threw sounded louder, fiercer, to my ears, until a cold sweat broke out across my skin.

"Enough," Mom commanded.

He stopped, letting the man drop to the hard floor.

Nausea rolled through me as I watched blood pool out of the bruised man's nose and mouth. I wasn't the one who hurt him, but that didn't stop the guilt from flooding in anyway.

"Leave us. And take our guest with you."

I jerked at Mom's commanding voice and looked up at her watching me with cool eyes. Her soldiers immediately hauled the bruised man out, freeing me of my restraint, but not the target still on my back.

"You embarrassed me, Leo," she said too calmly. "You made yourself look weak. Our soldiers will no doubt gossip about it to the rest of the organization. Now I'll have to focus on damage control for my leadership and yours."

"Are you kidding me? I'm making us look weak for refusing to punish a man trying to pay his medical bills?" I countered. "You should be helping him. Not making his life a living hell. What kind of woman are you?"

"The kind that wants to keep this family *alive*," she fired back. "Get a hold of yourself, Leo. If we let even a single person take advantage of us, we'll all be dead by next week. This family *cannot* be weak fools others walk all over. No matter the reasons or excuses people give. You have no idea the choices I've made to keep us from being constantly targeted. Do you think after your father was murdered that the violence directed at us ended? That my family sent extra protection simply as a precaution?"

I swallowed, hating that I didn't know the answer.

"Of course you think that." She crossed her arms and moved around the cellar staring at the rows of bottles surrounding us. "When in reality, I protected you from seeing the rest of it. The Nicastros put a target on *all* our backs when they went after your father. Their betrayal was an invite to other gangs to attack us once it became clear we were on their hit list.

"You never saw the organs that were left on our doorstep with messages saying the Danesi bloodline would be wiped out. Or the members of our Mafia who were gunned down by other gangs thinking we were with them. When your father was killed, hell took over our household until I became acting boss and started retaliating more viciously than ever before to prove the Nicastros hadn't weakened us." The ghost of a long-buried wound flickered across her face as she faced me again. "And through every second of that nightmare, I shielded my babies from it so they could grieve their father properly."

My breathing grew ragged as I forced myself to hold her steady gaze. I had no idea she made those sacrifices to protect us from that violence, even taking over our Mafia for that reason. But it didn't change anything.

"Did you seriously think I'd agree to hurt that guy?" I shook my head. "I won't let you make me into someone I'm not. Not a brute. And definitely not a killer."

Mom held perfectly still for a long minute. I thought she would lash out, bark some new orders or declarations that I had no choice but to be dragged into these situations again and again. Instead, the lines around her brown eyes softened.

"What I'm doing is no mother's dream for her child. If I had the power, I'd let you do anything you want with your life." She sighed, stepping closer. "But our world doesn't work that way, Leo. If you continue fighting against your future, against this family, there will be consequences to your actions. And they won't necessarily come from me."

My hands balled into fists. "What's that supposed to mean?"

Mom pressed one of her sharp nails against my arm, making the skin go ghost white. "You think I can wave a magic wand and dissolve the establishment your father's side built, that my family also comes from, but it's not that simple. You'll spend your entire life fighting against your familial instinct, and in the process, you'll betray the people you swear you love. People like Sophia."

"I can protect my sister without our Mafia," I replied quietly. "You'll realize that one day when we're long gone from here."

Her hand dropped back to her side. "Do you really believe Sophia would be safer if all she had was you protecting her?" She paused, letting her question sink in and rot to my core. "Your sister will always be in danger because of the world she was born into. It will never leave her or any of us no matter how far we try to run. We can stay safe if you accept your responsibilities to lead and grow our empire until we're untouchable. And despite how much it takes from us, how much we might hate it, sometimes that means retaliating against people you don't want to hurt."

I slumped my shoulders, exhaustion falling over me. There was no point arguing with her. Mom had sunk so deep into the darkness that she believed staying in it was the only way we'd be okay.

"I don't believe you."

Mom assessed me for a long moment. Until finally, she stepped away and the barbed armor she always wore reappeared. "Fine. Live in your naïve reality a little longer, but you'll be dragged out of it one way or another."

I watched her leave and stayed behind long after, wiping at the bloodstained floor.

CHAPTER
SIXTEEN

Tasha

"Are you sure you're ready for this?" Val asked me from the driver's seat.

I nodded, sitting motionless in the car. I'd snuck back to school twice, but that was before hordes of students trampled the campus's grass and scuffed the freshly polished floors. Victor and my mother asked me the same question throughout the weekend, their unique versions of worrying coming at me from both sides. I'd reassured them each time I was fine. I could go back to school with my head held high and finish my senior year as normally as someone in my position could. All I had to do was get out of the car.

Val reached over to squeeze my arm. "We can hang in the lounge for a bit."

"Sure," I whispered.

That was all the agreement Val needed before she jumped out of her Mercedes. I followed, prompting my security team to rush out of their vehicle the moment my shoes touched the pavement.

Moths to a flame, all eyes went immediately to me. Some discreetly while others outright gawked. I expected as much. The gossip of my father's and sister's deaths could nourish these people through the worst of famines.

"Line up!" Eric commanded. Immediately, the five guards created a half-moon around Val and me with their hands resting strategically at their gun-wielding hips.

If anyone wasn't staring before, they were now.

My saving grace was that they weren't allowed inside the school. It was the one rule I'd insisted on, and Victor eventually agreed. There was no damn way I was letting five tall traffic cones follow me around school.

I grabbed my book bag's strap and balled my other hand into a fist, clenching my nails deep into my palm. I could do this. I was raised by my father. Even though he'd lied to me all my life, he'd still taught me to command every space I was in no matter how large of a storm consumed my life. I wouldn't give anyone the satisfaction of seeing the loose threads holding me together. I was a Nicastro, and I owned this school.

"Gross," Val whispered beside me. "Could they be any more obvious?"

Holding my gaze on the school doors, I started forward with her staying close by my side. Some students hurried to get out of my way, as usual, but the rest stayed where they were—staring at me with repulsion in their eyes or a sour smile playing at the corners of their lips.

I ignored them, but I couldn't ignore the prickling uneasiness caked over my skin. Some news stations painted a story of tragedy and disgruntled retribution from a mystery person who had it in for my father.

Others questioned my father's backstory and why a man of his power and wealth would be brutally gunned down. No one ever said the word *Mafia*, thanks to Matteo and Richard pulling a lot of strings, but the hidden questions were layered neatly into the rest of the cake.

And unfortunately for me, the students and families of Scarsdale Country Day had colorful imaginations. A few minutes on social media was enough to see all the comments talking openly, eagerly, about who my father truly was.

But I would never let them see my cracks. How all my instincts wanted to scream that they had no idea what I was going through while they judged me from their cushioned lives. It would only fuel their fear and morbid curiosity, letting them shed my humanity.

The door clanged open, but not two steps in, two juniors spotted me and snickered.

"Is something funny?" Val whipped her attention to them. "Let me in on this amazing joke. I'll tell you how *funny* it is."

"Leave them," I replied, keeping my sight forward. "If they want to whisper, they can."

Val flared her nostrils, but backed down, giving my hand a squeeze as we walked on.

"Let's stop at my locker first," I said. "I want to get my stationery bag."

She agreed, the two of us chatting normally . . . until my locker came into view.

I froze. Val swore under her breath.

Slathered all over it was red paint spelling out two words:

MOB WHORE

The paint, so fresh it still dripped, was beckoning for other eyes. Students stopped to stare at the words.

Then turned to me, gauging my reaction.

I gave nothing away as I approached it. Somehow the words were more brutal up close, the contempt in each letter's stroke far more visible. Val went in to smear it until I put a hand up to stop her. The last thing I wanted was for her to be tainted by this, too.

I snarled at the students watching. "Which one of you greasy-haired freaks did this?"

A few more stopped to ogle the words before looking at me. Each of their stares a bullet piercing the reign I'd carefully crafted in this school for three years.

"Who knows?" someone called from the growing crowd. "But who cares? Someone had the nerve to say what everyone's been thinking."

My throat tightened. This was how far I'd fallen. Far enough for a mystery person to get ballsy enough to write this the morning I returned to school and know they were supported. But I couldn't let it get to me. My father would want me to be strong and face this taunt without an eyelash out of place.

I turned and grabbed at my lock, red paint smearing over my hands. Red. Like my father's blood that had coated my hands.

My body went limp. My skin went cold.

I couldn't be here. I couldn't do th—

"What the hell?"

Leo shoved through the crowd. He took one look at my locker and then at me, his eyes dropping to the red paint sticking to my fingers.

"Okay, everybody, shows over!" he yelled.

"I thought those two hated each other," a sophomore girl standing with her friend said.

Her friend, holding a sugary iced latte, made sure her voice was loud and clear. "Maybe it isn't just the mob she's a whore for."

Their words snapped me free from the nightmares replaying in my mind. Without missing a beat, I moved over to them and snatched the drink out of the girl's hand, pouring it over her head.

The girl screamed, but it was a hollow, distant noise in my ears.

"Gee, that looks messy," I said, letting each word drip from my lips. "But I'm sure your big mouth can clean it up fast."

I clenched every muscle so no one could see me shaking and turned back to Leo who hadn't budged. What was he doing anyway? Our reputations were on the line, clearly mine dive-bombing into hell. I didn't need him trying to stick up for me when it meant all the threatening questions that would sweep through our lives when it inevitably got back to our families.

"What exactly are you here for, Danesi?" I snapped. "Because your presence is as useless as you are to your family."

Leo studied me for a long, tense minute. I watched the gears shift behind his eyes until they settled on a choice I braced for from the wicked curl to his upper lip.

"Nothing interesting." Leo rolled his shoulders back and moved closer. "Or *useful*."

I stayed perfectly still as he walked past me and to my locker, pressing his finger to the paint. He turned to face me.

"All I wanted was to see you with a clown nose."

Before I could stop him, his finger pressed against the tip of my nose, leaving behind a smear of red paint. The crowd roared with laughter and Leo's wicked smirk turned into a full, toothy grin.

"What the *fuck*," Val exclaimed.

There was no damn way I was letting Leo get away with this humiliation. Without pausing to let the shock wash over me, I whipped my arm through the air and slapped my own painted-covered hand across his left cheek.

This time, the crowd gasped loudly as Leo reeled back from the blow. A smeared red handprint covered his cheek, the skin underneath already burning along with it. I flashed my teeth at him. "Don't ever touch me again."

Leo's shock wore off quickly, an icy stare appearing in his eyes. "Fine. I'll leave you with your new nickname instead."

"Thank God."

My eyes swept over the lingering crowd; the anger spread through my core, lashing out again. Fuck all of them. They wanted a show, and I was done giving them one.

I flicked my hand for Val to follow and kept my head high as we walked the remaining distance to the lounge despite the red covering my nose. But the second we were in the room, I rubbed at it, trying to remove the humiliation still seared inside me.

"Holy shit," Val said, slamming the door shut behind us. "That was barbaric. How the hell does anyone get the nerve to do that?"

I went to the bathroom to get the rest of the paint off my nose and hands. "Someone must have spread the news I was coming back today."

"It's disgusting." Val leaned against the bathroom's doorway. "I'm sorry, Tasha. I hope these horrible lies about your father end soon. You're going through enough."

I couldn't bring myself to look her in the eye and lie. Instead, I focused on washing off the paint, replying, "Me too."

"That was gross with Leo, too," Val continued, crossing her arms over her chest. "Is he behind it, and was that his screwed-up way of harassing you?"

I finished cleaning up and grabbed one of the freshly laundered white hand towels from a nearby basket to dry off. Val looked at me expectantly as I threw the towel in a hamper, but my buzzing phone saved me from needing to decide how I was going to approach that question.

Victor's name lit up my screen. I quickly picked it up, silently thanking him for saving me.

"Hello?"

"Hey, Tasha," he said in his usual gruff tone. "First day back going well?"

"Never better," I lied. "What's up?"

Victor took his time replying, sending my imagination on a joyride. Finally, he said, "I wish I didn't need to call you about this, but your mother isn't picking up and I assume she will for you. I got a call that your father's and Amelia's bodies need to be officially identified at the morgue before they can be released."

My hand gripped my phone harder than necessary.

"Oh" was all I could say.

"I'd be there to do the job, and so would Matteo or Richard, but we've got a lead on Julian staying at the Plaza and need to follow it right away in case it goes cold," Victor continued. "Your mom is the next best person to do the job."

I swallowed, my throat like sandpaper, but still had it in me to reply, "What if I do it?"

"Absolutely not." Victor practically jumped through the phone. "You've been through enough to last you a lifetime. Let us handle this part, Tasha. Got it?"

"Fine. I'll call Mom." I sighed.

"Good. I'll call again if I have updates. Otherwise, I'll see you at dinner."

I slowly lowered the phone once he'd hung up. Hardly thirty seconds passed before I was facing Val. "Up for a field trip?"

The chill from the basement air-conditioning raised every hair on my arms. In the fluorescent lighting, the white walls nearly glowed. Just like the bodies stored throughout the building. But that thought was nothing compared to the crushing weight threatening to topple me to the floor.

I couldn't do this.

I *had* to do this.

For them. It had to be me.

Val linked our arms. After she'd agreed to join me at the morgue, we'd snuck out a side exit on the east end of school. Barely anyone realized it existed other than smokers and students looking for a make-out spot. The oblivious group included my security team.

The coroner escorting us stopped at a wooden door. It was the one differentiating detail compared to the gray ones lining the hall. "They're waiting in the autopsy room. Your sister, Amelia, had significant damage to her features, but I found other markings like a mole on her right shoulder and a small heart tattoo on her ankle you can use to identify her." She paused, assessing me through careful eyes. "I can give you a moment if you need to prepare yourself."

I'd been preparing myself for this moment the second the bullets pierced my father and sister, but I kept that thought to myself.

My face remained blank. "No, I'm ready."

Inside, I was hit with the sharp scent of formaldehyde and a tinge of floral trying to mask it. A tray of autopsy tools with prongs and sharp ends sat on a metal table with large looming lights hanging over the top. All this silver and white. It was almost unbearable.

I paid no attention to any of it. My entire focus zoomed in on the bodies lying on the tables, covered in white sheets up to their necks.

They were waiting for me.

Val squeezed my hand as if she were scared I might collapse to the ground. But I was stronger than she realized.

Yet no matter how hard I tried, I couldn't get my legs to move.

"All the police need you to do is confirm these bodies are your father's and sister's. I won't ask you to be in this room any longer than necessary." The coroner picked up a clipboard with a slim set of sheets on it. "Will you be able to handle that?"

A cold sweat coated my neck and palms. The memory of my fingers pressing down on the bullet hole in my father's stomach roared in my mind. The light seeping from his eyes. Amelia's body laying still on the floor.

The blood.

I swallowed and pressed the back of my hand to my forehead, but nothing was cooling the heatwave across my skin and swimming in my head.

Val squeezed my shoulders. "Tasha, are you—"

I pushed her away, hurrying to the waste bin near the door to hurl my guts up.

So much for keeping it together.

"I'm"—I took a deep breath, spitting some of the remaining vomit taste out of my mouth—"fine."

Val rushed over to the sink. "I'll get you some water. She can drink this, right?"

The coroner nodded, sympathy wrinkling the corners of her eyes. "Yes, please go ahead. There are plastic cups in the top cupboard."

Val handed me the water and rubbed soothing circles on my back as I spat into the trash can.

"This is familiar," I said. "Though usually it's from a night of too much fun."

Val gave me a sad smile. "I know." After I was done, she placed her hands on my shoulders. "Do you want me to identify them? It's okay if you can't handle it. This is why I'm here; you can lean on me." To the coroner, she asked, "Is that okay?"

The coroner's forehead creased. "If you can accurately identify them, then yes, I can't see why not."

"I've known Tasha and her family for years." She gave me a reassuring smile. "It won't be a problem."

Maybe I couldn't do this. With the lingering vile taste in my mouth and a sheen of sweat covering me, I wasn't exactly at my best.

"Okay," I whispered.

Val nodded, giving my hand one last squeeze.

I looked over at the bodies again as Val viewed my father, careful to keep her hands close to her sides, while the coroner hovered behind. It wasn't Val's family lying on that table, but it was still amazing how well she kept her composure through it. The exact opposite of my messy self.

My teeth grazed across my bottom lip. I was such a coward. Letting my friend do such a morbid, devastating task. I'd chosen to defy Victor and not call my mother, telling myself *I* could handle this. What kind of closure could I ever get if I failed my family now?

Val whipped her head around, her eyes going wide as I approached. "Tasha?"

I put a hand up. "I came here for one task and I'm going to finish it."

"Are you sure?" Val hastily replied.

I nodded, meeting her worried gaze. Finally, Val relented and stepped out of the way to give me a full view of the body on the left.

My father.

Everything dissolved when I looked down at him. The sheet was rolled up to his neck, hiding the gunshot wounds underneath, but there was nothing wrong with his face. In life, his angles had been honed sharp from years of stress and constant danger. That was the face I usually saw. But now, those angles had smoothed, showing the father who had it in him to express his love unadorned by the pressures of his world. I'd savored those moments with him and I still did despite those memories being overwritten by truths I couldn't erase.

I nodded. "Yes, this is my father. Gabriel Nicastro."

"All right," the coroner replied softly. "Now your sister."

My heartbeat was a siren in my ears, the remaining nausea swimming in me surging.

There she was. Or at least, what I could make of her. My breath hitched as I took in Amelia's lifeless form. Her caramel-brown hair was pulled neatly behind her neck and tied in a low ponytail. The creamy tone of her skin was so pale she was nearly translucent. The white sheet was pulled up tight to her chin, but unlike my father, her face was all wrong. I could see exactly where the bullet had hit based on how the coroner had stitched her skin back together. The tiny object had torn through the right side of her jaw, shattering the bridge of her nose and ripping across her cheeks, grabbing some of her left undereye in the process.

The backs of my eyes burned with enough force to melt my vision. This was Amelia. My sister. My world. Now her beautiful face wouldn't go in the ground without being permanently marred.

I let out a few ragged breaths and shuffled down to her right ankle to see the tattooed heart. She'd gotten it a few months after she turned eighteen—the one time she ever rebelled—but in the end, she couldn't do anything too outrageous. Sure enough, it was in the same spot. The smooth line inked just below the bone. I could still see the moment clearly in my mind. The devilish smile that had crossed her face when the tattoo artist had revealed the finished product. The nervous giggles we'd shared.

"It's her," I gasped, practically leaping backward.

The coroner assessed me with a wary gaze but nodded all the same. She scribbled on her clipboard while Val descended upon me with her soothing touches and encouraging words.

"All right. Thank you, Miss Nicastro. I understand how difficult this is. Once I've given the police my findings, they'll release the bodies to you."

I clenched my jaw, taking one last long look at the bodies. My father and Amelia should be *alive*, not lying cold on those tables. Someone out there was relishing this hell I was living. And there was nothing more I wanted than to destroy them, even if it meant diving deeper into my father's world.

Val grabbed my arm. "Come on, Tasha, let's grab lunch."

"Okay," I mumbled. I couldn't stomach an ice cube, let alone a plate of food, but I didn't have the energy to say no.

We made our way back to the lobby where the edge of Val's car was visible through the windows.

The lingering summer heat prickled my skin as we stepped outside. I followed Val to the Mercedes, riffling around in my bag for my sunglasses.

It was why, at first, I didn't notice them approaching.

"Natasha Nicastro."

My name came out as a statement, said with the guttural voice of someone who had a perpetual layer of phlegm blocking their vocal cords. I stopped in my tracks as two men in frayed, unbuttoned dress shirts approached the car, their eyes glued on me.

"Can I help you?" I said.

"Yeah, you can," the second one grunted. The remains of his hair looped around his head like the wisps of a tiny crown. "We were at the meeting. A bunch of us have taken it upon ourselves to keep an eye on you since."

The cold from the morgue swept right back through me. "You've been *stalking* me?"

The first one waved an indifferent hand. "We followed you here to give you a message. Victor has clearly gone soft thinkin' you're a worthy inheritor after the Great Lion, sayin' he wanted to put you in charge. A lot of us think that'd be a big mistake."

I tried to stay calm, hiding how much stress controlled my muscles. "My father believed I was worthy of the title. If he thought I was capable, then who are you to say he was wrong?"

That wasn't the answer these two wanted to hear. A shadow passed over the men's faces as they stepped closer to me. It didn't slip my notice that the balding one deliberately pushed his shirt slightly back, showing off the gun hidden at his side.

"Emotions make people not think straight. Even the Great Lion ain't immune," the throaty one replied, tilting his chin up. "This hostility you're showin' is unwarranted. We are, out of the kindness of our hearts, giving you a clear path forward. All you gotta do now is tell Victor you're out."

I stared them down, moving nothing but my lungs to draw in air. "And if I don't?"

The second one frowned and clasped his hands in front of him. "Then that would be a very unfortunate move. A pretty little girl like you has a lot to live for."

From the corner of my eye, I saw Val hesitantly reach into her purse. For car keys to get us out of here or her phone to call someone, I wasn't sure. Neither option would work in our favor. Not with these men.

I ran my teeth over my bottom lip, blood throbbing in my temple. For the first time, I wished I hadn't ditched my security.

Faintly behind me, I picked up on a car door slamming shut, but it was quickly canceled out by my current problem standing in front of me. That was, until the two Nicastro mobsters glanced over my head and their unchecked confidence stuttered.

"Hey, lady, the entrance is that way."

"I know where I'm going," a familiar voice declared, before my mother appeared beside me. Her honey-blond hair was pulled behind her ears, showing off the full rage sharpening her features. "And it's to get you worthless scum away from my daughter."

"*You're* the Great Lion's wife?" the balding one replied. "You got a lotta nerve comin' back here. He'd have your head if he was still alive."

The two men smirked at first, until my mother stepped in front of me—pulling a gun.

Val gasped but otherwise stayed quiet. All I could do was stare at my mother as she stood her ground.

She moved closer, clicking the safety off. "But not before he strung both of you up for threatening his pride and joy, which Victor would be happy to fulfill if you don't get out of my sight."

The two exchanged a look before they, miraculously, backed off.

"You'll see soon enough," the throaty one grumbled to me.

My feet stayed firmly rooted to the ground until they retreated to the parking lot next door and roared away in an old, rust-covered Toyota.

Once they were gone, my mother sighed, and spun around to face us. "And Gabriel wondered why I hated this place."

"Oh my God, Mrs. Nicastro," Val exclaimed breathlessly. "I didn't know you had that in you. Who even were those people?"

"Some ex-employees of my dad's," I half lied, glancing between my mother and best friend. "Mom, what was that all about? How did you know I was here? Why do you have a *gun?*"

My mother shoved the weapon back in her purse, her *purse*, and glared at me. "I got it after the reading of the will. I only knew you were here because Victor wouldn't stop harassing me with calls until I picked up. That's when I learned *you* were supposed to have told me about identifying the bodies. I put two and two together." She tucked some loose strands behind her ear. "Really, Tasha, can you see why we hired a security detail to protect you? You're lucky I got here when I did!"

"I didn't know you could handle a gun," I replied.

She scoffed. "I was married to your father for twenty years. I've handled far worse."

"We're sorry for not telling you," Val said. "But thank you for stepping in."

My mother gave her a tight smile before turning back to me. "I'm telling Victor about this."

"No!" I replied, jumping forward when she pulled out her phone. I lowered my voice so Val wouldn't hear. "Not yet. He'll flip and the organization is already on the cusp of rioting."

My mother put her phone back in her purse. "Fine."

I slumped with relief, but I should've known there'd be a catch.

"In the meantime, I'd like for you to come with me."

I frowned. "Where?"

"To a café nearby," she replied, turning to nod at Val. "We can first follow Val to make sure she gets back to school safely."

I scrunched up my face. Other than a few awkward attempts to ask how I was feeling and dredging up old memories I could barely remember, my mother hadn't seriously tried to reconnect with me. She was either too busy arguing with Victor about the business or avoiding any of my emotions that were too big for her to handle. "Why?"

She sighed, breathing out all the vitriol that had made her look severe in front of those men. "To talk, of course." When she saw the look on my face, she added, "Is that somehow suspicious to you?"

"Yes," I replied. "But if you're ready, then I am, too."

CHAPTER SEVENTEEN

Tasha

THE ESPRESSO MACHINE SCREECHED LIKE A VISCERAL WARN-ing while it made our cappuccinos. My mother finally wanted to have A Talk, the kind of language usually saved for the *when two people like each other* conversation. I would gladly take it right now over whatever was in store for me.

We sat at a two-seater by a window in the cramped café. I watched my mother set her leather Saint Laurent purse begrudgingly on the floor and rub away the mascara smudged underneath her eyes. She had made no move since the car ride to start talking about whatever was on her mind. And based on the care she was taking looking at herself through her compact mirror, that wasn't changing anytime soon.

"Is it true Amelia sent you a wedding invite?" I asked, because I was curious and needed to get this train out of the station. My sister had broken the news to me on one of her venue walk-throughs. At the time, I thought nothing could horrify me more. Looking back, it all felt childish and inconsequential compared to my new reality. "She told me she'd sent you one."

My mother closed her compact mirror and nodded. "She did. I wanted to go with all my heart, but I wasn't planning to. Your father made it very clear I wasn't welcome anywhere near you two after I decided to cut ties with him."

"And I'm supposed to believe that?" I replied. "Along with everything else you've told me after not hearing from you for four years?"

"You never questioned what your father told you," she said, stuffing her mirror back in her purse. "Now you know how truthful he really was. Is it really that hard to believe?"

The barista brought over our drinks then, giving me the distraction I needed. My father let Amelia and me think our own mother wanted nothing to do with us. All the moments I desperately needed her, cried out for her in my sleep, she wasn't there. Was he really the one who stole her from me? If it was true, I could never confront him about it, never scream and demand he beg for my forgiveness. I wasn't sure which hurt more.

"The wedding invite wasn't the first time Amelia reached out," my mother revealed. "Somehow, she'd tracked down my address in Milan not long after I left. It started around the time that boyfriend died. What was his name?"

"Tyler Walsh," I answered though I was still reeling from the first half of her statement. Amelia had known where our mother lived and had been talking to her for *years*?

She snapped her fingers. "Ah, yes. That was his name. Sweet boy. If a bit rough around the edges."

Tyler was my sister's first boyfriend. They'd met when she was sixteen at Greenwich Country Club when Tyler was a lifeguard there and we still had a membership. Our father thought he'd be a summer fling, but that turned into three-and-a-half years of dating. While he never approved, I had liked the guy *far* more than I liked Julian. He didn't come from money, but at least he didn't act like a relentless prick.

Adding an extra heap of oil to our inferno, Tyler drowned off a beach in Long Island during a bonfire party a few weeks after the fighting broke out with the Danesis. Amelia and I had been with our nonna Donatella in Monaco.

When we returned, the Walshes refused to speak to Amelia or let her attend the funeral. It was all so chaotic and strange. In a matter of weeks our lives had been upturned in every direction.

But what if it hadn't been chaotic? What if it was all calculated and string-pulled by one man alone?

I looked at my mother in horror. "Do you think Dad was the reason Tyler died? To get him out of the picture?"

My mother sighed, giving a small shake of her head. "I don't know. Your sister never alluded to thinking that."

That made me feel about point five percent better. I hated not knowing the answer, especially now that everything in my past was tinged with doubt. From my father, mostly, but with my sister, too. Why was there a growing list of things she never told me?

I took a sip of my cappuccino and immediately ripped two packets of sugar to dump in. "Why would Amelia secretly marry Julian? It doesn't make sense."

"Love can make you do things you never expect," my mother mused. A glint caught in her eye as she assessed me. "I caught Matteo before he picked you up the other day. He wouldn't say it at first, but I finally got him to admit you were in Greenwich. In an area suspiciously close to the Danesis'."

I set my drink down too roughly, causing it to splash onto the saucer below. "I wasn't anywhere near their house."

"Sure, honey," she replied, cupping her chin in her hand. "I may have been gone for some time, but I still remember what things were like before I left. I take it Leo's back?"

I stayed tight-lipped, watching her closely. Anything I said could send a hand grenade straight into our plans, but not saying anything would make her more suspicious.

"I've seen him around school, so yes."

She chuckled. "You don't need to get all secretive with me. I don't mind that you're spending time with him again. Though I know Victor would have different thoughts." Her face lit up as she flashed me a playful grin. "It can be our little secret, okay? I'll even make sure to get rid of your security team. You just need to tell me when you're going to see him so I know where you are and that you're safe. Does that work for you?"

"Um—" I didn't know what to say. I was caught off guard, not only by her complete acceptance of me hanging out with Leo again but by the unbridled hope she wasn't afraid to show me. "Sure. Thanks, Mom."

"Of course, honey. I've always liked that boy. Making sure you're safe and happy is all I care about." But then the glee that had filled my mother's face drained out of her. She lowered her voice, adding, "Which is why the parking lot incident scares me. I've experienced firsthand what it's like to have men feel entitled to run your life, and it never ends nicely. Unless you impress them, which is nearly impossible, you'll spend every day avoiding people who want you dead. And unfortunately, you're an easy target."

"Where are you going with this?" I replied.

She reached across the table and clasped my hand, a thin layer of tears coating her eyes. "I want you to move to Milan with me. We can sell everything and start fresh." She choked out the last few words as tears escaped down her cheeks. She pulled away to wipe them. "We've lost some precious years together, Tasha. And I know there's a lot to rebuild between us, but if you're willing, I'd like to try. I can't lose my second baby."

The sip I took of my drink burned going down. She couldn't be serious. New York was my home. I couldn't abandon it.

"You won't lose me, Mom," I replied. "But I don't know if I can do that."

Based on the firm set to her mouth, she wasn't a fan of that answer, but her opportunity to argue evaporated when the chimes on the door tingled and Victor and Matteo walked in.

I jumped to my feet as my mind went in a dozen different directions. Had they found Julian? Did my mother tell them we were here?

Victor stopped in front of me, a wrath of disapproval hovering around him. "I can't decide if I should employ more guards to keep track of you or lock you in a tower until further notice."

"Knowing Tasha, she'll find a way to get out of both," Matteo replied with a delicate smirk.

I nodded at Matteo. "Exactly."

"We came as soon as we got a text from your mom," Matteo continued. "While it's inspiring how good you are at evading your security, you really shouldn't play games like this, Tasha."

"I'm not playing any games," I snapped before I could rein myself in. I didn't want to lose my cousin's support or look like a whining child.

"You're playing games with your *life*," Victor replied. "I know the two who approached you. You're lucky all they did was threaten you. I've had to restrain their violent sides many times."

I turned to glare at my mother who barely looked remorseful for blabbing. That was the *one* detail I asked her not to say anything about.

"You need to start understanding that you aren't a normal teenager with normal teenager problems. You can't keep doing things behind our backs, Tasha." Victor crossed his arms, jerking his chin sideways. "Let's go. I'll drop you off at school where you'll *attend* your remaining classes for the day."

Matteo turned to my mother. "Mind if I drive with you, Auntie?"

"Not at all," she replied, grabbing up her things. "I could use a pleasant companion who wants to spend time with me."

I ignored my mother and met Victor's fierce gaze. Saw the

righteousness in his eyes. He really thought I should dutifully follow his orders without question when he was as bad as my father for lying to me all my life. None of them deserved my obedience.

But I needed to pick my battles wisely, so I grabbed my book bag with a huff and followed him outside.

"Did you find Julian?" I asked.

Victor grunted as he unlocked his SUV. "A dead lead. If he was at the Plaza, he's moved now. Matteo insists he wouldn't stay close to home, but I keep telling him someone like Julian doesn't have the creativity to properly go into hiding. A witness saw him blatantly eavesdropping by the dining room door the night of the party for one."

I agreed with Victor, but I wasn't in the mood to say that out loud. Instead, I got into the passenger seat quietly while he jumped into the driver's side.

Neither of us spoke for a long part of the drive. I watched the rows of storefronts and houses turn into thick clusters of trees and cycle back again. I'd avoided Victor since I got back from Leo's house, afraid he'd see my betrayal written all over my face. But I couldn't put off the questions echoing around me forever. I needed to know the truth of Angelo Danesi's death. Even if it was brutal.

"Was Angelo Danesi shot to death?"

I turned to see Victor's reaction head-on. A small piece of my heart that ached to hold on to my innocence wanted him not to react. To assure me that Leo was full of shit. But the more I uncovered about who my father really was, the more that felt like an impossible wish. And the brief shock that crossed over Victor's face confirmed it.

Leo wasn't lying. My father was the reason our lives had imploded.

"How could you?" My vision filled with tears, blurring the edges of Victor's features so I could almost pretend it wasn't him sitting in the driver's seat. "You lied to me. Made me believe it was some tragedy that destroyed the tie between our families."

I didn't have it in me to lash out any more than that.

Victor sighed. "What gave you that idea, Tasha?"

"Does it matter?" I replied. "My father lied about so much. It makes sense that Angelo's death was just another one in his long list. Now, tell me what really happened."

His fingers went ghostly white around the steering wheel. "It's true. Your father ordered the hit. A group of Nicastro men followed Angelo after the Yankees game and fired at his vehicle when they approached a red light. It was over before any witnesses had a chance to realize what was happening."

"And he ordered it knowing Leo would be in the car with him?" I asked, my voice barely above a whisper.

Victor's jaw tensed. "Your father didn't want him hurt, but, yeah, he knew."

I wanted to cry. For fourteen-year-old Leo who had to experience something so horrific that could've led to his death and for myself for loving a father who could ruin lives without having the nerve to watch it happen. No wonder Leo couldn't speak the words out loud. Bringing it up must've stirred those violent memories alone.

Angelo Danesi was my father's *friend*. Our families were friends. How could he decide to destroy all of it? They hadn't been fighting before then. From what I knew, their friendship had never been stronger. My mother had been enthusiastically talking about us taking a trip to San Sebastián, Spain, together. Obviously, that trip never happened.

I stared down at my hands. At my fresh set of nails paid for by a monthly allowance my father set up for me. At the Van Cleef bracelet bought on one of the credit cards nestled in my wallet. All the money funding my life was tinted the same shade as Leo's. I only had the luxury of being unaware of it until now.

"Why would he order his friend's death?"

For a long minute, it looked like Victor wouldn't reply. Finally, he scratched his short beard and gave me a sideways glance before speaking. "Your father never had an issue winning the approval of the Nicastro Mafia after your nonno stepped down because of his kidney failure. They saw him as a perfect reflection of the boss they'd taken orders from for years. But that all changed when your father put his trust in someone that ended up being a rat for the FBI. It nearly got your father and our entire organization taken down."

I squeezed each individual finger on my left hand as I processed the mixed emotions running through me. Would it have been so bad for the thing that inevitably destroyed my life to have ended long ago? I still would've gone through the pain of my father going to prison, but at least he and Amelia would be alive. Our mother would never have left. We'd still have a friendship with the Danesis. Leo and I . . .

Anyway.

"Who was it?" I asked, pushing the rest of my thoughts about it aside.

"Uncle Francesco," Victor replied.

I leaned back against my seat. That wasn't entirely surprising. Uncle Francesco had been one of my father's close friends for reasons I never quite understood. He had been a stout man who brought over a new bottle of rye for my father every visit and always seemed to dose himself in enough cologne to make my eyes water. I assumed he disappeared from our lives when his attention started to linger on Amelia for too long, but it would line up with the timeline of everything.

"He was . . . eliminated," Victor continued, staring forward. "But that didn't stop your father's men from losing trust in him. There were rumblings of whether he had the right judgment to be their leader and if he deserved the power he'd inherited. It got bad enough that other families and their organizations that had once respected and feared your father started to lose faith, too. He had to do something bold and ruthless that would cement his reputation as a powerful boss for good."

I turned to face Victor. "So he destroyed all our lives to protect his own. *I* was the one who gave Leo those Yankee tickets, because Dad told me to. He knew he was involving me when he did that."

"He didn't want to," Victor replied quietly. "But once it became clear it was the only way forward, he had no other choice but to order a hit on him and get you involved. Angelo wouldn't suspect anything if you were the one to hand them over. We all knew how close you and the Danesi kid were. It was the hardest decision I ever saw your father make, knowing it would destroy the deep friendship your families shared.

"You need to understand he wasn't just protecting his reputation," Victor continued. "He was protecting you, the family. If he didn't take a vicious approach, others would've seen that as a sign of weakness and gone after all of you. He did it knowing it'd break the three of you, but at least then you'd be safe."

A flame of anger tore through the hollowness in my core. "Look how well *that* worked out. Those men mentioned Uncle Luca died by the Danesis' hands and not in the boating accident you all made me believe. Was he an expendable chess piece for this power struggle, too?"

But Victor didn't take my bait for a fight. He gently shook his head, his lips pressed into a thin line. "I know, Tasha. Your father never expected Sloane to retaliate and have Luca killed. It devastated him and cemented the bloodbath between our mobs. He told me once if he knew how this would all go down, he wouldn't have made the choices he did.

"But this is our reality," he continued. "And all we can do is fight for the future we want from here."

The flame that had surged in me flickered out, leaving exhaustion to sink into my bones. Now I knew everything—for better or for worse. No matter the reason, I couldn't forgive my father for the choice he made. But that didn't mean the rage I felt for his death was any weaker.

Because of my new enemy, my future no longer included him or Amelia. There would never be another gentle touch or affectionate word spoken. All our moments of laughter or ridiculous arguments were gone, too. All of it was. The only things I had left were a vicious family legacy and a growing hunger for revenge that needed to be fed.

"If I said no," I began, "and decided I didn't want to be boss, what would happen to the Nicastro Mafia?"

Victor didn't hesitate with his answer. "It would crumble like the rest of your family's empire."

"Does that mean you couldn't find the people responsible for the hit?"

"We could still find them," he replied. "But taking them down without the strength of our soldiers? That's another story. And one I have a hard time believing would go well."

Running away meant putting my extended family in jeopardy. I didn't want that. But it also wasn't the main reason I hadn't immediately rejected the role.

"But with me in power, we could crush them," I quietly replied.

"Exactly." Victor met my gaze. "I'm confident the organization would come around if they learned you took up the role to get revenge. Then there'd be no question of your legitimacy after we retaliated swiftly and fiercely with you leading the charge."

I clasped my hands together, focusing on evening my breaths.

You're a fighter, Tasha. That's why I know you can do this.

I couldn't deny what Matteo had said. Just like I couldn't deny my family history. My life had been destroyed the day the hitman broke into my home. Running meant destroying what remained and fueling the orchestrator's success further.

And there was no damn way I would let that happen.

This choice would stay with me forever and take me down a path I still couldn't fully comprehend. But it was the one that gave me a chance to satisfy the beast that had roared awake inside me when my family's blood had coated my hands.

"Then I know what I need to do," I replied.

CHAPTER EIGHTEEN

Tasha

THE OVERCAST SKY SHROUDED ME AS INTIMATELY AS THE black Alexander McQueen dress clinging to my figure. I sat in the Costas' sitting room, staring out the window at the saltwater pool lapping against the walls. Maybe I could back out of this. Jump into the water and float on my back until the salt dissolved me into nothing.

Anything would be nicer than going through with today.

"Ready?"

I turned to Val standing in the doorway in her own Alexander McQueen tuxedo dress. We got them together one Saturday morning in April, never in a million years thinking we'd be using them for a dual funeral.

"No." I rose from the couch and approached her. "But I also never expected to bury my sister and dad on the same day."

Val nodded, her lips pressed close, and took my hand.

The black car waited for us out front along with four other vehicles. Richard and Isabel Costa, Victor, Matteo, and my mother stood in formal wear under the front porch arches. My security team had also changed into a collection of gunmetal-gray suits for the day.

Once I'd identified my father's and sister's bodies, they'd been released to us the next day. The police barely tried to hide their disinterest in the case, stating they'd keep looking for the shooter, but made sure to remind me how "difficult" it was to solve "crimes of this kind." I didn't care though since I already had my own plans for retribution.

I'd wanted to help plan the funeral, but I couldn't find it in me to do it. My mother and Matteo took up the torch and organized it all. Now the service was in less than an hour. Then I would really, truly have to say goodbye forever.

"Honey," my mother said, clasping my hand in hers. She wore a string of pearls with a diamond droplet resting at the base of her throat. The one my father gave her for their wedding anniversary the year before she fled. She must've found it somewhere in the house, left behind with everything else. "Why don't you ride with me?"

I shook my head, releasing myself from her grasp, and stepped back. I wasn't ready to forgive her yet for tattling to Victor or deal with the endless hints she dropped about moving to Milan. Today, all my energy had to go into being strong for the funeral. Especially when everyone expected me to be a fragile mess instead. "I'm going to ride with Val."

Hurt swept through her eyes, but she nodded. "Okay."

The driver for our car opened the back door and I slid inside. Val followed and held my hand the entire way over, not speaking a word—exactly as I wanted it.

I focused on the cars rushing past us and the forests lining the highway to numb my mind as best as I could. But despite all my efforts, every scrap of pain I'd felt since the party forced its way back in once the driver made it to the Catholic church.

My heartbeat quickened at the sight of hundreds of mourners watching our procession. In a sea of suits and modest dresses, I couldn't tell the difference between my father's two worlds. He'd done a good job separating them, but now they blended together with ease. All to say goodbye to him and my sister.

When the car slowed to a stop, I let go of Val and got out before I lost my nerve. Within seconds, my security surrounded me, escorting me inside. Bouquets of flowers bursting with azaleas to snapdragons flanked the entrance of the church. I spotted my aunt Giana and uncle Edward hovering off to the side with Matteo's sisters, the five of them keeping to themselves.

I stepped inside and immediately stopped and stared at the two closed caskets at the front. A gold cross stood in front of the stained-glass windows, cutting through the light streaming onto the smooth mahogany wood. My body went heavy at the sight of them.

No. I couldn't do this. I—

My legs buckled under me. The pain in my chest seared through my rib cage. I was done for.

Strong hands wrapped underneath my arms, holding me upright, as a familiar smoky wood scent enveloped my senses.

"Hey, hey, I got you," Ravi's soothing voice spoke quietly but quickly in my ear, his firm hands holding on to me.

Before I knew what was happening, I was turned against his chest while he rubbed circles onto my back.

"Cover us," Ravi ordered to my security. He carefully moved me so our eyes locked. "You don't need to be strong today. I can be the person you lean on to get through this."

I closed my eyes, shaking my head. "I have to be. They'll never take me seriously otherwise."

Ravi wiped away the tears smudging my makeup. "*I* take you seriously. Who cares what anyone else thinks?"

"It's not enough," I whispered. "Not if I want to keep my family's empire from being snatched away. I need everyone in this church to support me."

"I *am* enough, Tasha." A muscle worked in his jaw. "None of these people would question you if you stood by my side again. My family's influence would award you that."

I stayed quiet. The Ferreiras were influential, but it wasn't the kind of influence I needed.

"But why does it have to be you?" Ravi continued. "Running an empire as big as your family's isn't for the weak."

My eyes flashed up to his. "You think I'm weak?"

"Of course not," Ravi replied. "But that kind of role will demand a lot of you. You're still young." He brushed my hair back behind my ear. "I'm afraid of how much you'd have to sacrifice. How much it'll change you. My mother became a hard woman once she took over Aurora Technology."

I shook my head. He couldn't know that revenge fueled my decision, but the reason shouldn't matter anyway. *I* wanted this. "People always change, Ravi. I don't *want* to stay the same forever. Even if it makes me too 'hard' for your liking."

"You'd risk a multimillion-dollar empire to make a point."

To make a point? I scoffed, pulling away from Ravi and recentering myself. "I can't do this right now."

Ravi's face softened. "Wait, Tasha, I overstepped."

But I wasn't interested in his apologies. My security moved out of the way to let me back into the public eye, leaving Ravi to sit with his regret. More guests had trickled in. All of them pretending like their attention wasn't solely on me. For once, I had no desire to be in the spotlight.

Val hurried over to stand beside me as I made my way up the long aisle to the front. The two caskets were both covered in a giant pile of white roses with a regal picture of my father in front of one and a beaming picture of my sister in front of the other.

"Are they really in there?" I asked breathlessly.

Val rubbed my shoulder, the side of her head resting against mine. "Yes, Tasha. They are."

Everyone was here to pay their respects, but they were also here to watch me. This was the first moment of many where I'd need to show the woman I would one day be. The one they could throw their support behind or rise against.

But all that slipped away as I stared at the caskets. What mattered was that they were in *there* and not standing out *here*. Leaving the burden of all the things left unsaid for me to hold on to.

Another hand wrapped around my other shoulder. I turned to look at Victor. The lines on his face were taut with grief, but he held himself together with the same level of control he'd always maintained. Strangely, it was what brought me the most comfort.

"Let's go, kid," he said. "We can't keep your father and sister waiting."

My legs stiffened on the cemetery's gravel road, every part of me fixated on the wide, gaping mouth of the mausoleum entrance, ready to swallow the two caskets whole. This was it. There was no going back.

I breathed in a long, deep lungful of air and straightened. I looked at my mother, at Victor, at Matteo, and at Val. At Ravi watching me carefully, waiting for one signal that I needed to lean on him. But I got through the service, and I was going to get through this, too.

"Let's get this over with," I said to everyone, but mostly to myself.

The priest started a hymn, with everyone singing along. I kept my mouth shut, focused on the feel of the air cycling in and out of my lungs. As everyone sang, the pallbearers carefully carried the caskets one at a time into the mausoleum's dark interior until both were placed inside.

When the priest said his final words, Val brought forward the special item I'd requested for the service. All eyes were on me as I stepped up and stared the crowd down.

"Now, Natasha." The priest gestured to me. "You'd like to say a few words?"

"Yes." I clutched the basket a little tighter.

"There was never any doubt in our house that Dad would protect and cherish Amelia and me over everything else," I started, making sure my voice carried. "Through him, I learned what my own strength looked like and that it was my right to demand respect."

I paused, picturing the smile on his face when he said how capable he always knew me to be. "He never tried to diminish my spirit. Instead, he praised it and encouraged me to stand strong against anyone who tried to extinguish my fire. Even when the person I had to stand strong against was him.

"And my perfect sister, Amelia." Without warning, my throat thickened with emotions. "She seized the role of older sister and went beyond expectations. People reserve the word soulmates for romantic love, but Amelia defied that definition. Every time pain or chaos entered our lives, she reached for me before anyone else. That was her way of saying I was her soulmate. I was the one she thought of when our worlds were shaken."

My eyes began to burn, so I paused to center myself. I'd come here today to bury the two most important people in my life. But I also wanted it known I wasn't backing down.

The crowd waited for me to continue, silent and watchful. Up close, I recognized a few of the men who worked for my Mafia from their cocky stance and their suits not quite as polished as the rest. Judgment oozed off them, but I ignored it. I already knew one day they'd have no choice but to bend a knee.

"My father and sister were two of the most resilient people I knew. When they set their mind to something, they didn't stop until they got exactly what they wanted," I began. "I know there are many who don't want me to take over. But I won't dishonor my family's memory by burying the Nicastro legacy with them."

I took in all the faces watching me. Their breaths hitched at my every word, fanning my spirit to keep going and say what could damn or glorify me.

"Whoever's behind their deaths thinks this was all it took to destroy us. I want them to know, wherever and whoever they are, they won't win this war, because I'm taking over this empire." Pausing, I curved my fingers along the underside of the lid before declaring my final promise. "And I'm coming for them."

With one flick of my wrist, the lid flew open, releasing into the air a flock of white doves. I watched the birds soar high above with hot tears escaping down my cheeks.

This time I didn't care that everyone saw me cry, because if they looked close enough, they'd see the rage heating those tears—ready to scorch whoever stood in my way.

Flying above the guests, the doves took off with my words harbored in their feathers. I lowered my gaze to watch the crowd's reaction only to notice a person standing at the edge of the graveyard.

Leo.

He stood alone with his hair swept back and his tie properly secured against his black suit. I almost believed he was a mirage come to taunt me. Standing hip width apart with his hands resting in his pockets, he looked more like the son of a Mafia boss than ever before.

I didn't know what to make of it. This boy from another life I was never supposed to go back to choosing to be at the funeral of the man who sent his own father six feet under.

Our eyes locked; the ends of his suit jacket fluttering like the doves in the sky. As I stared at him, the briefest of smiles played across his lips. Telling me that he'd heard every word. It made me certain of my choice.

A new era had arrived, but it would be mine to rule.

CHAPTER NINETEEN

THE FINAL BELL RANG, MARKING TWO WEEKS OF TASHA'S absence. I shoved my school laptop in my bag and heaved it over my shoulder, eyeing her empty desk.

She'd been strong at the funeral. Had something happened?

I shouldn't care. I *didn't* care. But the kind of declaration she made wasn't a joke or an exaggeration. Whoever was behind her father's and sister's deaths wouldn't take kindly to it.

But if something happened to Tasha, the wildfires of gossip would've reached my ears by now. It was a waste of my energy and time to wonder about her. I'd already texted her twice with no response and held myself back when my fingers itched to follow up a third time. I got the hint, but I wasn't sure if it also meant our partnership was off, too. Probably was after the way things went the last time we talked. I had been an idiot. Humiliating her more when she was already up to her neck in it. But I couldn't do anything to fix what happened if she didn't come back to class or answer my texts.

Out in the halls, I'd barely filtered through the masses when a tiny frame hurled themselves onto my back. I snagged my footing right before toppling to the floor as Scarlett squealed with delight behind me.

"Leo! Thank God, I found you before you left," she exclaimed. "A bunch of us are heading over to Derek's. He told Jonathan, who told me, that his moms had to go on a last-minute trip to Massachusetts because their family friend's dying or something. He gets the whole house to himself for the night! Isn't that amazing?"

I slowly blinked as my brain processed the onslaught of information coming out of her mouth at two times her usual speed. All I remembered was Derek and party and death. I nodded anyway. "Yeah, sounds like a great time. I'm down."

"Perfect," Scarlett purred, her fingers trailing over my chest. "I'll ride with you then. Let me grab my emergency overnight bag and I'll meet you at your car."

She was gone before I could say anything else. Which was how I wound up following Jonathan's car to Rye.

"You've got your fake ID, right?" Scarlett asked once we'd pulled into the parking lot in the downtown core. A cool autumn breeze carried a salty tang to it, making her pull her fall coat tighter around her. "We're getting the drinks while Derek orders a ton of takeout from this sushi spot he says has the best nigiri."

I should've been listening, but I'd tuned her out when my eyes landed on a store directly in my line of sight.

Golden Age Antiques and Collectibles.

"Actually, I need to grab something from another shop," I said. "Get me my usuals?"

Scarlett made some noises like she was about to protest, but I quickly squeezed her shoulder, saying, "Thanks, Scarlett," before lightly jogging over to the store. I didn't need her deciding to tag along with me.

My heart rate picked up once I was across the street and standing in front of the doors, the brightly lit interior and OPEN sign inviting me in.

I'd only stared at this shop from Tasha's car a few weeks ago, admittedly getting us nowhere. But here was an opportunity to get closer and see if this Ivan Romano was connected to the company calling themselves Salvator. My family was still in dangerous territory as long as the people who threatened them hid in the shadows. I needed to know from his lips if they were the organization I was looking for. Maybe it'd bring Tasha out of hiding, too.

And for all Ivan Romano knew, I was just some teenager. He didn't know who I was since he never spotted me at Greenwich Country Club. So there was nothing suspicious about me asking some prying questions.

I grabbed the handle and turned it with an extra dose of confidence, triggering a chime to ring throughout the store.

I was greeted with the sharp tang of polished copper and dust-filled corners. Shelves groaned under the weight of silver plate sets and clusters of figurines from different parts of the world. I passed life-sized statues and elaborate grandfather clocks with gold detailing, careful to avoid hitting any of the stacks of tea cup collections sitting in ornate boxes or picture frames leaning against any available surface.

The store was quiet except for the soft clicking of a keyboard somewhere in the back. I walked to it until I reached a counter with a cash register straight out of the Victorian era. Behind the counter was a small office with walls made of glass and a man I recognized instantly sitting in front of a desktop. He perked up when he saw me, rising to his full height and coming out around the counter.

"Good afternoon," Ivan Romano said with the typical pleasant tone of a salesperson. "Is there anything I can help you with?"

Up close, I could see there was nothing distinct about the guy. He had on a dusty-pink dress shirt and sleek loafers I'd seen guys Carter's age wearing, but a few speckles of gray cooled the scruff on his face, and he had the most average comb-over I'd ever seen. He could be anywhere from thirty-six to fifty-two. An unremarkable nobody. The perfect chameleon.

"Hi," I said, keeping my stance as relaxed as possible. "I'm looking for a nice antique for my mom's birthday. She loves them. I saw your store and was hoping you'd be able to help me out."

Ivan raised a brow at me. "Of course. Is there a particular type she likes? As you can see, we have an extensive list of options."

I hesitated. *That* was a detail I should've thought about before stepping in here. My mind whipped through everything I knew about Mom that didn't involve conning people out of their money or promising violence on men who betrayed her. Finally, I blurted out, "She loves to drink. And, um, eat good food."

Smooth one.

Ivan, though, didn't seem fazed that I insinuated my mom's personality revolved around gorging herself and gestured for me to follow him down one of the squished aisles.

"A connoisseur then. I have many unique pieces for you to choose from." Ivan stopped, turning back to me. "And what's the budget you have in mind?"

I shrugged, looking around at the paintings and candelabras placed around me. "No budget. Throw your best at me."

Ivan smiled and continued forward, sidestepping boxes on the floor full of sterling silver items and vases that would shatter into a million pieces with one accidental bump. I couldn't believe how blasé he was about his setup, especially when the majority of price tags had four or five zeros.

"Here's something she may like," Ivan said, grasping a tall silver pitcher with intricate details of cherubs and ivy entwined from the base to the handle. "A Tiffany & Co. pitcher from the late eighteen hundreds. Not many in this format exist, but one just like this is in the Met's collection."

I pursed my lips, pretending to closely inspect the antique's neck and spout before I straightened. "It's nice. Though I'm not sure she'd want a gift she can only have on display. Do you have something she can admire and use?"

Ivan considered my question for a minute before he trailed through the narrow path, prompting me to follow him again. I couldn't spend this crucial time pretending I was only here for a present.

"So," I started in a lighthearted tone anyone who knew me would call bullshit on. "You've got a lot of cool antiques here. Where do you get all these pieces?"

Ivan scanned shelves of mostly handblown glass décor before moving on to the next pile.

"Here and there. In my business, you have long bouts of famine before you get the big feast. Things tend to pile up until the right owner comes along to claim an item. You forget exactly where everything came from. Only where it was born."

I did my best to keep a straight face. If I laughed at his odd way of describing his line of work, he could easily clam up. "That makes sense. But do you have a general country you get your items from?"

Ivan plucked what looked like a single glass goblet from a shelf before putting it back. "Europe mostly. Some from East Asia. The best come from places in Austria, Switzerland, and deep within China, but everyone clamors for their items. It makes acquiring my own pieces for the shop a difficult endeavor. Worth the effort though."

Europe. That was where Salvator was based and sent art over from. But it was also too broad and didn't necessarily connect Ivan to them. I needed to dig further and put my questions to rest one way or another.

"Yeah, I bet. Do you have suppliers you partner with? That would make it easier, wouldn't it? I'm sure it'd help you find your big buyers, too."

Ivan didn't break his gaze from whatever search he was on, so it was hard to get a read on him. "You have a deep interest in antiques, do you?"

My right hand was stuffed in my leather jacket, letting me fidget away my nerves. "Inherited trait. My parents love them."

That answer seemed to satisfy him, because he replied, "It's always refreshing when a young man like yourself shows interests in maintaining the past." He smiled. "Yes, I do work with business partners across the States and in European countries. My main partner as of now is based in France."

I studied him closely while all the alarm bells went off in my head. "What're they called?"

Ivan turned his back on me, a man without any suspicion in his arsenal. "Salvator."

I needed to follow him around the store. To not show him the name meant something to me. But I couldn't get my legs to unhook from the chains that had snaked up and held me to the floor.

I knew what a front looked like. I'd grown up with a family business that thrived off them. This revelation wasn't damning evidence that Ivan and Salvator were running one, but it brought me much closer to uncovering what could be going on and how it related to everything. If I piled enough coincidences on each other, all I'd need to do would be to give a light push and topple the whole thing over.

"They're fairly new, but they've provided me with many unique items already," Ivan went on from somewhere else in the store. "One being a piece I'm trying to find for you. Ah! Here it is."

Finally, I broke free of the shock rooting me in place and hurried after him to the front of the store. He pointed to a polished wooden box displaying a large porcelain platter with individual grooves carved in the shape of oyster shells. Embedded around the scalloped work was mother-of-pearl with a thinly painted nautical design in the center of each oyster indent. The handles of the accompanying tools had the same details as well to pull it all together.

"A beauty, isn't it?" Ivan asked. "Perfect for any dinner party or for any day of the week your mother craves fresh oysters."

It was nice, Mom would love it, but I hadn't finished spiraling from the bomb of information he'd dropped on me. Somehow, I got myself to nod and mumble a few words of agreement.

"Should I assume this is the one?"

"Not sure." I pretended to muse over it before asking, "What other items does this Salvator company have? Can you show me?"

The corners of Ivan's mouth tightened. "I'm afraid not. This is the only piece I currently have from them that hasn't already been claimed."

"I didn't realize there was such a market for antique oyster trays."

Ivan didn't laugh. "The antique and art world are still quite strong. Now. Can I assume this is the perfect gift?"

My tongue ached to keep asking questions about Salvator. To demand he tell me the truth. But he never would, and I couldn't show him all my cards. No one knew I was here, and I had no clue how dangerous this guy was or what he'd do to keep his secrets safe.

So all I did was nod.

"Wonderful," Ivan smiled. He packed up the wooden box and lifted it into his arms. "I'll ring you up at the counter."

I walked with him back to the register, spotting a white credit card machine tucked beside it.

"Salvator is an interesting name," I blurted out as Ivan checked the price tag. "Isn't it Italian? Why would a French company choose it over a French name?"

"It is," Ivan replied. "But I believe they love art from the Italian Renaissance."

"So it's not a family name?"

Ivan stilled, deciding to keep his gaze on the box. "I wouldn't know. I like to give my suppliers their privacy when requested, as long as shipments arrive."

I smelled bullshit on that answer, but wouldn't let him see my suspicion. If the rare art business was a front, there was likely a family pulling the strings from behind the scenes and using guys like Ivan to smuggle their wares. Whether they'd use their real last name or not was another question.

I pulled out my wallet, tapping my foot on the floor so hard that it made a tiny figurine sitting on the counter wobble. This gift was about to take a bite out of my funds, but it was worth it.

My attention trailed back to Ivan's office. This time I took in the chaos that had slinked from the store space into all four corners of the small room. Other than a bit of space for Ivan's desk and computer, any remaining square footage was taken over by old filing cabinets and antiques. The majority being more of those life-sized statues he had spaced around the store. Could he be hiding anything back there? And if he was, what would I be looking for?

"Card or check?"

"What?" I asked, blinking back at him.

Ivan wasn't fazed and said again, "Card or check? I accept both."

I cleared my throat, about to reply, when my eyes landed on a sign behind Ivan's head.

It read, ID REQUIRED FOR ALL PURCHASES.

"Oh," I said, flipping open my wallet to find my fake ID. No way was I giving him my real name. "I'll pay by card. Let me get my ID for you, too."

But as I pulled out my fake, Ivan held up a hand. "No need. I know who you are, Leo. Many of my patrons are connected to your family."

Our eyes locked. Ivan gave me one of his neutral pleasant smiles again, but it did nothing to temper the static hissing above. Every layer of warmth in my skin went biting cold like I'd dove headfirst into the Atlantic.

He knew who I was this whole time.

I nodded and exchanged the fake ID for my credit card, barely looking at him as I went through the motions. How could he know who I was without ever meeting me?

But the answer was obvious. He'd done his research on my family.

Now I'd walked right into his store asking questions I shouldn't be interested in.

I inserted my card in the payment machine. I needed to get out of here as fast as possible. I needed time to think. Should I believe him? Carter said he wasn't interested in the art he was selling, but he didn't explain how he got on Ivan's radar. And if Ivan was telling the truth, what did my family's connection imply?

"Do you need help taking it to your car?" Ivan asked after the transaction went through.

I shook my head and pulled the box toward me. "I'm good. Thanks for your help."

If I didn't have a heavy weight tucked underneath my left arm, I might've sprinted for the exit.

Some of the tension in my shoulders relaxed once I was in reach of the door. I grasped onto the handle with my free hand and basked in the frost-touched breeze that glided in when it opened.

"Christ, man!" I shouted when Ivan materialized beside me. If my muscles weren't already tense, I would've dropped the box.

Ivan held out a slip of paper. "You forgot your receipt."

I took it from him and searched his eyes for any sign that he was onto me. But there wasn't a wrinkle too deep or a twitch at the corner of his mouth. His mask was seamless. And it made the alarm bells in my head ring louder.

"Thanks," I muttered, basically leaping out of the store.

"I hope your mother enjoys her birthday present," Ivan called out to me.

Despite knowing I shouldn't do it, I turned back to look the man up and down once more. He waved, but I didn't reciprocate. Instead, I hurried across the street and toward the liquor store to find my friends. I wouldn't go straight to my car with Ivan watching. Though it seemed pointless. If the man already knew who I was, then there was a high chance his knowledge of me stemmed deeper than I could imagine.

And that scared me the most. A guy I knew nothing about knowing everything about me and proudly saying it to my face. Only someone who was confident in his safety would act like that. I'd seen it before. It was in every person who stood close enough to my family that they could taste our version of power, while knowing they could never grasp it for themselves.

It only made my suspicions about this Salvator company grow. If there was a new criminal family running it, a lot of questions Tasha and I had could get answered.

The more I considered it, the more I became sure of my theory. Only another family with strong ties to the underground world would plan and orchestrate such brutal attacks like the ones our families experienced. Especially a criminal family who wanted to rise up the ranks fast.

My grip tightened on the overpriced gift tucked under my arm. Tasha could ignore me all she wanted, but I wouldn't let this go until I talked to—and warned—her about this. Even if that meant breaking and entering into her house.

CHAPTER
TWENTY

Tasha

THE PAIN HIT ME FROM ALL SIDES AS I WALKED THROUGH the quiet halls of my home. It still hadn't gotten easier being back here. I was beginning to wonder if it ever would.

After the funeral, the police finished their investigation without finding any useful evidence and released the house back to me. Since then, my mother and Victor had practically locked me inside with guards hovering twenty-four seven. It was punishment for making my big declaration at the funeral, scaring them more than anyone else. Instead of going back to school, I was forced to work with an online tutor and complete my school assignments from home indefinitely. Victor even took my phone away for the first few days. Like being isolated to the house wasn't punishment enough.

But I couldn't be totally pissed. Victor made sure to bring in a trusted group to clean and secure the property, sealing up the tunnel system for good and locking off the dining room so I didn't have to see it. My mother wouldn't leave my side for a week after we returned, bringing my favorite snacks when I didn't have it in me to eat a full meal or tucking me in when I drifted off on the couch or in bed.

We still didn't know how the hitman got into the secret passages and how they knew about them. Either they figured out the house's secret on their own or someone I was supposed to trust turned on my family.

Like Julian. Mr. I-Can't-Be-Found.

Neither theory was an easy pill to swallow.

Miraculously, all our staff had stayed on, giving me some comfort when I saw their familiar faces.

Our wasn't the right word anymore, was it? It was *my* home now, including everything and everyone in it. It was a concept I was still coming to terms with day by day. Heartbreak by heartbreak.

I reached the foyer, the gentle rise of the Saturday morning sun leaking through the windows and onto the hardwood floors. Nobody else was up—the small reward I got for waking at 5:00 AM—leaving me with the sound of my breathing and the thoughts in my head to keep me company. My gaze went to the slightly ajar door of my father's office. It was the place he used to retreat to after a long day or where he'd take private meetings with special clients and suppliers. Now I realized *special* meant "Mafia-related."

I couldn't go in. I couldn't go into a lot of rooms in this house.

Pulling my long cashmere cardigan tighter, I turned away from his office and nearly started for the kitchen when a rattling noise caught my attention.

I whipped my head around, trying to decipher where the sound was coming from. It grew in intensity as I searched until, finally, I found the culprit.

And thank God I did.

Outside, Leo stood at one of the first-floor windows in the piano room, shaking the frame and trying to pry a stick into the corners. I inhaled sharply when I saw him, rushing over to the window and lifting it up.

"What the hell are you doing?" I gasped, my voice strained. "Security will see you!"

Leo staggered back a step and met my gaze. A red flush filled his cheeks, and a hazy glaze was in his eyes. "I'm trying to get inside. This window never closed properly."

"Are you breaking into my house *drunk*, Danesi?" I hissed, gripping the bottom of the window frame. "It's five in the morning! The day has barely started!"

He grinned at me, swaying slightly. "Not if your last day hasn't *ended* yet."

I looked around the front yard for any drunkenly crashed cars. "Did you come all the way from Greenwich? Please tell me you didn't drive."

"I'm staying at Jonathan's house. He lives three streets over. I walked here when he passed out." He said it far too proudly for a guy who looked ready to pass out on *my* couch and drool all over the carpet. With the stick, he pointed over to my Porsche. "That's your car."

I sighed. I really needed to figure out what I was going to do with him soon. "And what about it?"

"I can tell it's yours because it's yellow. Your favorite color."

I stared at him, a little lost for words that he remembered.

Leo turned back to me, smirking like a fool. "It's like a neon highlighter. I knew you were a weirdo for liking it, but I didn't realize how far that weirdness went."

"It is not *neon*. And liking yellow doesn't make me a weirdo, you prick." I looked around once more and pulled the window up farther. "Get in here before I have to explain to my security why they shouldn't shoot you for trespassing. Leave the stick."

Leo obliged. Well, *attempted* to. I stepped back so he could climb in, looking more like a strange creature of the night with too many limbs as he heaved himself inside with his right leg and left arm first.

I winced when his body loudly collided with the ground and quickly closed the window behind him. Once Leo had staggered to his feet, I grasped his wrist and dragged him to the caterer's prep room.

I spun around, only to realize Leo was standing right behind me. The room was small compared to other parts of the house, but not small enough that he needed to be breathing down my neck. I took three steps back to stand by the prep sink, crossing my arms. "Explain yourself. And it better be worth the massive risk you took coming here."

"You were ignoring my texts and not coming back to school," Leo replied. "So I thought, what's the point in waiting around forever to find out if she is or isn't still looking for this new mob with me? Why not go talk to her *right now*?"

He had a slight wild look in his eyes that made me roll mine. After a night of partying, *this* was the bright idea his alcohol-soaked brain came up with?

"I wasn't intentionally ignoring you," I replied. "Victor took my phone away. Apparently, I'm a menace to my own well-being. I've been housebound for the past two weeks."

That got a chuckle out of Leo. It shocked my nervous system, shooting new energy through my veins. Not because I'd never seen Leo laugh before, but because this one wasn't shielded by the layers of arrogance he'd begun to wear. It was, for a moment, Leo in his simplest form. The boy I once knew.

"Hard to argue with that," he replied.

We grew quiet, a heavy unease building between us. Leo absently rubbed at his cheek while staring at the floor, and my stomach twisted painfully when I recalled the last time we spoke.

"Danesi . . ."

He whipped his gaze up to mine. The anticipation in his face made my tongue stick to the roof of my mouth. Apologizing didn't come easy for me, but I had to do it.

Finally, I cleared my throat. "I'm sorry for what I said to you at school. You were trying to help, and I got scared of everyone finding another reason to think I was weak. You didn't deserve that."

"Don't worry about it. I shouldn't have said or done anything either." Leo crossed his arms, the muscles in his jaw flexing, as he leveled his gaze with me. "You're a better person than I am anyway. I never apologized for all the accusations I threw at you four years ago. What I said was cruel and meant to cut deep. I knew you had nothing to do with my dad's death, and yet I was so angry and broken, I didn't care if I lashed out at you. I'm not surprised you hate me now. That's what I deserve."

My heart beat faster. Through all the years of hurt and heartbreak Leo caused, I never expected him to ever apologize for it. Hearing those words now released the final snare holding me to that resentment.

"I don't hate you," I replied softly. "Not anymore."

A sad smile appeared on Leo's face. One that made my chest pinch.

"Well," he said. "I'm glad for that at least."

I pressed my knuckles into the cold counter, not sure if I trusted myself to say anything else. But then a sobering curiosity shifted into Leo's eyes. Probably the most sober he'd looked in the last ten hours.

"Is it true what you said at the grave site? That you want to take over your family's empire—Mafia and all?"

"My dad thought I could handle it," I carefully replied. "It isn't what I thought I was signing up for, but there's too much at risk to let it go."

I pressed my lips together, waiting for the deep lines to form in his forehead and a proclamation that I shouldn't want or fight for this. Instead, Leo shrugged and nodded.

"Makes sense to me. You've always had that murderous glint in your eyes; why not put it to good use?"

I swatted him with a nearby tea towel, but inside, my chest warmed from his response. He actually believed I was capable. It was more than I could say for some people.

"My mom wants me to take over ours one day," Leo admitted. He leaned against the counter, crossing his arms. It accentuated his toned biceps before I quickly looked back up at the profile of his face. "I could ignore her pushiness when I was in California, but I can't anymore. She's been trying to get me to do things for her since I got back. I hate it."

I studied him. It was likely the alcohol making him open up to me, but I was too interested in this new detail to care. "If you hate it, why don't you tell her that?"

"I have. She doesn't care."

That wasn't surprising. Sloane Danesi had always been the most stubborn woman I'd ever met. When she set her sights on something, there was no stopping her from getting it. It was why I used to aggravate her; she couldn't handle that same stubborn streak in someone else.

"Thank you for coming to the funeral by the way," I said. "I didn't get a chance to tell you since you disappeared right after, but it...meant a lot. You had every right not to be there."

Leo looked down at the floor. "I know."

Silence stretched out. My thoughts went back to the car ride I had with Victor when I demanded to know the truth of Angelo Danesi's death. I still didn't know the full extent of what happened. What Leo was forced to experience.

And maybe it was wrong to take advantage of his drunken state, but I really wanted to know.

"I know you weren't lying about how your dad died," I said.

He looked at me, the rise and fall of his chest deepening. "Do you?"

I swallowed, nodding. "Tell me your side of it. What you witnessed."

Leo searched my face. It was a risk, being bold with my request. Leo already shut me out once and he could easily do it again. But finally, he spoke.

"We were...on our way home from the Yankees game. It was the two of us if you don't count our security. Everything went down at a red light just before Connecticut's border." Leo paused. He squeezed his knuckles and the color in his face paled. I almost scrambled to find a bucket for him to be sick in when he continued. "Dad...Dad was shot four times in the chest before he could reach for his gun. All his security were taken down, too. I hid under the dash until the gunfire stopped...watching his blood soak his shirt. I thought I was next."

My heart pounded against my rib cage. It was one thing to hear Victor tell me the blunt facts of what happened and a whole other to hear it in detail from the lips of the boy who was there.

"You knew it was my dad who ordered the hit," I said. "How?"

"The bullets," Leo replied. "I picked one of them up off the road. It had a lion etched into it. Your dad showed them to me once. Talked proudly about how he had a guy who made them in the thousands. And then he ruined my life with them."

"I didn't believe you," I murmured. "For a long time."

Leo pushed off the counter, locking his eyes on mine. "I know that, too."

With the intense way he watched me, I nearly forgot he came over here drunk out of his mind. Not until he swayed too much to the right and went tumbling to the floor.

I jumped forward to catch him and regretted it instantly. Leo took me down with him and we smacked onto the tiles in a heap of tangled limbs. I groaned when a shot of pain went straight up my back. It took me a minute to realize Leo was half on top of me and made no attempt to move.

"Get *off* me!" I shoved my sock-covered feet at his torso, making an inch of progress.

He listened—sort of. Leo hauled himself into a sitting position, but instead of completely shifting away, he grabbed my left ankle and started massaging it gently. He wouldn't look up or speak as he did it, putting me into a brief trance.

"Danesi," I said, trying to keep my voice level. "Let me go."

Finally, he did. I scrambled to my feet and ignored my skin going flush underneath my clothes. Leo gingerly stood up as well.

"You've been here too long," I said, grabbing an electrolyte drink from the fridge and handing it to him. "Here's your to-go gift. You're going to need it."

"Wait!" Leo exclaimed when I hurried to the closed door. "I *did* come here for a specific reason. I learned some stuff about Salvator."

Now he had my attention. I turned, narrowing my eyes. "What did you find?"

"They're working with Ivan Romano," he replied. "I went to his store and he confirmed it. Took buying one of his insanely priced items though. I think the Salvators could be a new criminal family, and Ivan is one of their middlemen."

A shockwave went through me, but I quickly recovered. *Finally*, we had something to work with.

Leo rubbed the back of his neck. "I don't know where we go from here though. It's not like he'll lay out all his secrets. I think he's using the store to smuggle things in for them since he wouldn't show me all their products or tell me who's running the company. He mentioned a lot of his customers are connected to my family, and obviously, I saw Carter talking to him. I don't know anyone who's close to us who doesn't have some type of shady background themselves."

"We don't need him to tell us anything," I replied as an idea formed. "Because we can break in and find those secrets for ourselves. Did you see a computer? An external hard drive?"

"Yeah," Leo replied hesitantly. "But if we do successfully break in without getting caught, how are we supposed to get into his computer? I doubt he's the type to use his birthday as a password."

I smirked and put my hand on the doorknob. "You don't need to worry about that, because I know how to hack into any hard drive."

A deep line formed between his brows. "Am I supposed to believe that?"

I shaped my mouth into a perfect circle, feigning mock offense. "Such little faith, Danesi. You shouldn't question the determination of a teenage girl with a grudge."

Leo sighed. "Fine. I'll believe you. When are we doing this?"

"Tonight," I replied. "Assuming you marathon through the worst of your hangover. As long as we're careful and quiet, we can get in and out as quickly as possible."

A slow, mocking smirk appeared on his face. "I don't hear girls say that to me very often. Usually, they like to take things slow before any action."

I curled my lip up at him and scoffed. "Oh my God, are you still fourteen? I'd rather make out with a dissected frog in the science lab before I did anything with you."

"Interesting," he replied, cracking the drink open and taking a long swig. "You *would* do something with me."

I flashed him my best venomous glare despite a wave of goose bumps snaking down my skin. It was from too many sleepless nights. Nothing more.

"You'll pick me up," I said, bringing the conversation back to where it was *supposed* to be. "I'll send you the details. But you have to promise you won't freak out when I show you how I'm going to hack in."

Leo rubbed at his mouth, wiping away the smirk he'd given me like it was lipstick.

"Sure, Nicastro. I'll be there."

We lingered for a breath longer. I snapped us free by opening the door and checking to make sure the rest of the house was still asleep before gesturing for him to follow me back to the window. He got in through there and he could see himself out the same way.

When Leo was back outside and had slipped out of sight, I closed the window and pulled out my phone.

I wasn't some secret computer genius, coding in my spare time and using the dark web to figure out how to hack into any laptop. I had better things to do with my time.

What I had were connections. And while Leo and I promised we wouldn't rope anyone else into this investigation, I couldn't let this prime opportunity pass us by.

I went to my messages and found the name I was looking for. Typing in a new text, I hesitated for a second before hitting send.

Ravi, it said. I need your help.

Tasha

"YOU'RE REALLY SERIOUS ABOUT THIS," LEO SAID AS WE QUIetly locked his mother's black Cadillac.

We were three blocks away from Ivan Romano's antique store. I zipped up my dark hoodie right to my collarbone and pulled my hair into a tiny ponytail. Security cameras would be everywhere inside the store, so I'd sent instructions to wear dark clothes and a face mask for when we broke in. Neither of us needed to be on the news tomorrow, or worse, have a group of unsavory visitors at our doors later.

"Why wouldn't I be?" I replied, pulling on black gloves and throwing him a pair, too. "Do you think I make a hobby of breaking and entering into alleged mob fronts?"

The edge of Leo's mouth kicked up in a grin. "You have the face for it."

I turned away, not sure if I wanted to smile or smack him for that comment.

My mother knew I was out with Leo. I'd told her as much so she would help me sneak out of the house and avoid my security team. She gave me a knowing smile and promised to make up a good excuse for Victor. I didn't have much of a choice and accepted it, not questioning her ability for my own peace of mind.

"Come on," I said. "We don't want to be late."

"Late for what?" Leo said as we speed-walked to the store's back entrance. He'd gotten over his drunken bender surprisingly fast, but I still caught him rubbing his forehead a few times and grimacing when we hit some bumps on the way here. "No one's expecting us."

I winced. It *might* have slipped my mind to tell him we weren't going into this break-in alone. Deliberately.

"Actually"—I tilted my head to the side—"someone is."

Leo stopped. I could already see in my mind's eye the horror on his face, the slump of betrayal in his lean muscles.

"*What?*" he exclaimed. "We said this would stay between us. Who else did you invite?"

I shushed him and hopped over the fence leading into the parking lot behind Ivan's store.

I'd told Ravi as much as he needed to know. Details like why I was searching for answers and why Leo was involved, the suspicions that made me want to break into the store. I told him about how it was potentially linked to the mob, though I kept out the parts where my father had ties to the underground world and had saddled me with them, too.

My window for warning Leo and explaining my choice closed fast when Ravi stepped out from behind a parked van.

"She invited me," Ravi replied coolly, his green eyes flashing in the darkness.

Leo growled out a slew of swear words as he followed me over the fence and up to my ex-boyfriend. I instinctively put myself between them and raised my hands up midway. I'd planned for Leo to be upset, but I had *not* expected him to bleed venom all over the damn concrete.

"Are you kidding me, Nicastro?" he snapped. "Of all the people, you told *him* about this?"

Ravi's already strained expression hardened into stone. "Don't talk to her that way."

"*Shut up*, you two," I hissed, eyeing our surroundings. Downtown Rye was quieter than the dead at this time of the night; any noise we made was an orchestra. "I asked Ravi to come for a good reason. He can help us hack into Ivan's hard drive." My gaze met Ravi's, immediately creating a small smile on his lips. "And I trust him. He knows how important this is to me."

If a person could be a frown, Leo would be one. His forehead knotted with wrinkles as he grumbled out a reply. "He has 'bad idea' written all over him."

"I said the same thing about you," Ravi replied.

I rolled my eyes at their dagger-glares, pointing at the backpack slung over Ravi's shoulder. "Enough. We're doing this as a team. Ravi, show him why you're our tech guy."

Ravi unzipped his backpack and pulled out a small silver device with a black cord attached to it.

"What's that?" Leo asked.

"A piece of tech Aurora Technology uses on the daily for our clients," Ravi replied. "It lets them get into any computer even when there's intense security protecting it. We sell to mostly legal groups trying to retrieve evidence or monitor dangerous criminals. Though my mother also uses it on every new romantic interest my siblings or I bring home to make sure they're not hiding something."

I groaned. "I remember that special first meeting. My dad was *not* pleased when she tried it on my phone."

Ravi blushed and let out an awkward chuckle. "She's extreme, but it's worked. That's how we found out one of my sister's new boyfriends was a conman from Sweden who scammed millions out of girls he met at prestigious events."

"I'm sure your family is a load of fun at parties," Leo replied.

My throat went dry. That used to be an exciting story the Ferreiras worked into every conversation. I used to find it hilarious, but all I could think about was how differently his family would view me if they knew the truth about mine. They wouldn't want me anywhere near their son.

I shook those thoughts away, focusing on the quiet, dark surroundings and the two hormone-fueled boys who'd gone back to glaring at each other.

"Come on," I said, flicking my wrist. "Let's get in and out as fast as possible. I'm sure there are alarms that'll sound when we break in."

Leo and Ravi silently nodded and the three of us secured our masks.

The back door was locked—unsurprising—but with three swift kicks at the handle, it broke loose.

I snapped my attention to the guys. "Okay, the timer's started. Let's go."

The inside of the store was stiff with silence. It took a few seconds for my eyes to adjust to the thick darkness. Once they did, I was glad I waited. Hoards of old, dusty items consumed most of the floor, making it nearly impossible to walk through without risking a cacophony of noise erupting.

"Why's there no alarm blaring?" Leo whispered. He took the lead and trailed through the expensive mess like he was intimately aware of the space.

I glanced up to the ceiling, spotting two security cameras. "There is one, but we can't hear it. If my suspicions are correct, we have fifteen minutes max before someone swarms this place—and it may not be the police."

Ravi's eyes went wide, and I could practically hear the thoughts racing through his head.

But we didn't have time to linger. I followed Leo to the office and carefully maneuvered around the dozen life-sized Greek and Roman statues spilling out.

The desktop screen came to life at Leo's touch, prompting a password immediately. Ravi got to work, and after a breathless minute, the screen shifted, blessing us with the home page.

I released a rush of air. "Okay, we need to find names of Ivan's customers and if they have any link with the company Salvator. If there's any mob connections, I want to find them."

Ravi got to work searching through the computer's folders, pulling up files with sheets of data none of us had time to read, and typing in key words that might speed up our search. My palms were coated in sweat, beads of it forming along my hairline with each second that ticked by.

"Stop!" Leo jabbed a finger at a file labeled SALVATOR. "There! That should have names!"

Ravi double-clicked the file, opening a spreadsheet of data with names of customers, items they purchased, and prices.

I started scanning the spreadsheet in a frenzy, my eyes glossing over names and orders without fully absorbing what I was reading. But as I continued to go through the columns, that frenzy deflated.

"This is a normal log of things Ivan's sold to customers that he's gotten from Salvator," I said.

Leo squinted at the screen, his lips pressing close together. "It is. I don't recognize any of these names from my family's circle either. They're just regular people."

"We can't spend long looking," Ravi said, glancing at the front doors. "Are you sure this group is connected to the mob? I've never heard of them."

"Why would you?" I replied.

Ravi stayed quiet.

"Maybe Ivan has a separate log for their black-market orders," Leo said. "He's gotta keep a tighter eye on how much and how often those items come in and out of his store. The file wouldn't be labeled obviously either."

He was right. I considered the details I knew about the Salvators, how a criminal family liked to use a symbol to represent them, until an idea hit me. "Look up the words *La Colombe*. It means dove in French."

My guess paid off. Ravi typed in the two words and up popped a file under the name immediately where a shorter, but more detailed, list of names appeared.

Ravi sucked air in through his teeth. "Damn. Here it is. What do you want to do with this information?"

I pulled out my phone. "The fastest option is to snap pictures of the entire spreadsheet and review it later."

Carefully, I got to work taking as many photos as possible while Ravi slowly scrolled through. They were titled vaguely, like "Maiden" or "17th Century," making it difficult to figure out what these goods were.

"What is it?" Leo asked, when I instructed Ravi to pause.

I squinted to make sure I was reading everything correctly. Somehow, I was. "This isn't only showing the prices of these weirdly described secret items. It's showing the sums of money Ivan *sent* to people." And those sums were in the high six figures. Some cresting into seven or eight. "A store doesn't send customers money. I would assume even when they're dealing in illegal goods."

"They aren't supposed to." Leo propped his hand against the desk and leaned closer. "Especially not to men like Tobias Green."

I inhaled sharply. Tobias Green had been sent fifteen million dollars in installments over the past year.

Why was Scarlett's father, the owner of a pharmacy chain, receiving that kind of money from an art dealer?

Seeing his name lifted a film from my eyes. Suddenly, I was seeing more familiar names on the list. Police chiefs my father had invited to parties, business tycoons who donated hoards of money to charity galas I attended, high-powered lawyers my father had worked with. A quick search on my phone revealed many of the other names came from heads of major hospitals and border patrol. No one I looked up had a simple background or job. There was a pattern, creating a web that filled me with more dread the longer I connected each string.

But the real shock came from a name near the bottom of the list. A name that reinforced my suspicions and shed any doubt I had.

"There it is," I whispered.

Julian Henderson.

Unlike many of the other names, he *gave* money to Salvator through Ivan. A whopping amount that couldn't be for a bunch of these dusty old things. Julian wasn't a man who collected antiques or old art. He preferred to have everything new, throwing out items that bored him without any guilt or hesitation. Once, I caught him throwing out his toothbrush after a single use. I later learned from Amelia he had a "quirky habit" of never using a toothbrush more than once.

He sent the money for another reason. Now he was toying with us, hiding out God knows where, evading all of Victor's searches. I was sick of his games and wanted answers. It was about time I got them out of his smug little mouth myself.

"This has to be bribe money," Ravi said, snapping me out of the heated plan forming in my mind. "Which makes the chances that this store is a front for money laundering or something darker much higher. I can't believe some of the names on this list. Whoever this Salvator group is, they're not playing in the small leagues."

A dark look passed over Ravi's face, but I was too busy grabbing a photo with Julian's name in center focus to care. The more I saw, the more I was convinced they were a lot more than a simple art dealership. Leo's assumptions had to be right. The Salvators must be a criminal family violently manipulating us from the shadows.

"I can't believe this. I need to talk to Scarlett," Leo said.

He stepped back while still staring at the computer, hands on his head. I watched in horror as he *kept* moving backward, oblivious to our tight surroundings, directly into one of the statues.

"*You idiot!*" I shouted.

I lunged to try and stop it from tipping over, but it was too late. The statue fell to the floor and cracked open like a fresh egg, spilling its contents over the hardwood.

Wait.

I inched forward to get a better look, my breath catching when I realized what I was staring at.

Leo swore. "That thing is filled with drugs."

He was right. I picked up one of the hundreds of small plastic bags filled with capsules and round white pills.

I whipped my head up and pointed to a large Japanese vase sitting on the ground. "Break that one," I told Leo.

His eyes went wide. "You're kidding?"

"*Do it.*"

Thankfully, he listened and edged over, careful not to touch anything else. With a grip on the neck, he picked it up and gave it one good whack on the floor.

All three of us winced at the loud crack, but it was worth its sacrifice when more of the tiny bags poured out.

Leo bent down, wiggling free a wide chunk of the white interior. "They put in a fake wall to hide them."

Which meant one thing.

"They're working with Ivan to bring illegal goods into the country," I said. "And they're using this 'rare art' to smuggle everything in."

Suddenly, Ravi was on his feet, ripping his family's hacking device out of the computer. "We need to get out of here *now*."

I dropped the plastic bag and flew to my feet. Through the glass walls, the silhouette of a man threw open the front door.

"*Shit*," Leo hissed. "That has to be Ivan."

Without hesitation, we raced out of the office, not caring what items we sent crashing to the ground.

Ivan roared, throwing every colorful word he could think of at us as he tried to catch up. I hurled myself past all the antiques until the door was within sight, but just before I reached the cold air of freedom, a heavy thud and moan sounded behind me.

I spun around. Ravi was right behind me, but Leo's feet had gotten caught up in a chandelier, sending him to the ground.

Ravi gripped my arm, his jaw severe behind his black mask. "Leave him!"

I saw the pleading fear in his eyes and read the thoughts that likely flashed over his face. *You don't care about him. Don't risk your life for his.* Maybe at another time, when I was at my angriest with Leo, I would have felt the same and left him there. But I couldn't do it, despite the huge risks.

I wrenched out of his grasp and raced over.

"Get up," I ordered, heaving the chandelier off him. "We are *not* getting caught because you suck at burglary."

Leo groaned as he pushed himself to his feet. "Says the one who put a flashing arrow above our heads by violently shoving her way out of here."

The bit of light from outside illuminated the space behind him, giving me ample warning that Ivan was barreling toward us.

Clasping our hands tight, I hauled us out of there, savoring the sweet feel of a shiver rippling over my skin once we were outside.

Ravi was already on the other side of the fence and waving us down.

We sprinted to catch up to him and down the street, throwing ourselves to the ground once we were back at the Cadillac.

I ripped my mask off, gasping for air.

"Damn, that was way too close," Leo said, pressing his head against the back tire. "But we got what we came for."

Hanging my head, I gulped in a final lungful of air to calm my breathing. "You're okay, Danesi? No sprained or broken ankles?"

He nodded, glancing at me through one open eye. "I'm good. But my hand is still questionable. I can't believe how hard you gripped it."

I glared at him to hide the fact that I wanted to smile. Leo on the other hand didn't try to hide his grin. We sat like that, me forcing myself to glare, him stupidly smiling at me. It took way too long to remember we weren't alone.

Clearing my throat, I turned toward Ravi. "Thanks for your help. We wouldn't have gotten anywhere without you."

Our eyes locked. Ravi hadn't removed his mask yet, but I didn't mind. Not when he looked at me the way he did. Like he didn't recognize the girl staring back.

"That was incredibly dangerous," he said. "If I'd known how that would go, I'd never have said yes or let you go through with it."

"Let her? Don't be a shit about this. You knew exactly what you signed up for," Leo snapped. "And she can handle herself."

Ravi glared at him before focusing back on me. His searing gaze made my chest ache.

"I know how important it is to you to find answers, but this isn't it, Tasha. Let me handle it instead. I can ask my parents to call in some favors to help find the people behind this organization. You don't need to put yourself in harm's way anymore."

My mouth went dry, caught between not wanting to upset Ravi and needing to follow my own instincts. One of us was walking away from this disappointed no matter how much I tried to find common ground.

Ravi was used to me giving in and letting him take charge of protecting me, but that was before my world turned upside down. I couldn't betray myself, the person I was trying to be, and give up control. Not this time. And honestly, never again.

"I'm sorry, Ravi," I replied with a shake of my head. "This is something I need to do and nothing you say is going to change my mind."

He tore off his mask, revealing a deep frown, and rose to his feet. "Then we have nothing else to talk about."

I rose as well, making a spark of hope light in Ravi's eyes. But whatever he hoped I would say wasn't coming. "I need you to keep my investigation to yourself. Can you please do that for me?"

He shoved his hands into his pockets, staring me down. "Why should I?"

I clenched my jaw. He was bringing out the side in me he disliked by forcing my hand. But I wouldn't let myself feel guilty for it. "Because if you do anything to jeopardize my search, I'll hate you as much as the people responsible for murdering my family."

Ravi's nostrils flared. He looked behind me before shaking his head and taking a few steps back. "You aren't acting like the girl I loved for three years."

"Because that was never the full me. All I showed you were the parts I knew you would like, but I'm not doing that anymore," I replied. "This is who I am and I'm not ashamed of it."

He held completely still for a long moment. I almost thought he would snap out of it and come back over, but then he faced away from me and melted into the shadows without another word.

CHAPTER
TWENTY-TWO

I STARED AT THE OVERSIZED WOODEN DOOR, ITS LONG METAL handle reflecting my sullen expression. I'd stood under this awning with its massive potted plants more times than I could count, waiting for the door to slide open and for Scarlett's beaming face to greet me. My gut had never churned with dread—the total opposite—but there was a first time for everything.

My gut rolled again as I reached for the doorbell. I squeezed my eyes shut and pressed it anyway. Here we go.

Scarlett knew I was coming over after school. I'd texted her in fourth period after debating all day if I should confront her about her dad.

In the past, our one-on-one hangouts always ended the same way. We'd exclusively date until I had to catch a flight back to California. Other than that one-off make out session, this was the first time I'd asked to hang privately since I'd returned. I hadn't asked to turn our relationship back on at my house, so I already knew Scarlett expected this to be the moment it happened. Only one of us knew this visit wasn't going to be like the others. All I could do was hope she wouldn't be too pissed off when she caught on.

My lungs rattled as I breathed in and out. Whatever happened, I couldn't let myself chicken out. Not for something this major.

The front door slowly swung open, revealing Scarlett beaming ear-to-ear.

"Leo!" she squealed, throwing her arms around my neck. "You made it!"

I hugged her back even though I couldn't shake the stiffness in my arms. She'd changed out of her school uniform into a low-cut top tucked into a silky, formfitting skirt. Up close, her perfume of sweet vanilla and orange blossom hit my senses. The one she knew I loved the most on her.

Shit. She really expected this to be our get-back-together day.

Scarlett hopped back, swatting me playfully on the shoulder. "You were taking so long that I thought you forgot where I live."

I gave her a closed smile. "Took the scenic route."

More like, I'd spent twenty minutes in my car wondering how I was going to approach the subject of her dad potentially taking huge sums of money from the mob.

Scarlett took my hand in hers and led me inside, throwing looks over her shoulder that used to rile me up. It would be easy to toss myself back into her arms—into her bed. After Tasha ambushed me with Ravi last night, maybe starting shit up with Scarlett again for a little while would put my head back on straight. Things had gotten too messy, too . . . close recently. I hadn't told Tasha I was coming over here, and it was nice to have a secret she didn't know about again. Especially after the blunder I made at her house the other day.

"You're here now," Scarlett said, pressing herself up close to me with a coy smile on her glossy lips. "What do you want to do first? Watch a show or . . . ?"

I pictured Tasha's face when I eventually told her I went to see Scarlett for information. How I'd let the air hang with the question if anything else happened while I was over there. Realistically, she wouldn't care. There was nothing between us, maybe there never had been, but a small part of me still imagined her lips pinching and the slow rise and fall of her chest as she tried to keep her breathing even. Wondering. Hating the possibility of what I implied.

But it was all bullshit. And frankly, I wasn't interested in being in any bed but my own today.

I stepped away from Scarlett, nodding toward her family's formal living room. "Can we talk for a bit?"

Scarlett pulled a flyaway blond lock behind her ear, a deep crease forming between her brows. "Um, okay."

"Great." I led the way as if it were my house. "Is your dad home? Or Yeva?"

"No, they're out." Scarlett placed a hand on her hip as I made myself comfortable in one of the armchairs in front of the polished stone fireplace. "Did you come over here to talk to them?"

I shook my head. "I came here to see you."

She planted herself at the edge of the blindingly white couch that took up most of the wide room and crossed her arms. "What do you want to talk about then?"

I leaned forward, clasping my hands together. There was no easy way to edge into this.

As the Greens' only child and miracle baby, Scarlett was adored by her parents. They'd been an indestructible unit when I first met them as a kid. Never once did her parents go somewhere without Scarlett tagging along or having her opinion listened to. They used to spend all their free time together that getting her to hang outside of school was a challenge. It was why her dad's affair and the inevitable divorce rocked Scarlett's world so dramatically.

Scarlett was more observant than most and her dad didn't deny her anything. If he was involved with the Salvators and Ivan Romano, she would know about it—and my hunch told me she did.

"I need you to tell me if you've heard of a man named Ivan Romano."

Right away, I could tell I'd caught her off guard. It was the reason her eyes widened and her jaw went slack before it was replaced with a fixed disinterest that people with secrets wore.

"Am I supposed to?"

I exhaled, keeping my gaze settled on hers. "Don't play this game with me, Scarlett. We've known each other long enough. Your dad is connected to him, and I need you to tell me why."

Scarlett searched my face. "I've heard of him. He's my dad's rare antique dealer. What does it matter?"

"You're still doing it," I replied with a shake of my head. "You're giving me half-truths. Ivan Romano is more than an antique dealer, and he has connections with some dangerous people."

"Where did you hear *that*?"

I kept my expression stony. "Do you really want to know, Scarlett?"

Thankfully, she didn't. Scarlett looked away, tapping her fingers against her knee before she let out a heavy sigh and turned back. "Ivan approached my dad at the beginning of the year to partner with him on this new project. Apparently, he needed people in high places to help him get it off the ground. My dad has always wanted to get in with the art and antique world, so he jumped at the opportunity."

She was still hiding key details thinking I didn't know enough to catch on. "Scarlett, come on. Can we be done with this dance? Because I'd rather we move on and start telling each other the full truth. It'll save time."

She huffed, rising from the couch to wander over to the windows. Her hand wrapped around a chunk of the sheer curtains flanking them. Silence hung between us for a stretch of time, tempting me to speak first, but I watched and waited for her to crack. I knew Scarlett well enough that eventually she would. The one thing she hated more than anything was giving free lodging to someone else's secret.

"You have to keep this between us." She spun around. "Okay?"

I nodded. "Okay."

Did I feel badly for blatantly lying? Sure. But keeping Sophia and the rest of my family safe was more important to me than maintaining my integrity.

And maybe I felt compelled to help Tasha get justice. Not for her dad's death, but for the devastating pain that had consumed her the day she lost him and her sister. I knew that kind of all-consuming grief far too well. I couldn't give her the kind of comfort she needed—she'd never accept it in the first place—but I could give her this.

"Fine. Ivan approached my dad to partner with a group called the Salvators. Ivan's their contracted middleman," Scarlett replied.

"Do you know who's behind them?" I asked.

Scarlett shook her head. "No clue. Ivan is the only one Dad has spoken to. He thought it was sketchy at first and questioned how legit they were. Ivan responded by telling him to ask for any type of art he wanted. Nothing was out of bounds. Three days later, an original Van Gogh arrived at our doorstep."

"An *original*? Aren't all those in museums?"

"Not all of them," Scarlett replied.

She walked past me to the doorway connecting the formal living room with the dining room and beckoned me to follow.

I did, taking one hesitant step after the other until we were standing in front of the long table, staring at a landscape painting of a sunflower field in the artist's famous style.

"You're positive it's real?"

Scarlett nodded. "My dad had it discreetly appraised. It's real."

I moved closer to the painting. I wasn't some art enthusiast, but I could still appreciate how momentous it was to have a work of art like this hanging in your own home. If the Salvators had the connections and power to obtain a hidden painting of Van Gogh's, where else did their influence reach?

"Why did they want to partner with your dad?" I asked, facing her. "The Salvators gave him this painting." *And lots of cash*, I wanted to add but kept to myself. "What's he giving them in return?"

Scarlett's throat bobbed. "You won't see him the same way if I told you."

My heartbeat quickened, because all at once I connected two questions together. Tobias Green owned Evergreen Pharmaceutical. And the sculptures Ivan Romano had piled in his store were filled with drugs. "He's selling their drugs, isn't he?"

This time, she didn't try to act naïve.

"Scarlett..." I ran a hand through my hair as I approached her. "Do you realize how bad that is? Your dad is using his legitimate business, a business people put *a lot* of trust into, to smuggle illegal drugs into peoples' hands. That's fucked up in a lot of different ways."

"Why do you care so much?" she asked, the question coming out clipped and accusatory.

"Because I'm worried about what this organization really wants," I replied. "I don't think this ends at drug trafficking and selling rare art as their front."

Not if the names on that spreadsheet were true. Tasha sent me the photos she took of the list after we'd gone home, and I'd spent a sleepless night researching every name. One pattern stood out more than any other. The Salvators wanted power across North America, and lots of it, with a titanium-made web that the law couldn't—or wouldn't—take down.

"So what?" Scarlett said, wrapping her shaking arms around herself. "It's not worth standing up to a group like them. My dad is far from the only one they've brought in. Ivan made it clear that we'd be safe under them and heavily compensated as long as our pharmacies helped their dealers sell the drugs as real prescriptions. No questions asked. So he took the offer, even though he ..."

"What?" I asked.

"Dad didn't want to at first," she replied after a brief pause. "He tried to give the Van Gogh back. He told me he didn't want to get into business with a group whose leaders stayed nameless but expected him to smear the legitimacy of our family business. They didn't like that."

Scarlett turned away from me, her fingers clenched so tight against her arms that the skin turned porcelain. I gently touched her shoulder, coaxing her to turn back around.

"What happened, Scarlett?" I asked quietly.

She hesitantly faced me again, her careful composure pulled down to reveal something she couldn't hide. Something that made me tense all over.

Fear.

"We found one of Yeva's greyhounds the next day floating in the fountain out front. He called to accept the offer before they went after her second one. Or worse."

"Holy shit," I replied.

She sucked her cheeks in and let out one loud, rattled sigh, but it didn't seem to help her shaking. "Dad thinks they've been around for a while and are now making their presence known. Whoever the Salvators are, they know exactly what they're doing and how to force people to comply."

Her story was too familiar and part of a growing pattern. How many other families were out there being threatened into "partnering" with the Salvators? I thought of my own family, what happened to Sophia. They must have approached Mom, too, and she turned them down. It would explain why she already had suspicions of who was behind everything. And why she was more concerned than triumphant that Gabriel Nicastro was dead.

"That must be what happened to the Nicastros."

I cringed all over the second I blurted those words out. Scarlett paused, staring hard at me, before she moved back into the formal living room. At first, I thought she might let my comment slide, but instead, she went for the jugular.

"Why haven't you asked to get back together yet?" She spun around. "Whenever you've texted asking to hang out, it's always led to us officially dating again. I thought it'd happen when you invited me over the other day, but you practically shoved me out of your house after feeling me up for an hour. This was also to get information, not to spend time together."

I stayed quiet, not knowing what to say.

"You know, there's a rumor going around that you went to the funeral. Before that, at the party, you were seen following her away from the crowd," Scarlett continued, her eyes searching my face. "Is it true?"

The muffled sounds of music playing from the kitchen floated in, pressing through the thick silence filling the rooms. I shoved my hands in the pockets of my jacket. "Will you believe me if I say it's not?"

She let out a dry laugh. "Unfortunately, no. I know you too well at this point, despite how little I should care about you after the way you've treated me."

My hands gripped the car keys resting in my pocket. It was something to do, somewhere to put my discomfort at the surety in her voice.

"Every year, you use me to hide from your grief, and every year, I let you do it. Even now, here you are using me, just with a different ribbon tied around it," Scarlett said. "You always dumped me the day before you left for California, and yet every time, I secretly hoped things would change and you'd realize what a good thing we have."

"Scarlett—"

She put up a hand to stop me. "I don't live my life around when you're home. I have friends who truly care about me. I've gone on plenty of dates with other guys. I have my tennis club and a smooth path to Princeton laid out for me. I don't need you, but I can still want you. And for some ridiculous reason, my heart keeps pointing in your direction."

An invisible hand clamped around my throat and made it impossible to speak. She wanted more from us, something I wasn't able to give. I didn't know what I could say that wouldn't hurt her further.

A relationship between us would always fail, because she wasn't the girl I truly wanted.

Her brows pressed close, but it didn't hide the shine in her eyes. "Can't you say anything to that?"

"I don't know what to say," I replied softly.

"You can answer this." The pain laced in the soft lines of her face tightened. "Are you still chasing a fantasy, or are you finally ready to come down to reality and be with someone who actually wants you?"

All I could focus on was my breathing as she stared at me. Scarlett never questioned where she fit into my life before. It made it easy to pretend the truths harbored in my chest were make believe. But now she toed a dangerous line. One that I didn't have the courage to cross.

Instead of giving her the answers she deserved, I pulled out my car keys and gestured vaguely to the foyer. "I have to go."

"You're a coward, Leo Danesi," Scarlett whispered.

Maybe I was a coward. But a coward was easier to be than a hopeful fool.

Slipping past her, I made my way back to the front doors with her disappointment following close behind.

CHAPTER TWENTY-THREE

THE TOUCH OF THE GLASS DOORKNOB SENT A SEARING PAIN straight to my heart.

The last time I stepped into Amelia's bedroom was the day she died. I'd avoided it since. But if anything in there could help me track down Julian, I had to find it. Yet every time I tried to open the door, the same pain flared up inside me, holding me back.

I closed my eyes and took a few breaths to calm my nerves. I couldn't spend my whole life avoiding this room until someone packed up everything she'd ever owned.

If she were here, Amelia would push me to go inside and encourage me to get one step closer to avenging her death. This was all for nothing otherwise.

With my breath held, I grabbed the doorknob and slowly turned it.

Afternoon light streamed through the bedroom windows, catching on the millions of tiny particles floating in the air and illuminating the ethereal wallpaper of delicate flowering vines rising to the ceiling.

I gently closed the door behind me and surveyed the room. There was the smooth white duvet with a Hermès blanket draped over the end, a slew of decorative pillows placed on the bed, the art prints she'd bought from every country she'd visited, her colorful shelf of luxury perfumes.

Time had stilled in here.

I breathed in Amelia's lingering scent, nearly convincing myself she would walk in after me, excitedly chattering away. That our father would call our names, a wide grin on his face as he gifted us sweets he picked up near his office.

Heat burned behind my eyes, forming tears that clouded my vision.

"For the love of God, pull yourself together," I muttered.

Scolding myself worked for all of three minutes. I moved around her bedroom, opening drawers and riffling through my sister's things while a dam kept my feelings at bay. There were so many beautiful, expensive things Amelia had bought or received over her twenty-three years. And I'd throw them all away, burn it in a big heaping pile in the backyard, if it meant I'd get more time with her.

When I got to her planner for this year, all my bottled-up heartbreak came pouring out.

Amelia loved to use physical planners. She had everything saved in her calendar on her laptop, but every year, she went out and bought herself a new planner to handwrite in.

When she allowed me in her room, I would lay on her bed and watch precision flow from her pen as she went through each week writing down her to-dos, her big events, her hopes for that week. I'd inspect each page like she was my student, admiring the small doodles she'd put in the corners and on special days like my birthday or our annual week-long trip to Martha's Vineyard.

I rubbed a shaky hand over my mouth. What was I thinking coming in here by myself? The wounds of Amelia's death were too fresh and deep.

Before I realized what I was doing, my phone was in my hand ringing the last person I should be calling. But my limbs had gone on an instinct I thought I'd buried long ago.

I tried to hang up, but my blurry, wet vision made me too slow. I bit my bottom lip as Leo picked up the call.

"Hello?" he said. When I didn't immediately reply, he asked, "Nicastro? Are you there?"

Sighing, I replied, "Yeah, I'm here."

"Is something wrong?" he asked, a hint of concern and suspicion in his voice. As if we didn't call each other every day way back when. I guess I would be suspicious, too, if the roles were reversed.

"Nothing...catastrophic." I blinked up at the ceiling. "I'm in my sister's room trying to find something on Julian."

A long pause stretched between us. I gripped the phone a little harder, hating myself for falling back into old habits. Could I *be* more embarrassing?

But then he spoke. And his words, the tenderness that came with them, pulled me back onto stable ground.

"Why don't you talk to me while you go through her things?" Leo replied. "You don't need to do this alone."

I closed my eyes and focused on my breathing, while my heart pinched at the kindness in his voice. I didn't deserve Leo's comfort when my father brought so much grief into his life.

"Don't give up on me now, Nicastro," Leo went on. "What have you found? Tell me all about it. *Especially* if there's some scandalous diary entries. Don't leave any of those details out."

I rolled my eyes. "You're disgusting."

His laugh set off a flutter in my chest, warm and soft, prickling across my arms. "I'm *thorough*. Can't leave any stone unturned."

Leo was teasing, but he wasn't wrong. I went to Amelia's desk and searched through her drawers and piles of books for her personal journal. Her bookshelves had two rows dedicated to her old ones, but she kept her most recent one somewhere on her desk.

"What're you doing?" Leo asked.

"Your little joke gave me an idea," I replied. "Amelia loved keeping journals. It was a daily ritual for her that no one else could read."

"You're sure going through them will help?"

I nodded, stopping myself when I remembered he couldn't see me. "It's better than rummaging through her walk-in closet."

Mostly because her scent was more heightened in there.

"Can't argue with that," he replied.

The journal sat nestled underneath a stack of wedding magazines and hardcover books. Amelia didn't stay loyal to one type of journal, but instead gravitated toward whatever design spoke to her at the time. The current journal was from Dior with the brand's vintage motif of a blue-and-white illustration adorning the cover.

I opened it, revealing more of my sister's signature handwriting in sentence form. The first entry was dated March of this year and was a few simple lines. Most of them were that way, giving a brief window into what Amelia was thinking that day rather than a long paragraph.

"Way to leave a guy hanging," Leo said. "Either you've been swallowed by a pile of clothes or you're reading through the notebook. Or is this a prank call I haven't caught onto yet?"

His voice made me jump; I'd forgotten for a minute that he was still on the line. "Yeah, I'm reading."

"And? What do they say?"

My eyes scanned two pages from June when she was feeling extra frustrated by the wedding planning and Julian's demanding parents. "Nothing that relates to finding Julian or anything to do with Ivan and the Salvators. Just a lot of stress about work and the wedding."

Maybe there wasn't anything suspicious about her and Julian's elopement. From the endless venting, I'd have gotten fed up and done the same.

But then I flipped the page and my gaze landed on one entry that made my breath catch.

"What?" Leo exclaimed. "Did you find something on Julian?"

I hadn't. Instead, I'd stepped on another landmine of a revelation.

> *Dad thinks he can spend his whole life making decisions for me like he does for all the men in his mob. I'm tired of being leashed to his gold chain and nothing but a pretty pawn. I won't let him do the same to Tasha.*

"No," I replied, my jaw sagging as I reread the entry. "But now I know my sister lied to me in more ways than one."

Amelia knew about our Mafia and never told me. From the way she carried herself around me, I never would've known she harbored this secret. This... resentment. But then, she hid her marriage from me, too.

"How?"

"She knew about the Nicastro Mafia, at least since June, and she didn't tell me. I don't think our father was aware."

Leo whistled. "Damn. Your sister was really an island unto herself."

"Hardly," I scoffed. "We leaned on each other for everything, even when we fought. I was her rock as much as she was mine."

A long pause carried through the line before Leo spoke.

"Are you sure?"

Sunlight streamed through the crystals hanging in my sister's window, casting colorful light on the gray carpet below. I stared at them as the silence of the room pressed in on me.

Amelia and I told each other everything. The painful, the embarrassing, the scary.

But this wasn't some irrelevant secret. Just like her elopement with Julian wasn't. Amelia chose to push me away by hiding these things while I went on believing we were still an unbreakable force. The truth pulled from the shadows possibilities I hadn't ever considered or wanted to believe.

Blood pulsed in my ears. "I used to be."

Leo sighed. "We don't need to linger on this discovery. What else does the journal say?"

I was grateful for the permission to move on. His encouragement pushed me to turn the page and continue scanning, until I neared the back of the journal and stopped.

My fingers grazed over a piece of paper hidden between the pages. It had the letterhead for the Carlyle, a luxury hotel in the Upper East Side of Manhattan, and on the paper was a quick note. I inhaled sharply.

> Thanks for a wonderful secret honeymoon, wifey. Can't wait to have more slow dances with you at our favorite place. —J.

"What did you find?" Leo asked.

Wifey? *Ugh.* Gross. "A note from Julian. He must've written it after they got married because he mentions their honeymoon."

"Hmm." Leo didn't say anything at first. Yet, somehow, I could practically hear the grin stretching out on his godforsaken lips. "Guess that's where they—"

"Do *not* finish that sentence," I snapped.

He chuckled, probably saying something else infuriating, but I didn't hear him. I was too fixated on the photo taped to the back of the note. It was of Amelia in a formfitting white gown with her hair falling behind her back, gazing at the camera with a bemused smile on her face.

There was one entry on this page.

Julian can be such a softy. He'd buy this hotel and live in it because it'd remind him of this day.

"Danesi," I exclaimed, pressing my phone close to my ear. "Drop whatever you're doing and meet me in downtown Scarsdale. We need to head to Manhattan."

Leo must've jumped up from his bed from all the rustling that came through the phone. "Why?"

"Because," I replied, holding the photo up. "I know where Julian's hiding out."

CHAPTER
TWENTY-FOUR

Tasha

"ARE YOU SURE YOU'RE READY FOR THIS?"

City lights shone against the fading daylight, glittering like a scatter of diamonds across the skyline.

I glanced over at Leo. His broad shoulders pressed into the driver's seat and his bicep flexed as he grasped the wheel a little too tightly.

"Of course." My gaze narrowed. "Don't tell me you're having second thoughts."

Leo nodded to my fingers. "All I'm saying is if you keep using that thing so aggressively, you won't have any nails left. Remember when you competed in that pageant and you didn't notice some were bleeding until you wiped it all over your dress? If you're too anxious, we should turn around."

I looked at my ring finger. Sure enough, I'd filed the nail farther down than the rest of them. It was an annoying bad habit I'd had for too long. I couldn't believe Leo remembered anything about it, especially the year I competed in a junior pageant.

"I'm not anxious about finding Julian," I replied. "I'm hoping my mom doesn't suddenly decide she's *not* okay with us hanging out alone and spills our secret."

Leo went rigid, the whites of his knuckles flashing. "You told her we were working together?"

"No, all I told her was I'm spending time with you again to get her off my back about ditching my security. She was fine with it and didn't ask for further context, and I didn't give it," I replied. Though now that I thought about it, what *did* she think we were doing each time I told her I was seeing Leo? Heat crawled up my neck and settled in my cheeks when I made a guess. After sneaking a glance over at him and seeing the same red flush tinting his skin, I knew he thought the same thing.

"And excuse me," I said, shifting from our current topic. "You said you couldn't make it to my pageant! How do you know about my botched nail disaster?"

"Yeah, I couldn't make it." He cut a sly look over to me before focusing back on the road. "But I got my mom to film when you were on stage, and I watched afterward. You never spoke about it, so I figured I'd help keep it that way."

I stared at him, appalled, mouth wide open. There were way too many avenues I could take with that revelation, but I wasn't interested in going down any of them. Instead, I put away my nail filer and watched the apartments and skyscrapers of Manhattan grow closer.

We reached the Upper East Side soon enough with the Carlyle sitting prettily on Seventy-Sixth Street. An American flag swayed above the carpeted entrance, while around the glass doors, black-tie security eyed those passing by, daring them to try and put themselves where they didn't belong.

"Pull over."

Leo obeyed, snagging one remaining spot behind a silver Audi. "What's the plan? Do we march through the front doors asking questions?"

"Something like that," I replied. "Find a place to park and meet me inside."

He jerked as if I'd slapped him. "Hold up, Nicastro, I wasn't serious. You shouldn't—"

I jumped out of the Ferrari and slid my sunglasses back on despite the setting sun. The hotel's guards quickly moved out of the way, giving a warm welcome. I held myself like any haughty, powerful rich person stepping into this hotel would do. That way no one would give me a second glance when I went looking for my wanted man.

I was greeted by a floor polished until it had its own reflection and the latest renowned modern art gracing the walls. Thankfully I'd stayed here plenty of times, so the layout wasn't foreign to me. Going to the front desk and asking if Julian was hiding here was out of the question. He wouldn't use his real name anyway. The only way to know if my hunch was true was to get a little creative.

I slipped around the corner and past the elevators, speedwalking down the hall until I spotted a staff entrance. I quickly pushed it open. Inside, cement walls and carts of dirty dishes replaced the vases of fresh flowers and moody lighting out in the lobby.

This hotel was frequented by celebrities and high-powered professionals throughout the year. Which meant confidentiality was tattooed over the staff's lips the moment they accepted the job. Finding Julian would be difficult but not impossible. What I needed was one employee who's wallet was too hungry to take the code of silence seriously.

A young employee rolled a cart of freshly cut bouquets down the hallway. Eyes heavy-lidded, shoulders sagging. A gold name plate was pinned to his pressed blazer with the name STEVEN engraved on it. A walking, overworked zombie. Perfect.

I stepped in front of the cart and slammed my hands against it. It lurched to a stop, nearly toppling the bouquets to the ground.

Steven jerked out of his daze. "Excuse me, miss. Guests aren't supposed to be back here."

I ignored him. "Is a man who looks like a Henderson staying here?"

Steven arched a brow at me. "A who?"

"Don't act like you don't know. Anyone working in a luxury hotel knows who the Hendersons are, and I know one of them is staying here."

A dicey but necessary bluff.

Steven hesitated. "I can't give out guest information."

Bingo. Julian was here. I could have done a happy dance but restrained myself to a small smile.

"Really?" I pulled out four thousand in cash and slid it over to him. I'd brought this kind of money for a moment like this. "Are you sure?"

He stared at the money for less than a second. "He's on the twenty-first floor. In twenty-one-oh-two, our premier two-bedroom suite."

"Thank you. Now stay quiet." A thought hit me, and I extended my hand. "Give me your access card."

His scratched at his wrist before shakily handing it over.

With the room and access card in my arsenal, I slipped back to the lobby. Leo could catch up later.

At the elevator, the door swooshed open, letting a family out and allowing me to move in. I steeled myself for what came next despite how much my heart pounded and my palms were slick with sweat.

On the twenty-first floor, I took the gun out of the holster hidden underneath my jacket as I tiptoed toward room 2102. If Julian was behind my father's and sister's deaths and tied to the Salvators, I had to be prepared.

I leaned against the door, listening. Although I paid off that employee, I couldn't trust security wouldn't come running up here anyway. Which meant I had to act fast.

I quickly texted Leo the room number. Then with a racing heart, pressed the access card against the door handle. The light turned green.

There was no going back now.

The door clicked open, but a stereo playing inside drowned it out. I moved into the foyer, stepping carefully through a bedroom first. Empty. Back in the hall, I padded on silent feet past the small kitchen and second bedroom until I reached the living room. Windows let in warm evening light onto the plush lapis-blue couches. The pillows were thrown out of place and drink stains covered the glass coffee table with garbage overflowing from the trash can. Clearly Julian refused to let the housekeepers in.

Immediately, I spotted room service laid out on the black table. There was no physical sign of Julian, but the half-eaten plate of dinner meant he was recently here.

My gaze flicked to the door leading out to the long balcony. It was the only area I hadn't checked.

With my gun unlocked and raised, I moved over and quietly opened it.

And there he was, leaning against the railing.

I cocked my head to the side as I stepped outside, my gun aimed at him. "Julian. So nice to see you again."

Amelia's fiancé—scratch that, husband—sprang back from the railing. An old fashioned dropped from his hand, shattering on the ground.

"You're a difficult guy to track down." I stepped farther onto the balcony. The wind picked up, sweeping through my hair. Views of Central Park and neighboring Upper East Side buildings surrounded us.

"Tasha, I . . . I can explain."

Seeing him here, in a woolen sweater with rosy cheeks and freshly gelled hair agitated a knot deep in my stomach. One I'd been trying to ignore. He was alive. *I* was alive. And my father, *my sister*, were lying in a cold mausoleum for the rest of eternity.

"Amelia is *dead* and you're the one who gets away," I growled. "Are you going to hop between hotels until, what, the problem goes away? Sounds to me like a coward with a secret. Or in your case, several."

He raised his hands slowly up to his chest. "I know, Tasha. I can't stop thinking about it. Every night I picture what her face and your dad's must've looked like in those final moments. It's like the bullets struck me, too."

I stepped closer, teeth bared in a snarl. "Don't you dare pretend like you have any idea what they felt. You fled and left them to die. And then I find out you secretly *married* Amelia before the hit, making you entitled to our money? Why don't you explain that one?"

"I know how it looks." Julian waved his hands in front of him, his face a groveling mess. "Amelia and I decided to elope one afternoon. She said how frustrating the whole wedding planning was and didn't want to wait anymore. After she was shot...I didn't know what to do. I was terrified I'd be next." He shook his head. "You have to understand that I can't come out of hiding to talk to the authorities. Not when the people behind Gabriel's and Amelia's deaths could come after me. I was supposed to be in the dining room *with* them! The reason I'm alive is because I got pulled away by a call from my dad first."

I watched him closely, reading his body language and the desperation behind his eyes. His excuse made sense, but it didn't mean it was the truth.

"Victor told me a guest saw you eavesdropping by the door that night," I said. "What did you hear?"

His lips parted, a deep line forming between his brows. "What does it matter?"

"It matters to *me*," I snapped before I reeled my anger in. If I wanted to get answers, I had to stay calm and in control. "Tell me."

"I only stayed outside of the room because I heard the two of them arguing. Amelia sounded pretty angry." Julian closed his eyes as if transporting himself back to that night. "Then there was a bang like a door hitting a wall before I heard the first shot."

In the distance, a siren blared. Julian's chest rose and fell as he waited for me to reply.

My gaze stayed steady on him, not allowing myself to even blink. "What did you do when you heard the gunshot?"

"I..." Julian stared at me. "You have to understand. I *wanted* to open the door, but I..."

"But you what? Ran?"

He didn't need to answer. It was written all over his pouting face.

I jerked my head toward one of the lounge chairs pressed against the brick wall. Unfortunately for him, this interrogation was just beginning. "Sit."

Julian lowered his arms. "How did you find me?"

"I'll be doing the questioning and you'll be doing the answering," I replied. "The hitman got into my house through the secret passages. Something few know about, but you do."

He stared at the gun in my hand, pulling at the collar of his shirt. Suddenly his knees buckled, and he fell to the ground, hunched over like a beggar. "I'm sorry, Tasha. I know you're not a bad person. Please don't shoot me! You have to believe I'm innocent."

And here I thought there wasn't anything more he could do to aggravate me.

I lowered my gun to get him to stop blubbering. "I'm not going to shoot you, Julian."

Julian paused the cry fest, peeking up at me through his hands. I bristled at the way he looked at me, recognizing a second too late I'd been played.

"Perfect."

Then he bolted for the door.

Hot anger flared through me. Oh, *hell* no.

I hissed, rushing after him. But before he was out of view and into the suite, Julian backed out again, arms raised.

Leo stepped onto the balcony, holding a gun to Julian's chest.

"Whoa, man, is the gun really necessary?"

"Yes," Leo replied. "Because she might not shoot you, but I will."

A shock went through me. At the wind sweeping through Leo's hair, his cut-glass profile, the darkness coating his soft eyes. He glared at Julian, all heat and poison with his gun molded to his hand. Like it was always meant to be there. A glove made only for Leo, waiting patiently for him to finally put it on.

It scared me to see him this way. How easily he fit into the Mafia clothes his mother wanted him to wear.

I forced my attention back to Julian and pointed my gun at the chair. *"Sit."*

Julian darted glances between the two of us. "Holy shit. Are you guys working together? Tasha, you don't realize the Danesis are likely the ones behind the murders. I overheard Victor and Matteo talking about an ugly secret your dad kept from you about— "

"They aren't behind it." I interrupted before he could relay what I already knew. Clearly, he was an expert in "stumbling upon" other people's conversations. I pressed my nails into my palm. This was officially aggravating. I came here for *answers*. "We have a common enemy, and all signs point to you."

Visibly trembling, Julian fell to his knees again, this time with actual tears streaming down his face. "I know you think the worst of me, Tasha. But I swear I had nothing to do with their murders. I loved your sister; I would rather die before hurting her. I don't care about some inheritance. Why would I? I'll have more money than I can use for the rest of my life."

That last part was true. The Hendersons' wealth was a major factor in why my father approved of Julian.

But it didn't matter how much money or influence he came from. His name was still on that list in Ivan Romano's shop.

"Then explain to me why you sent huge installments of money to a criminal group called the Salvators before Dad and Amelia died," I replied, my voice tinged with venom.

Julian blinked up at me, an indent forming in front of his left brow. "Who?"

"I'm getting really tired of this innocent act," I snapped. "Tell me why you sent money to the Salvators. Did you pay them to kill my sister after you convinced her to marry you sooner? Or is this group something you dreamt up yourself?"

"I don't know what you're talking about!" he replied, head shaking back and forth, hands trembling. "I haven't paid anyone *anything*, much less to kill my wife! I've never heard of these Salvator people."

Leo frowned when our eyes locked. Did I believe him? Could I afford to?

And if I did... what kind of larger truth was waiting for me?

"Did my sister have access to your bank accounts once you two were married?" I asked.

I didn't want to ask, but I had to.

Julian considered my question for a hair-pulling amount of time before he finally nodded. "We gave each other access to our accounts. But mine have all been frozen since I went into hiding. The only person who knows where I am is my oldest brother, since I need him to pay for my stay here and anywhere else I go."

My eyes narrowed. All I wanted to do was reach forward and pry his forehead open to see if what he said was true or a lie. Because if it wasn't, it forced me to ask a bigger question. One that had my sister's face plastered all over it.

Tears continued to fall down his face. "I'm trying to keep a low profile until my brother can get me the hell out of the country. You won't have to worry about me taking your family's money. I wouldn't if I could." Julian went quiet for a moment, his breathing heavy. "Sometimes a part of me wishes I never met your sister."

People shouted from the sidewalks and car engines hummed down below. On a nearby rooftop, a flock of pigeons cooed together. Yet all of it was a muffled echo compared to the roar in my head.

Julian ran his hands through his hair, messing up the pristine style. "That's the lowest, most selfish thing I can say knowing Amelia's gone, but it's the truth. I'm terrified of what could be waiting for me around every corner."

"It is selfish." My words came out quietly, my gaze and gun trained on him. "My sister loved you more than anything, and all you can think about is wishing you never got tangled up with her in the first place?"

Eyes puffy and red, Julian looked up at me and replied, "I'm sorry, Tasha. Amelia never deserved someone like me."

"No, she didn't." I lowered my gun. "Get up."

Julian's stare widened as he watched me put it away. "What—"

"Get in whatever car you have on standby and leave. I don't care where you go, but leave New York before I change my mind and let Victor know you're here."

I shielded myself from the emotions threatening to break me. Would my father have approved of this? Or would this be a disappointment, making him second-guess his belief in me?

Julian stared at me with his lips slightly parted. Then in a frenzied rush, he rose to his feet and hightailed it out of the suite. I kept my focus on the apartments across from us, as Leo slowly put his gun away in my peripheral vision.

"Why'd you let him go?"

I sighed, closing my eyes, and pictured the hundreds of times my sister reached for me. The foggy details of those memories now blended together, forming a kaleidoscope version that would slowly fade with each passing day.

There really was an infinite number of ways a heart could hurt.

"Because I got my answer."

"I can't say I'm following."

"He's not behind it." I crossed my arms and stepped back inside, heading for the front door. Better to get out of here now before the Carlyle's security arrived. "Julian has always been a terrible liar. I saw it when he faked the same interests as my dad. It was painful to watch."

I did one more scan of the suite, thinking of the note and photo I found in Amelia's diary. "When I said the Salvators, there wasn't an inch of recognition in his face. I would've caught it. Julian really didn't know who I was talking about."

Leo moved closer to me, his brow slightly arched. "Then why was his name on their list?"

I pressed my lips together. If Julian wasn't the one who sent the money and my sister had access to his bank accounts...

"Amelia did it." I wrapped my arms around myself. "Probably."

Leo sighed, kicking at the base of the door, and looked at me. "We don't know that for sure."

"It's a possibility though. And if she did, it would make more sense that she was targeted, too, instead of caught in the crossfire."

If Leo could explain away any involvement my sister might've had, I'd have accepted it with glee. But he stayed quiet, and I was forced to let my mind go further down this rabbit hole as we made our way outside, wondering just how deep Amelia's connection to the Salvators went.

Out on the sidewalk, a group of young girls kicked at a scattering of golden and rusted amber leaves with their schoolbags slung over their shoulders. A cyclist darted past, and a mom and daughter with Brunello Cucinelli shopping bags eased around the girls, laughing. Life went on. As long as the wheel kept turning for everyone else, it didn't matter how much my world crashed around me.

"Who do you want to question next?" Leo asked, sliding up next to me. "We could look into Tobias Green more. Based on what Scarlett told me, there could be something there."

I tried to get my mind to think of what came next. To get the fire in my core blazing, but it was snuffed out by the weight of the reality I walked out of. Julian wasn't our guy. He was just someone with too much money and a flimsy spine.

If I could find the person behind the Salvators, I'd get the justice my father and sister deserved. *I* deserved. And then there'd be no damn way anyone from the Nicastro Mafia would cross me. But all I had was a dead end and a pile of useless hopes.

As if reading my thoughts, Leo asked gently, "What's wrong, Nicastro?"

Without warning, my chest crumpled inward. It was hard to tell if it was his words or the way he said them that caused it. Maybe a mix of both. Whatever it was, I couldn't let myself fall into the emotions stirring through my veins and settling across my skin. It was wrong. Terrifying.

I moved farther into the blare of New York's traffic. If I didn't get away from this hotel, from my failures, I might scream.

"Hold up." Leo's footsteps struck the ground as he followed. "Where are you going?"

"I need a walk."

"I'll come with you."

Irritation bloomed through me. I ignored him. The layers of stone dividing Central Park's lush greens from the cobblestone street were a block away now.

There was no need for him to be so...*protective* of me. We weren't friends. We were far from anything good. And before the two of us watched my family get shot, nothing but a shared resentment of the other lived in us. Anything more wasn't right, not unless we both wanted our fathers' bodies to roll in their graves.

"Hey!" he called. "Nicastro, wait!"

At the corner of Seventy-Sixth and Fifth, I stopped. My cheeks burned as pedestrians gawked at us. I crossed my arms and turned to watch him finish jogging over.

Once he'd reached me, Leo ran his fingers through his hair, letting out a long sigh. "You shouldn't go off by yourself. It's dangerous. You don't have your security with you, remember?"

"I've been training with Victor to protect myself since I was twelve," I replied. "It isn't high on my priority list to worry about wandering these streets alone in the evening."

"It's still safer if we stick together." He pointed loosely behind him. "Why don't we go back to the car? Maybe get dinner at a place in the West Village I know. We can figure something else out."

I stepped closer to Leo. "You can drop the act. I know you don't actually care about me."

"Act?" Leo's lips parted as he stared me down. "Despite how we left things, Tasha, I would still be devastated if anything happened to you. That's never changed."

My body froze, the blare of a horn sharp in my ears, and a cold breeze lifting the hair from my neck. This Leo wasn't the one who swaggered into my party with a bottle of champagne trying to embarrass me. This version tempted both of us to go back to how things used to be. Maybe beyond that.

I could drop it. Keep walking until he gave up. The Met was across the street, its grand staircase basking in the glow of the sunset. But my thoughts tumbled out before I could stop them.

"We may not hate each other anymore, but that's where it's supposed to end. Now you're saying you *care* about me, too?" I scoffed, but inside my heart beat double time. "I don't appreciate the obvious lie."

Leo stepped closer, frustration flashing across his face. "It's *not* a lie. Are you really this stubborn that you refuse to see that I can care about you despite what happened between us and our families?" He paused, sunlight cutting across his face. "Or maybe that's exactly what you're afraid of."

"I'm not *afraid* of anything." I pressed a finger beneath Leo's collarbone. This was the way we were supposed to be, at each other's throats with a snarl on our lips.

But with one breath, the hardness Leo sheathed himself in fell, leaving nothing but a quiet tenderness on display. "You are. You hide it well in front of everyone else, but I've seen it before. And I saw it again that night when you were trying to stop your dad's bleeding. You were so"—he glanced at the ground and back up again—"vulnerable. You've tricked everyone, pretending to put yourself back together. But this isn't a broken arm you can easily heal. Losing your family has completely cracked you in two and now you're acting like a few stitches is enough to keep yourself together."

I should hate him. Scream that he had no idea what he was talking about, that he didn't deserve to still be fluent in reading me. But I couldn't make myself say it. Because everything he said was true. Despite the time that had passed, he was still the one who saw every part of me and accepted all of it.

A smolder appeared in Leo's eyes, and before I knew what was happening, he grabbed my hand and pulled me close. I forgot how to breathe as he pressed our clasped hands against his beating heart and brushed his other hand along the edge of my jaw.

"Maybe I'm an ass for assuming anything; I definitely was when I hurt you years ago," Leo continued, running his fingers up into my hair. "But I can't stop myself from believing you still care about me as much as I care about you."

I searched his face, my throat thickening with a range of emotions building inside. "Why do you believe that?"

Leo didn't say anything for a moment. I held my breath when he tilted my head forward to rest his forehead against mine, my entire body turning molten with each heavy beat of his heart.

"Because," he said breathlessly, closing his eyes, "every time I've been at my lowest, you've found me, even when I stupidly pushed you away."

My eyes squeezed shut along with his. I'd kept myself at a distance from everyone since the hit, terrified that any touch would shatter my scarred walls and make them collapse around me. But the comfort of Leo's hand covering my own, the feel of him so close to me, sent a coil of unexpected longing in my heart.

I angled my chin upward, letting my lips brush briefly over his. Electricity singed through my bones at the touch, a hint of what could come if I went all in. Leo arched closer, waiting for me to take us further.

But before I pressed my lips fully to his, I froze. None of this was right. How could I enjoy any kind of happiness when I still hadn't gotten justice for Amelia's and my father's deaths?

With a gasp, I ripped free of Leo and stepped back as if his hand burned. His eyes went wide, those soft lips I almost kissed parting.

Whatever feelings or thoughts I had were overflow from my younger years. Nothing more.

I shook my head, clenching and unclenching my hand. "You don't have any type of hold over me, Danesi. Stop letting yourself believe in fantasies or else you'll find out the hard way that I can be a heartless bitch when I want to be."

"We both know that's a lie," he replied. "You're not heartless. But you're scared of someone using it against you."

He was right.

The roar of buses, the screaming laughter of children, the blaring music from a passing car surrounded us.

But the sounds were hollow against the raw truths I was forced to hear.

"It'd be better if I was heartless," I replied softly. "Then I wouldn't need to live with all this pain."

Leo didn't say anything at first. When he did, his voice was wrapped in sincerity. "You don't have to carry all of it."

My chest ached. If only I could give away some of this burden.

But letting Leo in—a boy who already ripped my heart apart once—was far more terrifying than if he put a gun to my head.

I lowered my chin as hot tears suddenly pushed out of my eyes.

"Tash—

"No." I raised a hand, rubbing at the tears as more rolled down my face. I hated that he saw me like this. "I need some time to myself."

Leo stepped toward me even as I backed away. "Where are you going to go?"

The Met. That was the place I needed right now. With its hushed galleries and history woven in each piece. Where I could be with the art and feel closer to Amelia.

"The museum."

He nodded, like he understood exactly what the Met meant to me. Because of course he did. There was nothing I hadn't told him when we were close; all the walls I held up now were once nonexistent. When I never considered if he would one day hurt me.

"I can hang out here until you're ready to go back to Scarsdale."

Why did he have to make this difficult?

I forced myself to harden, to put up walls neither of us truly wanted. But I had to do this. "I'll find my own way home."

The hope in his face fell. "That's it?"

I let a venomous layer go over my skin like a callus. Leo's softened jaw and deepened forehead lines asked me to stay, but I couldn't risk knowing what came after.

"What else do you expect from me? We're not friends anymore," I said. "We're not anything."

The muscles in his arms twitched, but he didn't move to keep up with me.

"Don't go," he said, his voice low and hoarse.

I bit my lip and forced myself not to cast another look at him as I hurried across the street.

CHAPTER
TWENTY-FIVE

She didn't make it easy, did she?

My lips still burned where Tasha's had briefly grazed them—desperate for more. Since she left me standing on Fifth, I'd replayed our conversation and the choice we nearly made over and over again. She had been pressed close enough that her pounding heart felt like my own. The softness of her skin and her dark hair against my fingertips were better than I had imagined. Kissing her would've been the fatal blow to the volatile ground we already stood on.

And I had been ready to let it explode.

I parked and headed over to my favorite restaurant on this side of Manhattan. The faux bursts of pink azalea flowers covering the front entrance was unmistakable from two blocks away. A few couples hovered by the entrance, and the hum of chatting customers inside grew as I got closer. I should've expected another busy night.

Dad used to bring all of us here once a month. He'd make sure to clear his schedule and fill a weekend afternoon with fun things to do before we headed to our reservation. I would order the same thing every time, and Carter would make fun of me for it until Mom told us to quiet down while she sipped her glass of wine and held Dad's hand. Sophia would order something we all told her she was too young to like, and when we were inevitably right, I shared my food with her while she waited for her next option to arrive.

When I wanted to remember what it was like for my whole family to laugh—to be a rock-solid unit—I pulled up one of those memories.

The inside was a cyclone of enthusiastic people chatting at max volume while they sipped wine and put forkfuls of pasta in their mouths. I blinked to adjust to the dimmed lighting. An entangle of rich cooking smells hit me as I approached the host.

"Got room for one?" I asked, breathing in the mix of different sauces coming from the kitchen.

The host nodded, maneuvering around chairs and stressed servers in classic black-and-white suits, to an empty seat at the bar. At least it was something.

I took it and peeled off my coat then checked to see if Tasha had texted me. But there were no new messages on my phone. I didn't know why I expected any different. Or why a pang of disappointment shot through my chest. She kept to her word no matter what. I wasn't sure if I should be frustrated by it or impressed.

The bartender placed a tall glass filled with ice and soda in front of me before taking the rest of my order. I fiddled with the paper straw, checking and rechecking my phone until I was ready to dunk it into the restaurant's dishwasher.

Text me if you decide to take the ride, I'd messaged not long after she'd left.

We'll find them, Nicastro, another said.

Then I'd texted her something that reeked of desperation.

Any interesting paintings?

I groaned out loud as I reread that one. If I could hire a guy to steal her phone and delete that text, there was no price too steep.

It was aggravating caring about her. My head was filled with all the worst-case scenarios that could play out because I wasn't there to be her second pair of eyes. But I didn't want to be that guy who ignored her request to be alone, even if it tore me up inside.

I shoved my phone in my back pocket and let out a heavy sigh.

The restaurant was packed with families wrangling their kids and couples out for a casual date. My jaw tightened when I spotted one family with three kids teasing their youngest sister while their parents told them to be nice. The older kids complained she started it while the youngest glared. Eventually all three went into a sibling stalemate.

I missed that life. When no burdens weighed on any of us except for when I gave Sophia piggyback rides. When I could look across the table at Dad's humored face and assume this meal we shared would blur together with the many more to come.

I clenched my hands together and nearly turned back to my soda when a face caught my eye. A shock of surprise rattled through me.

Carter?

He sat at a two-person table facing the restaurant with nothing but a sbagliato cocktail in front of him. His ash-brown hair was slicked back, and the first two buttons on his shirt were loose underneath his navy-blue blazer. There was no one with him, but a half-full iced tea sat on the other side of the table. He stared down at his phone, totally oblivious to my presence.

My brows pulled close. What was he doing down in the city?

I slid off my barstool and moved over to him. As I approached, Carter looked up, startling, before he quickly recovered.

"Leo! What the hell are you doing here?" he asked, a sly grin kicking up the edge of his mouth. "Did you drag a date all the way to this place? Should I expect Scarlett to pop out at any moment?"

"No, I came alone," I replied. "I should be asking you though. Who's with you?"

Carter shrugged, twirling the liquid in his drink around. "No one for me. I got a craving for this place and decided to make the trek."

I rested my hand against the back of the empty chair, nodding to the glass of iced tea. "Do you generally order two drinks at once?"

My brother smiled at me. "You know I'm terrible at making decisions."

The server brought out my carpaccio appetizer, hesitating when he saw me standing over by my brother. I motioned for him to bring the plate over before I asked, "Feel like a dinner companion then?"

"Why not? For old times," Carter replied.

I pulled the seat out and lowered myself onto it as my server placed it in front of me. He blocked my view for half a second, but not long enough to miss the way my brother's eyes flashed toward the bathrooms as he stretched his neck side to side.

"Did you order anything?" I asked as I dug in.

Carter had picked up his phone again, his fingers flying over the screen before he looked up at me and replied, "Not yet. I was taking my time. Savoring the memories we have here."

The carpaccio turned into a hard lump on its way down. I nodded, scanning the bustling space. The ghost of my memories hovered at different tables all over the restaurant, but no one else would ever notice or care. No one else but Carter. They were ours to hold on to no matter how many thorns had grown since.

"Nothing about this place has changed," I replied. "I can almost forget what's happened. Like we stepped into a time capsule and at any second Dad's going to walk in and join us."

I met my brother's gaze. His ocean-gray eyes had sobered, every hard edge he wore like a weapon surrendering to the sadness he hid so well from the world. "I feel it, too."

"Do you miss him?"

"Every day," Carter replied. "Coming here fuels me. It's a reminder that everything I'm doing is in honor of him and the man he would've wanted me to be."

I nodded, about to ask what kind of man that was, when a deep, muffled voice caught my attention.

"Leo!"

The restaurant's noise was two octaves too high to be sure, but I could've sworn I heard him. Dad's voice calling my name.

I snapped my attention to the windows facing the street. There was a group of three hovering in front of a lamppost, but no one else.

It was impossible, wasn't it? That after all this time, despite what I saw in the car that day . . .

"Leo! Come here, son!"

"That's him," I said breathlessly.

Carter's face scrunched up. "What are you talking about?"

I sprang to my feet, throwing my chair back. I didn't have time to explain.

The restaurant was a blur around me as I rushed to the front doors. It was why I didn't notice a server carrying a tray of dirty plates until it was too late. Our bodies collided before I could pull back, causing an ear-splitting shatter when the plates hit the ground. The switch of the restaurant's noise flipped off immediately.

I should've stopped and apologized, offering to pay for dry cleaning and broken plates, but I couldn't focus on anything but Dad's voice calling my name.

I threw the door open and ran out onto the street, nearly knocking into another person. The light of the sun was almost gone, leaving a hushed twilight over the brick stone apartments lining the street and shedding trees.

"Dad?" I called, whipping my head around. I couldn't let him get away, not after so many years without him. "Where are you?"

A toddler's delighted screams caught my attention. He was across the street, his stubby legs trying to run down the sidewalk while his young dad chased after him. In a few long strides, the dad scooped his son up into his arms, burying his face into the nook of the toddler's neck.

"My silly boy," he said. "Were you trying to run away from me, Leo?"

I watched them until the dad put his son back in his stroller and they disappeared around the next street corner. When they were gone, I closed my eyes. The chill of the night air prickled the hairs on my exposed arms, but the hurt of it was nothing compared to the massive cave inside my chest.

It wasn't him. Of course, it wasn't. What was I thinking, running out here when I'd watched Dad die? I was chasing after ghosts, pleading with them to take me back to a time when I wasn't so broken.

I turned back to the restaurant, but immediately stopped.

Hurrying down the street was Val Costa.

I took a step forward, narrowing my eyes to make sure I was seeing her correctly. She had on a long black coat and a matching purse hanging from her shoulder with her hair wrapped up in a large clip. Her back was to me, but before she crossed the street, she glanced my way for one second, and our eyes locked.

She didn't register me, or if she did, she hid it well. I didn't bother jogging to catch up to her before she hurried farther down the street and disappeared. What would I say anyway? Any conversation with her would lead into dangerous territory of her finding out I came into the city with Tasha.

But what was she doing here? Had she come from the same restaurant as me and my brother or one of the many others lining the street?

I sent a quick text to Tasha telling her who I saw. Not surprising, that one went unanswered, too.

Some people looked at me warily when I walked back inside the restaurant. Carter stood near the crash site, talking to the manager. The two shook hands as I approached.

"I need to apologize," I said as the manager slipped back into the kitchen.

My brother shook his head, placing his hand on my shoulder. "Don't worry about it. I explained who we are. Turns out Dad saved this place years ago when Nicastro Developments planned to demolish it and the two restaurants next door for a new condo building. They've been grateful to him ever since."

That was news to me, but it was something I could see Dad doing. If he loved a restaurant, he was loyal for life.

"Hey, you remember Valentina Costa, right?" I asked as we sat back at our table.

Carter arched a brow at me. "She's Tasha's friend. Why?"

I pointed absently behind me and jabbed some pasta onto my fork. "Did you notice her leaving this place just now? When I was outside?"

My brother propped his elbow on the table and flagged a server down. "I was a little busy fixing your blunder to notice the mess of people coming in and out of here." Before I could say anything else, he turned to the server. "We're going to hang here for a while. Enjoy some of your best liquor and wine. What would you recommend?"

"Nah, I'm good, Carter," I replied. "I'll just eat my food and go."

"I'm offering to buy you a drink and you're turning it down?" My brother scoffed and faced the server again. "We'll have a bottle of your best red and two shots of bourbon to start."

"If I didn't know better, I'd think you're trying to get me drunk," I replied when the server was gone.

Carter leveled his gaze with me. "Leo, you burst out of here yelling about hearing Dad's voice. Clearly, being back here is making you go through some shit." The server brought over the shots and the bottle of wine. He eyed me closely before asking for my ID. Without hesitating, I pulled out my fake and handed it to him.

Once the server had returned it to me, satisfied, my brother picked up the shot and raised it. "I want to see you enjoying your life and not be wrapped up in the past. Dad would want that for you, too. Can you drink to that?"

There was no point arguing with him. Not after what I did.

I picked up the other shot and raised it, downing it at the same time he did. It slid down my throat with a satisfying burn, warming my gut and lighting up my senses.

"What are your friends doing tonight?" Carter asked a few glasses of wine—and beers—later. "You should invite them down here. I have to get going, but there's no point letting a fun night like this end."

I tipped back the last bit of my wine and pulled out my phone. The aftermath of my earlier embarrassment had stopped ringing through me, thanks to my brother.

"Not sure," I replied, opening the group chat I had with my friends. "But I agree."

Last minute party in Manhattan, I wrote. Who's in?

A grin spread across my face when everyone said yes.

CHAPTER TWENTY-SIX

Tasha

MY FORK SCRAPPED AGAINST THE PLATE OF RICOTTA SWEET potato gnocchi. I thought I'd eat in peace while I rehashed everything that went down tonight. Leo's forehead pressed against mine, his warm breath caressing my lips...

"That gnocchi must be *very* good for how quiet you are."

My mother pulled me right back to earth. I slid a glance to the high-top stool she'd planted herself on. Her arms rested on the cold marble with a bright grin spread across her lips.

"That's true," Matteo said from his spot at the breakfast nook. He sipped on his espresso martini, the trio of globe lights hanging above us casting a soft glow over his permanently cheerful face. "I've never seen you so quiet. You're usually passionately arguing about something or telling me the latest restaurant you want us to go to with Val."

I scowled at my mother for throwing me into the spotlight. She knew I'd been with Leo. I might've asked Matteo to pick me up near the Danesi house recently, but we never spoke about it again.

"It'd taste better if I didn't have two sets of eyeballs staring me down the whole time," I said, stabbing my fork through the air to point at them.

When they eased up, I seized the opportunity to check my phone. I braced for another text from Leo and sighed when my screen came up empty. Guess he finally got the hint. My insides rolled with each message he sent, watching his hope fade into desperation in real time, but I couldn't bring myself to reply. It was a habit of mine that Val complained about constantly.

Speaking of Val, I'd texted her once Leo told me he thought he saw her. I'd asked her what she was up to and if she wanted to hang. She'd sent an immediate yes and asked when she could come over. I'd made up some excuse then about my mother requesting one-on-one time and I'd get back to her. So that solved that mystery. It obviously wasn't Val he saw. Why would she bother lying about being down in the city?

I knew Leo wanted me to respond to his texts, but to make things up? *Ugh.* Cringey.

"I'm curious since you weren't home when I arrived," Matteo said, already breaking the stalemate of silence. He crossed his legs and tilted his head to the side. "When I asked Aunt Adriana, she said you were 'getting a pedicure with Val,' which I thought was strange since you hate people touching your feet."

I tried to catch my mother's eye, but oh-so surprisingly, she'd taken a new interest in the parmesan flakes scattered on the counter.

The damage control I was about to do though paused when Victor suddenly appeared from the front hall with Richard on his heels.

"We have a serious situation on our hands," he said.

I jumped up from my seat, heart going into immediate overdrive. "What's going on?"

But he didn't give me a reply. Instead, he disappeared back down the hall. Moments later, I heard the TV in the living room come on.

"There's a new *situation* in the Mafia every week," my mother huffed, making no move to follow.

Matteo jumped to his feet, and the two of us raced down the hall to catch up. I didn't know what I expected to find when I stepped into the living room and faced the TV, but any of the possible answers I could have come up with didn't prepare me for the news anchor's words:

"A car collided into a building near LaGuardia Airport this afternoon, killing the driver and passenger. One of the victims has now been identified as Julian Henderson, fourth son of the luxury hotel line, Henderson International. Sources say the driver of the SUV was chased off the road by another car before fleeing the scene. Police are still looking for the suspects and their vehicle. Those driving in the area are advised to be on the lookout for a black 2017 unmarked Dodger. If anyone has information, please contact your local police right away."

Hot, acidic bile rose up my throat.

Dead. Julian was *dead*.

I nearly stumbled as I tried to sit. Matteo was instantly at my side, his gentle but firm hands helping me lower onto the couch.

"This is a grim shock," Matteo said to Victor. "When did you hear the news?"

"About twenty minutes ago." Victor frowned, the lines on his face deepening. "Some of our guys were there to witness it. One of them got a sighting of Julian as he was heading to the airport and had a team ready to confront him. I was on my way, too, but once I got the call telling me what happened, Richard and I changed course to come over here."

"This was deliberate," Richard said. "We may not have questioned Julian in time, but we know he wasn't the mastermind behind Gabriel and Amelia's hit."

I put my hands to my forehead, the pulse of my blood throbbing on both sides of my temples. How could he be dead when I saw him just a few hours ago? This wasn't how things were supposed to end. I'd let him go to flee somewhere *safe*.

"Are you okay, Tasha?" Matteo asked, placing his hand on my hunched back.

I shook my head, lifting it to look at Victor. "No. I—I saw him at the hotel he was hiding in."

All three men's eyes widened in surprise, but it was Matteo who recovered first. "Tasha, please tell me you were hallucinating."

Heat flared through my whole body as I turned to my cousin and his concerned frown. This was *not* a conversation I had planned on having with them—ever. But I couldn't hide such a crucial detail when someone deliberately killed Julian hours later.

"I wasn't hallucinating," I replied. "I figured out where he was staying in Manhattan and went down there to confront him. He gave me his side of the story: how he was innocent and terrified that whoever was behind the hit would go after him next." I bit the inside of my cheek. "Guess he had a right to be worried."

"Tasha, I cannot *believe*—" Victor held his head in his hands, pacing back and forth, before he let out a frustrated grunt. "Do you have any idea how dangerous that was?"

"I knew," I replied calmly.

"And you didn't tell us? Aunt Adriana said you were with Val all afternoon." Genuine hurt passed over Matteo's face. "We could've helped you."

"I lied to Mom," I replied to keep her out of this. "I was worried Julian would find out one of you was with me and spook before I could talk to him."

None of them needed to know Leo was with me.

When that didn't satisfy Victor's outrage, I added, "I can handle dangerous situations. Isn't that what you've been trying to convince the Nicastro Mafia of?"

They turned to one another. None of them came up with a good enough answer to counter with, because they knew I was right.

"Someone wanting Julian dead meant he knew something we don't," Matteo said. He turned to me. "What did he tell you? Anything concrete we could go off?"

I pressed my lips into a thin line. "Nothing. He truly was in the dark. All he could tell me was Dad and Amelia were arguing privately in the dining room before the hitman came in."

I thought about everything else Leo and I learned. Should I tell them about Ivan Romano? The Salvators? And if I did, would they be grateful for my work or take it and turn me back into a bird in a gilded cage?

"He did mention an interesting name," I continued. "He said he thought a group calling themselves the Salvators might be behind the hit and that a man called Ivan Romano was working for them. Maybe it's a new Mafia trying to push their way in?"

No one said I couldn't use a loophole to give them information.

Victor and Richard's faces lit up, a knowing look passing between them.

"Our suspicions were right then," Richard replied. "We'd heard those names during our search, but couldn't find concrete evidence to follow our hunch."

Victor moved over to me, and I rose to meet him. He put his hands on my shoulders, a flush of pride appearing in his cheeks. "You've done well, Tasha. I'm still mad at you for putting yourself in danger, but I understand why you did it. Your father would be proud of you. *I'm* proud of you."

I straightened, blinking away the sting behind my eyes. I never knew how much I needed to hear those words until now.

Victor dropped his hands and spun around to Richard, the tender smile he'd given me shifting brutal again. "Richard, we have work to do before the cops mess it all up. Let's go."

The two men left without a backward glance or final word, leaving Matteo and me alone with the news channel circling back to the story about Julian.

"I'm going to catch your mom up on what's happened," Matteo said.

When he was gone, I put the TV on mute, but it didn't stop me from staring hard at the video footage. Cruisers were parked everywhere. The camera panned to an SVU crashed through layers of brick, but the center focus was on Julian and his driver covered in a tarp.

It churned my stomach seeing him like that. I never liked him, but he didn't deserve this. And yet, the Salvators pounced the moment he was out in the open. I couldn't understand why killing him was the best option when he didn't know anything. Not unless that was how they dealt with a minor threat.

My whole body went numb. He'd been in hiding safely for weeks until I showed up. Should I pretend that was a coincidence? Or should I acknowledge the ugly reality that the Salvators might have been following *me* and uncovering Julian's hiding spot inadvertently sent him to his grave?

If they had been following me that meant another ugly reality. Leo was with me. Which meant they would know we were working together.

I pulled out my phone and sent him a quick, blunt text.

Julian's dead. We need to talk.

I tapped my foot while I waited for his response. But nothing came, not even verification he'd read my message.

Yes, I'd ignored his texts for hours. But come *on*. This wasn't the time to get petty. We needed to figure out what the hell was going on and what to do next.

I groaned when ten minutes passed, raising my gaze to the ceiling, before I forced my thumb to press the call icon. The phone rang three times before Leo finally picked up.

Immediately, I knew he wasn't home. Club music thumped through the speaker so loudly I had to move my phone away from my ear.

"Hello?" Leo yelled.

"Danesi," I pressed, straining my voice to stay calm and not snap at him for being somewhere infuriatingly loud on a Wednesday night. "Julian's dead. It's on the news. We need to figure out what we're going to do."

"*What?*"

"Julian. Is. Dead!"

"Oh wow!" he said, still yelling, but this time with a slur to his words. "Sucks for him."

I balled my hand into a fist, lightly biting down on it to keep my composure. "Truly *sucks*. Go home right now. I think the Salvators were following us, and they could go after you next."

All I heard in response was a DJ hyping up the crowd until Leo eventually replied, "I'm *fine*. You can go back to staring at a bunch of naked people in paintings and stop worrying about me."

He hung up before I had a chance to process what he said.

"You idiot," I whispered, bringing up all of Leo's socials to figure out where he was.

I told him to leave me alone *one* time and he goes on a bender on a school night? The words we exchanged made me feel like I had swallowed an ember that hadn't stopped burning my insides, making me hot and agitated at the thought of him. While I didn't want to be anywhere near Leo right now, I couldn't let him drunkenly run around Manhattan when he could become roadkill.

Combing through Leo's socials gave me no hints. He hadn't posted anything all day, so I moved over to Scarlett's socials. If Leo was partying, then she'd be, too.

Sure enough, Scarlett made a bunch of updates in the past hour. She tagged the place on one of her posts—a club in Times Square known for outrageous events and bills that easily racked up into the thousands.

With a hard set to my jaw, I hurried into the kitchen where I found Matteo sitting back at the breakfast nook alone.

"Your mom went upstairs to run a bath to calm her nerves," he said. "I'm going to head out soon to help Victor and Richard unless you want some company."

"I do want your company . . . and your help," I replied. "If you promise not to say anything about this to Victor or my mom, I promise not to sneak out again."

Matteo's left brow quirked, but his eyes glinted. "Let's not make promises we know you can't keep. What is it?"

I placed my hands on the table, the molten ember inside me pumping new energy through my bloodstream. "I need to take a little car ride."

We stood outside the club, the thump of music pooling with the cigarette smoke from a group huddled by the door. The skin along my collarbone prickled from the cold night air.

I'd changed before we left to blend in better with the club's over-the-top environment, putting on a matching outfit that shimmered with a bralette top that sunk low.

"Are you going to tell me why we're here?" Matteo asked.

"Not yet." I grabbed his hand, squeezing it. "Please don't hate me, but I need you to wait out here."

He sighed and gestured toward the club's entrance. "Go on then. But if you're not back in fifteen minutes, I *will* be raising enough hell to embarrass you for a year."

I smiled and dropped his hand. Thank God I still had one semi-normal family member around here.

Getting into the club was far easier than it should have been. I sailed past the bouncers with a heavy stack of cash in both their hands, sinking deeper into the sultry shadows. The colorful lights of the club's main space hit me by my first step, giving me a clear view of the long stage in the center and the entertainers performing on it. Bartenders did tricks as they made drinks, getting whoops and cheers from the crowd when a lick of fire burst from one of the cocktails.

I scanned all the faces I could see, but they clustered together, making it difficult to spot Leo or any of his friends. Scarlett's video showed they had a VIP booth, so I pushed through the dancing crowd to start my search.

It didn't take much longer to find him.

Near the back of the room, Leo sat sprawled in a booth with his arms hanging over the back, a rich flush visible from the loosened buttons on his shirt. Empty bottles and glasses lay all over the table in front of him, the shine of spilled champagne and other alcohol soaking into the cracks. His head was lolled to one side, eyes closed, with hair sticking to his forehead.

No one else was in the booth as I approached, and the flair of outrage I clung to driving down here disintegrated. All I felt looking at him was a sharp ache. Without his smug grins and indifferent attitude to hide behind, he looked so much like the boy I once knew.

"Leo," I said gently, reaching over to shake him.

He stirred awake, blinking up at me with a glaze over his eyes. "Nicastro? Are you really here or did I take something weird?"

"It's really me," I replied, dropping my hand. "I need you to go home. It's not safe right now."

Leo's chest rose and fell. His gaze flitted over me, taking in my low-cut shirt and bare legs, but the look only sent a cold shiver along my spine.

"That's hilarious. Because you didn't have a problem leaving me alone on Fifth."

My jaw tightened, but I let the dig pass. "I'm sorry for that. And for ignoring your texts. I needed some time to think, but we really should go."

"How's that going for you? All that thinking?" Leo sat up taller, bringing his voice up, too. "Because I've done some *thinking* and I *think* I made a big mistake letting you back into my life. All you've done is stir up some shit I never wanted to go back to and use me as your little disposable puppet."

My body tensed. "I never went into this to use you. *You're* the one who pushed me away, and then forced yourself back in when you came to my party uninvited."

He grabbed a half-empty cocktail and chugged back the rest of it. "And what a stupid move that was."

I kept my breathing steady, not taking his bait. "What happened to you, Danesi?"

Leo leveled his gaze at me, the edges of his drunken amusement hardening. "Your dad came along."

His words were a brutal switchblade against my skin. Our eyes stayed locked on each other for a stretch of time, his unflinching.

"Whoa, why the hell are *you* here, Tasha?"

Jonathan and Scarlett appeared, hovering beside Leo like a shield.

"She's stalking me, obviously," Scarlett sneered, pushing her blond curls over her bare shoulder. "Why else?"

Our eyes locked briefly. Scarlett tried to smirk at me like this was all a game, but she couldn't hide the flush that snaked up the front of her chest. The worry that tugged at her brows. We both knew who I was here for. But unlike her, I wasn't in the mood to pretend otherwise.

I turned my gaze back to Leo's and the drunken sneer plaguing his features.

"Stay away from me, Leo," I said. "For good."

The cruelty in his face faltered as I said his name, but that didn't stop me from turning my back on him and walking away.

"Wait, I—"

But whatever Leo wanted to say was drowned out by the heavy music as I slipped farther and farther away.

CHAPTER
TWENTY-SEVEN

Tasha

I squinted up at the clear October sky through my sunglasses, zipping my fleece jacket right up to the top. Students milled around Scarsdale Country Day's campus. I waited by my Porsche for Val so we could go to a cute café downtown. It had been my suggestion, and while I did enjoy eating out, my real motive was to get an extra hour away from Leo.

He'd been trying to catch my eye in the hall since he'd sobered up last week, giving me the puppy-dog treatment as if that would work on me. I'd blocked his number and had been dodging him successfully, but the energy it took was wearing on me.

"How much longer do you think she'll be, Miss Nicastro?" Eric asked, surveying our surroundings like my personal watchtower.

I shrugged and checked my phone. Val said she'd be here as soon as she'd changed from her gym class, but with Val, soon could be anywhere from three minutes to ten.

Maybe if I hadn't been preoccupied, I would've noticed the pain in my ass striding toward the car.

"Nicastro," Leo called loud enough for heads to turn. "We need to talk."

My spine stiffened as he approached. Before he could get too close though, Eric and my other guards surrounded me.

"Hold on there, son," Eric said. "Leonardo Danesi, correct? I have strict orders not to let you anywhere near my client."

Leo barely looked at him, keeping all his attention trained on me. "I'm not going to hurt her."

That wasn't good enough for my security though, their hands positioned to get physical if necessary.

I was ready to throttle Leo for making a scene in front of half our peers. Already, anyone who was outside stopped what they were doing to stare, some with their phones out.

I should tell him to screw off. With this many witnesses, it would get back to the entire Nicastro Mafia that I let a Danesi speak to me. And God knows what he wanted to talk *about*. My father's soldiers were looking for any reason to question my authority and cement their belief that I didn't come anywhere close to his level.

My nostrils flared thinking about it.

To hell with it. Let them think whatever they wanted.

"Let him through," I commanded. *"Now."*

My guards broke apart hesitantly and let Leo close more of the gap between us. I crossed my arms, making sure I was ice cold.

Other students still hovered nearby like groups of cancerous cells, trying to inch closer. Eric and his team created a barricade though, giving us enough distance from the leeches to have a semi-private conversation.

"I already told you to leave me alone," I said. "And yet, here you are bothering me like it's the only way you can breathe."

A muscle worked in Leo's jaw. "I've been trying to apologize to you since I remembered what I said at the club. I was an ass—"

"That's putting it lightly."

"—to you," he finished. "I didn't mean what I said. I got in my head about my dad and let it get out of hand. I'm sorry."

I glared at him. "Oh, Danesi, you absolutely meant what you said. Your drunken mind brought it all to the surface."

He stepped close enough for me to smell his cologne. The ember resting inside me blazed to life again, sending goose bumps down my arms. I tightened my hold on myself, all too aware of our audience.

"Fine, you're right. I did mean some of it. But doing this"—he paused, gesturing from him to me—"*thing* between us hasn't been exactly easy for me. Your dad had mine killed, and I spent years thinking he wanted to kill me, too. That *you* somehow were in on it as well. A guy doesn't exactly get over that in a couple therapy sessions."

My throat was sandpaper as I swallowed. I didn't lower my gaze from his or soften my glare, but a coil twisted painfully in my stomach.

"Oh, I know all about that. I lost my uncle because of your family, too. Right after you told me I was the vilest person you knew and then never spoke to me again," I hissed with all the poison I could.

Leo shifted away, fiddling with his uniform's tie. It wasn't enough though. I wanted him to get down on his knees and beg for my forgiveness right before I stomped all over his heart.

"A lot of shit has gone down between our families. Between us." He wet his lips. "But I don't want to keep fighting. We make a good team. So, can we please go back to how things were?"

My breath caught when he looked back at me. His pained expression, the *please* he mouthed to me. It gave me whiplash when I was set on barring him from my life for good.

But he was right. We'd gotten this far because we were doing it together.

And maybe, somewhere *deep* inside of me, I still wanted him around. It hadn't been that easy to block his number anyway.

I tilted my chin up, looking at Leo through my lashes. "You are infuriating."

"Is that a yes?" Leo grinned.

God, he was really going to make me say it out loud.

"It is, okay? Now get out of here before Val shows up."

But Leo stayed rooted in place. "We need to talk about Val. You got my message about seeing her in the West Village, right?"

I rolled my eyes. "It wasn't her."

"It *was* though," he pressed, keeping his voice extra low. "And I noticed her right after I bumped into Carter, too. He was supposedly eating alone. Isn't that weird?"

I shook my head a little more aggressively than I meant to. "It *was not her*. I texted Val after you supposedly saw her. I asked her to come over and she enthusiastically said yes. She wouldn't have if she was in the city. You saw a doppelgänger."

"Did she come over?"

"What?"

Leo's face and voice stayed even. "Did Val come over to your house after you invited her?"

I twisted my lips, heat flaring through my chest. "No, I told her not to."

"Hm," was all he said, but I could've shoved him for the look he gave me.

This conversation was going nowhere good, so I snagged the opportunity to change the subject.

"I learned something *actually* helpful while I was ignoring you," I said, glancing around for eavesdroppers.

"Did you?"

I gave him a tight smile. "Scarlett told you Ivan approached her father at the beginning of the year, right?"

Leo eyed me wearily. "Yeah."

"That's where she lied," I replied. "A few days ago, my cousin let slip that Ivan wasn't in New York then. He was working up in Toronto until April for some hunting and fishing business that got busted for selling illegal weapons. Ivan left and moved down here just before the bust. So it *couldn't* have been him who roped the Greens in. It was someone else she deliberately didn't tell you about."

"And that person could lead us to the Salvators," Leo whispered. His lips formed into a hard line. "I need to find Scarlett."

I snatched a fistful of his jacket as he turned to storm off, pulling him back. Even though I wasn't truly touching him, a shower of sparks flowed up my arm anyway, going right to my beating heart.

Clearing my throat, I dropped my hand and glared at him. "Calm down, Mr. White Knight. You're not going to go charging after her to demand answers. You already did that once and clearly it didn't work out the way you wanted it to."

Leo clenched his jaw but stilled. "Then what's your grand plan?"

The minute Matteo told me what he'd learned, a plan started forming in my mind. Originally, that plan didn't include Leo and some light kidnapping, but I had always been flexible.

"You're going to ask her on a date to the Met," I said. "This Saturday. Have her meet you there. What she won't expect is I'll be there, ready to get real answers. The public setting should keep her from making a scene."

Leo wasn't convinced. "Are you sure that's a good idea? She'll know we're working together. I can ease into the topic when she's relaxed."

I shook my head. "No, you're too close. You won't be able to get a good read on her the way I can." I inched closer, lowering my voice some more. "Trust me, Danesi. We need to get real answers fast. With Julian's death, we don't know who's on the Salvators' hit list or what their next move is. Time isn't a luxury we have anymore."

And after this public display, it wouldn't be long before all of Scarsdale knew of the latest update in the Nicastro versus Danesi feud.

He searched my face. "Okay. I'll text her."

I wasn't sure if I wanted to say more or tell him to leave, but Leo made the choice for me when his eyes flashed above my head before he turned away from me.

I pushed off my car as Leo retreated to school and glanced behind me to see what caught his attention.

A familiar cobalt-blue Jaguar pulled into the private, Ferreira-labeled parking space. I watched as Ravi hopped out with takeout in one hand. His hair was styled differently, and a new pump of air was in every stride he took.

"Hey, stranger," I said, playing with the thin golden chain around my neck.

After breaking into Ivan's antique store and our heated discussion, Ravi had stopped reaching out. It didn't occur to me he was deliberately ignoring me until we passed each other in the halls and he hadn't looked my way. I'd spent weeks asking for space, and yet here I was, the fool who felt shaken when he finally listened. I never realized the influence Ravi had over me until I cut myself loose from him.

"Hey," Ravi replied, shoving his free hand into his pocket. "I was hoping to talk to you."

"Oh?" I kept my face neutral when really my skin seared. "What about?"

Ravi glanced toward the school, a frown tugging at his face. I knew who he was looking at, but I didn't have the nerve to follow his gaze.

"I've been thinking about what happened ever since we…hung out," he started. "And I decided I couldn't stay quiet about it forever. I love you too much to do that."

My spine snapped tight, waiting with rising dread for him to continue. "About what?"

His expression pinched before he let out a heavy sigh. "You mean the world to me, Tasha. And I know you asked me not to say anything about your search, but I can't keep pretending like doing this with *him* isn't incredibly dangerous. The Danesis have a shady background. Gabriel distanced himself for a reason."

My heart squeezed painfully. Ravi still had a rosy view of my father. Every time I withheld the truth, the guilt grew.

"I know you think teaming up with him is your best chance to find this Salvator organization," Ravi continued. "But I can tell you if you're ever in a situation where Leo needs to choose, he'll betray you. You shouldn't put trust in someone who's as weak as him. If you're really set on finding them, I can help you. I'll be far more useful anyway, which you should've known since the start."

The side of my head throbbed. "It doesn't sound like you have a very high opinion of me then."

Ravi's face fell. "That's not what I meant. You're one of the few people I genuinely respect."

"Then you have to trust I know what I'm doing," I replied.

A cloud passed over the sun, shadowing Ravi's face briefly. It made the smolder in his bright eyes heighten as he said in a low voice, "There isn't a girl I trust more than you, Tasha. But I can still worry. I spent three years protecting and loving you. I can't turn that instinct off, especially when you start hanging with guys like Leo."

I lifted my sunglasses up onto my head and placed my hands on my hips. "I'm my own person, Ravi. I don't need you coddling me like some child, and I *really* don't need you trying to guilt-trip me about who I choose to spend time with. We broke up, remember? And if we hadn't, you still aren't the one who decides what's best for me."

A flush burned across his cheeks as Ravi moved closer and took my hand in his. "You're right. I've been an idiot and promise to do better. Forgive me."

I sighed. Even with my blunt words, he still held on to the hope that we'd get back together. I couldn't fault him for it. For a while, I'd kept that possibility open by letting him stay close, but that door had now closed. Though I wasn't ready to tell him—or myself—why.

I raised my hand up to his cheek and cupped it, letting him lean in to my touch for a moment before I needed to hurt him again.

"You have to let me go, Ravi," I said gently. "I can't be the girl you're searching for."

Devastation shot into his eyes, but I didn't let it shake me. I lifted onto my toes and kissed his cheek. A final goodbye.

When I pulled back though, the hairs on the back of my neck stood up.

I wasn't sure what compelled me to turn toward the school. All that mattered was I did, my gaze passing everyone else and going straight to one person.

Leo stood by the front doors watching us. But when he realized I'd spotted him, he turned and hurried back inside with his shoulder blades pressed close.

CHAPTER
TWENTY-EIGHT

I fastened one of Dad's old Rolexes to my wrist, the platinum base nearly glowing against its gold counterparts.

A streak of morning sunlight pushed through my bedroom window, catching at the tips of my freshly buffed shoes. I'd already been up for hours, the anxiety of today's confrontation with Scarlett coursing through my bloodstream.

It was hard enough asking her to hang out, implying we'd get back together. Bitterness still coated my tongue. She ate up my bullshit without batting an eye.

Despite the secrets she was hiding, Scarlett deserved more than me.

Until Tasha gave the all clear to drive to the Met, I had to hover in this cold, large house with the new staff, Mom's unchecked guards, and my obsessive thoughts for company. And damn, were my own thoughts the loudest in this house. Especially when it circled right back around to the memory of Tasha pressing her lips to Ravi's cheek.

I should've known they'd get back together eventually.

Running a comb through my hair once more, I let out a frustrated sigh and headed for the door. If I was going to be a nervous mess, I might as well embrace it and chug some coffee.

The lights were already on when I stepped into the kitchen. The remnants of Sophia's and Mom's rushed breakfast before they left were strewn over the island, but thankfully, the pot of coffee still had a quarter left. I snagged a mug from the cupboard and poured until the dregs spilled in.

"All dressed before ten in the morning on a Saturday? I must've missed that the world's on fire."

I spooked at my brother's voice, whirling fast enough for drops of the hot coffee to spill onto the floor.

Carter leaned against the archway in an entirely black outfit. I'd heard him leave early this morning, and recalled him mentioning at our impromptu dinner that he had a job to take care of in Portland this weekend.

"You're back?" I replied, trying to wipe the coffee off my hand. "I thought the Maine issue would take you until Monday."

My brother's darkened gaze seared into me. "Change of plans."

I nodded, taking a sip from my mug.

"I came looking for you," Carter continued. "I hear you've been extra busy lately getting into trouble with a certain someone."

My hand stilled mid-sip. Was he talking about Tasha? I was prepared for my family to find out the truth eventually, but not *this* fast.

"Mom's been harassing me to do some of her mob shit, but I haven't gotten in trouble for it—yet," I replied. I'd play dumb until he forced my hand.

Carter smirked, moving into the kitchen to grab a macadamia nut cookie off a depleted platter.

"Isn't she the worst," he said.

I waited for the tease in his voice or a joke to follow, but neither came.

"There's something I was hoping to show you while we've got the house to ourselves," he went on. "A gift. It was promised to me, but I think you would appreciate it, too."

My ears perked up like they'd been slumbering, acutely aware of the quietness of the house. Now that I thought about it, where was everyone? I hadn't heard or seen any of our staff or caught a glimpse of a Danesi soldier standing guard over the house. It hadn't been this quiet since that horrible day with Sophia.

My phone buzzed loudly against the counter, snapping me out of my thoughts.

Carter's brow arched high. "Unless you have something more... important to get to?"

I snatched my phone before he could see it was a text from Tasha. What I needed to say was *no*, but my brother was dropping hints he knew what I was up to. It would be bad news if I left him hanging without first grinding the situation down to something manageable.

I set my coffee down. "Nope. I've got some time."

"Perfect," Carter replied, finishing off his first cookie.

I followed my brother out of the kitchen and through the second foyer, the light of the new day flooding over the river-blue granite tiles. He flicked his wrist at the back staircase when I hesitated.

"Come on. It's upstairs."

Whatever it was he wanted to show me, it'd better be good. Already my palms went slick, itching to send a quick text to Tasha to tell her our plan wouldn't be on schedule. I could picture the frustrated pout to her lips and the way she would stretch her neck from side to side to try and release her irritation.

My curiosity rose the farther Carter took me, winding down the halls, passing our bedrooms. Eventually, Carter stopped outside one of the guestrooms. "He's in here."

"He?" I asked as Carter opened the door. "I thought you said it was a gif—"

I stepped inside and froze.

Thick body odor forced its way down my throat, coming off a gang of men. But it wasn't their sweat that caused me to stop. It was their guns. Large, ugly ones gripped in their hands with a second smaller one hanging at their sides.

Carter shut the door behind me before strolling over to sit in an armchair beside a small glass table.

He nodded to one of the armed men. "Secure the door."

The guy shoved past me, giving me a chance to see the white lily tattoo hiding behind his ear and removing any chance of escape. But getting out was overshadowed by a dark reality kneeling in the center of the room.

Victor Callan.

Through swollen eyes and a gagged, bloody mouth, he stared at me without blinking.

I dragged my focus from Victor to my brother, ready to hurl my coffee.

"What the hell is this, Carter?"

"Retribution," he said. "I'm surprised you haven't figured this part out yet. Seeing as you've been running around New York with *Natasha Nicastro* looking under stones you shouldn't touch."

My jaw nearly locked from how much I clenched it. "I have no idea what you're talking about."

Carter's eyes flashed. "I've had guys tailing you for weeks, Leo. You're not as slick as you think you are."

The blurred image of Victor sat in the corner of my eye. What the hell was Carter doing?

"Fine, you caught me. You're pissed I'm working with Tasha to find who's trying to kidnap our little sister and leaving dead bodies in their trail?"

Carter crossed his legs. "I'm not angry. Actually, I admire your boldness. It's a quality we seek, and I have to say, I didn't expect to find it in you."

Dread pulsed through me. "What are you talking about?"

Slowly, Carter slipped a hand into his suit jacket's pocket and flashed a pin at me.

A dove pin.

My body went slack. No way.

"You're working with the Salvators?"

"They've given me more power and respect than I'm ever going to get in our family."

Tension crackled off my skin, ready to go off like a bomb. "You knew the Salvators planned on kidnapping Sophia, and you were going to let it happen? What the hell is wrong with you?"

Carter winced though it was short-lived. "I was never going to let anyone hurt her. Sloane wasn't interested in forming a partnership despite many strong arguments from my guy Ivan, so our boss felt more extreme measures had to be taken. It's unfortunate it didn't work, but we roll with the punches."

"And what?" I asked. "You were hoping traumatizing our sister would convince Mom to roll over?"

"Sometimes you have to put love aside," he replied, twisting the pin around between his fingers. "And hope you can fix things later."

His words settled over me like a thick layer of ash. "So...what? You're just some servant cutting yourself at the knees to join a new Mafia you barely know over your family's?"

I may have issues with ours, but I would never betray Mom—or Dad's memory—like this.

The corners of his eyes pinched. "Of course not. I'm trying to integrate our organizations. I came on board because unlike our dear *mother*, my skills are acknowledged within the Salvators. She can join and make all our lives easier, but I'll convince our soldiers to desert her in due time either way." He waved an indifferent hand to the men in the room. "As you can see, I've already started. Under the Salvators, our soldiers will have proper leadership and you won't be dragged into the role of boss. I'll be the one heading this division, as I should've been from the beginning."

I swallowed, hating the rush of excitement that shot through me at the thought of relinquishing the burden of being the heir. "Who else works for them?"

Carter rested his elbow on the table. "I need to know where you stand before I can give you that kind of information. I thought today would be a great opportunity to test your strength and dedication to the new future we're creating."

I studied him, waiting for the axe to drop and wishing I could live in ignorance instead.

"How?"

With a dangerous smile, Carter rolled back his sleeves. "There are two sides to everything, especially in our world. You act like it's possible to blur them into one, but when it comes down to it, there will always be a line you have to cross." He retrieved a handgun from his jacket and laid it on the table. "The question is, are you willing to cross it?"

I stared at the gun, at the silencer attached to it, refusing to let myself look at the man kneeling on the floor. Blood pounded in my ears and echoed every gunshot I'd ever heard.

Kill him. That's what Carter wanted. Kill one of the remaining people Tasha cared for. Doing something like that was unforgivable. If Tasha found out, there would be no moving forward. I'd lose her forever.

Somewhere through the time we'd spent together, the thought of resurrecting the bond we once shared, creating something greater, felt less impossible. But now . . .

I dragged my eyes back up to my brother. "Why are you doing this?"

"Because," Carter replied, lifting his chin, "Victor was part of my signing bonus. I join the Salvators, get the Danesi Mafia on board, and in exchange, I get the man who led the hit against Dad. But since I'm so gracious, saintly even, I decided to give you the honor. It only seems fair seeing that you were there when he was killed."

The room spun with nothing to keep me centered.

"We don't know if he was the one." My words came out breathless and desperate. I met Victor's gaze and immediately broke out in a cold sweat.

Carter pointed his gun at Victor casually. "Fine. Was it you, Victor?"

Victor stared at us for a heartbeat before lowering his head.

"There," Carter replied. "He was in charge of the hit. I bet more than one of the bullets were fired by his gun."

I paced a few steps, rubbing the back of my clammy neck. "Our guys already killed Luca and now Gabriel's dead. Killing him is going to cause more senseless violence. Aren't you tired of it?"

"Hardly." Carter was calmer than an eagle tracking its prey as he rose and stepped toward me. He leaned in close, his breath brushing the side of my cheek tenderly. "You need to do this. Or Tasha will be the next bound and gagged person in this room."

I jerked away from him. Threatening me was one thing, but Tasha was a whole other. In a foul way, he was right. I'd always have to choose a side—and right now, he was forcing me to choose whether I let Tasha fall into the Salvators' deadly hands or cement her hatred for me. "This isn't who you are."

Carter walked back to his chair, stone-faced. He assessed me for a long moment, rubbing his hand over his mouth. I nearly thought he would put an end to this insanity when a flicker of regret flashed through his eyes, but it disappeared as he lowered his hand.

"It is now," he replied. "So what will it be, Leo?"

I'd said no when Mom wanted me to beat her employee, but this was a deadlier situation with the consequences of my choices radiating stronger and harsher. And the more my brother stood firm in his position, the more I realized how little choice I had.

Extending a shaky hand, I took the gun and turned toward Victor. Although he couldn't speak, there was admission in his eyes. He knew before I did, he wasn't getting out of here alive.

I was an eighteen-year-old idiot too wrapped up in my own shit to realize what vicious creatures lurked in the deep end of the pool.

Sweat from my palm pressed into the handle, bile rose in my throat. Victor was Dad's killer, but that didn't change anything for me. He was still a human being. Still deserved to live. There were a hundred different ways he could be brought to justice. But I couldn't take Carter's threats lightly; not when I'd seen what the Salvators were capable of.

The click of the safety being removed was thunder in my ears. The press of the trigger a thorn stabbing my skin.

And the bullet's release was lightning flashing in my eyes.

CHAPTER TWENTY-NINE

Tasha

ECHOES OF AMELIA SURROUNDED ME. IN THE SHUFFLING steps of other patrons. The long squeak of a gallery door closing shut. An attendant asking for someone to move back from the art. I stood on the second floor of the Met in the European Paintings and Sculptures wing. It was easy to get lost in time as I sank into the endless priceless works.

Despite being a Saturday, the grand halls and intimate galleries were still on the quieter side as the morning crowd slowly filtered in. I used to relish when Amelia got us early access to the museum. We'd float through the rooms with no one else around like little thieves in the night. Now the empty galleries and memories they conjured pressed down on my chest.

I checked my phone again. Nothing. Leo should have responded to my text forty minutes ago, telling me he was on his way.

We'd gone over the plan plenty of times: meet in this gallery ten minutes past opening. I'd find a hiding place before Leo met Scarlett down in the lobby and brought her up here. Then came the easy—or hard—part depending on how Scarlett reacted. The plan *had* to stay on track. So where the hell was Leo?

A security guard watched me with suspicion. I didn't blame him. Twenty minutes ago, the Met opened, and I'd walked directly up here with my security team following, pacing through the rooms with the jitteriness of someone up to no good. I'd told them to spread out and not look obvious. They had grumbled about it but listened. I caught a glimpse of Eric pacing through a gallery two rooms down, keeping his focus squarely on me. He wasn't happy when he learned I wanted to come here, knowing he couldn't bring any weapons into the museum.

"Breathe, Tasha," I mumbled, readjusting my top for the umpteenth time. My outfit was a bit more extravagant than necessary. I had on a one-shoulder shirt that cut diagonally across my chest and tucked into a pair of distressed jeans with a bold red shade on my lips. Even the perfume I chose was more than necessary, with vivid scents of pistachio and creamy vanilla.

I wasn't entirely sure why I did it. But the more I thought over this plan, thought of Leo taking Scarlett's hand, smiling at her, Scarlett grazing her fingers easily and comfortably over his body...

The perfume was spritzed and the lipstick painted on before I had a chance to decide otherwise.

All of this was speeding toward disaster though if his sorry ass didn't walk into this gallery *immediately*.

"And here I thought staring at art was supposed to be a relaxing experience."

I spun around, coming face-to-face with the girl of the hour as she quietly approached me.

Scarlett's hair was pulled into a ponytail with braided pieces woven in above her ears. A light pink blush covered her round cheekbones, bringing out the soft gray in her blue eyes. I did one sweep over the long sweater dress hugging her delicate frame before meeting her eye again.

"What are you doing here?" I asked.

"Spare me the innocent act," she replied, her hand wrapping tight around the golden chain of her Dolce & Gabbana purse. "I saw you hurrying up the steps as I was being dropped off by my driver. Leo said to meet here at ten thirty, but I decided to come earlier, and magically, you're here. I don't believe in coincidences, so I suspect you were in on this *date* from the beginning."

I stiffened all over—uncertain how to respond.

Scarlett's top lip arched up in a grimace. "Either you're hooking up or you two are more serious than that. And I can't tell which one I hate more."

"We're not doing anything like that," I rushed out. It shouldn't matter what Scarlett thought of me or what I was doing with Leo, yet I couldn't help explaining myself.

She gave me a long look. "We tell ourselves the stories we want to hear."

"Is that what you did when you lied to Leo about Ivan Romano?" I asked. If she was going to catch me off guard, I would do the same to her.

But Scarlett didn't flinch. She stepped closer, gazing at the Edgar Degas painting hanging in front of us. "He's lied to me plenty of times."

"This isn't some stupid relationship squabble," I snapped. "There's way more on the line. Are you that pissed at Leo you'd feed extra support to criminals?"

"I'm not pissed at him," she eventually replied. Scarlett faced me, her eyelids heavy. "Dating Leo has always felt like I was with a ghost. Someone I desperately wanted to be with, see and touch, but was never fully present. Then just as I was getting comfortable, starting to believe this time things were real, he'd disappear again without warning. Leaving me to pick up the pieces until the next time he came around."

I should've yanked the conversation back to the topic of Ivan and the Salvators, but I was too entranced by the temptation of knowing what was behind the curtain of Scarlett and Leo's messy relationship to say anything. The boy I once knew would never use a girl so brazenly. It was another example of how we'd become strangers over the past four years, even when fragments of our past tried to tell me otherwise.

"My friends kept telling me to stop letting him back in, and I could see how embarrassing it all was," Scarlett continued. "I would try dating other guys, but the moment he sent that first text at the start of summer, I was roped right back in. I know part of it came down to hoping I'd finally make him realize I was more than a placeholder for the girl he truly wants. But each time he left was another reminder he was still as hung up on her."

A knot formed in my stomach and snaked up my throat. I didn't have the nerve to ask her who she was talking about. Not when the answer hung between us. Over me.

"Remember when we were eleven years old and we all went to Leo's birthday at the Rockefeller's observation deck?"

I frowned. Of course I did. It was long before the friendship between our families was slashed apart, and every kid that came through the doors of my home was a friend—including Scarlett. *Especially* Scarlett. But I couldn't see what that memory had to do with anything we were talking about.

"He shoved an entire tray of rainbow-sprinkle brownies into his mouth and almost ruined my new dress by running around with a hot chocolate in his hand," I replied dryly. "We spent the rest of the party waiting for him to stop puking in the bathroom so he could open his presents. I'm not *allowed* to forget that party."

A rare smile brightened Scarlett's face. It reminded me how far our fragile, simple friendship had fallen.

"Then you must remember when a huge group of kids and parents were lined up waiting for the elevators that day. There were only two operating, so it was taking forever to get all of us to the top. You and I were with our moms."

I nodded, waiting to see where she went with this trip down memory lane.

"When our turn finally arrived, Leo showed up with his family. Everyone made way for the birthday boy. You'd gotten into the second elevator and waited for me to join you, but I took the last spot in the elevator with Leo."

I remembered that, too. Leo and I had been arguing over some ridiculous, inconsequential thing. Days later, when I got sick with a bad flu, he came over to watch movies and play games to help distract me. All was forgiven. If only all feuds and heartbreak could be patched up that easily.

I searched her eyes and saw the exact moment water filled them.

"I didn't realize then how that decision would lead me down a new path, a path away from you." Scarlett looked down at the floor, a streak of light catching in her diamond earrings. "We drifted apart slowly. At first, I wasn't aware it was happening. Then all at once, any hope I might've had to go back to how we used to be was yanked away when Angelo Danesi died. My father saw the bad blood as a way to finally get into the Danesis' inner circle and convince Sloane to let him open small Evergreen stores inside all their casinos. He made me choose the Danesis." Scarlett lifted her gaze to mine. "But if I could go back, I would've gotten into the elevator with you."

A sandbag of weight settled on my chest, making it hard to think, to breathe. I remembered so many big memories between us and so many smaller moments. We were too young to know what to do when the fighting started, to stop our friendship from breaking. When it did, I took Scarlett's indifference as a sign she never cared to begin with.

But even if we wanted to go back to what we once were, new layers had shoved their way in, making it more difficult than ever before.

"Then tell me who approached your dad about the Salvators," I replied. "Who gave him the Van Gogh and put the order in to kill your stepmom's dog? You can finally make up for all the regrets you have over our friendship."

My phone buzzed incessantly between my fingers. I discreetly glanced down at the lock screen where three new messages from Leo waited.

It's a setup.

Leave.

NOW.

A shower of icy dread swept over me. I carefully lifted my gaze back up and put my phone away. There had to be some other explanation, a misunderstanding on Leo's part or some disgusting prank he was pulling on me.

But when I faced Scarlett, that dread intensified, getting cold enough to burn.

"Don't you get it?" she said. "When I got in that elevator, my path was made for me. There's no coming back."

Blood pounded in my head as I looked around us. The Met's security guards and all other patrons had disappeared, but more importantly, my security team were nowhere to be found. Instead, the gallery had a scatter of suited men hovering in strategic locations. They pretended not to be interested in us, but when one of them too casually turned in our direction, I spotted the bulge of a gun secured to his hip—

And a splatter of fresh blood on his white shirt.

"Maybe it's time you realized there's no changing our fates." Scarlett's voice was firm despite the faintest bit of melancholia laced through it. "And finally accept yours."

Our eyes locked; my heart lodged in my throat. "That's where you're wrong. My fate is whatever I decide. It could be the same for you if you fought for your own happiness as much as you do everyone else's."

Her lips parted but I didn't give her the chance to respond. I whipped around and sprinted from the gallery, flying past the armed Salvator soldiers toward the main hallway. If I could get outside to the busy streets, I had a much higher chance of dodging whatever plans they had for me.

The men charged after me as I made it to the hall. I turned right when I caught sight of the EXIT sign hanging above a stairwell.

"Don't move!" one of them roared.

No way was I listening to *that*. I raced over to the stairwell door, throwing myself against it and not pausing before charging down the steps two at a time.

It didn't take long for the door to crash open again, the weight of multiple shoes pounding above me. I grabbed the handrail and swung myself over to the next set of stairs. One floor. That's all I needed to get through, then I'd be home free.`

The men shouted as they chased me down the stairwell. I had my hand on the first floor's emergency exit, nearly ready to leave them behind, when someone suddenly gripped my shoulder and ripped me backward.

I stumbled, regaining my balance in time to thrust my elbow into the mobster's gut. It wasn't enough to get him off me, so I spun around and sent my fist toward his nose.

The crack of bone was the first thing I heard before his screams.

"You bitch!" he shouted, clutching his nose.

I didn't savor my win. Instead, I slammed my hands against the emergency exit and pushed, the alarm blaring seconds after.

A sheet of rain hit me on my first step outside, the density of the storm leaving mini pools of water in grooves and a slippery glaze over the ground. The streets were mostly empty because of it, and anyone walking hurried to get to their destination or blocked out the world with their umbrella.

Still, I raced down to Fifth Avenue, moving on intuition more than with an actual plan.

When I reached East Seventy-Ninth Street, I jaywalked across the road, searching for any café or store I could hide out in until I was positive I'd lost them.

But instead, I walked straight into the arms of two men with doves pinned to their shirts.

"Not so fast, little lady," one said, locking my hands behind me while the other held my neck.

I shoved at their hold as they dragged me toward an idling car with tinted windows. But it was useless; they weren't leaving empty-handed.

Just before we reached the car, another vehicle's engine roared. A heartbeat later, a black Ferrari hurtled into view.

My heart leaped into my throat at the sight of it.

Leo flew out of the car. A rage I'd never seen before erupted off him as he descended upon the two men holding me. He took out a gun from inside his jacket and slammed it between the first one's eyes, not wasting any time before he spun and did the same to the second one's temple.

Both men collapsed to the ground. Leo took my hand, pulling me to his car.

It didn't matter I never expected him to be here, only that enough God-thanking relief washed through me to baptize the Devil himself.

The moment I slammed the passenger door, Leo put his foot on the gas and sped away.

Tasha

"Holy crap. Holy crap."

"*Stop* saying that!"

The heat blasted across my skin, soothing every rain-soaked hair on my body and my racing heart. I sank into the soft leather of the passenger seat and squeezed my hands together.

"I just attacked two Salvator men in broad daylight. One of them could be dead with how hard I jammed this gun into his head. Sorry if I'm a *little* on edge." Leo gripped the steering wheel, both arms shaking as he sped down the street. He stole a glance at me, all furrowed brows and raindrops dripping from his wet hair. "The Salvators might kill me for what I did."

My mind whirled through everything. The first thing we needed to do was get somewhere safe. Then regroup and figure out next steps. "They won't. My family's penthouse is nearby. We can hide out there until we figure something out."

Leo nodded and followed my directions.

"I can't believe what happened." I ran a hand through my hair, tugging at the short locks just to make sure I was, in fact, awake. When nothing woke me from this nightmare, I turned back to Leo. "Where the hell were you? And how did you know I was being ambushed?"

He chewed on his lip. "I kind of found out through my brother."

"*What?*"

"I was getting ready to leave, but then"—his throat bobbed—"I overheard Carter on the phone with someone and the conversation made it clear he's working with them. After I confronted him, he told me they've been tailing us. They thought it was *funny*. He admitted their boss wants to meet you, and they were going to kidnap you while Scarlett distracted you."

My mouth fell open. "Oh my God. And here I thought we were being careful."

The Ferrari weaved around other cars and bright yellow cabs, closing in on the twenty-story sandstone apartment building. My family had owned the penthouse for years. Most of the time it sat empty except for when Amelia stayed overnight after working late at the Met...or when our father decided to spend time there. But now that it was in my name alone, I'd have to figure out my plan for it.

Leo rubbed his chin. "Guess not."

A concoction of emotions swirled through me. I was horrified Carter was part of the Salvators, yet I wasn't surprised at all. I hardly saw him since the bad blood was spilled, but before those days, my body still went on high alert when he entered a room.

And then there was Leo. He had raced down here without hesitation, not knowing what kind of danger he was barreling toward, all to save me.

The image of the rage rippling off his muscles and the feral look on his face when he got out of the Ferrari replayed in my mind's eye. When I flicked my gaze to him, nibbling at my bottom lip, I took in the defined profile of his face, the strain wrapped around his toned arms.

"What made him decide to tell you?"

Leo put a hand on the gear shift, his arm still trembling. I hadn't seen Leo openly shaken in a long time.

"I don't know," he finally replied. "But he wants me to join them."

Brick buildings and chic designer storefronts passed by, but I kept my gaze on Leo. "If they know we're investigating them, why would they bother to kidnap only me? And why would Carter let you go knowing you'd come down here to rescue me?"

"I . . ." He rubbed a hand over his mouth. "That hadn't crossed my mind."

"Why?"

Leo took his time replying, his teeth grinding harshly together. "I didn't want to push too much for answers. After he told me what was going down"—he paused when we reached a red light and swept his honey-brown eyes over to me—"all I could think about was you."

My cheeks burned. The air between us pulsed with too much tension—too much opportunity—for words to be said that couldn't be taken back. So I stayed quiet.

We reached my family's apartment building, where it held more secrets and wealth than any vault ever could. I pointed to the garage and pulled out my keys.

"What's the plan?" Leo asked as we stepped into the parking garage elevator. "You're going to hide out here until the Salvators give up on tracking you down or . . . ?"

I sighed, rubbing at my forehead. The elevators swooshed open, and we stepped out onto a plush cream carpet with lavender wallpaper. One door stood in front of us for the penthouse. I approached it and inserted the key.

"No, we're going to form a plan. But right now, I need a place to think for a second without worrying they'll try to grab me again." I peeled a straggly, wet strand of my hair off my cheek. "And fix my hair, too."

I unlocked the door, immediately flicking the lights on as I stepped inside. The chandelier hanging in the small foyer brightened, dazzling the eye and drawing us in to the rest of the spacious apartment. My mother had redesigned the space after marrying my father, then redesigned it again right before she left. Plush ivories and shiny gold accents coated every nook as though the luxuries of a Parisian apartment flew in one day.

When I turned to close the door, I realized Leo was still standing in the hall.

"What are you doing?" I asked, jerking my chin. "Come in."

He lowered his gaze and shook his head. "I don't think that's a good idea."

"Why not?" When he wouldn't give me an answer, I grabbed his hand, shocking both of us. I quickly recovered though, and added, "Exactly. Get in here."

I pulled him through the door and shut it. We stood there for a restless moment staring at each other, until it finally occurred to me that neither of us had let go of the other's hand.

The realization must have hit Leo at the same time because we both looked down at our interlocked fingers and back up to each other.

He let go first. "I made sure you're safe, but I think it would be better if you called someone else to come stay with you."

"Like who?"

"Someone you trust." Leo's eyes flashed. "Like Ravi. Since you're back together with him."

Of all the things I expected him to say, the words *Ravi* and *back together* weren't it.

"Why do you think we're back together?"

Leo shoved his hands in his jacket pockets. "I saw you two making up in the school parking lot. You kissed him."

I couldn't help it. A cackle bubbled up from deep within my core. I walked farther into the penthouse and tossed my purse on a nearby side table.

"We're not back together," I replied, leaning against the couch. "Not every bit of affection or touch means something romantic, Danesi. It's just my way of showing I care about someone."

Though clearly for *him*, it meant exactly that.

His brows pulled close. "I don't remember you being like that."

"I've gotten more liberal with my affection over the years. Here." I flicked my wrist, gesturing for him to come closer. Although he hesitated at first, eventually he did, and I took his left hand in mine, palm side up. "Let me show you."

Leo's eyes seared into mine as I traced my finger over the tender skin of his hand and interlocked my fingers with his. I tried not to think anything of it. Not the steady pulse kicking at the base of my throat or the heat blooming in my lower core. I'd held many hands before. Some romantic, many more platonic. Leo wasn't any different.

"This means nothing to you?" he asked.

His voice was rough, sending a shiver down my spine. I looked up at him. At the pools of rich, inky black expanding over his irises. How far would I need to go before they completely took over?

I licked my lips, Leo missing none of it, and arched forward, whispering, "Absolutely nothing."

Our breaths wove together. I leaned closer until I was inches from his cheek, the bits of stubble more visible than ever. When I pressed my mouth to his skin, millions of tiny, dizzying fireworks surged through me. I nearly forgot to pull away if not for Leo sharply inhaling.

"See?" I let his hand go and braced my own against the couch. I wasn't sure if it was to keep myself upright or to stop the greed flowing through me for more. "We're completely fine."

When Leo stepped back and turned away from me though, my stomach twisted. It was too much. I should have left it and told him I wasn't with Ravi.

But within the next heartbeat, he turned back around, coming closer than ever to brace his hands over mine. His darkened eyes flashed with something that made me ache all over and the shock of his breath against my neck sent electricity down my arms.

"Are we, Tasha?"

The part of me that had stirred awake when he came back into my life flared wider. It spread from a hidden spot in my core throughout my body, following the vessels of my blood until it had fully absorbed every part of me. All because he'd said my name like a spoken desire.

My chest rose and fell. Each time pressing against Leo's and deepening my sudden need to feel him all over me.

I searched his eyes. "What would you do if I said no?"

In response, he kissed me.

An explosion of want seized my body. I didn't hesitate. I leaned even deeper into the kiss, pressing our bodies together and opening my mouth so my tongue could graze his. Leo groaned at the sensation, lifting one of his hands off mine to grip my jaw and arch my head back to trail his lips down my neck then back up to my mouth.

I trailed my fingers over the muscles underneath his shirt until I reached his hips.

As I touched the button on his pants though, Leo ripped away, taking three deliberate steps back. My lips were hot all over and tender to the touch, and yet my body was desperate for more of him.

He wiped my smeared lipstick from his mouth, refusing to look me in the eye.

"What? Is that it?" I said, breaking the crackling silence. "You got a taste of me and you've decided you don't need anymore?"

"No," he replied hoarsely. "I can't...be with you. It wouldn't be right. You deserve better."

I blinked and pushed away from the couch. So much of us had been connected, but I could already feel him slipping away. "Where is this coming from?"

He finally looked at me. "From a place of reason. You're a Nicastro, Tasha. And I'm a Danesi. We've already seen what kind of nightmares are created when our families get tied up together. I can't go any further knowing how easily I could cause you pain."

"That's not fair," I replied quietly. "You nearly confessed your feelings for me after we found Julian and I pushed you away then. Now you kiss me with all this passion and suddenly decide to reel it back in? Pretend none of it happened?" I scoffed to hide the crack of pain going through my heart. "Must be *so nice* to finally have control over your emotions."

Leo shook his head. "You have *no* idea how difficult it is to rein my feelings in when I'm around you. I've spent the past four years convincing myself I hated you more than I loved you. It was the only way I could keep my sanity, and it's part of the reason I left for California. I had to put as much distance as I could between us. Then I came back, and all that effort vanished when I saw you again."

He paced around, finally stopping at the kitchen's long island. "I nearly lost it when I saw those guys dragging you away. The fear I felt in those seconds shut down everything else. All I could think about was how I was willing to do anything to make sure I didn't lose you again."

My mouth went dry. "Years?"

Love?

"Yes," he replied, his voice lowering. "I never told you because your dad wrung Carter out for flirting with you one time. Then when my dad was killed, and I said those horrible things to you..." Leo's lips formed into a tight line. "There was no hope after that."

I frowned. "I know your brother flirts with everyone, so I didn't take him seriously. But my father thought I would and didn't want me getting my heart broken. He wouldn't have had an issue with you."

A spark of hope appeared on his face but died a moment later. "Well, it doesn't matter anymore. I can never make this real with you. You're better off with a guy like Ravi who can keep you safe and happy."

A lick of anger lashed through me. At Leo for believing he knew what—or who—was best for me and at my father for fracturing so many relationships when he had Angelo killed. I'd gone years thinking the first boy who held a place in my heart didn't feel the same invisible string tying me to him. Now I had him so close, my chest pulled wide open to those old feelings, only for us to be further apart than ever.

My loss was still piling up, close enough to smother me.

"You don't get to decide what's best for me," I replied, approaching him. When he wouldn't meet my gaze, I grabbed his chin and forced him to face me. "I've spent my whole life having others do the same. Don't be like them, Leo. If you still love me, then love me fully, because that's all I've ever wanted from you."

Leo stared long and hard at me, our breaths close enough to merge. Until finally, he hissed through his teeth, grabbed hold of my waist, and lifted me up into his arms.

I wrapped my hands around the back of his neck and my legs around his hips as he kissed me. He sat me on top of the kitchen island, removing his shoes and jacket. I pulled his shirt over his head, running my fingers down his chest, causing a hot ache to burn through my core.

His lips made their way down my neck and to my collarbone while he pulled the single strap of my top below my shoulder. I moved my legs apart to let him fit his knee in between and the ache inside me intensified. Leo pressed me down against the island, the chill of the granite sending a wash of goose bumps across my skin as he removed my pants and tossed them away.

I let out a soft gasp when his lips kissed my inner thigh. Then all at once, I was in his arms again, his teeth gently biting my bottom lip.

"Which room is yours?" he asked.

The ache inside me throbbed. I could have swatted him for the tease, but instead, I pointed to the bedroom at the far end of the penthouse.

We were a fluid unit. Shifting and laying bare every vulnerable part of ourselves. It wasn't my first time, but this wasn't like anything before. I was terrified and thrilled by how much I was filled with more longing, more *want*, the further we went. I'd wanted him more than any other boy and here he was, fully, irrevocably mine.

I breathed in his unique Leo scent when he moved inside me. I guided his hands, lips, teeth to new places and let him do the same for me.

I relished in all of it. Despite the dangers that waited outside these walls, we had found our way to each other. And nothing would ever take that away.

The Egyptian cotton sheets brushed against my back, tempting me out of bed. I let out a small groan, rolling onto my side, and bumped into another figure.

I cracked my eyes open to Leo staring at me, his lids drooped and a crooked smile on his face.

"Hey."

"Hi." An evening haze had settled over the city as day quickly retreated for night. Everything that happened rushed back in. The tangled limbs, the satisfied desires. Leo had pulled me into his arms afterward and traced his fingers over marks and lines not visible to him before while we talked about everything and nothing. We must've drifted off. "What time is it?"

"You just woke up in bed with me and you're worried about the time?"

I rolled my eyes and dragged my finger down his neck to his chest. "Unfortunately for your pride, waking up next to you doesn't suddenly make everything else in our lives disappear." Leaning in close, our lips were inches from each other's, as I whispered, "Even if I could stay like this for a long time."

He grinned and closed the distance between us, pressing a deep kiss onto my mouth. When Leo broke away, he threw back the sheets and got to his feet. "You're right though. We need to figure out what we're going to do now that the Salvators tried to kidnap you."

"I'll call Victor," I replied. "He'll be pissed I didn't call him right away, but he'll know what to do."

Leo pulled on his briefs, avoiding my eye. "I'm gonna shower."

I propped myself up on my elbows, a grin creeping onto my face as I gave him a once-over. "Aw, don't go. I'm enjoying the view."

A strained smile swept over Leo's face before he headed for the bathroom. With him gone, I dragged myself out of bed and pulled a silk robe on as I went to retrieve my phone in the living room.

There was a hurricane of missed calls and frantic text messages from my mother, Val, and Matteo, but one message stood out to me.

A video. From a blocked number.

I stared at the blurred preview, my heartrate rising as I pressed the play button.

At first, nothing in the video clicked. All I could see was a large bedroom with a group of rough-looking men standing around in silence. Then the camera shifted and revealed two more figures, one kneeling on the ground while the other stood over him. Two people I knew far too well.

Hot nausea swam through me, but I couldn't look away. My eyes stayed tethered to the image while my body shook uncontrollably.

"So, what will it be, Leo?" Carter Danesi said off camera.

Silence. Leo stared into the distance with an unreadable look on his face.

Then he stepped closer to the screen, this time with a gun clutched in his hand. I waited—praying—he dropped it. But he turned back to the kneeling figure and raised his arm.

The audio exploded with noise and died back into silence. One shot. That's all it took. One shot to take Victor from me forever.

I crumpled to the ground, a hand to my mouth, tears bursting from my eyes.

I wanted to scream. Tear this room apart. Tear *him* apart. First my father and sister. Now Victor. A man who was family. *Murdered.* And by the person who held me close just now, making me think there was no one else in the world I could trust.

I dialed Matteo's number, my chest heaving until my cousin picked up.

"Tasha! There you are. I've tried getting a hold of you and Eric all day. Where are you? Your mom and I are worried sick!"

I stared at the closed bathroom door, steam snaking out from under the crack, and rose from the floor. "I'm at the family penthouse on the Upper East Side. The Salvators tried to kidnap me and got rid of Eric and the security team. I need you to come get me right now."

Matteo swore under his breath and told me to hold tight until he got there, but I had already tuned everything around me out. I kept my attention trained on the bathroom door and the sound of water shutting off while I inched toward the kitchen countertop.

The bathroom door opened, and Leo stepped out with a towel wrapped around his waist. "Hey, I was thinking—"

I raised his gun at him, tears streaming down my face. "Why'd you do it?"

Eyes wide, Leo stared at me and the gun for a heartbeat, every pore in his face going pale. "Tasha, what are you talking about?"

"*Don't*," I snapped, "fucking lie to me."

I moved closer to him, clicking off the safety. Everything inside me begged to pull the trigger and get revenge for Victor.

"I know you killed Victor. Is this some kind of game to you? One elaborate, sick joke to amuse you? It wasn't enough I watched my dad and sister die, you had to go one step further and ruin every facet of my life. Who's next? Matteo? Val? Ravi? I know how much you hate him in particular."

Leo raised his hands up, sidestepping over to grab his clothes off the floor. "I know how bad this looks, but I swear to you, I didn't kill him. Carter did. I wanted to tell you what happened, but I—"

"Didn't want to hurt my feelings?" I sneered. "How exactly were you thinking of broaching the subject? *That was a great time in bed. Oh, and by the way, I shot Victor before my second cup of coffee.* Let me guess, you and your entire disgusting family have been working with the Salvators from the beginning. *You're* the one I should've been going after this whole time."

In the middle of putting his clothes on, Leo paused, squeezing his eyes shut. He had the nerve to look distraught, as if this was destroying him from the inside out.

"None of this was a game, and I'm not working with them. I had *no idea* my brother was either. He tried to get me to kill Victor, but I didn't pull the trigger. I never would. I *swear*. Please, Tasha. You have to believe me."

A fresh set of tears flowed down my cheeks. I stared at him, thinking of Ravi's warning. He told me Leo would be too weak to stand by me. And I'd brushed him off, believing *this* boy was different. I'd been a complete, reckless fool.

"I don't," I said, my voice lethally calm. "Get out."

"Tasha—"

"Get out!" I screamed. "Or I swear to God, I *will* shoot you."

He threw on his shirt and zipped up his pants. For a moment, it looked like he would listen to me, but as he stopped to grab his car keys, Leo faced me again with pleading eyes. "You have to believe me, Tasha. Please."

I walked over to the door and threw it open. "I don't and I never should have."

Leo stared at me for a long, desperate moment. But his lies wouldn't work on me anymore. I'd been foolish enough to dive headfirst into his charmed web. I wouldn't make that mistake a second time.

After what could be a lifetime, the hope drained from Leo's face and he stepped out of the penthouse—and my life—for good.

CHAPTER THIRTY-ONE

THE FERRARI'S TIRES SCREECHED ON THE PAVEMENT AS I arrived home. I barely had the engine turned off before I was storming inside to find one person.

My brother.

"Carter!" I roared, hand gripped around the car keys. "Carter! Where the hell are you?"

My booming voice echoed up the high ceilings and vibrated down the long halls. I charged through, meeting nothing but cold, empty interiors.

I wasn't sure how I was ever supposed to step into this house again after becoming a prisoner to Carter's vicious mind games. Yet here I was a few hours later, ready to slice his neck for framing me.

I would've told Tasha.

I *should've* told Tasha.

But I was a coward and there was no excusing that. My brother had walked me into a trap I hadn't caught onto until it was too late.

When I'd held the gun in my hands and stared down at Victor, all

I could think about was Dad. For years before he died, I pretended like the truth of his life was a part of my made-up stories, the sounds I heard or the things I saw were nothing but daydreams for a bored kid.

The second I held the gun and faced a man about to die, I felt the truth I'd tried to hide from. The violence, the cruelty. If I'd held it for any longer, maybe that poisonous violence would have reached my heart and taken me for good.

But it hadn't. I couldn't tell whether Carter ever expected me to go through with killing Victor or not. I was too hung up on the brutal reality that had been in front of me.

I'd looked in the eyes of the man who killed my father. Who Tasha loved. And before I had a chance to consider the consequences, the bullet was fired, landing right on its mark.

The minutes that followed had been a blur.

All I could recall was Victor's body being taken away and Carter telling me he got exactly what he wanted from me.

Because he hadn't only put his gun away. He'd put his phone away, too. And I'd been too stunned and locked in the moment to register the walls of my brother's trap narrowing in.

It was painfully obvious looking back. I'd checked off every box of his plan to ruin my relationship with Tasha.

My brother clearly didn't know me as well as he thought he did though. So when I threw open the doors to the solarium, a genuine look of surprise crossed his face.

What neither of us expected though was for Mom and Sophia to be present, too.

"Leo?" Mom asked, a book in her hand. "What's with your aggressive entry?"

My gaze vaulted between her and my sister lounging on separate couches like this was any other Saturday night in. Like a man wasn't murdered in cold blood up in one of our guest rooms hours ago.

But they wouldn't know what the hell went down. The bastard casually sipping his sbagliato cocktail in Dad's old armchair would have made sure of that.

"You *asshole*," I shouted, charging toward Carter. "You're framing me for what happened to Victor Callan?" My hands balled into fists, armed and ready to meet their mark. "I should kill you right here."

My brother set his drink down and sprang to his feet, but the relaxed angle to his body didn't fool me. He was as tense as I was. Ready for a fight.

"You want to kill me for getting you away from Tasha Nicastro? You've told me countless times you hate her guts," Carter replied. "Come on, Leo. I was doing you a favor. Don't be fueled by your dick."

I clenched my teeth, but it wasn't enough to restrain me. My fist flew for his face faster than either of us could process, hitting Carter square on the upper left cheekbone. He reeled back, barely holding himself together from crashing into the coffee table.

"Boys!" Mom shouted, her tone snapping to the militaristic one she saved for the Mafia. "Stop this *immediately*." Her hand was around my shoulder within seconds, pulling me back. "Leo, what's come over you? Why are you screaming the name of the Nicastro underboss?"

"Because he killed him!" I roared, jabbing my hand through the air toward my traitorous brother. "He shot him dead because he's defected to that new Mafia, the Salvators!"

Sophia gasped from her seat, reminding me too late that she was here, while Mom's eyes bugged out of her head. She turned to Carter slowly, asking, "Is this true?"

My brother's jaw moved from side to side, a hot flush rushing up his neck. "Dad is dead because of that man. I wasn't going to turn down the chance to finally get revenge."

Mom put a hand to her mouth, her horror burning into fury. "You've betrayed our family for some half-brained revenge scheme? That organization tried to *kidnap* your sister because I refused to hand power over to them and they have spread their control through different industries and families like some parasite for months!"

"It was all I could do to gain some real respect in my life!" Carter shouted back. "After I messed up one time, you acted like you *might* give me another chance to take over, when we both know you've *never* planned on giving me the role of boss. Not even underboss or consigliere. All you've done is use me, and I was the desperate idiot who went along with it hoping one day you'd change your mind."

"Clearly, she had a good reason not to trust you," I exclaimed, stepping in front of Mom. "She isn't perfect and we butt heads often, but everything Mom does is for the *family*. While everything you've done is for yourself."

Carter shook his head, having the nerve to look at me with sympathy creasing the sides of his eyes. "I spent years believing I was worthless. That I'd done something to forever disappoint her and make me unworthy of her love. Dad was the only person who'd ever look at me and actually see me. Mom focused on you from the start. When I messed up and fell for that FBI scheme, she clung to it. I probably would've gone my whole life believing it, too, and broken myself trying to win her back if the Salvator boss hadn't shown me the *real* reason. I was doomed from the day I was born."

I froze at the same time Sophia asked, "What are you talking about, Carter?"

Carter brushed his messed-up hair off his forehead, keeping his razor-sharp gaze on Mom. "Where's all that anger and passion now, Sloane? You don't want to tell them the truth you tried to keep from me?"

Mom's face stayed as steady as an anchor, but she couldn't hide her overly bright eyes, the distant look in them.

I stepped closer to Carter, most of the adrenaline-fueled anger pumping through me now at a simmer. "What shit are you trying to start now?"

"I'm not starting anything," Carter replied solemnly. "I'm showing you the layers of cruelty Mom has hidden from us. She would rather birth a dozen sons before ever letting a bastard inherit the Danesi empire."

My heart was in my throat, pounding against my neck like a trapped animal desperate to get free. I couldn't look at Mom. Not when a reality I never thought possible was rising to the surface, ready to shatter my already scarred worldview.

"Sophia," Mom said. "Leave us."

"But—"

"Now!"

Sophia glanced at me and Carter before finally obeying and hurrying out of the room. Mom followed after her, shutting the door with more force than necessary.

"What's he talking about, Mom?" I asked.

"She hasn't confessed for this long that I doubt she has the nerve to say it now," Carter replied. "I'm the son of Dad's mistress. The Salvator boss showed me my real birth certificate and her death certificate when they were trying to recruit me. My birth mom died of cardiac arrest after I was born." When Mom inhaled sharply, his upper lip curled up. "Guess you didn't destroy *every* copy like you thought. It would've been a perfect con, too. With her gone, you could take me in and pretend I'd always been yours. No one knew who this woman was aside from you and Dad. You could wipe away her entire existence and have full control over your new little enemy. Indulge my curiosity, did you use foxglove or nightshade? Or maybe it was wolfsbane. You really did have so many options to make it look natural."

My body slumped, stunned by the accusations Carter was making, and I waited for Mom to deny it.

Nothing came.

Holy *shit*.

"It's true." My eyes widened. "That's why you're stuck on me inheriting the Mafia."

"Exactly." Carter threw back the rest of his cocktail, wiping his mouth with his wrist, and set the empty glass down with a sharp smack. "She's been lying to both of us our whole lives. You're nothing but a means to an end, Leo, just like me. Someone she could keep a leash on until our usefulness was used up. She'd force you into a position you hate rather than let a bastard son take over. I've been breaking my back for years trying to prove myself to her."

Mom stepped forward, her pearl-white teeth ready to tear a chunk from him. "I did what had to be done to protect the Danesi name. That woman would have ruined your father and our empire by using you as her pawn. She was about to go public with you before I put a stop to it."

"You did it to protect your *own* livelihood," Carter retaliated. The cocky aloofness he wore like a dirty shirt was ripped off, revealing layers of caked-in rage. "That's why you got pregnant right after you killed her. Lucky for you, you gave Dad another son with your first try, so you could easily convince him to replace me with Leo as heir." He turned to me. "Learning this truth was the launch point, but I joined the Salvators because they accepted me for who I am and didn't make demands that I could never satisfy. I get the life I want rather than the one others try to dictate. They can give you the one you truly want, too. Everything I've done, little brother, has been for your benefit as much as mine."

"Don't you *dare* try to warp his mind!" Mom yelled, jabbing her finger through the air. "I raised you as my own, giving you everything I gave Leo and Sophia. The only reason I won't make you the heir is because of how much of a wild card you are. All you've done with this massive betrayal is confirm my instincts."

"And here I thought you might finally have a change of heart," my brother replied, his voice straining, eyes tightening. "After everything

I've done to try and make you look at me with pride. To look at me like I'm your *son*. I could've found it in me to forgive you for poisoning my birth mom. But instead, all you can do is look at me with disgust. You've never given me the same as you've given them. If you did, I wouldn't be standing here ready to walk out of your life for good."

Mom studied him for a long, painful stretch of time, her eyes glistening in the hushed lamplight, then her expression shifted. Hardening. "If that's the way you see it, and you want to paint me as a monster, then fine. Walk out of this family, but don't ever expect open arms if you try to return."

The grief etched into Carter's skin dissolved, making room for a tight, vicious smile. "With pleasure. I bet you haven't noticed a bunch of your soldiers have already deserted and are gladly working under the Salvators now with a hefty pay increase."

Mom gasped, propelling her to yell a few choice phrases at him.

It was all too much. Mom killed a woman and took her baby. A baby that was my half brother. And now he was trying to overthrow Mom with the Salvators' help. What kind of Shakespeare shit *was* this? I came in here to confront Carter for framing me for murder and getting Tasha to hate me. This wasn't how things were supposed to go.

The room spun as I threw open the door and fled, not giving either of them an opportunity to force me to stay. I didn't move with any real intention. My mind was detached from my body, caught in a web of toxic secrets-turned-realities slowly suffocating me. I didn't realize I'd gone into the backyard until Carter was calling my name.

"Leo! Hold up!"

I finally stopped, coming back down to my unrelenting world. My brother jogged to catch up to me. Though the remaining daylight was fading fast, I could still make out the red patch on his face where my fist landed and a bruise would soon form.

"Stay away from me," I growled. "You've blown up enough of my life today."

"I didn't come out here to 'blow up' anymore of your life, and I didn't want to involve you in the first place, but I had to follow orders when you got in the way." Carter let out a heavy sigh. "I came to tell you that I can give you an out. If you really don't want to be involved in the underground world anymore, I can help you. You can graduate early and go anywhere in the world you want. I won't keep you here like Sloane wants to."

My brows drew close. "And what's the catch?"

"There's only one," he replied. "You have to make sure you never try to contact Tasha again."

There were tons of signs warning me he would say something like this and yet the shockwave still crashed through me. I couldn't let myself fall into my anger though when another massive warning sign was grabbing my attention. Carter was trying to act casual. My brother was anything *but* casual, which meant he was hiding something.

"It sounds like you have plans for her."

Carter assessed me through a narrowed gaze but said nothing.

My mouth went dry. "Tell me."

"Unfortunately, that's none of your business," he replied, sliding his hand into one of his pockets. "Especially not after you failed the test I gave you earlier. I *let* you know what our plans were, because I was hoping you were worthy of coming into the organization and I could make a strong case for you. But you've disappointed me, Leo. You'd rat your own mother out to the feds and let your empire fall if you dreamt up a good enough excuse." Carter shook his head, pulling out a packet of Marlboros and a lighter. "All because of this moral high ground you think you stand on. I love you, little brother, but it's why I had to make the choices I did. I couldn't stand back and watch you ruin everything Dad built. The Danesi Mafia will be much stronger under the Salvators' reign once its off the life support Sloane has given it. Which is why I know you'll understand and forgive me one day."

I watched him light the cigarette, blowing a few puffs of smoke into the air before I replied. "Maybe I'd let it fall if it meant stopping the constant cruelty and broken people this world creates."

Carter held my gaze for a long minute before dropping his Marlboro to the ground and grinding it beneath his foot.

"Stay out of the way, Leo," he said, walking away from me. "Or you'll face consequences I won't be able to protect you from."

I stayed perfectly still until he slipped around the side of the house and melted into the darkness. Once he was gone, I sank to my knees with my hands gripping my hair.

What the hell was I supposed to do now?

"Leo?"

My head snapped up to the sound of my sister's hesitant voice. She appeared from behind the landscaped hedges, backlit by the golden glow of a porch light.

I quickly staggered to my feet. "Sophia, hey. I'm sorry you had to see all that."

She stepped closer, shaking her head. "I didn't come out here to get an apology from you. I need to tell you something important. I overheard Carter talking on the phone earlier."

I tried to keep my cool, hoping she wouldn't notice my muscles shaking with anticipation. "What did you hear?"

Sophia pulled her golden-brown hair behind her ear, glancing sideways to the house. "There's a party happening tomorrow night somewhere in Rye. By the ocean, maybe? Carter was going over details with someone. He doesn't want any of us finding out. Especially you. After what happened...I thought you should know."

Yes. My next move. I planted my hands on her shoulders. "You're a miracle worker. Thank you."

Sophia frowned, searching my eyes. "Don't make me regret telling you, Leo. Promise."

I kissed the top of her head before letting my hands fall back to my sides, whispering, "I promise."

It was the first time I lied to her.

Tasha

THIS KIND OF HEARTBREAK WAS A WHOLE NEW LEVEL OF hell. I wrapped my arms around myself, staring blankly out the window as my new reality settled like hazy smoke around me.

Victor was gone. My father, Amelia...now Leo. He may not be dead, but everything I thought we could be was. Even after all I'd been through, I was still as naïve as ever, believing I knew the people closest to me when that couldn't be further from the truth.

I wiped away a tear, watching the rain continue to drench the city's dark skyline. It was fitting for the grief pumping through my veins.

I had been pushed so much since this all began. Now I'd reached my limit.

Maybe I should let the Salvators take over and forget about getting revenge. I was tired of searching for justice that wasn't there. My mother had been right. Sometimes it wasn't worth bruising your skin and draining every vein to fight a battle you had no chance of winning. My Nicastro stubbornness had gotten me this far, but I'd worn it down to the bone and now it could barely stand. What would happen if it collapsed entirely?

Two knocks rapped on the penthouse door. I braced myself before hurrying over. I hoped it was my cousin and not Salvator mobsters here to snatch me again. Yet despite calling Matteo, desperately asking him to come down here, I still dreaded having to confess everything to him.

When I opened the door though, I realized I'd have to confess everything to a lot more people than I anticipated.

"Tasha!" my mother exclaimed, rushing forward to throw her arms around me.

I stumbled back a step as she collided with me, my system still shocked at the other faces. Clearly Matteo made a few calls before he arrived.

Because it wasn't just my mother who was here. Richard and Val were, too.

"Are you hurt?" Matteo asked, his eyes wrinkling in concern.

A golf ball-sized lump suddenly lodged in my throat. I had to say the words out loud.

"No," I managed to say. "But I've made a terrible mistake."

"You need to tell us *everything*," Val said, rushing over to me. "My dad won't tell me what's going on. I wouldn't be here if I didn't overhear him on the phone with Matteo talking about you nearly being kidnapped!"

I glanced at Richard who stood rigidly by the door.

"I let her come down with me, but I can make her leave," he said. When Val whipped around to glare at her father, he added, "Tasha, it's up to you if you want Val to know."

I faced my best friend again as she looked at me hopefully.

"Please, Tasha," she said. "Whatever's going on, I can handle it. If you're in trouble, I can help you, but I can't do that if I'm in the dark."

I worried my bottom lip. I never wanted to involve Val, but I couldn't ignore her standing in front of me. Keeping her in the dark was a double-edged sword. If she didn't know what she was connected to, she couldn't begin to defend herself if anyone tried to come after her next.

"Okay," I replied, squeezing her hand. "Here's the truth: Your dad is the consigliere for my family's criminal organization. It's been running in the shadows of our empire for generations, and now I've inherited it all. That's why I was nearly kidnapped, because the organization who killed my father and sister is targeting me."

Val gasped, pulling away to put her hand up to her face. She looked from me to her father in horror before shaking her head. "Are you serious?" Our sober expressions must have been enough of an answer because she turned to point accusingly at Richard. "I can forgive Tasha for not telling me anything, but you're my *dad*. Are you seriously telling me you've gone this whole time lying to Mom and me about what your real job is?"

Richard let out a heavy sigh. "We'll talk about it later."

Val fumed until I stepped closer to place a hand on her shoulder. "You know now. Can't that be enough?"

She frowned for a moment before finally casting her furious gaze to the floor. "I guess it'll have to be."

"Yes, it will have to be, Valentina, because we need to move on to the much more pressing matters here," my mother interjected, throwing her fall coat onto a nearby chair. Her hair was pulled back in a messy bun and dark circles hung under her eyes. "Tasha, what's going on? You've scared us royally saying you were nearly kidnapped, and now Victor isn't answering his phone either. Matteo said your security team were *taken out*?"

I squeezed my hands together. I needed to tell them everything, no matter how difficult it was.

Once I was done explaining how I was ambushed at the Met and I got the video of Victor's death, Matteo whipped out his phone.

"We need to get you to a safe house within the next hour," he said, his wobbling voice the only emotion sneaking through. "After that we can figure out next steps."

"Wait, hold up," Val said. "Tasha went through all this and now you're going to make her go into hiding?"

"That's *exactly* what needs to happen and then some," my mother replied. "I've been saying from the beginning she's not safe in New York. Next steps need to be getting her out of this country."

Matteo shook his head, raising a hand up. "Aunt Adriana, please. Let's not start making passionate assumptions here. We still need Tasha around to lead the Nicastro Mafia."

"No, you *do not*," she declared.

Val turned to me when my mother and Matteo started arguing. "I know I'm new to all of this, but is that what you want, Tasha? To abandon your whole life here and the rest of the people who care about you?"

I clenched my hands together. It was difficult to look her head-on as she stared at me with an accusatory look in her eye. I'd said I would stay and fight for my empire, to avenge my father and Amelia, and yet all that fire in me was barely a tendril of a flame right now. "I don't know anymore."

Val frowned as she shook her head. "What does this Salvator organization want anyway? Would it be crazy if you talked to them?"

My eyes widened at *that* statement.

"You're joking," I replied. "I can't go anywhere near those people!"

"But they didn't kill *you*," Val argued. "They've had plenty of opportunities. Don't you want to find out why?"

"Valentina," Richard snapped. "I'm appalled by your suggestion."

My mother, apparently done with her argument with my cousin, whipped her attention to Val also. "So am I. My baby will not go anywhere *near* those horrible people."

I gripped my hands together in my lap, keeping my focus on Val alone. "If I did, I have no way of contacting them. I'd rather not perch out on the sidewalk waiting for them to try and kidnap me a second time."

As if they could hear me, another knock sounded on the front door.

Matteo and Richard stiffened, both of them suddenly wielding guns. They gestured for us to stay quiet.

Blood roared in my ears, but I listened. My hands gripped the back of the chair while they stalked over and looked through the peephole.

"Hello, Miss Tasha?" an older male voice with a pleasant ring to it said. "It's Albert."

The adrenaline pumping through my chest deflated. Albert was the doorman for the building and had been since long before I was born.

I straightened and waved at Matteo and Richard to stand down as I walked over and opened the door.

"Ah," Albert said, a wide smile spreading over his white-bearded face. "Good evening. It's been a while since I've seen your lovely face around here."

He had on his usual double-breasted black coat with gold buttons and a matching hat. I was fairly sure he hadn't updated his uniform in forty-odd years. The only change was the youth that slowly sucked out of him with each passing year.

I smiled. "It's great to see you, too."

"Albert?" My mother popped her head into frame and beamed at him. "Oh! It's been too long."

The doorman startled at her presence but quickly recovered. "Miss Adriana! How lovely to see you, too. I didn't know you were back in town."

She grasped my shoulder. "I needed to be here for my baby."

I could tell my mother was about to launch into a whole conversation with him, so I quickly jumped in. "Albert, what's up?"

He raised his hand, revealing a large white envelope he was holding.

"I normally wouldn't bother you at such a late hour, but someone dropped this off and insisted I give it to you right away. I hope you'll forgive me for the intrusion."

"Of course," I replied, taking the envelope. It was blank and smooth except for my name engraved in a gold cursive in the center. "Thank you, Albert."

He tipped his hat to me. "Of course. And please let me offer my condolences for the loss of your father and sister. Mr. Nicastro and Miss Amelia were wonderful people that I'll miss seeing around."

I gave him a tight smile and closed the door as he got back into the elevator.

"What is it?" Val asked.

Matteo put out his hand, but I didn't hand the envelope over. Instead, I moved to the kitchen and grabbed a knife to slice the top open in one clean sweep.

Inside was a postcard-sized piece of paper made of a thick matte material. One side was blank, but the other had the same engraved gold lettering on it.

"It's an invitation," I said.

> *Dear Miss Nicastro,*
>
> *We are pleased to invite you to celebrate our launch into New York and beyond tomorrow evening. Invitations are limited so please do come alone. Our director of operations would be honored to meet you.*
>
> *Time and location will be revealed through a phone call one hour before the event starts. Our entire organization looks forward to your presence.*
>
> *S*

A tiny dove was printed below it. Just in case I didn't get the hint.

They had to be mocking me. A delivered invitation with a clear message that I couldn't hide from them.

"They know I'm here," I said, turning to everyone. "And now they're inviting me to a *party* they're throwing tomorrow night like some underground debutante ball."

A fearful glint appeared in my mother's eye. "Throw it out, Tasha. Right now."

I held it close to my chest and sidestepped her when she tried to come and take it from me. "I'm not throwing it out. At least, not yet."

"Leo must've told them where you were hiding out," Val suggested.

Matteo extended his hand. "Let me and Richard see it."

I gave it to him this time. After a few seconds, Matteo shook his head and looked up at me, putting the invite on the kitchen counter. "This is absolutely a trap. They know you're more vulnerable now that Leo killed Victor and the Nicastro Mafia still haven't accepted you as their boss."

"You can't go anywhere near their party," Richard added. "We can still figure out how to put them down but walking into a place where they have the upper hand cannot be it."

I stared at the invite sitting innocently on the counter, the tendril of fire inside me growing again with each second.

The right answer was to agree and stay far away for my own safety. But this was the biggest chance I'd been given to find out who was behind my father's and Amelia's deaths and get the revenge I craved. A *literal* invitation. If I rejected it, fled to a safe house instead, all I'd ever be was a spineless coward.

My resolve hardened quietly. If I wanted any chance of successfully getting into this party, my decision had to stay a secret. I didn't know how I was going to get away with it yet, but somehow, I would.

"Okay then," I replied, keeping my face free of emotion. "I'll throw it out. We have to stay on the safe side."

My fake proclamation satisfied my mother and Richard. Val shook her head, frustration creasing her brows. Matteo, however, studied me with unwavering eyes. I tried to give him a reassuring smile, but it did nothing to break him—or ease my now pounding heart.

"See? Tasha agrees," my mother said.

"Apparently, she does." Matteo rubbed his facial hair for a moment before suddenly clapping his hands. "All right, then. We need to get moving on this plan. Richard, I need you to take Aunt Adriana and Val back to the Nicastro house until you hear from me about the safe house. I'll let you know which one we're going to when I call. In the meantime, I'll stay here with Tasha."

My mother's eyes widened. "I'm not leaving my daughter, Matteo."

"But you need to. For now," he replied. "Tasha can't leave this apartment until she goes directly to the safe house. She'll need clothes and other supplies though. That's where you and Val can help."

"That works for me," I quickly replied. "Val knows what my essentials are."

"I—" Her brow furrowed, but then she sighed. "Okay. I'll do it."

My body ached to vibrate with anticipation, but I kept myself calm to avoid suspicion. Sneaking away from one person would be much easier than four.

"It's settled then," Matteo said, going over to the door. "Richard, I'll be in touch soon."

Val and my mother gave me a big hug while Richard nodded stiffly. The three of them left a minute later, leaving me with one remaining obstacle.

The front door shut with a soft click. Matteo kept his back to me at first, so I busied myself in the kitchen.

"I know what you're doing."

I froze and looked up. Matteo had crossed his arms, the side of his lips slightly curved.

"But you don't need to panic," he continued. "Because I support it."

I let out a shaky breath. "You know I want to go."

My cousin nodded. "It's why I sent them away. So you can without pushback."

"There's a catch though, right?" I narrowed my eyes at him. "What is it?"

Matteo sighed, sitting on one of the barstools stationed at the kitchen island. "I was already planning on telling you the news before you called. Now it feels more pressing than ever. I got word that a bunch of Nicastro soldiers have defected to the Salvators. They've already decided not to trust your leadership. Or me for siding with you. Once word gets out that Victor's gone, it'll get worse."

My heart plummeted into my stomach. "*What?* But they haven't given me a chance! Barely any time has—"

"I know, Tasha," he interrupted. "And with everything that's happened, our options are more limited than ever. Which is why you need to use your last ace if you want any chance of taking the Salvators down and getting the Mafia on your side."

"What ace?" I replied.

"You'll know soon enough." Matteo checked his phone, sucking through his teeth. "And look at that, he's already here after I called him on the way down. That guy moves fast when it comes to you."

I could've asked him who he was referring to, but my gut told me I already knew the answer. I just didn't understand why he was my ace.

A few minutes later, my prediction came true.

Ravi stepped into the foyer, his presence consuming the small space. He had on a ribbed turtleneck tucked into a pair of dress pants with his dark hair pulled off his tanned face.

"Tasha," he said, striding over and pulling me close to him before I could react. "Matteo told me you were attacked by that Salvator group; I got down here as fast as I could. I should've protected you knowing you were tracking them. I'm so sorry."

"It's okay. I didn't expect you to," I replied, quickly springing free of his embrace. I hadn't changed my mind about our relationship, so I couldn't give Ravi false hope. My attention turned to Matteo. "But I don't understand. Why did you ask Ravi to come?"

The two exchanged a knowing look, putting me on high alert. Irritation bloomed in my chest. I'd already been kept in the dark over too much, and yet here I was again, in the dark about something *else*?

I glared at both of them. "What aren't you telling me?"

"Tasha..." Ravi took my hand and guided me over to the couches to sit with him. "There's something I've had to keep from you. Now that you finally know about your family's Mafia, you should finally know the truth."

I balked at his calm acknowledgment. "Wait, how do you—"

"I know about all of it. I have from the start," Ravi said. He lowered his gaze, squeezing my hands in his, before looking back up at me. It would've been better if I pulled away, but I couldn't bring myself to while my focus was saddled to whatever confession Ravi was about to reveal. "You know my family has influence and connections around the world because of Aurora Technology. What I didn't tell you is that the underground world is also part of that list."

I squinted at him. That confession didn't feel big enough, which only told me there was more to it. "You're saying your family has ins with criminal organizations?" When he nodded, I asked, "How many?"

Ravi pressed his lips together. "All the major ones globally. My mother decided long ago that offering our spyware technology to any recognized group who wanted access built priceless relationships with them. We don't ask for money. When we need something, we ask for favors."

I finally pulled my hands free of his, rising to my feet to pace over by the windows. My mind whirled with this bombshell of a secret, piecing it together with all the memories I thought I fully knew. If the

Ferreiras were well respected by criminal groups here and internationally, it would give them the kind of power a warehouse full of weapons could never achieve.

"Is that why my dad was so excited we were dating?" I asked, spinning back around. "Because he knew the truth?"

"Yes," Matteo answered for him. "Anyone who's involved in our world knows about the Ferreiras. They're nearly untouchable. Those associated with them are, too."

"I wanted to tell you," Ravi said. "But it was too much of a risk to my family while you were unaware of your own family's true empire. I thought it was better if I didn't overwhelm you more by immediately telling you my family's secret, too."

I placed my hands on my hips. "Okay, fine. Then what are you doing here? Why does Matteo think you're my chance at stopping the Salvators?"

Ravi turned to my cousin. "I'm not sure. Why did you ask me to come down here, Matteo?"

"Well, originally it was to talk about what's been happening within the Nicastro Mafia," Matteo replied. "But now there's a new reason for you to be here. The Salvators have invited Tasha to a party they're throwing tomorrow night. She needs to go if we want any chance of infiltrating this group and finding their boss, but she needs backup to cut them down."

"And you could ask other organizations nearby to help me," I finished, suddenly understanding Matteo's thinking.

I wanted to go into the party and make the person who ordered the hit on my family cower at my feet. To look them in the eye and demand answers before I retaliated. The only way I would ever feel a sense of healing was by living with the satisfaction that those behind my family's murders got what they deserved.

But I was one person. I couldn't go up against a group that had proven how merciless they could be. I needed support—an army of my own—and here was a person who could make that happen. My final ace.

"Ravi," I said evenly. "You said you would always be there for me."

He rose from the couch but didn't meet my eye. I watched the curve of his jaw harden, his breathing grow shallower. I'd already pushed him away, dragged a line through the sand between us, but I needed him now more than ever. And if he didn't help me, I didn't know what I'd do.

"Your plan is incredibly dangerous," he eventually replied. "And my family doesn't like getting involved with mob wars. We stay neutral at all times unless it becomes personal."

"I'll go either way." I followed him, stepping closer until he finally looked at me. "But with your help, we can make sure this is an immediate win, and I can finally get justice for my father and sister. Can't your family make this one exception?"

His green eyes softened the longer he looked at me, until finally, he took my hand again.

"All right, Tasha. I'll do this for you." Ravi paused, glancing over at Matteo before turning back to me. His breathing grew heavy as he ran his thumb across my fingers. "There's one thing I need from you to secure their support though. It's the only way my parents will allow me to call in these favors."

I steeled myself, replying, "And what's that?"

CHAPTER THIRTY-THREE

"I *WON'T* ALLOW IT AND THAT'S FINAL, LEO," MOM ANSWERED.

I stared her down. We'd been in her home office for at least forty minutes looping through the same argument and it was getting old. Yesterday, I'd put a tracking device on Carter's car to find out where the Salvators' party was happening. When his car had pulled into a property in Rye and stayed there overnight, I knew I had my spot.

But I couldn't waste any more time hanging around here. I needed to sneak in as soon as I could for one reason.

Tasha.

She would be at the party. Somehow and someway, she would find out about it, and she wouldn't be able to stay away. And when she did walk willingly into this snake pit, I would be there to protect her right to my last breath.

I didn't care that Tasha had banished me from her life and hated my guts; I'd never be able to walk another step if I let her go into this trap alone.

But my biggest opponent wasn't anyone from the party. It was Mom.

All because she happened to see me getting ready, securing one of Dad's guns to my side, and realized immediately I wasn't going to any normal party.

"You can't hold me back from doing this," I said. "We're talking about Tasha here. A girl you've known all her life. She deserves to have someone care about her safety."

Mom let out a deep sigh, her jaw tightening. "You want to go into an unknown environment we *know* is dangerous to try and protect Tasha all on your own. I know you two have shared a special bond since you were little and that Tasha isn't her father, but this is a guaranteed bloodbath."

I clenched my jaw as the clock on her desk inched closer to nine. Outside, the sky was dark with hardly a sliver of light shining from the moon. It was the perfect night to get around without detection. I needed to make sure that worked in my favor and not the Salvators.

"Exactly. Tasha *isn't* her father, so she doesn't deserve to face the grudges you have for her family," I said.

Mom took off her glasses and pushed away from her desk, pacing in front of the built-in bookshelves lining the wall. I watched her think through what I'd said as my gut churned.

"I don't have any ill will toward her. She was a devilish little sweetheart when she was a child, running around our house and teasing you and Carter. It made my affections for her stronger," she finally said, and turned to face me. "But this group took down New York's most powerful crime boss within his own home. No matter what I might want to do, I cannot risk your life like this. If you died, it would be the end of us. The end of *me* as your mother, knowing I let you go."

She crossed her arms, her resolve solidifying. "You will not take yourself to this party. I'll have security tie you to a chair if it means keeping you safe."

"Are you kidding me?" I exclaimed. I pressed my palms against my head, feeling the heavy thump of fury against my hands.

If I couldn't be there for Tasha, there was no excuse or reassurance in the world that would stop the guilt from suffocating me.

"I love her, Mom," I said, my voice wobbly as I lowered my arms. "I have since I was a kid. Even after Dad died and I knew it was wrong."

Her chest deflated. "Oh, Leo."

"She wants nothing to do with me, but I couldn't live with myself if I let her go alone and something happened," I continued. "I care about her as much as I do our family. And that's the most important thing, right? Protecting our family?"

The house was silent as a graveyard, making the roar in my ears louder than ever. "I haven't been the easiest son. I've defied you and caused a mountain of headaches over the years, but this is the first time I've ever asked for something this huge. So you have to understand how important this is to me."

She pulled her hair behind her ear, her foot tapping at the floor. A spark of hope lit inside me, until it disintegrated with one shake of her head.

"I'm sorry, Leo. I really am," Mom replied. "But I can't risk losing you. You're too valuable to me as my son and as the Danesi Mafia's heir."

My body went ice cold, vision sharpening to a single point while everything else in my life blurred into the background. I couldn't let this be the end. Mom was seeing what was directly in front of her while I was seeing the dark descent our lives would take if we did nothing. It wasn't just Tasha I was fighting to protect. We would all be at the mercy of the Salvators eventually if we didn't stop them now.

There was one thing that would persuade her. It was the only real leverage I had, even though I'd spent my entire life fighting against it.

Which was why I had to use it despite everything I stood for begging me not to.

"If you don't help with this, I'll be dead to you anyway. I'll find a way to disappear from your life for good," I said. A flash of horror passed over her face, so I continued before she could respond. "But if you let me go tonight, I promise to finally take up my role as the Danesi Mafia's future boss and do whatever has to be done to secure it."

Her eyes went wide, but still she kept her guard up. "That offer changes nothing, Leo. Not when you could die at this party."

My teeth ground together. She was right, unfortunately, and I couldn't think of anything that would reassure her enough to let me go.

"Here's my counteroffer," she said, breaking me out of my panicked thoughts. "I will let you go to this party, but you'll take every Danesi mobster with you for *your* protection. They'll have orders to keep you alive no matter what, even if that means abandoning your goal of protecting Tasha and dragging you out of there. And afterward, when they bring you back home, we'll begin your official initiation, and I'll assign a right hand that'll never leave your side. In case you get any urges to fall into old habits of thwarting your responsibilities toward the family."

I wanted nothing to do with her offer, but my choices were limited. Either I took it or I surrendered Tasha to whatever horrific plans the Salvators had.

After a reluctant pause, I nodded. "Okay."

"We have a deal then," she said. "But we're agreeing on *your* future, Leo, not to a relationship with Tasha. Regardless of what hopes you're harboring, I can already see all the different ways the story between you two could go. All of them end with heartbreak."

I'd spent years believing the same, but this short time with Tasha back in my life made me realize we still had a chance at being together. There was a connection between us I'd never been able to sever. I knew with unbridled certainty we'd always find our way back to each other.

Neither of us moved as her words hung in the air, locked and loaded and waiting for me to respond. Mom's shoulders were stiff with anticipation, but I wasn't going to give her the outburst she was expecting. I didn't need to.

"Start rallying our soldiers right away," I replied. "I want to get out of here and to the party before Tasha does."

"How exactly do you plan on protecting her, Leo?" Mom asked as she went over to her desk to pick up her phone. "Do you really think you can stop her from putting herself in danger?"

I moved over to a mirror hanging beside a framed abstract painting, smoothing my hair back until every strand was pressed firmly down. I searched my own face, saw the hardened edge around my brows, the sharp cut of my nose. The only part of myself I still recognized was the scatter of freckles that had grown with me during my time in California. But the rest was all new. Or rather, a homecoming with a ghost I'd tried to run away from for the last four years.

When I stared into the mirror, I stared at my father.

I fixed the collar of my shirt and turned back to Mom. "I know I can't, but I'm going to try anyway."

Tasha

WHEN THE TOE OF MY HEELS HIT THE BLACK MARBLE, I knew there was no going back.

I stepped into the mansion the Salvators occupied in a glittering Paolo Sebastian dress as dark as a raven. The array of perfumes and expensive wines brushed against the edges of my lips and nose, creating a seductive orchestra to the senses.

At any other party, I'd expect everyone's attention on me, but tonight, I was surrounded by the enemy. Blending in was far more attractive, though I had high suspicions I wouldn't get that wish.

"Here we go," I whispered to myself.

When I extended my invite to the guards at the door, they looked briefly at my name before ushering me in without hesitation. It took all my willpower not to freak out at how eager they were to have me inside.

But I had to be positive. I was here to make the Salvators think they had nothing to worry about. To get them to lower their guard, bring me right to their boss, and then I'd go in for the kill.

I glided with the other new arrivals into the ballroom directly off the foyer. My heels clicked against the stone, getting drowned out by the soft mellow voice of a singer the farther I walked into the party. The ballroom was filled with guests in swaths of muted silk and playful satin, paired with a heavy dose of power clasped at their necks or wrists, while uniformed servers carried around trays of caviar-spread crackers, slices of Wagyu, and a hoard of other decadent small plates.

If I wanted to, I could pretend this was some billionaire philanthropist's private charity event or an A-list celebrity's extravagant birthday bash. But those illusions were like balloons popped midair as I looked at the rows of suited Salvator soldiers eyeing the room with their handguns in full view.

I touched the dark emerald pendant resting on my chest, feeling my heart beating underneath.

My breaths turned deep and forceful looking at the party guests. Was the Salvator boss already in the crowd quietly watching me? Or would they appear in a grand entrance surrounded by guards looking for violence, demanding everyone's attention?

Those questions came to a screeching halt when my eyes caught on the last person I wanted to see.

Leo hovered by a mantel with ornate tilework framing the antique fireplace. Because of his height, he stood above half the guests, though by the way he hunched his shoulders and kept his chin lowered, it didn't look like he wanted others to notice him. With a black tux that pulled at all the right curves and his windswept hair smoothed at the edges, staying under the radar was nearly impossible. And I hated how quickly I betrayed myself by noticing.

I didn't have a chance to decide what I would do though. In the next second, Leo descended upon me, barely stopping himself from shoving people aside to make his way over in record time.

"Tasha," he exclaimed, an edge of desperation in his voice. "I knew you'd show up. You have to get out of here. Before my brother or someone worse gets their hands on you."

Seeing Leo again caused thunder to boom in my head and a raging fire in my stomach. The image of him standing over Victor with a gun in his hand hadn't left me. Now here he was enjoying a party that Carter no doubt invited him to.

I flashed my teeth. "I trusted you and you turned out to be a traitor. What makes you think I'll listen to you now?"

"I swear I don't work with the Salvators. My brother doesn't even know I'm here," Leo pleaded. "You need to get the hell out of here. It's not safe."

"Funny you think you need to rescue me from danger when *you're* the one I should've stayed away from," I said. "How dense do you think I am, Leo? I know exactly what I stepped into. I'd ask if you'd like to participate in my little mission to find the boss, but you've already contributed *plenty*." I stepped closer until his tense breaths caressed my collarbone, my body betraying me when it sent a trail of electricity down my arms. "Was it before or after you saw my dad and sister get shot that you decided my life wasn't horrible enough and you needed to contribute your share?"

His thick brows pulled close on his cruelly handsome face. "Tasha, please. Hate me for good, but don't stay here."

"Look at that, we're finally on the same page about something. But I won't be leaving until I meet the person running this show."

"Carter already told me the Salvators have something planned for you," he said in a low, harsh breath. "I have Danesi soldiers ready to get us out."

A sharp slice of dread went through me. I had wondered if Leo would show his face here, but I hadn't anticipated him bringing anyone. If I let myself believe that he was telling the truth and wasn't working for the

Salvators, that meant he had an explosion of chaos ready to descend here at any moment.

"What's wrong with you?" I snapped. "You'll start a bloodbath with that many violent men charging in here!"

And destroy my own plan after I found the boss.

"*Good evening, everyone!*" someone said, their voice blasting through speakers spread around the ballroom. "I have the pleasure of announcing our next singer. Please welcome her to the stage!"

A celebrity pop star's voice filled the speakers. I recognized her right away—along with every other guest within earshot.

Before I could brace for it, the crowd rushed forward to get closer, shoving without thought and elbowing into tender joints. In the flurry, I tried to maneuver away from the overly excited guests, just for a woman with a massive handbag to clock me as she charged forward.

I lost my footing, but instead of stumbling, I tipped forward and crashed to the floor. My hands smacked against the black marble right before the rest of me followed.

"Animals," I groaned to myself.

With a throbbing wrist, I heaved myself to a sitting position to get my bearings, then got back to my feet when I was sure no one would send me falling over a second time.

I looked for Leo, but in the sea of the party, there was no sign of him. Despite taking my eyes off him only for a minute, he wasn't anywhere in sight.

I breathed deliberately and slowly, trying to relax the nerves prickling across my skin and goading my heart to beat harder. The crowd had swept him somewhere else in the room. Anything else I couldn't— wouldn't—consider right now.

The audience clapped at the end of the singer's song, their simultaneous praise an explosion of noise beating down on me. I moved away from the crowd to get a better view of my surroundings, scanning everywhere for Leo. I'd come into this party alone, but I couldn't forget about him after having his presence dangled in front of me.

By some miracle, hands clutched my arm, and I turned with a swell of relief.

"Leo, God, you can be so fru—"

The words fell from my mouth when I came face-to-face with my best friend instead.

"Val?" I asked, taking in her dark crimson dress.

"Tasha!" she replied, her face flushed and her eyes wide. "There you are."

I sucked through my teeth, glancing around us. "Val, *what* are you doing here?"

"We didn't become friends yesterday. I knew you wouldn't be able to stay away once you were invited and I followed you after getting your things packed. I couldn't let you walk into this party alone."

My chest warmed from her protectiveness, but a riddle of questions snuffed it out quickly. "How did you get in?"

But Val wasn't listening to me. Her attention was elsewhere as she slid her hand down my arm to grasp my own, tugging me toward the hall where the servers were flying in and out. "Come on, let's go somewhere calmer to figure out what our plan is."

I held still, forcing her back. "Wait! Leo was just here. I need to find him first."

An odd shadow passed over Val's face before she gave my arm another tug. "Forget about him."

Maybe I would've listened to her, disappeared into whatever room she tried to take me to … if her dress's off-the-shoulder sleeves hadn't shifted out of place.

Like a smear of red lipstick, a long, thin scar traced across Val's left upper arm.

The same spot where my father shot at the hitman as they ran away.

I looked up at Val. The fragment of hope I grasped onto that this was a major misunderstanding, that I was misremembering what happened that night, disintegrated when my eyes locked with hers.

"How could—"

A shout rang out above the music, cursing and saying my name. I whipped my head around until I spotted where and who it came from.

Leo was across the room by a set of back doors leading out onto a patio, struggling against the grip of four Salvator soldiers dragging him away from the party. Two other suited men—Danesi soldiers I assumed—struggled against the confines of security as well, trying to get close to him with no luck. With one swift move, both soldiers went limp with cloths pressed to their mouths and were immediately dragged out of sight.

My whole body went into high alert. Whatever was going on and whatever was true, I couldn't let the Salvators take Leo away.

But when I tried to rush over to stop them, a guard suddenly appeared, blocking my path.

"It's over, Tasha," Val said from behind me. "For him and for you."

I ignored her and jumped away from the guard, trying to run to Leo. Instead, our eyes met for barely a heartbeat before one of the men firmly pressed a cloth over his mouth, too.

"No!" I cried.

Leo made one last effort to lunge toward me, but the drugs in the cloth were too powerful and his eyes sagged shut.

CHAPTER THIRTY-FIVE

I CLAWED AT THE DARKNESS PINNING ME DOWN. I COULDN'T remember why I was desperate to be released from it, but a deep instinctual force told me it was the one thing I had to do. It grinned gleefully at me as I used all my effort to fight.

I'd had plenty of nightmares before. Enough to be the envy of any demon, but I'd never had one that wouldn't let go of me.

Eventually, I got my wish.

I gasped awake, getting one second to clock that my arms and legs were tied up and I had been chucked into the ocean, before I started to sink.

The world stilled beneath the salty depths. I tried to kick back up to the surface, but those bastards tied my ankles tight and added two heavy weights, making it impossible. Only the drum of my blood reminded me I was still alive.

I forced my eyes open in the stinging water. My black tux and white dress shirt billowed around me like death's shadows creeping closer, preparing to consume me for good.

But I wouldn't let it come for me. Not without a fight.

My hands were pinned together in front of me, but a few seconds of struggling to get rid of the zip tie proved how useless that effort was. I wouldn't be able to hold my breath for much longer, so if I wanted any chance to get out of this alive, I needed to find a new option. Fast.

Heaving my torso forward, I grabbed the rope on my right ankle tying me to a weight and pulled against its knot. One tug, then two, but the rope was stronger than it looked.

My eyes burned. My vision blurred. A soft voice whispered for me to relax and stop struggling.

Come on, come on.

Miraculously, the rope loosened and slipped off my right ankle. I clenched my teeth as I watched the weight descend into the darkness below.

I didn't stop to enjoy my victory though. Immediately, I moved to my left ankle and pulled against the binds for it, too.

Pain shot into my lungs without warning and mini lights danced in my vision. I struggled to keep going, but the lightheadedness took control, weakening my arms and tempting my mouth to open for non-existent air.

Shit, shit, shit.

The shadows moved closer this time. They climbed up my legs, stroking, caressing. Telling me it was easier to let go.

I closed my eyes. The temptation was intoxicating as my muscles went numb and the ache in my lungs pushed toward the edge.

But Tasha's face filled my mind. Her laugh echoed in my ear. Sophia appeared beside her, a childlike smile lighting up her whole face.

I couldn't leave them behind.

My eyes flew open, and I used my last bit of strength to push past my jacket and get to my ankle. Unlike the other one, this rope refused to budge out of the knot.

My fingers slipped, scrapping against the coarse rope and breaking skin. Droplets of blood floated out of the cut and dissolved against my face, trailing upward.

I reached for the second rope again, but my hands could barely grasp it as the force of the salt water pushed back against my remaining strength. There was one weight tied to me now, but there might as well have been a dozen swaying back and forth.

The gravity of my situation crashed around me. The withheld oxygen in my lungs had withered to scraps. I couldn't swim. Even without a weight holding me down.

My heart seized.

I'm going to die.

I managed to look up once more at the waning moonlight above the dark waters, but as I passed out, something exploded from the surface.

Though my vision blurred in and out, I could make out a figure swimming toward me. It had to be a mirage, my brain bringing to life one last fantasy before giving itself over to death, because there was no way what I was seeing was real.

Tasha swimming toward me.

When she reached me, she pressed her face up close to mine and wrapped one arm underneath my armpits. Heaving with more strength than I realized she had, she pulled the two of us up toward the open air. But the movement snapped the last of my willpower to keep the ocean out. My tightly closed lips broke open, letting the dark waters rush down my throat.

Bubbles floated out of Tasha's mouth as she gritted her teeth and swam faster. In seconds, we broke the surface to the sweet, cold night air, but I couldn't enjoy it. The water that had gone down my throat was a noose around my neck. Choking and squeezing the life out of me.

Tasha pulled me to shore and threw me onto my back. While the black dots in my vision pooled wider, she came closer and pressed her mouth to mine. In another time, I would have savored the feel of her lips, but instead I could barely keep myself awake as she breathed air into my lungs.

"Come on, Leo," she said, her voice strained and fearful as she pressed her hands against my chest.

I tried to speak, but thinking of words to say became a struggle, too. I'd lost feeling in my entire body.

Her hands continued pumping against my chest, up down, up down, touching my heart with each attempt to keep me here.

"Don't leave me, Leo. *Please.*"

She pumped her hands against my chest one more time, my name a desperate prayer on her lips, and with a jolt, the noose around my neck finally released.

Tasha

I GOT OUT OF THE WAY WHEN LEO TURNED ON HIS SIDE AND hurled the salty water out as gracefully as a backfiring engine.

Though my vision no longer stung from the salt water, my head swam with dizziness from diving so deep. I pressed my palm against my forehead, reorienting myself before I tried to stand or move in any way.

I hadn't known what the Salvators were planning when they grabbed Leo. All I knew was that I couldn't watch him be dragged away to meet whatever deadly fate they had in store for him.

While everyone was distracted by the commotion, and Val was pulled away by someone I assumed also worked for the Salvators, I had a prime opportunity to sneak after the men who had taken Leo outside. Thank God I did. I'd secretly watched them take him down to a dock extended far off the water's edge and tie weights to his ankles. But after he was thrown in, they wouldn't leave right away. I'd spent those excruciatingly long minutes wondering what my options were, heart lodged in my throat, when they finally went back inside.

Once Leo was done throwing up and breathing again, I moved to his ankle and unfastened the second weight. A snarling red line had formed along his skin, but otherwise it didn't seem to have caused any damage.

When the weight was free, I grasped his arm, trying not to focus on the way his white dress shirt clung to his chest or the way I felt a drop of relief that his rigid hairstyle had fallen back into a tousled look. "Are you okay?"

Leo shrugged off his drenched jacket and tossed it on the ground. "Of course. I try to drown myself for fun at least once a week"

I let out an exasperated sigh. "Good to know your sarcasm is still intact."

We both struggled to our feet. Even though he was the one who nearly drowned, Leo helped *me* stand. But I didn't push him away immediately. I slid my hand down to his, savoring the steady pump of blood through it after the cold embrace of the ocean.

"You need to get out of here," I said, looking around the property. Most of it was covered in shadows with hints of the partially covered moon and the distant glow coming from the party to guide us. "*Now.* Before someone realizes I'm gone and comes checking on you."

"I'm definitely *not* leaving without you. I'll get my soldiers swarming in here in less than a minute if we need backup," he replied. Realization dawned in his eyes though. Leo shoved his hands in every pocket on him, hissing through his teeth when he pulled out his soaked phone and nothing he pressed turned it on. "Shit."

"They tried to *murder you*, Leo," I said, peeling my drenched hair from my forehead. "And I can't leave before I meet their boss. I've done more than you deserve after what you did to Victor." I squeezed the puddles of water out of my dress. "So if you'll excuse me, I have places to be."

Leo jumped forward, the muscles in his neck tightening. "Tasha, please don't go. I don't care if you think I'm a monster. All I care about is knowing you're safe, and that can't happen if you stay here."

My heart betrayed me, yearning to believe his earnestness. But I'd let myself fall for it plenty of times up until now, just like I'd fallen for the lies Val had swaddled me in. The only way to keep myself protected was to put a wall up between us, even when an ache swelled in my chest.

"Let me go, Leo," I replied softer than I meant to. "And think of yourself. You've done it plenty of times before."

Leo stepped closer, a plea on his face. "Tash—"

A safety clicked off behind us. I stiffened before we spun, facing a gun and a too familiar face.

Carter.

He let out a strained sigh when he saw us, throwing furious glares at his brother. "For fuck's sake, Leo. I told you to stay the hell away. Instead, I find out you've caused a scene and were 'being taken care of'? I had to pretend like the thought of you getting killed didn't matter to me! I fought hard to keep you out of this war, but the boss made it clear if you tried to sabotage us again, I couldn't do anything to protect you."

Ocean water dripped off Leo's drenched shirt as he glared at his brother. "Don't bother trying. I'm not here to be coddled; I'm here to keep Tasha far away from your group. I'll burn this whole place down if I have to."

Carter stepped closer to his brother, darting a glance into the darkness behind him. "I've given you more than one chance to leave with a sack of cash and your freedom intact. But now you've put me in an impossible position where I can't let you run off. If you won't join the Salvators tonight, your fate will be determined by our boss." He hissed with frustration. "You were supposed to keep your head down and stay out of the way after I put a bullet in Callan's head."

Bile burned in my throat as his words, the casual tone of them, settled over me. "What did you say?"

Carter flicked his attention in my direction, rolling his shoulders back. "Uh—"

"I told you he shot him," Leo said breathlessly. His eyes met mine. "And he did it to pull us apart."

Carter frowned. "It had to be done."

The air became difficult to breathe. Leo hadn't been lying. Carter truly did frame him and sent the video to split us up. I wanted to tell him how sorry I was for not believing him and to bask in the swell of relief that overcame me. But I couldn't focus on anything when a flash of crimson caught my eye and Val emerged from the darkness.

"There you are, Tasha! I should've known you'd go rushing after Leo." She held up fistfuls of her dress from the ground, her breaths coming out in exasperated huffs as she looked at Carter. "What are *you* doing down here, Carter?"

"Fixing your blunder," he replied, giving her a sideways glance.

Val rolled her eyes while mine saw red.

I bared my teeth at her. "You lying *murderer.* I spent weeks grieving with you over my family's deaths and you sat there comforting me when all this time *you* were the one who shot them! You tried to shoot *me!*"

Leo cursed.

"I was following orders, Tasha. Not everything revolves around you," Val replied, her mouth pinching. "And I didn't know that was you behind the one-way mirror at the time. You spooked me with your screaming; we didn't expect anyone to be in the passages."

My gaze seared into my best friend's—scratch that, *former* best friend's face. "*Everything* about this is personal, Val. We grew up together; you were like a second sister to me. And for what? Were you promised some batch of followers you get to control or a pretty little crown you can wear?"

"I wouldn't have done it if we had another option. But I was promised a better life for myself—for *all* of us—if I went through with it." She glanced over at Carter and Leo, then back to me. "I know you don't get it yet—I'd be feeling the same if I was in your position—but there's a bigger picture here. We've all been miserable, including you, with the current way our families have been controlling us. My dad never gave me the time of day because he was always focused on the needs of your family, and you've been begging for scraps of respect from people who looked down on you for years. Eliminating your dad was the only way the Salvators could get us the life we want, where we *matter*. It wouldn't be possible if we were always fighting to keep him from shutting us down."

My body shook from the cold, salted ocean clinging to me and the October air sealing it in. I couldn't believe what I was hearing. Val had rationalized killing my family, letting herself decide it was best for *my* future on top of her own.

"He was still my father. You took him and Amelia away from me," I replied, tears burning my vision. "I hate you for justifying what you did to him, but I hate you more for how you dragged my sister into this as well. How would you feel if I shot down your dad? Your little brother?"

Val shook her head. "What happened was all necessary. You'll understand soon enough." She turned her focus to Carter. "Let's go. The boss is ready to meet with Tasha. We can deal with your brother later."

"Fine." Carter waved his gun at us to start walking. "Let's get going, you two."

Adrenaline pumped through me. The Salvators' boss. This was the reason I came here, even though I wasn't supposed to be doing it soaked all over and with Val's betrayal stinging across my heart.

Carter directed Leo and me at gunpoint, the music from the party and the laughter of guests trailing close. I braced myself for their snarls and narrowed eyes, but Carter and Val pushed me away from the party and over to the east side of the mansion.

Two guards flanked an unassuming door and nodded to Carter as we approached. Shock and nausea knotted tightly in my stomach. I wanted to know who the boss was, but not like this. No one would know what happened to us in a house this size and with walls thick enough to hold in the loudest of screams.

At the base of a staircase, another set of guards stood waiting for our arrival. Spotting us, they stepped forward and grabbed hold of Leo's arms and mine as Carter and Val led us up to the second floor.

Salt water dripped from my dress and my hair clung to my neck like a siren pulled from the sea. I shivered all over despite the heat inside as we moved across the runner on the hardwood floors and past the eggshell-white walls. I couldn't falter now or I might lose the last bit of strength I had to face what came next.

We halted at a set of double doors with crystal knobs and elegant swirls carved in. I stared straight ahead as Val stepped up to it. The person who orchestrated all this was behind those doors. Whoever they were, they would see the bottomless hatred I held.

And if luck was on my side tonight, I'd be able to unleash the same amount of pain they ordered on my family.

Val rapped on the door. With a flourish, both opened from inside, revealing a ten-seater ornate wooden table with lavish dining chairs around it. Three brushed copper antique globe lights hung in a row over the top, casting a stark light across the room and the intricate molding running up the walls and curving into the ceiling.

One seat at the center of the table was occupied. One that made my heart stop and the air from my lungs disintegrate.

"No," I whispered.

Amelia, my kind, beautiful, perfect sister, rose. She rested the tips of her fingers on the table and locked eyes with me.

"Hello, Tasha."

CHAPTER
THIRTY-SEVEN

ALL THOUGHTS AND EMOTIONS SHUT DOWN INSIDE ME, leaving me with only the ability to breathe. My sister, *my sister*, was alive and well and—

"What's going on? You're supposed to be dead!" I said breathlessly. "I watched your coffin go into the mausoleum."

I stepped forward and a Salvator soldier yanked me back. But with one raise of Amelia's hand, he dropped his grip on me.

My sister stepped away from the table, her long natural curls tumbling down a pure white jumpsuit. In a few long strides, she made her way over to me and wrapped her arms around me and pulled me close.

"I know, Tasha," Amelia said, pressing her cheek against my drenched head. "You're understandably confused."

My arms were dead weight against my sides, more a doll than a living being. Amelia didn't seem to notice or care. I breathed in her familiar scent from Jo Malone, but where it used to be a delicate, refreshing smell, it now scratched at my throat with a sharp, rancid undertone.

When Amelia finally let go of me and stepped back, I stared at my sister, somehow praying into existence the chance that she would drop this ruse and explain that it was all some horrible fever dream. "Amelia, this can't be what I think it is."

She searched my face, the composure in her own never breaking.

"It's exactly what you're thinking," she replied calmly. "I'm the boss of the Salvator Mafia. It exists because of me."

My heart dropped into my stomach. This whole time I craved revenge and my own sister was the one I was pursuing. My focus landed on a dove pin attached to her jacket. The same one that our father gave me while he bled out and the one I'd seen Salvator mobsters wearing.

Find her. Those were the last words he spoke before he died. I had assumed he meant go to her at the party, but our father had meant something greater. He *knew* Amelia was behind the Salvators and was about to fake her own death. He was trying to tell me she would be the one I needed to find.

Amelia's love of art history, all the money she convinced Julian to send to the Salvators, the secret marriage...so many signs had stared me in the face, and I'd been too naïve to see them. Too trusting that I knew my sister through and through to ever suspect she was capable of something merciless and calculated.

"No," I whispered.

But the Amelia I knew, the one who always had a soft laugh to brighten a room and a wistful look in her eyes wasn't looking back at me now.

I'd buried a dove, only for a cobra to be resurrected in its place.

"So you pretended to be dead?" Leo piped up, reminding me it wasn't just the two of us in this room. "Why wouldn't you want everyone to know who's in charge?"

"That's always been the downfall of other Mafias," Amelia replied. "Practically the whole world knows who the boss is. If I'm going to keep my position, I can't have everyone knowing who I am, other than those

I've vetted personally. I used the body of a dead girl similar to me and had my team swap her in. Rest in peace to her."

Leo's brows furrowed tight as he gestured to the room. "How did you convince all these people to follow you?"

"Through years of pinpointing who was looking for change. I've had easy access to our father's Mafia and others in the underground world ever since I realized what our family business was actually for. Not everyone in it is a raging sexist. Some saw the vision I had—especially when they saw the price I was willing to pay for their loyalty. Once I had initial people I trusted, they went out and started bringing more in. No one in the lowest rankings of the Salvator Mafia knows who their boss is. I'm the intriguing, powerful boogeyman who decides if I'll fulfill their wishes or put them in hell. It took a lot of patience and momentum to get here.

"But anyway..." Amelia frowned, turning to Carter. "Why is *he* here, Carter? I thought we agreed that if your brother tried to cause any more issues for us, he'd have to be eliminated. Are you going soft on me?"

Carter went rigid, snapping his attention to me. "Tasha pulled him out of the ocean."

I held my ground when Amelia turned back to me, looking more like our father than ever. She let out an exasperated sigh. "Always the rebellious one."

"You let me think you were murdered," I said quietly, studying her face. There was an uncanniness to her now. She was familiar yet a stranger all at once. "I mourned you."

"I couldn't let anyone who wasn't in my close circle know the truth, and until now, that included you." Amelia cupped my cheek. "I'm sorry for that, Tasha. Truly. It broke my heart having to put you through everything, but I hope with time, you can understand why it was necessary."

The body at the party and at the morgue was never hers. The girl I thought was Amelia lying on the metal table with her stitched-up face was really the face of another. No wonder Val wanted to verify the bodies in my place.

But the second body *was* our father's. Take away everything else and there was no covering that up or excusing it.

"Dad is dead because of you." My vision blurred. "He loved you and you had him killed."

Amelia lowered her hand, a steel in her hazel eyes that could cut through diamond. "Love goes so far, Tasha. When he tried to stop me, I did what any boss would do with a problem. I got rid of it."

My skin was raging hot beneath my cold, wet dress. I bit the inside of my cheek to keep my body from shaking, even as every cell inside me trembled like an earthquake wanting to split me in two. "A problem? Dad was never a *problem*. He definitely wasn't a saint, but he did *so much* for us, and you heartlessly destroyed him and the life we had for... what? Your own lust for power?"

Amelia kept her lips sealed for a long minute before moving away from me and back to the long table where Carter and Val now lounged.

"I destroyed a life that was *imprisoning* us," Amelia finally replied. "When Dad found out about the Salvators, he told me to put an end to it, but I didn't listen to him, and he cut me off. I was forced to turn to that trust-fund weasel Dad forced me to date. I know you hated Julian. Do you really believe I ever truly loved him? That I wanted to be shackled to such an airheaded, entitled prick? I married him to gain access to his finances and get everything he owned transferred to my offshore accounts while he was still in the haze of our 'happy nuptials.' He was supposed to be in the dining room with us that night. Of course, plans changed there, but everything worked out in the end. "

My throat went bone dry as I tried to swallow. He was just a pawn for her plans. A means to an end. Images of Julian flipped through my mind, landing on the final one I had of him on his hands and knees, begging me to believe he wasn't behind any of this. It was true I had never liked him, but I couldn't imagine so violently and forcibly taking him out of my life—and everyone else's lives—for good.

"Despite how much of a monster you might think I am, Tasha, I never planned on killing Dad initially," Amelia continued. She locked her gaze with mine, a new fire burning in her eyes. "I was fine with him cutting me off from the money. He could've thrown me out of the house or done a dozen other things to punish me for not listening to him. But he didn't do any of those things. Instead, he threatened to take away the only thing he knew would hurt me. You."

I didn't dare breathe as my sister wiped carefully under her eyes.

"When you told me that he offered to bring you into the family business, it was clear he was moving his own chess pieces to ensure you would choose him over me if things got ugly. And I couldn't let him rip you away from me like he did with Mom," she continued. "So I had to make the order and save both of us from his cruelty."

I shook my head, the details she admitted swimming in my head and making me dizzy. "I don't get it. Why did you *want* to start your own Mafia? You always made it seem like you had no interest in the family business, let alone the underground world Dad was operating in."

"That's true. I didn't always want this life," my sister replied. "But to Dad, it didn't matter *what* I wanted. He'd already made up his mind about me and I came up short. I could've gotten multimillion-dollar projects for him, shot a hundred of his enemies in one sweep, and he would still see the version of me he had settled on. Someone once suggested he consider me as his successor, and he laughed. *Laughed.*" She clenched her teeth, running a trembling hand over her curls. "I was too weak. His silly little girl who liked art and cried too often. I was never..."

I stepped forward, my breathing coming in short bursts. "Never *what?*"

"I was never you," Amelia replied with an edge to her voice. "Dad started grooming you for the successor role years ago. You had the spark he was looking for. I once heard him say you were the miniature version of himself while I was too much like Mom. How could I ever change his mind when he thought like that? He chose *you*, and there was nothing I could do about it. Creating the Salvators was my way of proving how wrong he was. I'm not weak and never have been."

I stared at my sister as she poured herself a glass of water from a pure crystal carafe and took a long sip. It never occurred to me that our father had already set his eyes on me inheriting his crown. He seemed to keep me at a distance, dangling the idea of it just out of reach, but really, he was waiting until the right moment. While Amelia was forced to witness all of it from the sidelines.

A stab of guilt went through my chest for her. I couldn't help it. She was still my sister. "You shouldn't have gone through that. If I had known, maybe—"

"You didn't and that's okay," Amelia replied. She smiled gently, coming back over, and took my hands in hers. "None of this is your fault. Which is why I want you to come on board. Help me build a *new* empire. All the years of careful planning, pooling of money, and recruitment has been for this. *This* future. Not the one Dad or anyone else had decided for us."

Silence filled the room, expanding and absorbing every particle of air with each second that I didn't respond. Carter and Val watched me closely while Leo's gaze seared into my back.

A hole opened in the center of my chest, swelling with an intense ache. All because of how much *want* I felt for what she created. That despite how she orchestrated our father's death, how she gave Victor up to Carter as a gift, and all the other ways she'd torn my heart apart that would never be fully repaired, I couldn't stop myself from picturing this new future she wanted for us.

I'd come in here with the intention of taking down the Salvators' boss, but nothing prepared me to face my *sister* of all people. Going through with my original plan meant losing her a second time. Would it be worth it? Was I prepared for that?

If I joined her, I would have her back. I could hold power over men who once made me feel weak and alone. Force them to fear me if they wouldn't respect me. I wouldn't need to hold my promise to Ravi to gain my power. It would be so easy to let go of my outrage over what Amelia had done and melt into her arms again. To go back to a version of what we used to be, always there for each other no matter what faced us.

All I had to do was take her offer.

"And if I joined you," I said, "you would help get the Nicastro Mafia on board with me as their boss?"

She searched my face, a curious look in her expression. "You misunderstand me, Tasha. The only way I can build the Salvators into the Mafia I want is to absorb other mobs and gangs into it. That includes the Nicastro Mafia. I can't have you leading them; it'll undermine my authority."

The pull to join her froze. Revenge had fueled me to fight for the role, but that didn't mean I wanted to give it up now that I knew she was behind everything. Amelia knew I wanted to take our father's place in the family empire. He believed I could lead it. Yet despite that, she didn't want me to have this?

"Carter wanted me to think Leo shot Victor, knowing it would break us up," I said as a suspicion sprouted inside me, growing, and spreading with rapid speed. "Was that his idea or yours?"

"Mine," she replied, letting go of my hands.

"Why did you want that?"

Amelia stayed silent for a long time before finally answering, "If you must know, it's because I didn't want you two getting so close again and coming between us when you finally learned I was alive. If anyone was to find out you two had an alliance, well..." She inhaled deeply, flicking her attention to Leo and back. "It would've made things...difficult for me."

And there it was. My suspicion blooming into reality. I turned to look at Leo as well. Our gazes locked, an understanding passing between us. My sister didn't want us being close, because she was scared it would convince our families' Mafias to support each other again. We were powerful organizations on our own but still easy for Amelia to infiltrate. If we'd had an alliance, our Mafias would've been titanium and nearly impossible to compromise.

She'd broken us apart for her own gain. Not thinking of the pain I'd feel from losing Leo again and thinking he had betrayed me. Just like with Dad. With Victor. How could she stand here and reassure me the things she did were for my benefit as much as her own when I was the only one hurt by her choices?

Amelia pulled a piece of my wet hair behind my ear, grazing her fingers over my cheekbone. "Don't let this discourage you. I can make sure Leo's kept safe as long as he stays out of trouble. Whatever makes you happy and feel loved. All I want is you by my side."

A part of me felt for Amelia. Our father wanted to control who she was by smothering her strength and ambition. And yet, here she was wanting me to do the same. To become her obedient little sister sitting at her feet while she ruled our world without any equals.

I closed my eyes, the weight of the necklace pressing hard against my chest. My heart. After a moment, I knew what I had to do.

"I can't join you, Amelia," I replied, looking at her. "You didn't want to be in Dad's shadow, and I don't want to be in yours. The Nicastro Mafia is mine to inherit, and I won't let you take that from me."

My sister's mouth twitched as the warmth she offered flickered out. "I'm sorry you feel that way."

She stepped away from me, her hand going to her chest and sliding underneath the V-cut of her jumpsuit...

And pointed a gun at Leo.

"But I wasn't offering a choice," she said, walking over to him. "Either you comply or he dies."

My heart went into my throat while Leo's eyes widened, but it was Carter who jumped forward first, springing out of his chair and holding his attention firmly on my sister. "Hold on, Amelia. Let's figure this out together. My brother can be a pain in the ass, but I can work on him. It doesn't need to go this way." He tensed, adding, "*Please.*"

"Save the negotiations, Carter," she replied. "This is all on Tasha's shoulders now."

I tried to keep my voice even only to fail miserably when it came out wobbly and breathless. "You wouldn't."

"Wouldn't I?" Amelia replied, releasing the safety. "We've been raised in the company of killers all our lives, Tasha. It's in our blood. I wanted you to do this willingly, but if I have to force your hand, I will."

She didn't flinch. Not one lock of hair moved or brow twitched. Her expression was sharper than a surgeon's knife and snuffed of any emotions.

A loud bang erupted. I yelped, thinking Amelia had fired at Leo, until I realized it was coming from outside the massive windows facing the ocean.

Fireworks exploded into the dark sky. They illuminated the room in brilliant shades of violet, teal, and gold, flashing across my sister and highlighting the corruption within.

Watching our father and Victor die was its own kind of gut-wrenching pain. But watching the person I thought I knew, the one I unconditionally loved, shed into a merciless stranger was so much worse. This pain haunted every touch, every word, every gentle smile I'd ever experienced with her. Death was final. But this betrayal was infinite.

I couldn't let her walk free and escape the crimes she'd committed on our family. But I wouldn't stop her for our father alone, I would stop her for *myself* and for the death of who we could've been.

"All right," I lied, my words ringing clear in the large room. "I'll join you."

Sweat formed across my back as I stared Amelia down, willing her to lower the gun from Leo's head. I'd need her far away from him when I signaled to Matteo.

"I'm glad you have." Amelia's arm fell to her side. She nodded to the Salvator mobsters hovering behind Leo and they stepped back.

Relief swelled through me like the tide coming to shore. Without thinking, I hurried over to him. He wrapped his arms around me the moment I was within reach, pressing his mouth to the top of my head.

"I'm going to get us out of here," I whispered into his chest. "Get behind something when I tell you to."

Leo stiffened but didn't say anything.

"I have to say, I'm surprised your Achilles' heel is still him. I remember you telling me you'd never forgive him for how much he hurt you."

I pulled out of Leo's embrace and faced Amelia. Something had shifted in her expression, as if she was seeing me for the first time, too.

I placed myself in front of Leo, willing him not to move. Amelia already made it clear she had no issue shooting him, but I had to take the risky bet that she wouldn't touch me.

"Let's wrap up this conversation," Amelia continued. "I have a jet waiting to take me to France to set up shop there, and I want you to come with me."

I inhaled slowly, my heart a wild stallion beneath my rib cage. Whatever happened next, I couldn't let it end with my sister walking out as a free woman. "You've lied to me so deeply and cruelly, Amelia. Maybe one day I could've found it in me to forgive you for taking Dad and Victor, but what I can never do is forgive you for betraying me. Your own sister." I ripped the emerald pendant from around my neck, the delicate gold chain snapping free immediately. "Which is why I'm putting an end to this."

The fake stone shattered beneath my fingers. Shards of glass stabbed into my skin, sending shocks of pain through my hand, but it was worth it to get to the hidden wireless button beneath, calling on my final ace.

"What is that?" my sister snapped.

On cue, an explosion from some bombs my soldiers secretly attached to a wall on the east wing boomed through the mansion, rushing upstairs to reach our ears and shake the floor beneath us. My big, grand signal to tell Matteo it was go time.

I threw the necklace to the ground as blood dripped from my hand. I met Amelia's wide eyes and smiled; my head swimming with adrenaline. "There's your answer."

A fury I had never seen before flashed across Amelia's face. It was probably a look that made others buckle at the knees, but I held steady against it. All I needed was another minute. Then I could watch my sister and the world she had created come crashing down.

I smiled when a flurry of gunshots rang out downstairs.

"That's a raid!" Val exclaimed, jumping to her feet so fast her chair toppled to the floor. "Is it the FBI?"

"We have to get out of here, Amelia, *now*," Carter said.

Amelia whipped her attention to the closed double doors before coming over to me in two long strides. She grabbed my chin, digging in her long acrylic nails enough to ache. "Do you think getting a few allies in here will help you, Tasha? I had the most powerful Mafia boss in New York killed without any issue. What makes you think you can stop me?"

"Because I have something Dad didn't," I replied, my jaw so tight it ached.

On the other side of the walls, dozens of footsteps pounded down the hall, growing in intensity as they followed the tracking signal the Ferreiras' wireless device issued after I triggered it. Amelia's soldiers had their guns out and pointed at the door, but there were only eleven of them total in this room. A lamb of strength compared to the lions charging toward us.

"Boss, forget about her!" Val shouted, heading for a back door. "We need to get you to safety!"

"*Amelia*," Carter pressed. "Let's go!"

Amelia's chest heaved. Her nails pressed so deeply into the delicate flesh of my face that they drew blood. "You've just made an enemy out of me, Tasha."

"Then so be it," I replied. "You're already dead to me anyway."

With one swipe of my wrist, I ripped the dove pin off her as the double doors crashed open and a thunder of Nicastro Mafia soldiers and criminals from different gangs stampeded in with Matteo leading the charge.

"Now!" I screamed at Leo, as the first bullets began to fly from Matteo's gun.

Leo dove out of the way of one of the Salvator men right before a bullet could pierce his chest. I wanted him to stay down, but he swiped the dead man's handgun and whipped around to start firing at the remaining Salvator soldiers, too. I used the initial distraction to grab Amelia's weapon and twist her arm behind her, forcing her down and holding a firm grip on her while I pressed the nose of the gun between her shoulder blades. There was no way I was letting her escape during the chaos.

Well over forty criminals had swarmed the room, making quick work of the eleven Salvator mobsters. They surrounded Val, but she refused to drop her weapon.

If she didn't stand down soon, they would shoot her. I had made it clear to go after everyone who wouldn't surrender, not knowing that it included my former best friend. My eyes burned into her, willing her to listen to Matteo shouting at her to give up, though I couldn't help but wonder what it would feel like to watch the person who sent the fateful bullets into my father experience the same pain.

But she wouldn't listen. Not until one specific person rushed into the room.

"Put the gun down, Valentina!" Richard roared at his daughter.

And finally, she did.

"Fuck all of you," she spat. But the gun was on the floor and right after, my consigliere grabbed her.

With the ring of bullets over, Matteo turned to me, his face falling open with shock when he realized who I was holding on to.

"*Amelia,*" he breathed. "You're the one behind all this?"

"She is," I replied, letting go when a group of my allies surrounded her. "We've spent the last half hour catching up on every way she's betrayed our family."

Matteo closed his eyes for a moment, giving his head a shake, before he opened them again and looked at me. "The rest of the gangs helping us are downstairs holding the guests in the ballroom. Most of the Salvator Mafia didn't surrender, but the few that did are also with them. Incidentally, they're former Nicastro mobsters. Fools." He nodded to Leo who rigidly stood facing everyone; his skin flushed underneath the salted hair sticking to his face and the gun still firmly in his hand. "We had the Danesi Mafia appear and start firing with us. I thought they were on the Salvators' side, until they told me their orders were to keep their heir safe. They helped us when I told them we were trying to push our way to you. Apparently, they knew wherever you were, Leo wouldn't be far behind."

I smiled, but it was short-lived when a jolt ripped through Leo like a spasm. He whipped his head around. "Where's my brother?"

We all looked around the room. Sure enough, Carter was nowhere to be found. I looked down at Amelia when she let out a harsh laugh.

"That weasel," she said. "Abandoning us to save himself."

Matteo gestured to a few of our guys. "Tell those downstairs to find Carter Danesi and stop him from escaping."

The men nodded, rushing out of the room with their weapons gripped in their hands.

"What are we doing with her?" one of the guys with a gun trained on Amelia asked. "I can put a bullet in her skull right now to put an end to this."

My cousin sucked in a breath sharply, but otherwise waited silently for my response.

Amelia kept her face turned away from me. I'd wanted to take down the boss, have them on their knees begging for mercy as I towered over them. I had that, but now that I knew the person was my sister, I couldn't let them kill her. Not because of who she was, but because in death, Amelia would never have to face the consequences of her betrayal or see how well I'd do in spite of it. Death was the easy out. And I wouldn't be the one to give it to her.

"No. Tie her up," I ordered. "I want a group to discreetly leave her outside of a police station with concrete evidence against her. Do whatever you need to do to make it happen." The Nicastro Mafia eyed me warily and then one another, but I ignored their doubts.

Richard stepped forward, two Nicastro soldiers dragging Val along behind him. "My daughter has brought so much shame onto our name, but please, Tasha, let me handle her. I promise she'll suffer more from her actions than sending her to the law."

I stared hard at my former best friend who glowered at me. Finally, I gave one simple nod.

Matteo clapped his hands together, his gun back in its holster at his hip. "Well, let's get this next plan in action."

Hands wrapped around Amelia, hauling her to her feet, while Richard dragged Val out of the room and the rest handled the fallen Salvator soldiers. I was so absorbed in the scene, I didn't notice Leo approaching me until his arms were wrapped around my shoulders, pulling me to his chest.

"It's over," he said, nuzzling my neck. "But I can't believe it. These guys aren't all from the Nicastro Mafia, right? How did you get other organizations to help?"

I squeezed my eyes shut, my stomach twisting, but I ignored it and let myself sink into the feel of him. Leo didn't know what I'd done, but for a moment, I wanted to forget the secret I carried.

"Matteo made some calls," I lied. It made me a coward, but I wasn't ready to face the fallout of my choices. "Some groups owed him a favor."

Before he could ask more questions, I shifted to face Leo. I pressed my face into his chest, inhaling his unique, comforting scent.

Looking up, I took in every eyelash and every mark on his handsome face. "Thank you."

"For what?" he asked, his voice husky.

"For not giving up on me, even when I tried to push you away."

His eyes softened, and before I realized what was happening, his face was inches from mine. I parted my lips, wanting nothing more but to feel his mouth, but before I could let myself completely melt into him, Matteo appeared beside me, holding out his phone.

He gave me the kindness of not commenting on Leo and me. "For you."

I took the phone and stepped away from Leo, the pulse of my heart beating hard in the side of my head.

"Are you hurt?" were the first words out of Ravi's mouth. "Matteo said you've been through hell tonight. You know I could've been there to protect you; you didn't need to be so stubborn about it."

I cleared my throat, turning away from Leo. "I'm fine. The other gangs were incredibly helpful. I'm just reeling from everything I've learned."

"I'm glad you're safe," Ravi replied, the tension in his voice easing. "You can tell me all about it once this wave has settled. And remember to call me if anyone like the police tries to cause you trouble. I'll handle it."

"Thanks, Ravi," I said, soft enough that no one else could hear. "We'll talk soon."

Once I'd hung up, I took a long, steady breath to center myself again, before spinning back around. Until we were out of here and Amelia was in the hands of the law, I couldn't let myself falter. I placed a hand on my hip, striding over to Matteo to give back his phone.

"We should get out of here," I said. "We need to prepare our stories for the cops."

Leo studied me, searching for answers I wasn't ready to give, but he didn't argue. "I'll follow your lead."

I managed a small smile before facing the room.

The criminals from these different organizations had agreed to follow me after one simple yet wholly fraught deal I made with Ravi. I wasn't naïve about that. Despite the promises I had to make, one day I would forge a new crown that was all my own. One that would burn as bright as a fallen star and scorch every last drop of darkness that got in my way.

"Ready?" Matteo said with a sobering gaze. He and I both knew how loaded that question was. "We can leave by a side exit so no one from the party sees you two."

I nodded and moved to the open doors, but before I reached them, Amelia's voice stopped me.

"This isn't over," she snarled.

I paused, letting myself savor the feeling of this win. Despite how it happened, I'd shut down the Salvators, and I wouldn't let anything take that away from me.

"Oh, big sister." My voice was smooth as velvet as I spun around to face her. "It definitely is."

Tasha

THE WATER IN MY GLASS SHONE FROM THE FLUORESCENT lights hanging above as I lowered it back onto the table. Across from me, Agent Marquez sat back in his chair beside his colleague, Agent Stein.

Once my hand was checked out at the hospital and I had showered, I drove to the White Plains FBI office with my mother when they inevitably called about Amelia. With clean skin and comfortable clothes on, I sat in this windowless room for hours, answering endless questions while giving my best performance to date.

"It's true Amelia's *alive* and a *Mafia boss*?" I asked for the twelfth time. As if I truly couldn't fathom any of it. Every fed agent I'd spoken to since I got here lapped up my innocent act without batting an eye. My mother had done a great job with her performance, too.

Agent Marquez nodded with the patience of a seasoned teacher. I'd already put him and Stein through the ringer with my own slew of questions, pretending like I didn't already know every answer they gave and the ones they purposely sidestepped. To them, I was a naïve seventeen-year-old rich girl caught up in her family's malicious schemes. I planned on keeping it that way.

"As I already explained, yes, she is. Someone left her tied up outside the police station in Rye with a note stating who she was and a burner laptop that has her fingerprints all over it. Given the circumstances surrounding your father's death and faking hers, we've been investigating this thoroughly. At the very least, she's being charged with fraud on a number of counts."

My mother took my good hand in hers. She'd been crying on and off all night since I first broke the news to her that Amelia not only faked her own death but was a criminal mastermind, too. Now her eyes shone with her latest batch of tears. Without her hair done up and her makeup perfectly applied, the stress in her face was on full display.

"It's absolutely awful. I never realized she'd been corrupted. Did you really not see any signs?"

I shook my head, staying quiet. Getting deeper into this conversation in front of Agents Marquez and Stein would send me down a slippery path to revealing how not-so-innocent I was in all of this.

Agent Stein let out a sigh and pushed back his chair. "Everyone is grateful for the help you've given us, Tasha. Ms. Lemieux. I realize this has been a difficult night for the two of you. I'm sure you're eager to get home and rest now. We'll take things from here."

Home. It was a place I thought I'd always understand and find comfort in. But now it was also a stranger to me and full of a past I needed to get away from. At least for a little while.

I'd agreed to take time off school and go to Milan with my mother. After everything that had gone down, seeing the life she'd created for herself and laying low until the news had run its course on Amelia sounded like a blessing. Matteo agreed to run Nicastro Developments—and the

Nicastro Mafia—while I was gone. Neither of us were worried about a revolt over it. Not with Ravi's influence always hovering.

"I also want you to know that we'll be keeping your sister in custody until her trial," Agent Marquez added. "You may be asked to testify."

"We'll be talking to our lawyers before anything like that occurs," my mother replied.

He wordlessly nodded and rose to his feet with us. But when we were back out in the hall, I turned to the agents with one last need pulling at my heart. "I have one favor."

My mother and the two men stopped, waiting for me to continue.

"I'd like to see my sister again."

"Tasha..." The lines on my mother's face deepened. "I'm not sure you can handle that."

I shook my head. "After what I've been through, I can handle almost anything. News will break about her before lunch and then chaos will descend. I need to see her once more before then."

"She's still in the observation room for questioning," Agent Marquez replied. "I can take you there. Will that be enough?"

My mother touched my shoulder, but I ignored her silent plea and nodded, my pulse beating fiercely inside me. "I'll take it."

He escorted me down the hall to another wing and knocked on a door before letting himself in. I followed inside while my mother and Agent Stein waited in the hall. Two other agents reclined in chairs, keeping their attention on a one-way mirror in front of them.

My eyes slowly adjusted to the sudden dip in light, but that didn't stop my gaze from traveling to the figure on the other side of the mirror. My sister sat at a table facing us while an agent tried to coax answers out of her. She was still in her white jumpsuit, but now her thick curls were tied back and blotchy purple circles were underneath her eyes.

Surrounded by four gray walls without any of the glamor and power to shine over her, Amelia only looked like a privileged young woman who got into a tough situation.

But I knew better than to fall for it.

Amelia glanced up then. And although she couldn't see anything from that side of the mirror, her gaze landed on the area where I stood—almost meeting my eye.

My stomach knotted, but I refused to let myself waver. It didn't matter that my sister couldn't see me. Despite everything we'd put each other through, that sisterly link tied between us hadn't severed.

But this time, I wouldn't grieve for her. I saw now how the world our father secretly raised us in had warped her into someone unrecognizable. He caused so much of our pain, but Amelia still chose her path. Now it was time I chose mine.

I grabbed the dove pin our father gave me from my purse. It was such an innocent thing on the surface, yet underneath a sharp point waited to cut through the toughest of skin.

I stared at it for a moment, then chucked it into the garbage bin near the door.

"I have one more favor," I said.

"You keep saying that." Agent Marquez sighed. "What is it?"

I slipped my hand into my pocket, pulling out a small paper. There were no words on it. Just a simple sketch of a lion standing fierce and unwavering. I extended it to him.

"Can you give this to her?"

He took it, eyeing the image. "What's it supposed to mean?"

I smiled. "She'll know."

Our father used to say Nicastros were as powerful and regal as lions. It must have been why the family decided to use it to symbolize our Mafia. One less lion remained in this family since Amelia shed her fur for scales. There was nothing I could do to change her back, no regrets I could voice to save her from this fate.

But there was one regret I'd never feel.

I'd never regret throwing my sister into the fire she created. Just like I'd never regret standing back and watching her burn.

Casting one more look at her, I left the room—and Amelia—behind forever.

CHAPTER
THIRTY-NINE

I ASSESSED HOW I LOOKED IN THE MIRROR ONE MORE TIME before getting out of my car and taking the stairs up to the front doors. And yet smoothing my hair or fixing my tie couldn't stop my chest from feeling like it was filled with wings, fluttering so hard and fast that I was ready to take flight.

It had been six weeks since I'd seen Tasha. Six weeks of torture since she got on her flight and left for Milan with her mom. I hadn't tried to stop her or make her feel guilty for going, knowing this was more important than ever for her to do, when that meant accepting she wouldn't return any of my calls or texts during those weeks, too.

But that was behind us. She was back in time for Scarsdale Country Day's winter formal—and to be my date.

I exhaled a stream of nerves, pulling at the sides of my onyx-black suit before ringing the doorbell.

Charles answered the door, giving me a bemused look when he saw me fidgeting. "Miss Nicastro will be down shortly. Why don't you come in?"

I nodded wordlessly and stepped inside, patting my hands against the sides of my thighs. We'd exchanged a few texts and had one phone call since Tasha got back, but otherwise, we hadn't seen each other since she left. I wasn't sure what I would do once I saw her. All I did know was that she was the person I'd spend days, weeks, or months waiting to reunite with.

"Charles?" Tasha's rich and lovely voice called out. "Is that Leo?"

The house manager eyed me openly before calling back, "Indeed, Miss Nicastro."

I held my breath until she stepped into view from the second floor. When she did, my face broke out in a grin as my fiery lioness looked down at me.

Her golden gown hugged down to her ankles, the front scooping wide and low across her chest. The light caught on the shards of gold embellished across the fabric and the extra flourish trailing on either side of her. She was the sun incarnate. And I'd never seen a more breath-taking sight.

"Damn," I said.

Tasha smirked and descended the steps toward me. In a few strides, I moved over to the staircase and grabbed her hand on the last step, running my thumb over her soft skin as I helped her reach the ground safely.

"Does that mean you like my dress?" she asked, shaking her bangs away from her thick lashes and dark irises. "I got it in Milan. It's a Zuhair Murad."

"It does," I replied, squeezing her hand. "And I like the beautiful girl wearing it, too."

She narrowed her eyes at me, though I could still see the blush forming in her cheeks. "I'm sure you've said that many times."

"No," I replied. "I've only ever said it to you."

Tasha searched my face for a moment, her face softening the longer she looked at me. "Hi, by the way."

"Hey," I said quietly.

Letting go of my hand, she pulled the delicate chain of her purse over her shoulder, and asked, "Are you ready to go?"

"Where's your mom?" I craned my neck down the hall when I heard the gentle clatter of dishes in the kitchen. "Doesn't she want to see you off?"

Tasha shook her head. "We said bye earlier. Come on."

I wasn't going to argue about getting more alone time with her and hurried down the steps to open the passenger door of the Ferrari, taking the chance to admire how gorgeous my date was one more time.

We'd beaten the odds. I loved her all the more because of it.

"What?" Tasha asked with a small laugh.

I grinned. "I'm admiring how stunning you are."

She smiled back, but a muscle twitched in her jaw before she quickly slipped inside the car.

I noted it as I came around to the driver's side. Tasha wanted to ease back in after everything that happened. I could go along with that even when all I wanted to do was run my hands across her body and press my lips against hers.

Sighing, I got into the car and looked over at her. I could see a million city lights tonight, but the one that mattered was the one illuminating her. "I'm so happy you're here."

The sides of her eyes crinkled as she gazed back at me. "Me too."

Tomorrow was full of the unknown, but tonight was all ours. I'd spent enough years keeping my distance from Tasha to last a lifetime. I had no interest in ever going back to the sidelines of her life.

We sped down the highway to Manhattan where the winter formal was taking place. No one knew yet that we were together, but they would when we walked in. Announcing it this way was more on brand for us than anything else could be.

"Have you had any updates on your brother?" Tasha asked, breaking the silence that had built between us.

I shook my head. "Still haven't been able to track him down. I'm guessing nothing has changed with Amelia?"

She tipped her chin down, fiddling with a ring decorating her index finger on her right hand. "Not that I've heard. The media have been wild trying to get a photo of her. Some sites are offering six figures for a shot of her in an orange jumpsuit. It's disgusting. I was left alone most of the time in Milan, but paparazzi were waiting in droves when we landed back in New York."

I pressed my lips close together. An explosion erupted across every news station in North America when the story broke that Amelia Nicastro was still alive and was the one behind her own father's murder. They hadn't stopped talking about it since and probably wouldn't until her jury trial was over later next year. My brother hadn't made a dent in the story since no one knew he was involved. Val got off easy, too. It made sense though. Her parents whisked her out of the country to some remote center for troubled teenagers right away. It wasn't on a map and took in the worst cases.

"Have you heard anything about Val?"

A shadow darkened Tasha's unblemished face. "No. Nothing."

I reached over and gently squeezed her hand. "You did the right thing. With all of it. Remember that."

She locked eyes with me for a second before squeezing back. "Sometimes I'm not sure I did."

We held hands for another minute before I let go to exit the highway and submerge into the thick of Manhattan.

Our formal was being held at a venue on the edge of Central Park near Lincoln Square. The car guided us there, but within two blocks, it became clear which building we were headed to.

The road out front of the venue was blocked off with valets guiding incoming cars and helping students in sharp tuxes and expensive dresses out of their vehicles.

Once we were up next, I jumped out before an attendant could come over and rushed around the Ferrari to the other side. My heart pumped wildly in my chest as students turned to gasp when I opened it and revealed who was with me.

I extended my hand and Tasha took it as she stepped out of the car in one graceful flourish.

"Thank you," she purred.

I smiled, kissing her hand. "Of course."

Like a Red Sea of glittering silk and hand-stitched lace, our classmates parted to let us through. Every conversation halted as we moved up the front steps of the venue and stepped inside. But I didn't care what they thought or whispered about. All I could focus on was the fierce beauty walking beside me.

An archway of flowers in every color covered the grand entrance into the event. I breathed in the cacophony of floral scents as we passed through it and into the ballroom. Corinthian pillars swept around the room with thick burgundy curtains draped beside every door. On one side was a large stage where a DJ played remixes of popular songs in front of a dance floor while opposite, students hung at the bar sipping elaborate mocktails in long-stemmed glasses. Large round tables with shiny gold tableware and tall vases filled with the same flowers from the archway took over the rest of the space.

I turned to Tasha, brushing my fingers down her arm. "Do you want me to grab a drink for you or find our seats first?"

When she didn't answer, I followed what had caught her eye. Across the ballroom, Ravi hovered by one of the pillars by himself staring at us. After I learned he'd helped us take down the Salvators, I worried he'd made a move and swept Tasha back into his arms, but that all melted away once she agreed to come to the formal as my date.

I glared at him for a beat before leaning close to her ear. "Don't feel badly for him. He'll be okay with seeing us together after a while." My focus caught on a flash of blond hair. Scarlett stood with the rest of my Scarsdale group by the dance floor. When she caught me staring though, I looked away. "So will others."

Tasha's jaw tensed again as she turned to face me. "Let's get away from everyone for a little bit. Okay?"

"Okay," I replied and followed her from the room and down an empty hall that had nothing but a few cushioned benches and generic white orchids decorating the space.

She sat on one of the benches, her hands braced on either side of her, and stared at the ground. I carefully approached as she crossed one leg over the other, shaking her foot hard enough to make her entire leg move.

"Is something wrong?" I asked.

She wouldn't look up at me. "I was told you're spending more time with your family's Mafia lately. Is that true?"

I swallowed. It was, but since she left so quickly after the Salvators' party, I never got a chance to explain to her what deal I had to make with Mom beforehand. Clearly, she was upset she had to find out what I'd done through another source.

"Yes." I rubbed the back of my neck and took a seat beside her. "I meant to tell you everything sooner, but you were gone for so long and—" I sighed. "I've officially become the heir apparent to the Danesi Mafia. It was the only way I could convince my mom to let me go to the Salvators' party. Though I wasn't much help that night, was I?" A dry laugh escaped me. "While you were gone, I've started shadowing her and our consigliere in between school."

I braced for her shock. The questions and anger from not telling her right away. But none of that happened. She looked down at her hands instead, twisting the ring on her right hand back and forth. This time, I paid more attention to it. Noticing that it had a gold band with a rectangular emerald in the center and tiny diamonds lining all four sides of the gem.

"I'm grateful for all the help you've given, Leo," she replied. "But I wish you hadn't put yourself in such a position for me."

"I *wanted* to. Making sure you're safe is worth it, Tasha." I pressed my lips into a tight smile. "It does mean my extracurriculars entail spending way too much time with my mom and a bunch of rough dudes who think yelling is a normal conversation level. But it's not all bad. Honestly, maybe with us taking over, we can put any remaining bad blood to rest."

"I *do* want that. Truly." She lifted her gaze up from her lap and looked at me. "But it can't happen the way you want it to."

I searched her sober face. "What do you mean?"

She ran her teeth over her bottom lip, stretching the quiet long enough to put me on high alert.

"The Nicastro Mafia didn't have a change of heart about accepting me as their new boss before the party." Tasha paused, her throat bobbing, and moved the piece of jewelry off her right hand and over to her left. To her ring finger. "They agreed to accept me if I promised to marry a specific person when I turn eighteen. It was either take their offer or lose them entirely and let my sister win."

The world around us stilled. No music. No laughter. No clinking glasses. All I could hear was the blood pounding in my head—loud enough that the words I spoke were muffled to my own ears. "Who did you promise to marry?"

Remorse coated her dark eyes, and I knew before she spoke what name would leave her lips.

"Ravi."

This time, my heart stilled, too.

If I disintegrated into dust and every last part of me swept into the cracks of the floor, I wouldn't have noticed. Because all I could focus on was the way she said his name, the simplicity of it, and it cracked me in two.

"Why," I said, the one word coming out thick and hoarse. *"Why him?"*

Why not me.

Tasha's eyes shone with a thin coat of tears. "His family . . . they're powerful. *Far* more powerful than I ever realized. They hold the respect and friendship of nearly every criminal organization around the world. It was how Ravi convinced the organizations near us to come and help and why my father was so enthusiastic about us dating. He knew how much they could strengthen our own family. I wanted to win my Mafia over on my own, but I couldn't risk letting Amelia get away with her plan. Being engaged to Ravi is the only way I can get them to accept me. I'm hoping with time I can make the Mafia realize that I'm as strong as my father was, but for now . . ."

I knew just how deep the Ferreiras' influence went, but I didn't have it in me to explain that to Tasha. Ravi and his family were completely untouchable. It would make *her* completely untouchable in more ways than one if she went through with this marriage.

"I didn't choose this to hurt you," she continued, grasping my hand. "Please understand that. We wouldn't have stopped my sister if it wasn't for them. The Ferrairas wouldn't have agreed to help me if it wasn't personal for them, and being their son's fiancée made it that way. I *had* to do it. For all of us."

"Did he buy that for you?" My throat thickened as I stared down at the ring. "Or did he already have it?"

Tasha's brows knit together, her lips pressing close. "We picked it out in Milan. He surprised me with a visit a week after I arrived and insisted on buying me a ring to make our decision more official."

I closed my eyes. There it was. The reason she ignored my calls and texts while she was gone. I desperately wanted to believe this was an alternate reality I'd fallen into, one that I would snap out of and back to the reality I was supposed to be in, *we* were supposed to be in.

But when I opened my eyes, he was standing there. Waiting for her.

Tasha leaned in and kissed my cheek before she let me go and rose to her feet. "I'm sorry, Leo."

"Don't do that." I shook my head, my hands clenching and unclenching from the anger flowing through them with nowhere to go. "Don't talk to me like this is over."

Sympathy poured out of her gaze. I hated it. Hated the way she looked at me like I was an injured dog she had no choice but to put down.

"But it is," Tasha replied.

Ravi put his hand on her waist. He tried to keep his expression neutral, but I saw triumph flash in his bright eyes before the two of them turned their backs on me and walked away.

When they had disappeared into the crowd, I jumped to my feet as well. The world around me spun and my head pounded. Fire coursed through me as I made my way through the swirling party lights and students drunk off their perfect, untouched lives.

I didn't stop shoving through the beauty and wealth until I reached an exit door and pushed it open, stepping out to the barren trees of Central Park and the slumbering earth beneath it. The cold night air brushed over my heated face, a chill rushing across my skin.

The stillness nearly silenced the buzz of the city the farther I walked, though it didn't touch the pain that burrowed through me, digging down to bone with each reminder of what Tasha had done. Who she had chosen.

When I reached a divide in the path, I stopped and looked up as the first snowfall of the season drifted down from the clouded sky. I repeated her name under my breath, each mention tearing out another piece of me, until nothing but the memory of that name, of what we could've been, remained.

ACKNOWLEDGMENTS

This book exists because of so many impossibilities becoming possible, and for that I am forever grateful.

To the person who was my first impossible-made-real: Sabrina Taitz. My fiercely extraordinary literary agent and friend. You've guided us through the toughest of storms and kept me afloat through it all. I will never forget the first time you told me that this book and I were worth fighting for. You meant every word and then some. I used to hope and dream as I worked on my stories that one day a person would come along and have such an unwavering belief in me. Then that day came. You are wishes coming true.

With Sabrina came an introduction to the absolute best literary agency someone could ask for. I had no idea when I became a WME Books author that I would also get a huge group of dedicated professionals joining my team! Thank you to everyone, especially Cashen Conroy, Olivia Burgher, Lucy Balfour, James Munro, Gabriel Jotischky, Ty Anania, and Sian-Ashleigh Edwards, for everything you've done, and continue to do, for this book and my career. I am one lucky author to be championed by all of you.

It's not often you find someone who understands the heart of your story perfectly *and* wants to make your wildest dreams come true. I'm blessed that I got both from my editor. Ruqayyah Daud, you are the reason I get to write this Acknowledgments section and the reason this book has flourished to a level I'm extremely proud of. Your enthusiasm and belief in Tasha and Leo's story is a blessing I will never take for granted. Thank you for passionately championing this book and for helping me live out a miracle. Because of you, a childhood dream came true.

A gigantic thank-you also goes out to the entire Little, Brown Books for Young Readers team. There are so many of you who have helped strengthen and uplift this book in various ways, and I'm in awe of all of you! Special thanks to my managing editor, Esther Reisberg, and to Jill Freshney, Ariana dos Santos, and Su Wu, who polished the words in my book until they shined. Thank you to Martina Rethman for ensuring the production of this book went smoothly and making it possible for me to hold this story in my own hands. To Karina Granda, my head cover designer, as well as to Sasha Illingworth, Jenny Kimura, Elena Aguirre Uranga, and Michelle Gengaro-Kokmen, who worked so hard to bring this book to life vividly inside and out. And to Elena Masci for the stunning art of Tasha that graces the cover. Thank you to my marketing and publicity team—Sadie Trombetta, Stefanie Hoffman, Alice Gelber, Savannah Kennelly, Dominique Delmas, and Victoria Stapleton—for all your work and passion to get this book into the hands of readers. To the sales team: Shawn Foster, Danielle Cantarella, Cara Nesi, and Leah Collins Lipsett—thank you for your tireless efforts to ensure bookstores across North America make room on their shelves for my book. As well, thank you to Megan Tingley, Jackie Engel, and Alvina Ling for believing in this story so strongly.

To my UK publishing team at Hachette Children's Group: Thank you for your excitement and love for this book. Thanks especially to my editor Nazima Abdillahi for jumping on board so quickly and enthusiastically. It is a dream to have my stories published globally, and you are the reason I get to live out this fairy tale.

I have the absolute privilege and luck of knowing like-minded, genuine writer friends who have stuck by me and supported me through all the chapters of my literary journey. First, thanks go out to Alexandria

Rogers and Elora Ditton, my long-standing critique partners and dear friends. You have seen me through many variations of myself as a writer and as a person, encouraging me to keep building upon my craft, listening with a kind ear whenever I needed one, and always, *always* reminding me of my worth. I'm so proud to put your names down in this book. It exists, in many respects, because of you two. Love you, mean it.

To the many more writer friends who have loved and supported this book—and me—since the early days and everywhere in between. I love and appreciate all of you. A special thanks goes out to Jordan Gray, Chantel Pereira, Trisha Kelly, Emily Charlotte, Valerie Norton, Elizabeth Urso, Alexis Dent Hanes, Kat Korpi, Alina Khawaja, Daniel Aleman, June Hur, Skyla Arndt, Elle Tesch, Alyssa Eatherly, Tracy Deonn, Carolina Flórez-Cerchiaro, Alyssa Villaire, Kiana Krystle, Mackenzie Reed, Liselle Sambury, Rebekah Faubion, Adalyn Grace, Chelsea Hollerud, Carey Blankenship-Kramer, Cassy Klisch, Mallory Jones, Carrie Lewis, Sonia T., Katie Zhao, Isabel Ibanez, the Creative Cottage Group, and the Toronto Writer Crew for offering so much kindness and enthusiastic support whenever I needed it. Thank you so much to all the wonderful authors who provided blurbs for my debut as well.

My deepest gratitude to my family and friends who have listened to me talk about my big dreams of telling stories for a living since I was a single-digit age, and encouraged those wild fantasies until they became reality. Your faith that those dreams weren't too big—that it was inevitable I would make them happen—and your excitement when they came true means the world to me. Special thanks to Aunt Kathleen, Uncle Paul, Uncle Barry, and Aunt Karen in heaven. On the friend side, special thanks to Sara, Robynne, Rong, Claire, and all my St. John's, Newfoundland, friends.

To my parents: You are the ones I dedicated my first book to, so it only makes sense that I give you your own paragraph. Thank you for instilling in me a love for storytelling since birth (literally) and for not only accepting my creative side but for wanting it to flourish. No matter what quirky or grand dream I had, you always encouraged me and found your own creative ways to make it happen. It's a blessing to have parents like you two. All my love to both of you.

And finally, I'm ending this on my favorite person: Josh. You've believed in my ability to be an author since I first told you about my grand ambitions a decade ago, and never faltered in that faith. You've given me so much in the form of patiently listening to every thought I have about my writing and the publishing industry, letting me soak your shirt with my tears on more than one occasion *because* of said industry, and lighting up with joy whenever I've had good news like it was your own. I'm not sure I would have made it to this moment if it weren't for you. You're the type of guy authors write about when they want their leading man to be kind, genuine, thoughtful, and funny. Who loves the main character so unconditionally that it almost seems impossible for him to ever make it off the page. And yet, here you are. How lucky I am that I get the real-life thing.

Emily Williams

ELORA COOK

is an author who loves to write about ambitious girls living glamorous and dangerous lives. She grew up outside of Toronto and spent her formative years horseback riding, reading all the books she could get her hands on, and letting her imagination run wild. After earning her Bachelor of Arts degree, she worked on popular home reno shows and planned corporate events before finally achieving her lifelong dream of being a published author. Her name comes from the movie *Willow*, which she's certain destined her for a love of storytelling. She now splits her time between two cities to keep everyone on their toes. *In the Company of Killers* is her debut novel.